Fiction by Ben Bova

VOYAGERS
KINSMAN
MAXWELL'S DEMONS
COLONY
THE MULTIPLE MAN
MILLENNIUM
CITY OF DARKNESS
THE STARCROSSED
END OF EXILE
GREMLINS, GO HOME! (*with Gordon R. Dickson*)
FORWARD IN TIME
WHEN THE SKY BURNED
THE WINDS OF ALTAIR
AS ON A DARKLING PLAIN
FLIGHT OF EXILES
THX 1138 (*with George Lucas*)
EXILED FROM EARTH
ESCAPE!
THE DUELING MACHINE
OUT OF THE SUN
THE WEATHERMAKERS
STAR WATCHMAN
THE STAR CONQUERORS

Non-Fiction by Ben Bova

THE SEEDS OF TOMORROW
CLOSEUP: NEW WORLDS
NOTES TO A SCIENCE FICTION WRITER
SCIENCE: WHO NEEDS IT?
THROUGH EYES OF WONDER
WORKSHOPS IN SPACE
THE WEATHER CHANGES MAN
SURVIVAL GUIDE FOR THE SUDDENLY SINGLE (*with Barbara Berson*)
MAN CHANGES THE WEATHER
STARFLIGHT AND OTHER IMPROBABILITIES
THE NEW ASTRONOMIES
THE AMAZING LASER
THE FOURTH STATE OF MATTER
PLANETS, LIFE AND LGM
IN QUEST OF QUASARS
THE USES OF SPACE
REPTILES SINCE THE WORLD BEGAN
GIANTS OF THE ANIMAL WORLD
THE MILKY WAY GALAXY

VOYAGERS

Anthologies by Ben Bova

THE BEST OF OMNI SCIENCE FICTION

BEST OF ANALOG

ANALOG YEARBOOK

ANALOG ANNUAL

THE ANALOG SCIENCE FACT READER

ANALOG 9

CLOSEUP: OF FAME, YOUTH

THE MANY WORLDS OF SF

Voyagers

BEN BOVA

Doubleday & Company, Inc.,
Garden City, New York
1981

ISBN: 0-385-14890-9
Library of Congress Catalog Card Number 80–2836
Copyright © 1981 by Ben Bova

To Kathy and Bob, who care about the important things.

Either we are alone or we are not; either way is mind boggling.

LEE DUBRIDGE

Nothing is too wonderful to be true.

MICHAEL FARADAY

The only limit to our realization of tomorrow will be our doubts of today.

FRANKLIN D. ROOSEVELT

VOYAGERS

BOOK ONE

When I behold your heavens, the work of your fingers,
the moon and stars which you set in place,
What is man that you should be mindful of him?

THE EIGHTH PSALM

CHAPTER 1

Professor Ramsey McDermott leaned back in his creaking old leather chair and idly looked out his office window. The Yard was the same as it had been since the first day he had seen it, almost half a century ago. Trees bright in their October colors, students hurrying along the cement paths toward their classrooms, or dawdling on the grass in little groups of two or three, deep in earnest conversations.

A soft knock on his door snapped him out of his comfortable reverie. It's her, he thought.

As gruffly as he could, he called, "Come in!"

Jo Camerata stepped into the musty little office. I didn't realize she'd be so attractive, McDermott mused to himself. No wonder she's getting away with murder.

Jo was tall, with the dark, lustrous hair and ripe figure of a Mediterranean beauty. She wore the student's inevitable jeans and sweater, but they clung to her in a way that sent a surge through McDermott's blood. Her eyes were deep and midnight black, but wary, uncertain, like a trapped animal's.

McDermott smiled to himself.

"Put your books down and take a seat," he commanded. There! That'll convince her she's in for a long, tough grilling.

Jo sat in the straight-backed chair in front of his desk and held the books on her lap, as if they could defend her. Looking at her, so young, so luscious, McDermott realized that his office was gray with dust, littered with piles of old papers and stacks of books, heavy with decades worth of stale pipe smoke.

He leaned forward slightly in his chair. "I hear you've become quite a stranger to your classes these days."

Her eyes widened. "Dr. Thompson said it was all right . . ."

"He did, did he?"

"I've been helping him at the observatory—with the new signals they've picked up."

"And flunking out of every class you're in," McDermott groused.

"I can't be in two places at the same time," she pleaded. "Dr. Thompson *asked* me to help him."

"I'm sure he did." McDermott picked a pipe from the rack, toyed with it, enjoyed the way her frightened eyes followed every move his hands made.

"You've been helping Dr. Stoner, too, haven't you?"

"Dr. Stoner?" She looked away from him, toward the window. "No . . . not really. I'm working for Dr. Thompson."

McDermott felt a flush of heat go through him at the way the sweater pulled across her breasts, the helpless look in her eyes.

"You did some typing for Stoner. Don't try to deny it."

"Oh . . . yes, I did."

"What was it?" he demanded. "What's he written?"

"I don't know. I just typed it, I didn't read it. Not in detail."

Jabbing the pipe at her, "Don't try to play games with me, young lady. You're on the verge of being thrown out of this university. What did Stoner want typed?"

"It's . . . it's a paper. A scientific paper. For publication in a journal."

"Which journal?"

"I don't know. He didn't say."

McDermott leaned back, and the old leather chair groaned under his weight. "A paper about the radio signals?"

She nodded.

"And this object he's discovered?"

"That was in the paper, yes."

For a long moment McDermott said nothing. He sat back in the old leather chair, calmly stripping Jo with his eyes. Enjoying the fact that she obviously knew what he was thinking, but there was nothing she could do about it.

Finally he asked, "And what else have you done for Stoner?"

"Nothing!"

"Nothing? Really?"

"No . . ."

He pulled his face into its most threatening frown and growled, "Didn't you ask one of the secretaries in this department about making a hotel reservation in Washington?"

Jo shook her head. "That was only for Dr. Stoner. Himself. Not for me."

"Then you *have* done something else for Stoner, haven't you?"

"I thought you meant typing . . . mailing . . ."

"What about this Washington trip?"

"I don't understand what that's got to do with my status as a student, Professor."

He snarled back, "You don't have to understand, Miss Camerata. All you need to know is that I can toss you out on your pretty little rump if you don't answer my questions completely and honestly. Instead of getting your degree next June you'll be waiting on tables in some greasy spoon restaurant." He hesitated, leaned back, smiling. "Or maybe dancing at a topless joint. You'd be better qualified for that."

She glared at him, but answered sullenly, "Dr. Stoner is going down to Washington Sunday night. He has an appointment to see his former boss at NASA Headquarters on Monday morning. He wants to take his paper about the new discovery with him."

"He does, does he?" McDermott rumbled. It was just what he'd feared: Stoner was trying an end run. The ungrateful bastard. "Well, we shall see about *that!*"

He reached for the phone, picked the receiver off its cradle. "You can go," he said to Jo.

She blinked, surprised. "Am I still . . . you're not going to flunk me out?"

"I ought to," he growled. "But as long as Thompson vouches for you, I'll be lenient. Providing you can pass the finals."

She nodded and quickly got to her feet. As she headed for the door, McDermott added, "But you just keep away from that man Stoner."

"Yes, sir," she said obediently.

As soon as the door closed behind her, McDermott started dialing the special number in Washington that he kept taped under the phone's receiver.

CHAPTER 2

Jo drove straight to the observatory. Out through the narrow, traffic-clogged streets of Cambridge, past Lexington's Battle Green, past the bridge at Concord, out into the apple valleys and rolling hills bursting with colorful autumn foliage, her mind seething:

That slimy old bastard is going to hurt Dr. Stoner. I've got to warn him. I've got to warn him *now.*

But Stoner was not in his office when Jo got to the observatory. The little cubicle on the second floor of the observatory building was as neat and precisely arranged as an equation, but he wasn't in it.

Jo saw a stack of photographs carefully placed in the center of Stoner's otherwise bare desk. They were face down, and the back of the topmost photo bore the blue-stamped legend: PROPERTY OF NATIONAL AERONAUTICAL AND SPACE AGENCY—NOT TO BE RELEASED WITHOUT OFFICIAL WRITTEN APPROVAL.

She turned the pictures over, one after another. The paper was stiff, heavy, very expensive. The photographs showed views of a fat, flattened ball striped by gaudy bands of color: red, yellow, ocher, white. An oblong oval of brick red glowed down in the lower quadrant of the sphere.

The planet Jupiter.

Jo thumbed through all two dozen photographs. All of Jupiter. On some, two or three of the giant planet's moons could be seen: tiny specks compared to Jupiter's immense bulk.

She glanced at her Timex wristwatch. No way to get back in time for her first afternoon class. With a resigned shrug, she went to the window and separated the blinds enough to look out.

He was on the back parking lot, doing his karate exercises. Jo watched as he stood rigidly straight, his dark face somber and tight-lipped, his big hands bunched into fists just below the black belt that he was so proud of. For a moment he did nothing, merely stared blankly ahead, a tall, powerful man with jet black hair and brooding gray eyes, flat midsection and long, slim, athlete's legs.

Then he was all motion and fury, arms slashing and legs kicking in an intricate deadly pattern. It was like ballet almost, but violent, powerful, urgent.

Not a sound came from him as he swirled down the length of the blacktopped lot. Then he stopped just as suddenly as he had started, arms upraised and knees flexed in an alert defensive posture. He straightened slowly, let his arms drop to his sides.

She was afraid for a moment that he would glance up and see her at his office window, watching him. But he turned his back to the building, drew himself together and began another series of violent karate actions, kicking, slashing, punching the empty air all the way back to the far end of the parking lot.

Jo pulled herself away from the window. If she hurried, she knew she could make the last class of the afternoon. But she had to talk to him, tell him about Professor McDermott's strange interest in his trip to Washington. That was more important than the class.

Briefly she thought about putting a note atop the pile of photos on his desk. But she decided against it. She would wait for him, wait while he showered and changed back into his regular clothes and came back to his office. She would miss the late class, but that didn't matter. Seeing him was more important.

Not that he cared. She was just another one of the anonymous students who fetched and carried for the famous Dr. Stoner, the former astronaut who now worked at the observatory, alone, aloof, handsome and mysterious.

But he will care, Jo promised herself. He'll notice me. I'll make him notice me.

Keith Stoner let his shoulders slump and his arms hang wearily at his sides. He was covered with a fine sheen of sweat; it beaded along his brows and dripped, stinging, into his eyes. But the cool afternoon breeze would soon chill him, he knew, if he didn't get indoors quickly.

It hadn't worked. Nothing works anymore, he thought bitterly. Tae kwon do is a mental discipline even more than a physical one. It should help him to reach inner calm and self-control. But all Stoner felt was a burning anger, a hot, unrelenting rage that smoldered in his guts.

It's all finished, he told himself for the thousandth time. Everything's gone.

He pulled himself together, took the "ready" stance and heard his old Korean instructor hissing at him, "Focus. Focus! Speed you have. Strength you have. But you must learn to focus your concentration. Focus!"

He tried to blank out his mind, but in the darkness behind his closed eyes he saw the orbiting telescope gleaming, glittering in the harsh sunlight of space, a fantastic jewelwork of shining metal and sparkling mirrors floating against the eternal black of infinity. And scattered around it, like acolytes serving some giant silver idol, were tiny men in space suits.

Stoner had been one of those men.

Ex-astronaut, he thought grimly. Ex-astrophysicist. With an ex-marriage and an ex-family. Part of the team that had designed and built Big Eye, the orbiting telescope. Stuck now in a backwater radio observatory, alone, getting a paycheck that's more charity than salary.

But I'll show them. I'll show them all! He knew he was onto something big. So big that it would have frightened him if he weren't so determined to startle the whole world with his discovery.

But he was startled himself when the big antenna started to move. The grinding, squealing noise made him look across the empty lot to the sixty-foot "dish" of the radio telescope. It was turning slowly, painfully, like an arthritic old man trying to turn his head, to point itself toward the distant wooded hills.

They should have scrapped this antique long ago, Stoner thought as he watched the radio telescope antenna inch groaningly along. Just like they've scrapped me.

The antenna was a big spiderwork of steel frame and metal mesh, a thin shallow circular bowl, like a giant's soap dish. It had been pointing high up in the sky overhead, drinking in the radio waves emitted by unthinkably distant star clouds.

Stoner frowned at the radio dish. Somehow, it bothered him to realize that the radio telescope worked just as well in daylight as at night. It worked in rain or fog. The only thing that bothered the radio telescope was an accumulation of snow across its broad, shallow bowl. The bigger, more modern telescopes were housed in neat geodesic domes that protected them from snow. This old-timer wasn't worth the cost of a protective dome. The staff technicians went out and swept the snow off with brooms.

But this old dish has picked up something that none of the newer telescopes has found, Stoner said to himself. When the rest of them find out, they'll hock their left testicles to get in on the game.

He looked up into the bright, cloudless October sky. Autumn was being kind to Massachusetts. No hurricanes so far. The trees were in splendid color—blazing reds, glowing oranges, browns and golden yellows, with clumps of dark green pine and spruce scattered across the gentle hills.

But above the crest of the wooded ridge, invisible to human eyes in the crisp blue afternoon sky, the planet Jupiter was rising.

And the radio telescope was pointing straight at it.

Stoner shuddered and headed back inside the observatory. He did not notice the unmarked black Plymouth sitting in the tiny visitors' parking section out in front of the building. Nor the two grim-faced men in conservative gray business suits sitting inside the car.

Showered and back in his open-neck shirt, slacks and sweater, Stoner looked over the main room of the observatory, a slight frown of distaste on his face.

An astronomical observatory should look shadowy, sepulchral, like a domed cathedral with a huge optical telescope slanting upward toward the heavens. Men should speak in awed whispers. There ought to be echoes and worshipful footsteps clicking on a solid cement floor.

The radio observatory looked like the bargain basement of an electronics hobby shop and bustled like an old-fashioned newspaper city room. Desks were jammed together in the middle of the room. Papers scattered everywhere, even across the floor. Electronics consoles tall as refrigerators lined all the walls, humming and whirring to themselves. Men and women, all younger than Stoner, yelled back and forth. The room vibrated at sixty cycles per second and smelled faintly of solder and machine oil.

They were almost all students, Stoner knew. Graduate students, even some post-docs. But the regular staff itself was little more than thirty years old. Old McDermott was the nominal head of the observatory, chairman of the department and all that. The real day-to-day boss was Jeff Thompson, who was waving to Stoner from the far side of the island of desks set in the sea of paper.

"Want to hear it?" Thompson called.

Stoner nodded and started around the desks.

"Dr. Stoner," one of the women students said to him, reaching for his arm. "Can I talk to you for a minute? Professor . . ."

"Not now," Stoner said, hardly glancing at her.

Thompson was a sandy-haired middleweight with the pleasant, undistinguished features of the kid next door. An assistant professor at the university, he was nearly Stoner's age, the "grand old man" of the regular observatory staff.

"It's coming through loud and clear," Thompson said as Stoner approached him. With a relaxed grin he reached across the nearest desk and pulled a battered old set of earphones from under a heap of papers.

"We hardly ever use these," he said. "But I thought you'd like to actually listen to what we're getting."

Stoner accepted the headphones from Thompson and walked with him to the humming consoles along the wall. Thompson held the wires leading from the earphones in one hand. We must look like a man walking his dog, Stoner thought.

Thompson plugged the wire lead into a jack on the console and nodded to Stoner, who slipped the earphones over his head. They were thick with heavy padding.

All the noise of the bustling room was cut off. Thompson's mouth moved but Stoner couldn't hear what he was saying.

"Nothing," Stoner told him, hearing his own voice inside his head, as if he were stuffed up with a sinus cold. "Nothing's coming through."

Thompson nodded and clicked a few switches on the console. Stoner heard a whirring screech that quickly rose in pitch until it soared beyond the range of human hearing. Then the low hissing, scratching electronic static of the steady sky background noise—the sound of endless billions of stars and clouds of interstellar gases all mingled together.

He began to shake his head when it finally came through: a deep rumbling bass note, barely a whisper but unmistakably different from the background noise. Stoner nodded and Thompson turned a dial on the console ever so slightly.

The heavy sound grew slightly louder, then faded away. In a split second it returned, then faded again. Stoner stood in the middle of the silenced hubbub of the busy room, listening to the pulses of energy throbbing in his ears like the deep, slow breathing of a slumbering giant.

He closed his eyes and saw the giant—the planet Jupiter.

The radio telescope was picking up pulses of radio energy streaming out from Jupiter. Pulses that were timed more precisely than a metronome, timed as accurately as the clicks of a quartz watch. Pulses that had no natural explanation.

Slowly he pulled the heavy earphones off.

"That's it," he said to Thompson over the bustle of the room.

Thompson bobbed his head up and down. "That's it." He took the headset from Stoner and held it up to his ear. "Yep, that's what it sounds like. Regular as clockwork."

"And nobody's ever heard it before?"

"No, nothing like it. Not from Jupiter or any other planet." Thompson unplugged the earphones and tossed them back onto his desk, scattering papers in every direction. "It's not on the same frequency as the pulsars, or the same periodicity. It's something brand new."

Stoner scratched his thick, dark hair. "What do you think is causing it?"

Grinning, Thompson answered, "That's why we brought you here. You tell me."

With a slow nod, Stoner said, "You know what I think, Jeff."

"Intelligent life."

"Right."

Thompson puffed his cheeks and blew out a breath. "That's a big one."

"Yeah."

He left Thompson standing there, lost in his own thoughts, and headed for the stairs that led up to his second-floor office. The same young student fell in step alongside him.

"Dr. Stoner, can I speak with you for a minute?"

He glanced at her. "Sure, Ms. . . . ?"

"Camerata. Jo Camerata."

He started up the steps without a second look at her. Jo dogged along behind him.

"It's about Professor McDermott," she said.

"Big Mac? What's he want?"

"I think it's better if we talk in your office, with the door closed."

"Well, that's where I'm heading."

"You were out there, weren't you?" Jo asked, to his back. "You helped build Big Eye, out there in orbit."

They reached the top of the stairs and he turned around to take a good look at her. She was young, tall, with the classic kind of face you might find on a Greek vase. Black short-cropped hair curled thickly to frame her strong cheekbones and jawline. Her jeans clung to her full hips, her sweater accentuated her bosom.

An astronaut groupie? Stoner asked himself as he replied, "Yes, I was part of the design and construction team for the orbital telescope. That's why Big Mac invited me here, because I can sweet-talk my old buddies into sneaking some shots of Jupiter to us."

It was quieter up on the second floor, although the floor still hummed with electric vibrations. Stoner stalked down the narrow hallway, Jo trailing half a step behind him. He opened the door to the tiny office they had given him.

Two men were inside: one by the window where Jo had been standing earlier; the other beside the door.

"Dr. Keith Stoner?" asked the one by the window. He was the

smaller of the two. Stoner's desk, with the photographs of Jupiter scattered across it, stood between them.

Stoner nodded. The man by the window was inches shorter than Stoner, but solidly built. The one beside him, at the door, hulked like a football lineman. Professional football. They were both conservatively dressed in gray business suits. Both had taut, clean-shaven faces.

"Naval Intelligence," said the man by the window. He fished a wallet from his inside jacket pocket and dangled it over the desk. It held an official-looking identification card.

"Will you come with us, please?"

"What do you mean? Where . . . ?"

"Please, Dr. Stoner. It's very important."

The big agent by the door gripped Stoner's arm around the biceps. Lightly but firmly. The smaller man came around the desk and the three of them started down the hallway in step.

Jo Camerata stood by Stoner's office door, gaping at them. The expression on her face was not shock or even anger. It was guilt.

> . . . Jansky had unexpectedly recorded radio waves
> from the Galaxy while investigating . . . crackles and
> noises that interfere with radio communication.
> Jansky's discovery in 1932 marked the first successful
> observation in radio astronomy. It is indeed strange that
> it took so long to recognise that radio waves were
> reaching us from celestial sources.
>
> J. S. HEY
> *The Evolution of Radio Astronomy*
> Science History Publications
> 1973

CHAPTER 3

In Moscow it was nearly 11 P.M. A gentle snow was sifting out of the heavy, leaden sky, covering the oldest monuments and newest apartment blocks alike with a fine white powder. By dawn, old men and women would be at their posts along every street, methodically sweeping the snow off the sidewalks for the lumbering mechanical plows to scoop up.

Kirill Markov glanced at the clock on the bed stand.

"That tickles," said the girl.

He looked down at her. For a moment he could not recall her name. It was hard to make out her face in the darkness, but the golden luster of her long sweeping hair caught the faint light of the streetlamp outside the window. Nadia, he remembered at last. Sad, a part of his mind reflected, that when you pursue a woman you can think of nothing else, but once you've got her she becomes so forgettable.

Woman! he snorted to himself. She's only a girl.

"You're tickling me!"

Markov saw that his beard was the culprit and, moving his chin in a tiny circle, ran the end of the whiskers around the nipple of her right breast.

She giggled and clutched him around the neck.

"Can you do it again?" she asked.

"In English," Markov said to her in a gentle whisper. "Our bargain was that all our lovemaking will be done in English. It is the best way to learn a foreign language."

She pressed her lips together and frowned with concentration. Her face is really quite ordinary, Markov thought. Vapid, even.

Still frowning, she said slowly in English, "Are you able to fork me another time?" Her accent was atrocious.

Suppressing a laugh, Markov said, "Fuck . . . not fork."

She nodded. "Are you able to fuck me another time?"

"That word is considered to be in bad taste by the English and the Americans. Not so by the Australians."

"Fork?"

"No. Fuck. They usually employ a euphemism for the word."

"Euphemism?"

Markov's eyes rolled heavenward. She'll never pass the exams, no matter whose bed she flops into. As he explained in Russian the meaning of the word, he mentally added, Unless she can fuck the computer.

"Now I understand," Nadia said in English.

"Good," he said.

"Well, can you?"

"Can I what?"

"You know . . ."

"Ah!" Realizing that her mind had not deviated from its carnal goal, he replied, "Make love to you once again? Gladly! With white-hot passion. But not now. It is time for you to get back to your dormitory."

In Russian she bleated, "Must I? It's so cozy and warm here." Her fingers traced lines down his shoulder and back.

"It won't be cozy much longer. My wife will be returning very soon."

"Oh, her!"

Markov sat up on the bed. The room felt cold to his bare skin.

"She is my wife, dear child, and this is her apartment even more than it is mine. Do you think a mere university professor of languages would be given such an elegant apartment, in such a fine part of town?"

The girl got up out of the bed and padded naked to the bath-

room without another word. Watching her, Markov saw that she
was heavy in the thighs and rump. He hadn't noticed that before
they had gone to bed together.

Sighing, he pulled himself out of the bed and stripped off the
sheets. He kept two sets of bedclothing: one for the marriage
and one for fun. His wife had a keen sense of smell and was fas-
tidious about certain things.

Nadia re-entered the bedroom, tugging on her quilted slacks
and stuffing her blouse into the waistband.

"What does she do, this wife of yours, to rate such a fancy
apartment? A private bathroom, just for the two of you!" It was
almost a reproach.

"She works in the Kremlin," said Markov. "She is a secretary
to a commissar."

The girl's eyes widened. "Oh, I see. No wonder she is treated
so well."

Markov nodded and reached for his robe. "Yes. In our pro-
gressive society, the commissars work so hard and give so much
of their lives for the good of the people that even their secretaries live like . . . like we shall all live, once true communism
is established throughout the world."

She nodded without acknowledging the irony in his words. He
walked her through the little sitting room to the hallway door.

"This is a wonderful way to learn English," she said, "but I'm
afraid I'll need many lessons."

Markov patted her shoulder. "We'll see. We'll see. In the
meantime it might be a good idea for you to study the regular
lessons and spend more time with the tapes in the language lab."

"Oh, I will," she said earnestly. "Thank you, Professor."

He leaned down to kiss her lips, then swiftly ushered her
through the door and out into the dimly lit hallway.

Closing the door behind her, Markov leaned against it for a
moment. Hopeless, he told himself. Forty-five years old and you
still play childish games.

But then a grin broke out on his bearded face. "Why not?" he
mused. "It's fun."

He was an inch over six feet in height, lanky in build with
long legs and arms that swung loosely at his sides when he
walked. His reddish hair was starting to fade and his scraggly

beard was almost entirely gray. But his face was still unlined and almost boyish. The ice-blue eyes twinkled. The full lips often smiled.

When he lectured at the university his voice was strong and clear; he needed no microphone to reach the farthest rows of the auditorium. When he sang—usually at small parties where the vodka flowed generously—his baritone was remarkable for its fine timbre and lack of pitch.

He pulled himself away from the front door abruptly, hurried into the bedroom and finished changing the sheets. The soiled ones he stuffed into the special suitcase he kept behind his writing desk. Once a week he laundered them in the machine in the basement of the student lounge at the university. It was a good place to meet girls who didn't attend his classes.

Finally, he scrubbed himself down, pulled the heavy robe around his tingling skin and sat in his favorite chair in the front room, before the electric heater. He was just picking up a heavy tome and sliding his reading glasses up the bridge of his nose when he heard Maria's key scratching at the door.

Maria Kirtchatovska Markova was slightly older than her husband. Her family came from peasant stock, a fact that she was proud of. And she looked it: short, heavyset, narrow untrusting eyes of muddy brown, hair the color of a field mouse, cut short and flat. She was no beauty and never had been. Nor was she a secretary to a commissar.

When Markov had first met her, a quarter century earlier, he had been a student of linguistics at the university and she a uniformed guard recently discharged from the Red Army. She was ambitious, he was brilliant.

Their union was one of mutual advantage. He had thought that marriage would make love blossom, and was shocked to find that it did not. She quickly agreed to let him pursue "his own interests," as he euphemistically referred to his affairs. Maria wanted only his intelligence to help further her own career in the government.

Their arrangement worked well. Maria was recruited by the KGB and rose, over the years, to the rank of major. She was now assigned to an elite unit concerned with cryptanalysis—decoding other people's secret messages. To the best of Markov's knowledge, his wife had never arrested anyone, never interrogated a prisoner, never been involved in the tortures and killings that were always darkly rumored whenever anyone dared to whisper of the security police.

Markov was now a professor of linguistics at the same university where he had been a student. His career was unremarkable, except for one thing: his fascination with codes, cryptology and exotic languages. He occasionally wrote magazine articles about languages that alien creatures might use to make contact with the human race. He had even written a slim book about possible extraterrestrial languages, and the government had even printed it. He never bothered to wonder if he would have risen so far without Maria, except now and then in the dead of night, when she was busy at her office and he had no one else to sleep with.

"Aren't you cold, with nothing on but that robe?" Maria asked as she closed the door and let her heavy shoulder bag thump to the floor.

"No," Markov said, peering over the rims of his glasses. "Not now, with you here."

She made a sour face. "Been tutoring your students again?" She knew how to use euphemisms, too.

He shrugged. It was none of her business. Besides, even though she knew all about it, she always got angry when he spoke of it openly. Strange woman, he thought. You'd think she would have become accustomed to the situation. After all, she did agree to the arrangement.

"Why do you have to work so late?" he asked her without getting up from his easy chair. He knew that she would not answer. Could not. Most of her work was so sensitive that she could not discuss it with her husband. But once in a great while, when she was really stumped on a code or a translation, she would let him take a stab at it. Often he failed, but there had been a few times when he'd made a Hero of the Soviet Union out of her.

Maria plopped into the chair closest to the electrical space heater. Little puddles of melted snow started to grow around her boots, soaking into the ancient oriental rug. She glared at the heater. "This thing isn't working right," she grumbled.

"It's the voltage, I think," Markov said. "They must have lowered the voltage again, to save power."

"And we freeze."

"It's necessary, I suppose," he said.

She looked him over: her wary, cynical peasant's gaze of appraisal. Can I trust him? she was asking herself, Markov knew. He could read her face like a child's primer.

"Do you really want to know what's keeping me at head-quarters so late each night?" she asked slowly.

He pursed his lips. "Not if it involves anything you shouldn't tell me." Turning back to the book on his lap, "Don't let me tempt you into revealing state secrets."

"I know I can trust you—in certain things."

Markov concentrated on his reading.

"Kirill! Look at me when I speak to you! I need your help."

He looked up.

"Nothing like this has ever happened before."

She was really upset. Beneath her wary exterior he saw some-thing close to fear in her face.

"What is it?" he asked, taking off his glasses.

"You must come with me tomorrow to headquarters. You must be investigated and checked out."

"Investigated? Why? What have I done?"

She shook her head, eyes closed wearily. "No, it's nothing like that. Don't be afraid. It's a routine security investigation. Before we can show you the data, you must have a security clearance."

Markov's heart was thumping now. His palms felt clammy. "What data? If it's so sensitive, why should I be involved?"

"Because of that silly book you wrote. They want to talk to you about it."

"My book on extraterrestrial languages? But that was pub-lished six years ago."

Maria opened her eyes and leveled a bone-chilling gaze at her husband. "Nothing like this has ever happened before. The problem was brought to us by the Academy of Sciences."

"The Academy . . . ?"

"Academician Bulacheff himself. The chairman."

The reading glasses slid off the book on Markov's lap and dropped to the carpet. He made no move to pick them up.

"Kir," Maria asked, "do you know where the planet Jupiter is? What it is?"

"Jupiter?"

"Yes."

"It's the largest planet of the solar system. Much bigger than the Earth. But it's cold, far away from the Sun."

"There are radio signals coming from Jupiter," Maria said, her eyes closing again, as if trying to squeeze away the problem. "Radio signals. We need you to tell us if they are a language."

"A language?" His voice sounded strangely high-pitched, like a frightened boy's.

"Yes. These radio signals may be a language. From intelligent creatures. That is why we need you to study them."

CHAPTER 4

It was small, even by the standards of high school gymnasiums, but it was packed solidly with people. They sat on hard wooden benches and watched the slim, swaying blondish figure down at the center line of the basketball court.

Microphone in hand, held so close to his lips that every intake of breath echoed off the bare tile walls of the gym, Willie Wilson preached his gospel:

"And what is it that Jesus hates?"

"Sin!" cried the eager voices of the crowd. The noise exploded inside the gym, reverberating off the stark walls, pounding at the ears.

"What is it?"

"*Sin!*" they screamed louder.

"Tell me!"

"SIN!" they roared.

Fred Tuttle, lieutenant commander, United States Navy, clapped his hands over his hurting ears and grinned. He was up on the last row of benches, back to the wall. Unlike the blue-jeaned, tee-shirted crowd around him, Tuttle was wearing neatly pressed slacks and a turtleneck shirt. His jacket was carefully folded on his lap.

"This world is full of sin!" Willie Wilson was bellowing into his microphone. "It's dying of sin! And who can save such a sinful world? Who's the *only* one that can save this dying world?"

"Jesus!" they thundered. "JESUS!"

"Jesus Christ, our Lord and Savior, that's entirely right." Wilson's voice fell to a hoarse whisper, and the echoes rattling around the tile-walled gym died away. The crowd leaned forward, eager to hear Wilson's every word. "But Jesus can't do it alone. Could if He wanted to, naturally, but that is not God's way. Not God's way. God isn't a loner. If God went His way alone, He would never have created man. He would never have created this sinful flesh and this sinful world. He would never have sent His only Son, our Lord and Savior Jesus Christ, to come amongst us and show us His Way. Now, would He?"

A murmur of "No" rippled through the crowd.

"Jesus God wants to save this world. He wants to save *you!* He loves you. He made you in His own divine image, didn't He? He wants you to be just like Him, and with Him, in paradise forever and ever."

"Amen," someone called.

"Amen to you, brother," Wilson answered, and wiped sweat from his brow with his free hand. "Jesus wants to save us. Save the world. But He needs your help. He didn't design this world for Himself. He designed it for you—each and every one of us. And He won't save it unless we show Him—prove to Him—that we want to be saved!"

A trim-figured man with close-cropped brown hair pushed along the row of rapt listeners and squeezed down next to Tuttle.

"We got him," he said, leaning over to speak right into Tuttle's ear.

The lieutenant commander made a shushing gesture with his lips and held up a hand to silence the other man.

Willie Wilson, sweat drenching his sky-blue denim suit, was finishing his sermon. "This is *our* world. Jesus God made it for us and gave it to us. He made us to live in it, to be happy, to be fruitful and multiply. To worship Him and hate sin. He made us in His divine image, and when we commit sin—when we turn our backs on Jesus—we distort that heavenly image into something evil and ugly."

He paused and turned a full circle to peer at the crowd.

"Now, that's something to think about, isn't it? Something to ponder on. So let us pray. Let's meditate on how easy it is to commit sin and how hard it is to be righteous. And while we're meditating, the Sacred Rock Singers will praise the Lord in their own special way."

The crowd roared its approval, and a platoon of robed young men and women, armed with electric guitars and other implements, trotted out onto center court.

Tuttle turned to the man beside him. "Say again?"

"We got him. Picked him up this afternoon. They're driving him to the safe house."

"Good."

"I hope so. This isn't the old days, you know. We're out on a limb with nothing but your say-so."

"Did he offer any resistance?" Tuttle asked.

"No."

"Then technically, he went voluntarily."

"I hope that holds up in court."

"It won't go to court."

"You can't holler National Security and do whatever you feel like anymore."

The Sacred Rock Singers began to beat out a heavily amplified gospel song. The crowd immediately recognized it and began clapping in rhythm to it.

"I'll back you up," Tuttle yelled over the noise. "It was dog-gone important to get Stoner before he ran off at the mouth."

The man beside him said something in reply, but it was lost in the music and clapping.

"What?" Tuttle yelled.

The man shook his head in disgust, got up and pushed his way out of the crowd.

Dazedly, Keith Stoner sat on the bed of the room they had put him in. It was a comfortable bed with an old-fashioned tufted white coverlet spread neatly across it. The room was small but snug. An unused fireplace in one corner, a single wingback chair covered with a design of blotchy flowers. The bed table, one lamp, a digital alarm clock, a bureau, doors that led to a closet and a bathroom.

And the door that led into the hallway. Locked.

The two men who had identified themselves as Naval Intelligence agents had bundled Stoner into their unmarked black Plymouth without giving him a chance to say a word to anyone. Only Jo Camerata knew what had happened to him.

They had driven for hours, until Stoner felt they were deliberately trying to confuse him, to make certain he could not retrace their route. It grew dark and still they drove through the New England countryside, mainly along back roads.

"Where the hell are you guys going?" Stoner demanded.

"Just relax," said the agent sitting beside him on the rear seat of the car. He called himself Dooley. The bigger one was up front, driving, his massive bulk hunched over the steering wheel.

Stoner tried to keep track of the road signs, but they were swerving and lurching along back roads in complete darkness. They could have been passing open fields, or huge buildings, or even the ocean. The sky had clouded over and there were no lights along the roadside.

Finally they pulled onto a crunching, bumpy gravel driveway. Stoner saw thick boles of venerable trees leaning close in the dim light of the car's headlamps. A house loomed up ahead of them: big and old and boxy. The shingles were unpainted cedar. The car slowed, and in the headlamp glow Stoner could see a garage door swinging up automatically for them. They drove into the lighted garage and stopped.

"Wait a minute," Dooley said.

Stoner sat still and heard the garage door swing down again. Then the car's door locks clicked open.

"Okay."

The driver was out of the car before Stoner could get his door open, and stood waiting alongside as he climbed out.

"You guys don't take any chances, do you?" Stoner said to them.

Dooley let a slight smile cross his lips. "Against a black belt? We watched you working out."

Poor scared pigs, Stoner thought. All they've got is guns and bullets.

They led him into the house, an old Yankee farmhouse that had obviously been remodeled by a millionaire. The original rooms were small, with low ceilings that sagged so much the timber beams almost touched Stoner's head. Fireplaces in each room. And radiant baseboard electrical heating units. Thermal windows. A sparkling ultramodern kitchen, and another small kitchen just off the living room that served as a wet bar. The living room itself was all new, wide, spacious, with a high slanted cathedral ceiling. Beyond it were sliding glass doors that looked out onto a sunken swimming pool. Not quite Olympic size, but big enough.

They led him up a narrow staircase to the second floor.

"This will be your room, Dr. Stoner," Dooley said, opening a bedroom door. "There's some clothes in the closet that should fit you. Bathroom with shower through there. Socks and stuff in the bureau."

"How the hell long am I going to be here?" he asked. "Don't I get a phone call or something?"

Dooley gave another tight smile. "We'll bring dinner up to you. Somebody will be here to talk to you in the morning. No phone calls."

So Stoner sat on the bed and watched raindrops start to spatter on the dark window, listened to the rain drumming against the old house.

This must be how they felt when the Nazis bundled them off

to Dachau, he thought. Stunned . . . confused . . . totally off balance.

There could be only one reason for it, he realized. They wanted to keep him quiet, to prevent him from telling the world what he had discovered.

Which meant he was truly a prisoner.

I think, therefore, that we will get a message, but it will not be simple . . .

. . . which will come (perhaps in ten years, or a hundred, or maybe longer)—when some satisfactory radio-telescope work or something similar will acquire evidence of the deliberate beaming of a protracted message from space. First, the most important issue is the recognition of the message . . .

PHILIP MORRISON
Life Beyond Earth & the Mind of Man
Edited by Richard Berendzen
National Aeronautics and Space
Administration
NASA SP-328
1973

CHAPTER 5

"Professor Markov, you are a Party member?"

Markov nodded at the woman.

"But you have never been admitted to the Academy?"

"Not yet," he answered with a frosty smile.

They were sitting in a tiny interrogation room, a cramped, blank-walled windowless chamber. One of the fluorescent lamps in the ceiling was flickering; Markov could feel it tapping against his brain like a Chinese water torture. Deliberate? he wondered. Part of the interrogation? Or simply the usual sloppy maintenance?

The woman sitting across the small wooden table wore the tan uniform with red tabs and insignia of a lieutenant. She could not have been more than twenty-two, and she was taking this interrogation very seriously.

Markov decided to be charming.

"My dear young lady, you have my entire life story in those papers spread before you. It hasn't been a very colorful life, I admit, but if there is any special part of it that you want me to relate to you . . ."

She glanced down at the checklist on which her left hand rested. She held a chewed pencil in her right.

"You are married?" she asked.

She's going to go through the whole damned list, Markov groaned to himself. This will take hours.

"Yes. My wife is Maria . . ."

"Not yet," the lieutenant said, diligently making another check mark in the appropriate box. "Children?"

"None."

"Wife's first name?"

"Maria."

"Maiden name?"

"Kirtchatovska."

It made no impression on the lieutenant. She apparently had no idea that Major Markova had the power to make a lieutenant's life very uncomfortable.

"How long have you been married?"

"All my life."

She looked up sharply. "What?"

Markov smiled at her. It's really quite a pretty face, he thought. I wonder what she would do if I leaned across the table and took a nibble of that luscious lower lip?

"Twenty-four years this January," he said.

She looked down again and wrote on the checklist. Then her eyes rose to meet his. "Twenty-four years and no children?"

"I suffer from a sad malady," Markov lied cheerfully. "The result of a war trauma, the psychologists say."

"You're . . . impotent?" She whispered the last word.

Markov shrugged. "It's all psychological. Sometimes, on very rare occasions when I have found someone beautiful and truly loving, I am a tiger. But with most women . . . nothing."

"But how does your wife . . . ?"

The interrogation room door was flung open by a stocky man

in a captain's uniform. "Haven't you finished the forms yet? The colonel is waiting!"

Unfolding his lanky frame so that he had the advantage of height over the young captain, Markov suggested, "If you are certain that I'm not a spy or an assassin, perhaps I could meet the colonel and then return here afterward to finish the forms."

The lieutenant stood up too. "Or I could complete the interview after the working day is finished."

Markov said carefully, "I wouldn't want to put you to any trouble."

"I often work late," she said. "And these forms are strictly routine. There's nothing sensitive about them. We could even complete the interview at your apartment, if that is more convenient for you, Professor."

The captain snapped, "We don't conduct security interviews in people's apartments!"

With a sad shrug, Markov reached for his chair. "Very well then. I suppose we'll have to finish this here and keep the colonel waiting."

"No," the captain decided. "You will see the colonel now, and then return here to complete the interview. No matter how long it takes."

"Whatever you say," Markov agreed meekly. But he winked at the lieutenant.

She kept a straight face and said, "I will see you in this room, no matter how late it is."

It was difficult for Markov to suppress a grin as he followed the stocky captain down the featureless corridors. The walls were bare of decoration and even though they had apparently been freshly painted, the halls looked grim and almost shabby. Men and women, most of them in uniform, hurried through the halls. Although Markov could see no cameras anywhere, he got the feeling that everyone was being watched constantly.

The captain took him as far as an anteroom, in which a doughy-faced middle-aged civilian woman commanded a large desk with an electric typewriter and two telephones. She flashed Markov a disapproving glance, the kind that his wife often gave, the kind that automatically made him raise his hands to straighten his thinning lank hair and beard. Then she nodded to the captain and gestured wordlessly to the door beyond her desk.

The captain, motioning Markov to follow him, went to the door, knocked once and slowly—carefully—opened it.

Does no one speak here? Markov wondered. Are we at a shrine?

The captain would not cross the threshold, but he brusquely motioned Markov to go inside.

He stepped through into a sumptuous office. A broad desk of polished dark wood with crossed flags behind it. Oriental carpet on the floor. Windows that looked out onto Red Square. Plush leather chairs neatly lined against one wall. Gleaming samovar standing on a low cabinet.

The office was unoccupied. But before Markov could turn back toward the captain, the door at the far end of the room opened and his wife stepped through.

"Maria! This is *your* office?"

She was wearing her tan uniform, which made her look even squatter and heavier than usual. She scowled at him.

"My office? Hah! My office is smaller than the colonel's desk."

"Oh."

"Come on, come on. They're all waiting for you."

He crossed the fine carpet and entered the inner room. It was a conference chamber, the air hazy with cigarette and pipe smoke from twenty men and women seated around the long narrow table. Markov sneezed.

At the head of the table sat the colonel, a pudgy little man with narrow, squinting pig's eyes. Maria introduced everyone to Markov. He immediately forgot all their names except for Academician Bulacheff—the head of the Soviet Academy of Sciences, and an astronomer of first rank.

Feeling somewhat uneasy, Markov took the seat Maria indicated between a slight, bald man who puffed nervously on a long, thin cigarette, and a female secretary who had a notepad on her lap. Markov noticed that her skirt was up above her knees but her legs weren't worth bothering about.

"Now then," the colonel said with a single nod of his head that made his wattles quiver, "we can begin."

Markov remained silent, listening, as they unfolded the story. The planet Jupiter was giving off strange radio pulses, superimposed against the natural radio noises emanating from the planet. Could it be a signal of some sort? A code? A language?

One of the military men sitting near the colonel shook his head. "I think it's an American spacecraft that's been sent into a very deep orbit."

"It couldn't be," said the man beside Markov.

"A secret probe on its way to Jupiter," the officer insisted.

"For what purpose?"

The officer shrugged. "I'm not in the intelligence service. Let them find out."

"We have no indication of such a launch by the Americans," said a bleak-faced graying woman halfway down the table from Markov. "I doubt that the Americans could hide such a launch from us."

"What about the West Germans? They have a launching base in Brazil now, don't they?"

"It is under constant surveillance," the woman answered. "And it does not have the capability of launching interplanetary missions."

"Then it must be the Americans," the officer said.

Or the Jovians, Markov thought.

"It is not a spacecraft," Academician Bulacheff said in a mild, soft voice. "The radio pulses are coming from the planet itself. Of that we are certain."

"Have the Americans picked up the signals?" the colonel asked. Apparently Bulacheff's word was enough to silence the spacecraft theory.

"We have done a computer search of the American scientific journals," one of the younger civilians answered. "Not a word about this has been published."

"Perhaps they haven't picked up the signals."

"Nonsense! Their facilities are as good as ours. Better, in some cases."

"But do they have a radio telescope operating at the proper frequency? After all . . ."

The man beside Markov shrilled in a high, reedy voice, "We

know of at least four Western facilities that are devoted to studying radio emissions from the planets. The Americans are even
mapping Venus with radar! Do you have any conception of the
kind of equipment needed to accomplish that? No—if *we* have
detected these strange signals from Jupiter, *they* have detected
them also. That is sure."

"But why haven't they published any reports? It's been several
months now and the Americans are always in a rush to get into
print."

"Publish or perish," said Academician Bulacheff with a slow
smile. "Under their system, a scientist must publish papers constantly or be left behind in the competition for money and prestige."

The conversation drifted further and further into a guessing
game about what the Americans were doing. Markov slumped
back in his chair and studied Bulacheff. He was an elderly man
with a thin, sallow face. The little hair that remained on his
gleaming dome was pure white and wispy, like a spindrift of
snow blown across the tundra. The old man seemed slightly
amused by the proceedings. He caught Markov gazing at him
and returned a slight smile.

"The signals can be only one of two things," Bulacheff said.
His soft voice quavered slightly, but everyone turned to him and
listened.

Raising one finger, the academician said, "It could be some
natural process of the planet Jupiter that is giving off these radio
waves. Most likely it is exactly that and nothing more. After all,
we have been observing Jupiter's radio emissions for only a few
decades. The planet has been in existence for more than four
thousand million years. Who are we to say what is natural and
what is anomalous?"

No one challenged his statement. The colonel gave a little
coughing grunt and reached for a fresh cigarette.

"The second possibility?" Markov asked gently.

"It may be a deliberate attempt at communication by an intelligent race of Jovian creatures. Personally, I find that difficult to
accept, but we must consider it as a possibility until we can actually disprove it."

Everyone around the table nodded. A bit fearfully, Markov thought.

"Professor Markov," Bulacheff called, "you are a well-known expert on archaic languages—and you wrote a most interesting monograph about extraterrestrial languages."

Markov felt himself blushing. "The book was merely an amusement. It was not meant to be considered as a serious text."

Bulacheff smiled approvingly. "Perhaps. Still, it was a thoughtful piece of work. We must have your help. We would like you to review all the data we have obtained and have you tell us if, in your opinion, these radio pulses could be a language of some sort."

"Or a code," Maria added.

"I would be happy to do so," Markov said to the academician. "And more than happy to work with you, sir."

Bulacheff inclined his head slightly, accepting the compliment. "Now then, Colonel, if you are truly worried about the Americans, I suggest that we pay special attention to the international astronomical conference that will be held in Paris next month. The Americans will have a large delegation there, as usual. We should be able to learn how much they know."

"They talk that freely?" someone asked.

Bulacheff's wrinkled old face eased into a tolerant grin. "The Americans have a fixation about freedom of speech. They don't know when *not* to talk."

"But suppose," Maria asked, "they say nothing about these radio signals?"

The old man's grin faded. "That in itself would be significant. Very significant."

The colonel placed both his pudgy palms down on the tabletop. "Very well. Pick the people who should attend the conference," he said to Bulacheff. "I will add a few of my own."

Bulacheff nodded.

He's taken command of the project, Markov realized.

"But remember one thing," the colonel warned.

Everyone looked toward him.

"If it becomes clear that these signals really are from an intel-

ligent race, we must make certain that it is the Soviet Union—
and *only* the Soviet Union—that makes contact with them. Such
an advanced technology must not be allowed to fall into the
hands of the West."

. . . how might such a communication be effected? Space vehicles travel very slowly. A typical mission to the Moon lasts a few days, to the nearby planets a few months, to the outer solar system a few years. . . . Even quite optimistic estimates place the nearest civilization at a few hundred light-years, where a light-year is almost six trillion miles. It would take our present spacecraft some tens of thousands of years to go the distance of the nearest star, and several tens of millions of years to travel this estimated distance to the nearest other civilization.

A much quicker and more reliable means of interstellar communication is to send or receive radio messages that travel at the speed of light.

CARL SAGAN
Murmurs of Earth: the Voyager Interstellar Record
Random House
1978

CHAPTER 6

Stoner's eyes snapped open like an electric light turning on. He was lying on the bed, still dressed. He had fallen asleep.

It was morning now, gray and dank. Rain drummed against the window.

The hallway door opened and Dooley backed in, carrying a breakfast tray. It had been his single sharp rap on the door that had awakened Stoner. Through the open door he could see the other agent standing in the hall, calmly appraising him, ready for anything.

"Breakfast in bed," Dooley said cheerfully. "Not bad, huh?"

Stoner nodded blearily and Dooley quickly left. The door closed, the lock clicked.

Despite himself, Stoner found that he had an appetite. Juice, eggs, bacon, muffins, jam and coffee quickly disappeared into crumbs and stains on his paper napkin.

He went to the window, stared outside and tried to figure out where he was. The rain was stripping the last leaves from the trees. Low gray clouds were scudding past, most likely east to west, he thought. So north must be in the direction I'm facing, more or less.

There were no landmarks outside that he could recognize, only wooded hills that might have been anywhere in New England.

With nothing else to do, Stoner showered. He saw there was an electric razor in the bathroom. They're very thorough, he thought. And careful with their prisoners. Rummaging through the bureau drawers and closet, he found a blue pullover sweater and a pair of tan chinos that almost fit. The sleeves and pants legs were too short. At least they're not prison gray.

No books in the room. No television. No phone. The bed was a double. Its fluffy chenille spread, the kind a middle-class housewife buys for the guest room, was rumpled and sagged halfway to the floor. The wingback chair was still a decorator's nightmare. The carpet was thick, beige, ordinary. The night table was some unrecognizable variation of the furniture style carried by mail-order chains.

It was an odd room to be locked in.

Stoner shrugged to himself, thought about doing some warmup exercises, started pacing the room instead. He was by the window when the door's sudden opening startled him.

Turning quickly, he saw that the man coming through the doorway was the observatory's director, Professor McDermott.

Ramsey McDermott was a big man, physically big, with the heavy shoulders of a longshoreman and the rugged good looks— even in his sixties—of a campus idol. His blond hair had turned a dull pewter shade of gray long ago, but he still kept it in a bristling crew cut. His cobalt-blue eyes could still snap when he got angry.

Professor McDermott liked to loom over smaller people and convince them that he was right and they were wrong on the strength of precise logic and a booming voice. But to Stoner, Big

Mac looked old and flabby, living on past glories and younger men's achievements.

Stoner stood between the window and the chair as McDermott came into the bedroom. The hall door closed behind him.

"How are they treating you, Stoner?" No handshake. McDermott kept his heavy, blunt-fingered hands at his sides. He was wearing a tweed jacket, comfortable old slacks that bagged slightly at the knees, a checkered shirt with a hideous green tie.

"Rotten," Stoner snapped. "What's this all about?"

Looking over the room and seeing that the only chair was the little upholstered thing that Stoner stood in front of, the old man went across to the rumpled bed and gingerly lowered himself onto it.

"Damned arthritis," he grumbled in a deep, surprisingly rich voice. "Weather like this really gets to it."

"What's happening?" Stoner demanded. "Why have I been locked up here?"

"Your own damned fault," McDermott said, reaching into his jacket for a blackened briar pipe. "I know you were going to run down to Washington."

"I'm still a NASA employee . . ."

"Only technically," McDermott said. "You're on loan to me, and by God you'll take orders from me!"

"You can't push me around like this."

"The Navy can. The observatory's funded by the Office of Naval Research, sonny. At my suggestion, ONR has slapped a Confidential classification on what you're doing."

Stoner sank down into the chair. "How in hell can you classify a natural phenomenon? What I've discovered . . . why would the Navy want to keep it secret?"

Puffing blue clouds of smoke that smelled like burnt pencil shavings, McDermott answered, "You have no idea what's involved in all this, do you?"

"I've found extraterrestrial life, dammit!"

"Phah." The old man looked completely unimpressed. "Listen to me, sonny. I saved your career. If it weren't for me you'd be an unemployed ex-astronaut with a useless degree in astrophysics, teaching in some jerkwater college in Texas. Don't forget that."

"What does that have to do with it?"

McDermott puffed on his pipe. "Jupiter's giving off some strange radio pulses, the likes of which we've never seen before. So *I* get the inspiration of bringing an optical astronomer into the observatory, somebody who can get us access to the first pictures Big Eye is taking, from orbit."

"Okay, it was a good idea. A great idea."

"You bet it was."

"And it paid off," Stoner went on, "with the biggest discovery in history."

The old man snorted. "And you want to run down to Washington and tell your old buddies in NASA about it."

"For a start."

"And become a big hero. Publish a paper in *Icarus*. Get your picture on the cover of *Time* magazine. Become another goddamned Sagan and get on the Johnny Carson show."

"What's wrong with you?" Stoner asked. The man was talking in riddles.

McDermott blew a jet of smoke toward the ceiling. "What have you discovered, Stoner? What do those Big Eye photographs really show?"

"A spacecraft orbiting Jupiter, for Chrissake!"

"Bullcrap!" the old man bellowed. "It's a natural satellite. Another moon. The damned planet's got fifteen of 'em that we know about. This makes sixteen."

"With the kind of UV-to-blue indices we've measured?" Stoner countered. "It's much too bright to be a natural moon."

"How the hell do you know? It could be a chunk of ice that's been captured . . ."

"It's metal," Stoner said, quietly, firmly.

McDermott took the pipe from his teeth and shook his head sorrowfully. "You're grasping at straws, sonny. All you've got is a couple of photographs that show a tiny speck of light nobody's noticed before."

"Big Eye picked it up because it's too faint for telescopes on the ground to see."

"So why should you think it's artificial?"

Eagerly hunching forward in his little chair, Stoner ticked off points on his fingers. "First, your people pick up these radio pulses—something brand new. Nothing like them have ever come from Jupiter before."

"That we know of."

"Second, you bring me into the game so you can acquire the use of Big Eye before it's officially turned over to the universities. I get them to look at Jupiter and we find . . . something new."

"A sixteenth moon," McDermott muttered.

"Too much of a coincidence," Stoner insisted. "The new radio signals and the new . . . object. It's extraterrestrial life. *Intelligent* extraterrestrial life."

"No."

"Yes! Face it!"

Big Mac sucked on his pipe. It had gone out. Fumbling in his pockets for his lighter, he said, "Listen to me. Even if you're right it's too early to go running around yelling about it. It's a million-to-one shot, and if you're wrong about it, you'd be ruining yourself and the observatory by blabbing about it now."

"But other facilities must be picking up the radio pulses. We can't sit here and let them take the credit for discovering them."

"They don't have the Big Eye photographs," McDermott said. "That's our ace in the hole."

"For how long?"

"Long enough. That's why I got the Navy to classify everything."

Stoner got to his feet and paced the length of the bedroom. "We've got the greatest discovery in the history of science . . ."

"Maybe."

". . . and you want to keep it a secret."

McDermott gave a grunt that might have been a chuckle and, heaving himself up from the bed, jabbed the pipe stem-first toward Stoner. "It's out of our hands anyway, sonny. Come with me. Come on."

They went out the unlocked bedroom door, along the upstairs hallway of the old house and down the steep narrow stairs to the spacious new living room that bordered on the indoor pool.

Someone was swimming, methodically plodding his way slowly along its length in an overhand crawl stroke. Stoner couldn't be sure, but he thought the swimmer was Dooley.

Then he noticed that two men were sitting in the living room, in front of the empty dark fireplace. They got to their feet as Stoner and McDermott approached. Stoner recognized one of them as Jeff Thompson, from the observatory.

"Jeff," he said as he came toward the fireplace. "So they dragged you in, too."

"Not exactly," Thompson said, smiling a little guiltily. "I came voluntarily."

"Everybody's volunteered to keep this thing quiet," McDermott rumbled from behind Stoner. "You're the only one who's giving us trouble."

I'm the only one who's not on your direct payroll, Stoner answered silently.

The other man stuck out his hand to Stoner. "Hi. I'm Fred Tuttle."

McDermott explained, "Lieutenant Commander Tuttle is our contracting office in the Office of Naval Research."

Tuttle was in civvies: a neat tan corduroy suit with brown suede patches on the elbows. He was a small man, with the round freckled face of a Mark Twain character. But his grip was strong in Stoner's hand, self-assured. A salesman's grip, with the winning smile that they teach you in confidence courses.

"You're Air Force, aren't you?" the lieutenant commander asked.

"Inactive reserve," Stoner replied. "*Very* inactive reserve."

Tuttle's smile widened, showing even white teeth. "Well, we may be forced to put you back on active status, you know."

"No, I don't know. I don't understand what in hell is going on."

With a gesture Tuttle got them all seated. Stoner took the sofa that flanked the cold fireplace. It smelled of carbon and wet leaves. Thompson sat next to him. McDermott grabbed the big cushioned chair opposite. Tuttle remained standing, in charge.

"What we've got here"—the lieutenant commander's face went serious—"is something that may be vitally important to the nation's security."

"Important to the nation's security?" Stoner echoed, incredulous. "How can ETI be . . . ?"

"ETI?" Tuttle asked.

"Extraterrestrial intelligence," Thompson explained. "Astronomical jargon."

"Let's not get carried away here," McDermott rumbled. "All we've really got is these anomalous low-frequency radio signals and a few photographs showing what's most likely a sixteenth moon of Jupiter."

"Even if that's all there is to it," Stoner countered, icily, "we should publish the information. In *Science*. Or *Nature*. Before somebody else scoops us."

The old man glowered from behind his pipe. Tuttle clasped his hands behind his back and stared at his shoe tops.

Stoner felt the glacial calm that always descended upon him when he grew angry. Very quietly he asked, "What in hell happened to freedom of speech around here? Whatever happened to Faraday's dictum: 'Physics is to make experiments *and to publish them*'?"

"I'm not going to put my reputation on the line for some radio pulses and a couple of photos!" McDermott blurted. "I'm not going to make a jackass of myself claiming that we've discovered ETI and then be forced to retract it all when it turns out to be completely natural."

"Then publish what we've got," Stoner said in a cobra's whisper. "Forget the ETI conclusion, but at least let Jeff publish the radio pulses. He deserves that much. Get the priority. In print."

Thompson's eyebrows went up hopefully.

"The problem is this," Tuttle took over again. "If there's any chance at all that we *have* discovered extraterrestrial intelligence on the planet Jupiter, we've got to keep it confidential. It's important to the national security."

"How can intelligent life on Jupiter affect the national security?" Stoner asked.

Tuttle responded immediately, as if rehearsed. "If there is intelligent life on Jupiter, it must have a level of technology far ahead of our own to launch a spacecraft against a gravity field that's much more powerful than Earth's. We can't allow other nations—Russia, China, others—to get their hands on that technology. We've got to make certain that the free nations of the West get it."

Stoner felt his shoulders slump. "The same old shit," he muttered.

Undeterred, Tuttle went on, "Moreover, we've got to consider the possibility that the Jovians, whoever they are, might not harbor peaceful intentions. Maybe they intend to . . . well, invade us."

"Sure," Stoner said. "Maybe all those flying saucers the UFO freaks have been seeing for the past thirty years are really scouts from Jupiter, checking us out before they come here to rape and pillage."

"UFO's do exist," Tuttle said seriously. "And if there's intelligent life on Jupiter . . ."

"I'm starting to wonder if there's intelligent life on Earth," Stoner snapped. He got up from the sofa and headed back toward the stairway.

"Dr. Stoner!" Tuttle called. "You can't leave this house, you know."

Stoner glanced back over his shoulder and saw that Dooley was scrambling out of the pool. He stopped and stood where he was, seething.

Thompson was suddenly at his side. "Come on, Keith. Sit down and hear them out. It'll all work out, one way or another."

Clamping his teeth together so hard that his jaw throbbed, Stoner went back to the living room with Jeff Thompson.

"What you've got to realize, sonny," said McDermott once he was seated on the sofa again, "is that if you're right, if we *have* found extraterrestrial intelligence, the implications are enormous. Enormous!"

"The social impact alone could be incredible," Thompson agreed.

"And the psychological effects," McDermott went on. "The religious effects!"

"And the military implications," said Tuttle.

Stoner frowned at him.

"The gravity on Jupiter is more than three times higher than Earth's, isn't it?" the lieutenant commander asked.

"Not quite three," Thompson corrected, "at the top of the cloud deck."

"Okay," Tuttle said. "But down below the clouds the gravity

must be even stronger. Do you have any concept of the technology it would take to loft an artificial satellite against that gravity? And that spacecraft you found is in a very high orbit, isn't it?"

"Yes," Stoner admitted.

"We couldn't launch a satellite under those conditions. Take it from me, I know that for a fact."

Grimacing, Stoner said, "And while we sit around here stamping everything Secret, some other observatory stumbles onto the radio pulses and publishes the data. So then where are we?"

"But we're the only ones who know about the spacecraft," Tuttle said, excitement shaking his voice. "Nobody else has access to Big Eye and nobody will, I can guarantee that!"

"But somebody else could beat us into print with the radio pulses," Thompson said glumly.

McDermott shook his head. "Who? Haystack? Goldstone? They're not working down below six hundred megahertz, the way we are."

"What about Arecibo?" Stoner asked. "That's the biggest radio telescope of them all, isn't it? And Sagan's connected with it. Him and Drake. They'll be into print in ten seconds flat."

"Get yourself an ephemeris," said McDermott, smirking. "Arecibo can't point anywhere near Jupiter for another four months."

Stoner blinked and then remembered that the huge Arecibo radio telescope—a thousand feet across—was carved into a hillside and couldn't be steered or aimed the way the smaller radio dishes were.

"But we owe it to the rest of the scientific community to let them know what we've found," Stoner insisted. "It's only fair . . ."

"I am not going to risk my reputation, or my observatory's reputation, or the university's reputation," McDermott said, his voice steadily rising, "on the million-to-one chance that you're right!"

Tuttle added, "And there *is* the pressing military necessity to keep this under wraps. You can understand that, can't you?"

The hell I can, Stoner thought. But he said nothing.

"There's one additional factor," Thompson said. "Somebody

overseas might have already picked up the pulses. The Australians, the Russians, Voorne at Dwingeloo . . ."

Tuttle nodded curtly. "We're looking into that."

"And what do we do in the meantime?" Stoner asked. "Go to Leavenworth and wait until the Navy decides it's okay for us to return to work?"

"Nosir," said Tuttle. "The radio telescope observatory will continue to work as normal. All the staff have signed security oaths, and we've briefed them all on the need to keep this information absolutely secret. You'll have to agree, too."

"No, I won't," Stoner said flatly. "I'm just a consultant on this job. NASA pays my salary, not the Navy."

"Dr. Stoner, you are in the Air Force reserve. You could be recalled to active duty. This is an extraordinary circumstance. A real emergency."

McDermott chuckled. "They'll probably ship you to Greenland. Or maybe the South Pole."

"If you co-operate," Tuttle went on, "we'll set you up right here, in this house. You'll be incommunicado for a while, until we move the entire project staff to a more secure, government-owned facility."

Stoner realized they had him; there was no use arguing.

Glancing at his wristwatch, Tuttle said, "Well, I've got to get back to Washington. Lots to do. Dr. Stoner, I hope you appreciate the seriousness of this situation."

Without waiting for an answer, the little Navy officer strode briskly from the room. McDermott got up and lumbered out after him.

Stoner sagged back on the sofa, icy waves of anger creeping along his veins. Turning to Thompson, he asked, "Jeff, am I crazy, or are they?"

Shrugging, the astronomer answered, "Maybe none of you. Or maybe we all are. I don't know; insufficient data."

"McDermott's an asshole. He can't ride roughshod over people like this. He's *using* that kid. When the real Navy finds out what they're doing . . ."

Smiling tiredly, Thompson said, "That kid *is* the real Navy. And Big Mac isn't riding roughshod over anybody but you. The rest of us signed our security oaths as meek as lambs."

"You too?"

"Sure, me too. I can't afford to lose my job. Do you know how many openings there are for a second-rank radio astronomer? I'd have to start all over again, at the bottom." He shook his head.

"And you're willing to sign away your freedom to publish, just to hold onto your tenure at the university?"

"Look, Keith, I've got three kids to feed. And a wife. And a dog that eats as much as she does."

Stoner said nothing, but thought, I had a wife and two kids and if I stop working they lose the alimony and child support.

Thompson slapped him playfully on the shoulder. "Don't look so goddamned grim! This is all routine red tape. It'll all straighten itself out. We'll publish sooner or later."

"But how the hell did Big Mac find out about me?" Stoner wondered. "How did he know I was going to Washington?"

"Did you ask one of the secretaries to make plane reservations for you?"

Frowning, Stoner said, "No. I deliberately steered clear of them. Figured they'd go straight to McDermott with the information. I got one of the students to make my reservations . . . what's her name, the tall one with the good figure?"

"Jo Camerata?"

"Yeah. Jo. That's the one."

Thompson gave a low whistle. "Then she must've told Big Mac herself. Or at least, one of the regular secretaries."

"But I specifically told her not to."

Thompson shrugged. "And here I thought she was after your body."

"What?"

"She's had her eye on you for quite a while. Coming around the observatory, cutting classes, trying to catch your attention."

"Don't be silly," Stoner said. "She's just a kid."

"Some kid," Thompson grinned. "She's got the hots for you."

What of the occupants [of the UFOs] themselves? They seem to come in two sizes, large and small, with the former predominating. The Hopkinsville humanoids and many of those recounted . . . are much akin in appearance to the "little folk" of legend and story—elves, brownies, etc. Large heads, spindly feet, and, generally a head that sits square on the shoulders without much evidence of neck are often described. The larger humanoids are reported to be human size or a little larger and are generally very well formed. Sometimes they have been termed beautiful. The smaller ones are generally described as about three and a half feet tall. . . .

Therefore I must leave it to the reader's own judgment what weight to assign to Close Encounters of the Third Kind in assessing the whole problem [of UFOs], always remembering that it may yet be discovered that the humanoid cases are the key to the whole problem.

J. ALLEN HYNEK
The UFO Experience: A Scientific Inquiry
Ballantine Books
1972

CHAPTER 7

Kirill Markov stood squinting under his fur hat as the wind gusted down the street. No matter how long he lived, he would never become accustomed to the cold. It knifed through his fine coat and iced his bones.

Maria was speaking to the driver of the car parked at the curb in front of their apartment building, while Markov stamped his feet and waited at the doorway. Neighbors were peering out of their windows, discreetly of course, but Markov could see their shadowy forms behind the curtains. Even though the automobile was unmarked, everyone sensed that it was a government car. Markov could feel the mixture of curiosity and terror that rippled through the apartment blocks like an electric current.

"It's the professor!"

"They're taking him away? In broad daylight?"

"Look for yourself."

"His wife, too?"

"No, it doesn't seem so."

"They don't look upset, either one of them."

"Perhaps it's not what we think, then."

"Usually they come at night."

"Pah! I know how they work. The professor may *think* he's being taken to the airport or to some fancy university campus. Even his wife may think so. But take a good look at him. It's the last you'll ever see of him."

"No!"

"That's the way they took my brother, Grisha. Told him he was being transferred to a new job, in Kharkov. He went with a smile on his face. Into a cattle car that took him straight to Siberia. Eight years, they kept him there. He was a broken man when they let him back home to die."

"But what could the professor have done . . . ?"

"He's a thinker. It doesn't pay to think certain kinds of thoughts."

Markov smiled to himself as he sensed their whispered conversations swirling through the apartments all around him.

No, my neighbors, he wanted to say. It's not what you think. The government values me for my ability to think.

Maria finished her talk with the driver, straightened up and turned toward Markov. She was wearing only her regulation uniform, with nothing but the thin jacket to protect her blocky body. How she stood the cold was something Markov could never understand. Yet her feet were always like icebergs when she got into bed.

"Well, come on," she called impatiently.

Markov picked up his briefcase, trotted down the steps to the curb and reached for the car door.

"In the back," Maria said. "You sit in the back seat."

"Oh. I see." He pulled the rear door open and hesitated. Maria was standing next to him with her usual scowl on her face.

Markov looked into her eyes. "I . . . may not see you again for quite a while."

She nodded matter-of-factly.

"Well . . . take good care of yourself, old girl."

"You too," she mumbled.

He put a hand on her shoulder and she turned her face so that he could kiss her cheek. He pecked at it, then quickly ducked into the car. She slammed the door shut and the driver started the motor with a horrible screech of the ignition.

As the car pulled away from the curb, Markov turned to wave at his wife. She had already started back inside the apartment building. For some inexplicable reason he felt a lump in his throat.

The Naval Research Laboratory lies along the Potomac River, almost directly in the glide path of the commercial jetliners coming into Washington's National Airport.

Ramsey McDermott, squeezed into one of the Eastern shuttle's narrow seats between the window and the hyperthyroid businessman who had spent the entire forty-minute flight shuffling papers and tapping out numbers on a pocket calculator, smiled grimly to himself as the plane flashed past NRL. Atop the central riverfront building was the venerable dish antenna of NRL's fifty-foot radio telescope.

They can't pick up the Jovian pulses with that piece of crap, McDermott told himself.

He had "double shuttled" in his haste to get to a personal meeting with Tuttle, taking one Eastern 727 from Boston to New York and then immediately getting on to the New York-to-Washington plane.

Tuttle's office was not at NRL, or at the Pentagon. He had lucked into a plush new office building that the Navy leased in Crystal City, one of the high-rise glass and steel towers that had given the area its name.

McDermott phoned the lieutenant commander from the airport, and they agreed to meet at a restaurant downtown.

Impatiently drumming his fingertips on the rickety little table out on the chilly sidewalk in front of the Connecticut Avenue restaurant, Ramsey McDermott waited for Lieutenant Commander Tuttle to select his lunch from the oversized menu.

They bombed Pearl Harbor with less attention to detail, the old man groused to himself.

Tuttle had insisted that they meet at an outdoor restaurant. "Less chance of being bugged," he had whispered, quite seriously.

They discussed the problems of moving the staff to Arecibo, Tuttle clamping his mouth shut whenever a waiter or another customer drifted close to their table. McDermott, uncomfortable in the damp chill and the traffic noise from the street, struggled to keep his temper.

"If we need Arecibo," Tuttle said finally, "we'll get Arecibo, even if I have to get the President to declare a national emergency."

"You can do that?"

Tuttle nodded solemnly. "If I have to."

For the first time, McDermott felt impressed with the young officer's powers.

"But this man Stoner," Tuttle went on. "He's the key to it all. We need him to correlate the optical sightings with the radio signals."

"He'll do it," McDermott promised.

"He hasn't called for a lawyer or tried to get away from the house where we've stashed him?"

"No. He's going through a divorce; I think he's kind of glad to be safely tucked away where the lawyers and his ex-wife can't find him." McDermott chuckled to himself. "And underneath it all, he's got that old scientific curiosity—a fatal dose. It's an itch he can't scratch unless he plays ball with us."

"I don't want to call in anybody else if we can avoid it," Tuttle said. "God knows there's enough people involved in this project already. I don't want to let anybody else know what we're onto. Not yet."

"Stoner will co-operate."

"And he can get more photographs from Big Eye?"

"He helped design and build it. The telescope is being

checked out by the NASA people at Goddard, before they officially turn it over to the university consortium that'll run it. The official hand-over date is January first. Until then, the Goddard people are happy to help out an old pal. Stoner worked with those people for five years. They think they're just helping out a guy who got laid off by shipping him some photos of Jupiter."

"And Stoner himself won't cause any trouble for us? He'll stay where we've put him?"

"Yes."

"You're sure? Absolutely certain?"

McDermott leaned his heavy forearms on the wobbly little table. "Listen to me. He's got everything he needs up there at the house. But I'll tell you what I'll do. I'll get a girl for him— one of the students, a kid named Jo something-or-other. Hot stuff. She'll go prancing up there and we'll let nature take its course. She'll keep him busy. And happy to stay where he is."

Tuttle scowled disapprovingly. "That's sinful."

"It sure is."

"Well," the Navy officer said, "I hope she's signed a security agreement, at least."

Markov drowsed in the back seat as the car hummed through the gray October afternoon along the endless highway, kilometer after kilometer of flat, empty countryside. A thin coating of snow lay over the ground. The fields were bare. The trees stark and leafless against the dull sky.

Mother Russia, Markov mused, half asleep. The real strength of our nation: the soil, all its vastness, all its timeless power.

The sun was a dull yellowish blotch on the horizon when the car finally stopped at a chain link fence. A pair of soldiers stood by the gate. Except for their little wooden sentry house, Markov could see no structure anywhere. The fence seemed to be guarding emptiness, as far as the eye could roam.

The driver exchanged words with the soldiers and Markov opened his briefcase to show them his papers. They were very polite to him and quickly swung the gate open.

As the car accelerated along the blacktopped road, Markov re-

alized that he hadn't eaten anything since breakfast. The dreary
landscape stretched in all directions, empty and gray. His stomach rumbled. I might as well be going to Siberia, he thought.
This land is exile for a Muscovite like me.

It was fully dark by the time they came to the second fence.
The guardhouse there was bigger, and made of stone. Again soldiers looked over his papers, by the glow of a flashlight.

"Professor Markov, you are expected. One moment, please."

The guard disappeared into the stone building. In a few seconds a young lady came bouncing out to the car, long hair
flying, fur-trimmed coat unbuttoned.

"Professor Markov!" she exclaimed, opening the car door and
scrambling in beside him. "We were getting worried about you;
you're quite late." She tapped the driver on the shoulder. "Go
straight ahead and take the second left."

Before Markov could say anything, she turned back to him. "I
am Sonya Vlasov . . . I am only a graduate student here, doing
my doctoral thesis work, but the director asked me to be your
guide." She was almost breathless with excitement.

Markov paid no attention to the row upon row of huge radio
telescopes that glinted metallically in the lights from the road.
He saw only that Sonya Vlasov was young, eager, a little plump,
and had enormous breasts.

"My personal guide?" He smiled at her in a fatherly way.

"Oh yes. Whatever you want or need, it will be my pleasure to
see that you get it."

"How very thoughtful."

She pushed back her long, light brown hair with one hand, a
motion that made her coat open even more.

"Welcome to the Landau Radio Astronomy Institute, Professor
Markov!" she said happily.

Markov nodded graciously. Exile might not be so bad after
all, he thought.

I must now mention God—otherwise quite properly unmentioned in these scientific studies—and must go a step further and pose the question: Can a religious person, or even more, a theologian, possibly be legitimately involved in, even be excited by these discussions of the possibility of other intelligent creatures and free creatures out there?

As a theologian, I would say that this proposed search for extraterrestrial intelligence (SETI) is also a search of knowing and understanding God through His works —especially those works that most reflect Him. Finding others than ourselves would mean knowing Him better.

THEODORE M. HESBURGH, C.S.C.
President, University of Notre Dame
The Search for Extraterrestrial Intelligence (SETI)
National Aeronautics and Space
Administration
NASA SP-419
1977

CHAPTER 8

Stoner looked up from his frozen dinner and saw Jo standing in the kitchen doorway, a thick manila folder clutched in her mittened hands.

For a moment he didn't know what to say. Dark anger rushed through him; he could feel its heat in his face.

"What are you doing here?"

She stood her ground. "I brought the latest packet of photographs from Goddard Space Center." Her voice was low but steady.

"Brought me my homework. Thanks a lot."

Taking a step into the kitchen, Jo said, "Professor McDermott needed somebody to carry things from the observatory to you. He told me to do it."

Stoner said nothing.

"I had to get special clearance from the Navy."

"I'll bet."

"Look—I didn't think they'd do this to you." Jo's voice didn't tremble, but he could sense the tension in it. And there was something in her face, something in those dark eyes of hers: guilt, or fear, or . . . what?

"What did you think they'd do?" he asked.

She shrugged inside her heavy wool coat. "I don't know. I tried to warn you . . . to tell you that McDermott was uptight about you going to Washington . . ."

"How'd he find out, Jo?"

Her face fell. In a voice so low he could barely hear it, she answered, "I told him."

"Yeah. I know."

"He pressured me. I've been cutting a lot of classes to be out at the observatory. He said he'd flunk me out if I didn't tell him what you were up to."

He studied her. If she's lying, she's good at it. Anger was seething inside him. Or was it something else, something more? Anger usually left Stoner cold, his mind became as unemotional and unfeeling as an electronic computer. But now his hands wanted to grab and tear, his insides were jumping, blood pounding. Jesus, Stoner realized, it's been months since I've gotten laid.

"Come on in," he said, trying to make it sound calm. "Take your coat off. Sit down. Have some coffee."

Hesitantly Jo entered the kitchen. She put the thick manila folder on the Formica-topped counter, pulled off her mittens, slipped out of the coat. Stoner went to the range, where the glass coffeepot sat, half empty.

"No coffee for me, thanks." She took the stool across the counter from his and watched him pour himself a cup. "Are they treating you all right here? Is there anything I can bring you?"

"My car and the keys to it."

"They won't let me."

He carried the steaming mug back to the counter and sat down facing her. "That old car's the only thing I've got to show for sixteen years of marriage."

"Oh."

"I've become kind of attached to it."

"But they're treating you okay? They're not giving you any hassles?"

"Sure. Everything's fine—once I signed the security agreement. Now I've got the run of the house. Eight rooms. Or is it nine? I've lost count. Plenty of food. I have to cook it for myself, though. I'm a lousy cook."

"I could cook for you, sometimes."

He ignored it. Reaching for the manila folder, Stoner pulled out the latest stack of photographs. They showed the fat, flattened, gaudily striped beach ball that was the planet Jupiter. He could see exquisite details of the streaming bands of clouds that flowed across the planet: eddies and whirlpools the size of Earth, in burnt orange, brick red, dazzling white.

"Where are the background field pictures I asked for?"

"In the next batch," Jo replied. "They're still being processed."

"I need them," he said. "And a computer terminal."

She nodded. "Anything else?"

"Books. Every book on extraterrestrial life you can find. Empty the libraries. I want *everything* on the subject."

Another nod. "Anything else?"

He looked into her deep, lustrous eyes. "Why did you come here tonight, Jo?"

"Professor McDermott told me to. I'm a courier now."

"Why did you accept the job? You didn't have to."

For a moment she didn't answer. Then, "I wanted to see you. To tell you I'm sorry. If I'd stood up to Big Mac . . . maybe . . ." She looked away from him. "I'm sorry it turned out this way. Truly I am."

He reached across the table and grasped her wrist. "Prove it."

Without another word he led her out of the kitchen, through the tiny, close rooms of the old part of the house, up the narrow stairway to his bedroom.

He closed the door firmly. No need to turn on a lamp: cold moonlight filtered through the gauzy curtains of the window.

For a moment Jo stood in front of the bed. Then she turned

toward him. Stoner leaned his back against the heavy wooden panels of the door. Neither of them spoke.

He could see her face etched by the moonlight. She wasn't smiling. Her expression was strangely placid, tranquil. She began unbuttoning her blouse. Stoner watched. She unhooked her bra and tossed it aside. Reaching down, she pulled off her shoes, then slithered the jeans down her long legs. And finally the skimpy flowered bikini panties.

"Is this what you want?" she whispered.

His throat was dry. "Yes," he said, with an effort.

She stepped to him and started to unbutton his shirt. He stood there and let her do the work. Finally she was on her knees in front of him and he was naked. She kissed his erect penis.

"Is this what you want?" she asked again. But she didn't wait for an answer.

Just before he thought he would explode, Stoner dug his fingers into her thick black hair and pulled her away from him. Bending down, he scooped her into his arms and carried her the four strides to the bed. He put her on the coverlet and tented his body over hers.

Jo twined her arms around his neck and pulled him down onto her. He kissed her as he entered her and she was warm and ready and moving in rhythm with him.

It was like being in space again, floating weightlessly, drifting, drifting through the dark eternities while the stars solemnly, silently gazed down.

She clung to him as they convulsed together and then gasped out a single word: "Keith!"

For long moments they lay locked together, hearts racing, breath gasping. He lifted his face from the tufted coverlet and looked into her eyes again.

She smiled up at him. "That's the first time you've kissed me," she said.

"It's the first time you called me by my first name."

They laughed together.

He sat on the edge of the bed. His insides still felt fluttery. Jo traced a fingernail along the length of his spine.

"Is there anything else I can do for you, Dr. Stoner?" she teased.

Turning back toward her, "Stay the night."

"I have a class tomorrow morning."

"Oh." He frowned in the shadows. "Where in hell are we, anyway? Where is this house?"

"In New Hampshire . . . not far from White River Junction."

"White River Junction? Then how in hell can you drive to campus in time for a morning class?"

"So I'll miss the class," Jo said easily. "It won't be the first time."

"That's what got you under McDermott's thumb, isn't it?"

"I can handle Professor McDermott. He's just a big bully."

"White River Junction," Stoner mused. "Maybe you ought to bring up a pair of skis the next time you come."

"We won't be here for the ski season, from what Professor McDermott says."

"What do you mean?"

"He said the whole observatory staff will be heading south in a few weeks."

"Including me?"

She nodded. "And me. I'm going too."

"Where?"

"He wouldn't say. Just that the climate wouldn't be so cold."

"Green Bank?" Stoner wondered. "No, it's just as cold in those West Virginia hills as it is here. It can't be Arecibo. Not even Big Mac could swing Drake and Sagan out of there."

"What's it like to be an astronaut?" Jo asked.

He blinked at the sudden shift in subject. "Huh? I wasn't really an astronaut . . . not like the real rocket jocks. They used me as a construction engineer. I just rode up into orbit and helped put Big Eye together."

"But you spent months in space, didn't you?"

Shrugging, "Sure. And once they got the telescope working, NASA figured they didn't need an expensive astrophysicist who did construction work anymore. So I got RIFfed."

"What does that mean?"

"Reduction In Force. Laid off. Bounced. Fired."

"And that's when you came to the observatory?"

"Yes."

"And your family . . . where are they?"

So she's pumping me, Stoner told himself, knowing that

sooner or later she would have asked him about his wife and children.

"My wife took the kids back to her parents in Palo Alto," he said flatly. "The day I got the RIF notice, as a matter of fact. Strictly coincidence; poetic timing. We hadn't gotten along in years."

"How old . . . ?"

"Fifteen and twelve," he answered automatically. "The boy's the oldest. I don't see them at all. Last time I flew out to Palo Alto they wouldn't even come to the front door to say hello to me. Let's change the subject."

Jo reached over and pulled him down to her and kissed him. "I'm sorry," she said softly. "It must hurt a lot."

"It should, I guess. But mostly it just feels kind of numb."

"You're covering it over."

"With work. Right. My work comes first. Doris always said that it did, and she was right."

"And now?"

"Now I'm onto the biggest goddamned discovery in history. Nothing else matters. I'm going to *prove* that we've found extra-terrestrial intelligence. No matter what Big Mac or the Navy or anybody else does—I'm going to prove it to the world."

Jo leaned her head against his shoulder and made long, soothing, soft strokes of her fingertips down his chest.

"So fierce," she said in a whisper. "Do you know, you're just like me? We're two of a kind."

"You? You're kidding."

"I want them to notice me, too, Keith. I want to *be* somebody. I want to make the whole world know who I am."

He found himself grinning. "Well, you're on the right project for that."

But Jo said, "Who's going to notice a little technical assistant, next to the famous Dr. Keith Stoner or Professor McDermott. No. I'm going to become an astronaut. A real one."

"NASA isn't hiring."

"They will be, sooner or later. And women will get special preference, you'll see."

"It's not a romantic life. It's more like being a bus driver. Just a lot of hard donkey work. And risk."

"But you went into space. You became famous."

"And unemployed."

"Imagine making love in zero gravity!"

"Waterbeds are almost as good. Besides, astronauts don't make love in orbit. They're too damned busy. And scared. And exhausted."

"I don't believe it."

"It's a dull life, I tell you."

"No duller than being a computer programmer."

"Is that what you're studying?"

He could sense her smiling in the darkness, cradled next to his body. "That's what my parents think I'm studying. They want me to go to school and learn a nice, sensible trade until I meet a nice, sensible guy and get married and start having babies."

"And they're paying your way . . ."

"The hell they are! I got myself a partial scholarship. And I work weekends and summers. How do you think I got into the observatory? I get paid for helping out."

He grinned at the determination in her voice. "So now you've joined Big Mac's supersecret ETI project. I hope he's paying you well."

"I get a full technician's salary."

"Not bad."

"And I'm transferring to the Astronautics Department," Jo added. "I'm going to be an astronaut and nothing's going to stop me."

"Fine," Stoner said, fighting back a yawn. "But in the meantime let's not freeze to death." He peeled back the covers on his side of the bed.

"Don't worry," Jo answered. "We're going to be nice and warm this winter. We're going to Arecibo. I'm sure of it."

"McDermott can't swing that much weight," Stoner said, sliding into the bed. The sheets were already warm from the press of their bodies.

But Jo was on her feet, searching through the moonlit room for her scattered clothes.

"What're you doing?"

"I brought an overnight bag with me," she said, yanking on

the jeans without bothering about the panties. "It's in my car. I'll be back in a minute."

She was still buttoning her blouse as she went out into the hall, heading for the stairs.

Stoner yawned and wondered briefly how she knew so much about McDermott's plans. Then he thought about the overnight bag. The cocky little bitch! He didn't know whether to laugh or be angry. Yawning, he decided to do neither. He turned over on his side and drifted to sleep.

It is said that the freezing temperatures on planets like Jupiter or Saturn, in the outer Solar System, make all life there impossible. But these low temperatures do not apply to all portions of the planet. They refer only to the outermost cloud layers—the layers that are accessible to infrared telescopes that can measure temperatures. Indeed, if we had such a telescope in the vicinity of Jupiter and pointed it at Earth, we would deduce very low temperatures on Earth. We would be measuring the temperatures in the upper clouds and not on the much warmer surface of Earth.

CARL SAGAN
The Cosmic Connection
Anchor Press/Doubleday
1973

CHAPTER 9

A cocktail party in official Washington has an inbred hierarchical cast to it. Senators usually outweigh congressmen, of course, but there are all sorts of gradations among both senators and congressmen. A committee chairman is obviously more important than a subcommittee chairman—most of the time. But what about a junior Republican who happens to be an attractive woman? What about a congressman's aide who happens to be related to the governor of the congressman's home state?

Lieutenant Commander Tuttle was sensitive to the subtlest nuances of these parties. He knew that lieutenant commanders were slightly lower, in cocktail party echelons, than the average bartender. Still, much good work could be done at the right party if the lieutenant commander properly briefed his commanding officer. Besides, this party had a special extra dimen-

sion to it: the guest of honor was Willie Wilson, the Urban
Evangelist who was the brand new "catch" of the young social
season.

The party was taking place in the old Sheraton-Park Hotel,
still desperately trying to cling to its former elegance. The gilt
decorations of the function room were worn thin, the old
draperies dusty and frayed. But the rumor was that Wilson had
arranged the party for himself and gotten a special low price
from the hotel. The ostensible hostess had been dragooned into
fronting for the Urban Evangelist.

Tuttle's post for the evening was in a corner of the ornate,
gilded function room, dutifully chatting with the wife of his
commanding admiral.

"These parties are such a bore, don't you think?" bellowed
Mrs. Admiral O'Kelly. She held a heavy Bourbon on the rocks in
one beringed hand and was fingering her rope of artificial pearls
with the other.

Tuttle nodded. He was in dress uniform and felt slightly stiff
and foolish standing next to this old matron with her bluish hair
piled high atop her wrinkled, sagging face. But the admiral's orders had been firm: "Let me do the talking; you keep my wife
supplied with drinks but don't let her get drunk."

Not an easy task, thought Tuttle.

The big room was only half filled with guests in tuxedos and
evening gowns. Willie Wilson was the newest "in" subject of
Washington society, but the Sheraton-Park was not an "in" hotel
anymore.

Still, the noise level was climbing to the point where you had
to shout to make yourself heard by the person standing next to
you. The admiral's wife had no trouble with that: she had the
voice of a Marine drill instructor.

"Who is this Wilson, anyway?" she roared, leaning slightly toward Tuttle so she could yell directly into his ear. "Some
preacher, isn't he?"

"Yes, ma'am," Tuttle answered, wincing. "He's called the
Urban Evangelist. His mission is to reach the people in the inner
cities—the poor and disadvantaged."

"I saw him on television last week. He's a good-looking rascal!"

Across the room, Admiral O'Kelly was locked in earnest conversation with one of the President's Whiz Kids.

"My people over at Justice have picked up something that smells funny," said the earnest young man from the White House. He wore a three-piece beige suit with an open-necked pastel green shirt. "Have you guys been pulling any fast ones up in New England?"

Admiral O'Kelly let his impressive eyebrows rise. "Why, what on earth are you talking about, boy?"

The Whiz Kid's face went stiff with suppressed anger. "Don't play games with me, Admiral. And I don't have to be a hundred years old to know that something fishy is happening up there."

"It would help," O'Kelly said, lowering his voice a notch and putting some iron into it, "if you told me what you're referring to."

"Forcible abduction of a NASA scientist, that's what I'm talking about! Ring a bell?"

The admiral grinned at him, his face a leathery network of creases. "Can't say that it does. Sure you're not confusing my boys with CIA?"

"There haven't been any complaints," the White House aide admitted, "so you're in the clear—so far. But if I were you . . ."

"Let's put it this way, son." O'Kelly laid a heavy hand on the young man's shoulder. "If *I* were *you*, I'd pay attention to what's in my In-basket. I've been trying to get the attention of you West Wing boys for the past ten days."

"You have?"

"If you search diligently through your incoming memos, you'll find three of 'em from me. Last one's stamped Urgent and Top Secret. Dated three days ago. I thought sure you'd look at that one."

The Whiz Kid frowned. "I should have seen it . . ."

"I suppose you get so many Urgent and Top Secret memos that they just pile up on your desk," the admiral said, straight-faced.

"Yeah. Well, okay . . . let's get together, then. Tomorrow. I'll phone you first thing in the morning."

The admiral nodded cheerfully. "Good. I think you'll find what I have to tell you quite interesting. And important enough to bring to the President's attention—without any further delays."

The young man from the White House nodded. Admiral O'Kelly turned his back on him and let the natural tides of the party pull them in opposite directions.

That takes care of that target, O'Kelly told himself. One down and one to go.

He glanced across the noisy room and saw that Tuttle, stubby and loyal as a bullterrier, was still standing resolutely beside his wife. Alma didn't look too drunk. Still time to find Target Number Two.

And there he was, gliding toward the bar like a well-oiled smiling insurance salesman. O'Kelly headed for the bar.

Todd Nickerson had the bulbous red nose of a drunk. His eyes were always glazed over, even at important committee hearings and during vital votes on the floor of the House of Representatives. At parties he was loud, laughing, often lewd.

But Nickerson was the key man on the House subcommittee that examined ONR's budget every year. Not the subcommittee chairman. The chairman was an ancient party warhorse from Missouri whose only real interests were pork barrels and buxom black women.

Despite being half drunk most of the time, Nickerson was the real power of the subcommittee. And O'Kelly had to make certain that the subcommittee would not rise up to haunt him once he had put Tuttle's plan into action. The admiral elbowed his way through the crowd, stalking Nickerson like a submarine trailing an oil tanker.

They made a funny pair, once they started talking to each other in the middle of the party. O'Kelly, all steel gray with his bushy brows and piercing eyes, his uniform immaculate and pressed so well that the creases on his trousers could cut glass; Nickerson, weaving blearily, a tall, lank, alcoholic Ichabod Crane leaning over to hear what the stockier admiral had to say.

"The National Radio Astronomy Observatory?" the congressman yelled. "What the fuck are you talking about?"

Partygoers turned to stare, saw that it was Nickerson, and politely returned to their own conversations.

O'Kelly, feeling the collar of his uniform rasp against his neck, took the civilian by the arm. "Now, don't get crazy on me, Congressman. This is important. Very important. I'm not even certain that we can bring it up before the subcommittee; I'm afraid of leaks."

Nickerson focused his eyes on the admiral with an obvious effort. "Arecibo?" he asked, his voice lower. "That's what you want? D'you know what kind of headlines it'd make if the Navy takes over a peaceful research facility?"

"We already fund a large part of its operation," O'Kelly reminded the congressman. "We only need it full time for a short while."

Nickerson waved his glass in the air, miraculously without spilling a drop or hitting any of the people standing nearby.

"And what will the National Science Foundation do?" he demanded with a lopsided smile. "They'll go running to the media, tha's what they'll do. They'll start screaming that the good ol' Navy's screwing them outta the world's biggest radio telescope."

"That's why we need your support, Congressman. All of this must be done in utmost secrecy . . ."

"Secrecy my ass! The media'll make Golgotha look like a rehearsal. They'll crucify the Navy in general and you in particular. Ready to hang on a cross? In public?"

Suddenly O'Kelly looked as if he were on the bridge of a destroyer, charging into the enemy's guns. "If I have to," he answered firmly.

Nickerson blinked, then stared at him, mouth hanging open stupidly. The party babbled around them: raucous laughter, shrill voices, smoke, a blur of colorful women's gowns and men's somber formal suits.

"You're serious," Nickerson said at last.

"You bet I am."

The glaze left Nickerson's eyes. He was cold sober and alert. "Maybe you'd better tell me about it. In detail."

The admiral shook his head. "Not here."

"Outside then," Nickerson said. "I doubt that the grounds are bugged."

By the time the admiral came to reclaim his wife, the party had wound down considerably. The room was emptying, the noise level was down to a subdued buzz of conversations.

"Time for us to go, my dear," Admiral O'Kelly said to his wife, taking the glass from her hand and putting it on the table next to him.

"It's been a dull party," she said, slurring the words slightly.

"I'm awfully sorry, sweetheart, but it was important for us to be here." Turning toward Tuttle, "I was able to accomplish a couple of things that might have taken weeks, otherwise. Months, perhaps."

Tuttle beamed happily.

"I shouldn't have to go to boring parties," Mrs. Admiral O'Kelly said as her husband led her by the hand. "I didn't even get to meet the guest of honor."

"Some other time, dear. Some other time. Tuttle," he said over his shoulder, "thanks for taking such good care of the missus."

"My pleasure, sir."

"I'll see you in the office at oh-eight-thirty," the admiral said, by way of good night.

"Yes, *sir!*" Tuttle knew the admiral's tone meant: misson accomplished.

He felt exalted. He had won over the admiral to his plan and the admiral had taken on the White House and Congressman Nickerson. And won. The project was definitely *go*.

Scanning the dwindling crowd, excitement bubbling within him, Tuttle saw Willie Wilson. The Urban Evangelist was shaking hands, wishing people well as they filed past him on their way out. He pumped the admiral's hand, and then Mrs. O'Kelly's. She smiled girlishly at him.

"Thank you kindly, Admiral. The people of the inner city will appreciate your help and understanding." Wilson turned to the next couple in the impromptu line, as an aide whispered behind him. "God bless you, Senator. Hope you win by a landslide next year. . . . Thanks for coming. . . . Good to see you. . . ."

Tuttle hung on the fringes of the dwindling crowd, practically bursting to tell somebody his Good News. It was Top Secret, of course, but he couldn't keep all this excitement bottled up inside himself. Some of it *had* to come out.

Finally Wilson noticed him. "Freddie, is that you in that fancy uniform?"

"Hello, Will," said Tuttle.

The evangelist was in his trademark blue denim suit, with a white shirt and flowery bandana knotted at his throat. He was scarcely taller than Tuttle, and whippet thin. His face was bony, all angles. His hair was angelic golden blond; his eyes the cold gray of an Atlantic storm.

"I haven't laid eyes on you since—when was it, Freddie? Atlanta?"

"New Orleans," Tuttle corrected. "After the cops tried to break up your street meeting."

"Yes, I remember now. Two years ago. The Catholics were getting nervous in the service about me."

He's had his teeth capped, Tuttle saw. I guess you have to when you do so much work on television.

"I saw you over in Georgetown," Tuttle said. "You pulled a good crowd."

"A high school gymn," Wilson replied. "That's not much. Next time I come back to this town we'll fill RFK Stadium."

"I hope you do."

"We're getting bigger all the time."

"I know. People are starting to notice. Especially the TV spots. You put on a good show."

A small crowd was piling up at the doorway behind Tuttle, waiting to have their final word with the guest of honor. His aides fidgeted nervously and looked at their wristwatches.

"Well, we're trying," Wilson said. "It's a long, hard road."

"Yes, I guess it is."

"So why's the Navy at my party? Who was that admiral just went by?"

Tuttle laughed and heard himself say, "Maybe the Navy's getting religion."

Wilson grinned back at him.

"Something big is happening, Willie," Tuttle whispered suddenly, uncontrollably. "Something so big that it's going to blow everybody's mind."

"What do you mean, Freddie?"

Gesturing halfheartedly at the others milling around them, Tuttle whispered, "It's too soon to say. But it's big. Enormously big. As soon as we can verify that it's really true, I'll get word to you."

Wilson put on his best smile. "That's fine, Freddie. But what's it all about?"

Shaking his head, Tuttle said, "You'll know when I tell you. Nothing like it's ever been seen before. All I can say is—watch the skies."

"Lord, you make it sound like the Second Coming."

"Maybe it is," Tuttle answered, completely serious. "Maybe it is."

But even if we encounter life on the other planets of this Sun, it seems most unlikely that we shall meet intelligence. The odds are fantastically against it; since the solar system is at least five thousand million years old, it is altogether unreasonable to expect that other rational beings will be sharing it with us at this very moment.

To find our peers, or more likely our superiors, we must look to the stars. There are still some conservative scientists . . . who would deny that we can ever hope to span the interstellar gulf which light itself takes years to cross.

This is nonsense. In the foreseeable future . . . we shall be able to build robot explorers that can head to the stars, as our present ones are heading to Mars and Venus. They will take years upon their journeys, but sooner or later one will bring back news that we are not alone.

That news may also reach us, more swiftly and in richer detail, in the form of radio or other messages. . . . Even now, if it was felt worthwhile, we could build a transmitter that could send signals to the nearest stars.

ARTHUR C. CLARKE
Voices from the Sky
Harper & Row
1965

CHAPTER 10

Stoner pecked hesitantly at the computer keyboard. The typewriterlike terminal was perched shakily on the dining room table. The video screen readout unit sat next to it, flickering with pale green letters and symbols that danced across its screen. The dining room was littered with stacks of printout sheets and photographs. The entire side wall of the dining room was filled with bookshelves that Stoner had cobbled together out of boards and bricks, with the help of his security guards. Every shelf bulged with books.

He didn't have the house to himself, though.

In addition to the brawny young Navy guards who patrolled the grounds and prowled periodically through the house, cluttering the kitchen and checking all the doors and windows, there was a growing stream of visitors from Washington and elsewhere taking up the big living room, next to the pool. Military men, most of them, with bundles of logistical plans in their briefcases. Stoner could hear them arguing, sometimes shouting at each other, through the thick sliding doors of the dining room. Arguments about food requirements and bedding, insurance tables and electronic spare parts.

Stoner tried to avoid them as much as he could. They were welcome to the living room as long as they didn't interfere with his work. He shut their brassy voices out of his mind and concentrated on tracking the orbit of the spacecraft, using the Big Eye photographs and the computer to analyze its path.

It has to be a spacecraft, he kept telling himself. It can't be a natural object.

McDermott came to the house regularly, and not even the heaviest oaken doors could muffle the old man's deep, booming voice. Tuttle was there often, as well, but the little lieutenant commander was too deeply engrossed in planning their move to say anything to a mere astrophysicist.

Despite himself, Stoner could hear bits and pieces of their discussions. The project had acquired a code name: Project JOVE. And their arguing was mostly about where to place Project JOVE. McDermott kept bellowing about Arecibo. But more and more the other voices countered with another name: Kwajalein.

"What are you doing?" Jo asked.

She sat up in the bed, tucking the sheet modestly under her armpits. It was early morning, a quiet Sunday in mid-November.

Crisp sunshine filtered through the bedroom curtains of the New Hampshire house.

Jo had arrived on Friday evening, as usual, with a heavy folder of photographs from Big Eye under her arm. They were stamped Confidential and addressed to Stoner. The photos were beamed by laser from the orbiting telescope to NASA's Goddard Space Center in Maryland. From there they were transmitted by secure wirephoto cable to the Navy headquarters in Boston's virtually deserted waterfront. Jo picked them up at the gray Navy building each Friday afternoon and drove them up to Stoner in New Hampshire. And stayed the weekend.

He was sitting at the little maple writing desk the Navy guards had found for him, bent over a sheet of paper.

"I'm writing a letter," he replied, "to an old friend of mine. One of my former teachers. He's an astrophysicist: Claude Appert. Lives in Paris."

"He's French?" Jo asked.

"As French as the Eiffel Tower." Stoner finished addressing the envelope and turned in his chair to face Jo. "I want you to mail this for me when you get back to Cambridge."

Her brows arched upward.

"They won't let me mail anything out of here," Stoner explained. "Especially overseas."

"What's in the letter?" she asked.

He folded two flimsy sheets of paper and tucked them into the envelope. "I'm asking him if anybody in the European astronomical community has picked up unusual radio signals from Jupiter."

"That's a security violation, isn't it?" Jo pointed out.

With a shake of his head, Stoner said, "I didn't say we had found anything. I just asked if he's heard anything."

Jo said, "The Navy wouldn't . . ."

"Listen to me," he snapped. "They're using us, Jo. Do you understand? Using us. We've stumbled across an incredible discovery, and all they can think of is to keep it secret and try to turn it to their own military advantage."

"But . . ."

"But nothing! We spend our lives squeezing out every drop of knowledge about the universe that we can, and they treat us like civil servants. They take our knowledge and turn it into weapons. They throw us in the gutter whenever they feel like it, whenever they decide to cut down on the money they spend for research. Cattle are treated better! The government spends more money subsidizing the goddamned tobacco industry—causing cancer—than it spends on cancer research."

"What's that got to do with the radio signals?" Jo asked softly.

Stoner was on his feet now, lecturing, forgetting that he was naked. "When we come up with some hint of power, with some new idea that might help them control people or kill them, then they put us into harnesses and won't let us work on anything else."

"We don't live in a peaceful world, Keith."

"I know that. But what's Tuttle's first reaction to the possibility that we've found intelligent life? Not awe. Not even curiosity. Not even fear! They want to lay their hands on any new technology the aliens might have—so that they can improve their weaponry."

Jo said nothing.

"That's why they want to keep this news away from men like Sagan and Phil Morrison. Those men have international reputations. They can get the United Nations or some other international organization to make a united, worldwide program out of this. The military doesn't want that! They won't allow it! *That's* why they've got me bottled up here like a prisoner. That's why they want to move the whole damned operation off to some military base. They want to keep the whole damned thing a secret."

"I know that."

"Well, I'm going to blow the lid off this thing," Stoner said, waving the envelope in one hand. "That's what this letter is all about."

"Keith, you're only going to get yourself in real trouble."

"We're in real trouble now," he countered, "and as long as they can keep this thing secret, the whole world is in trouble."

"I don't know if I should mail this for you, Keith," Jo said.

He walked over to the bed, sat on its edge beside her. "Mail it. They can't put me into any deeper trouble than I am now. And it's important that the whole scientific community learns about what's going on here."

Reluctantly, Jo took the letter from his hand. She looked at the address, then turned and placed the envelope on the bed table beside her purse.

Stoner didn't tell her that the second sheet in the envelope was addressed to one of the authors whose book he had read a few nights earlier. A Russian linguist who had written an interesting monograph about possible extraterrestrial languages: Professor Kirill Markov, of Moscow.

More weeks went by, and Stoner patiently worked by himself while the wrangling went on in the next room.

McDermott promised us a warm winter, Stoner grinned to himself. It'll be April Fools' Day before we get out of New England.

Thompson brought the Englishman to the house on a bitterly cold morning, one of those New England days when the sun shines brilliantly out of an absolutely blue sky, but the air is a frigid mass of biting dry polar stuff that slides in from Canada and sends thermometers down to zero for days on end.

From inside the house it looked beautiful: bright sunshine glittering on pristine snow, trees stretching bare limbs into the crystal sky. Stoner spent all of two minutes admiring it when he first arose.

He was quickly down in the dining room, chugging away at the computer keyboard, exasperated because there just weren't enough early observations of the spacecraft to get a true fix on its origin. A blast of cold air told him that someone had just come in through the door in the rear of the kitchen.

Stoner didn't bother looking up. The computer terminal was starting to rattle off the answers to his latest equations, typing automatically, chattering across the paper at an inhumanly mad speed, numbers and symbols springing across the sheets faster than his eyes could follow.

Jeff Thompson called, "Hi, Keith. Busy?"

Stoner turned in the dining room chair, an acid reply on his tongue, but saw that Thompson had an older man with him.

"Keith, this is Professor Roger Cavendish."

Stoner saw a man of about sixty, tall but very spare, thinning white hair, bony skull of a face, deepset eyes, bushy eyebrows.

He stood there in his overcoat and scarf, gloves in one hand, and gave Stoner a quizzical half-smile.

"Professor Cavendish?" Stoner asked. "From Jodrell Bank?"

"Yes," Cavendish said softly. "Quite. Don't tell me my reputation has preceded me?"

"Your work on organic molecules in interstellar clouds isn't exactly obscure," Stoner said, getting up from his chair and extending his hand to the Englishman.

Cavendish's hand was cold, his grip lukewarm.

"And you're Stoner, the astronaut, eh?"

"Former astronaut."

"Yes. Quite."

Thompson took the coats and yelled in from the kitchen that he would put on a kettle for tea.

"There's instant coffee, if you prefer," Stoner suggested.

Cavendish actually shuddered.

Stoner walked into the living room. Cavendish's impressive brows went up when he saw the pool.

"My god, what splendor. Is it heated?"

"Yes."

"Of course, how stupid of me. Otherwise it'd be a skating rink in this weather, wouldn't it?"

Stoner grinned. "Well, there's a lot of hot air pumped into this room. The military and logistics types have their meetings in here."

"Ah. I see. Naturally, they'd take the best facilities for themselves."

Gesturing him to an armchair, Stoner asked, "What brings you to this place?"

Cavendish sat down and stretched pipestem legs. He was the perfect picture of an English academic: baggy tweed suit, sweater beneath his jacket, drooping little bow tie.

"NATO, actually," he replied. "Your intelligence people have been asking some interesting questions about radio signals, so our intelligence people put two and two together and finally NATO got into the act. One thing led to another, and here I am."

"You're representing NATO?"

"Quite."

"And you'll go with us when we move to Arecibo, or Kwa-jalein, or wherever they put us?"

"Lord, I hope not. Spent enough of my life in tropical para-dises."

Stoner sank back into his armchair, thinking, So they've brought NATO into it. Maybe my letter to Claude helped. I wonder if he forwarded the note to that Russian linguist?

Thompson came in with a tray bearing three mugs. Stoner took his and saw that it was black coffee. One sip, though, convinced him never to allow Thompson to make coffee for him again.

"Professor Cavendish was a prisoner of war for nearly five years," Thompson said. "In the Pacific."

"Burma, actually," said Cavendish. "Bridge over the River Kwai and that sort of thing. Very nasty. Best forgotten, if you can."

Within minutes their national origins and earlier lives were forgotten as they started talking shop.

"There's just not enough data," Stoner admitted, "to backtrack the thing's point of origin. I don't think we'll ever figure out where it came from."

"But you have enough to show that it couldn't have been launched from Jupiter," Cavendish said.

"I think so," Stoner said. "We've tried every possible launch window. If the spacecraft appeared near Jupiter at the same time the radio pulses started, there isn't any possible way it could have been launched from Jupiter itself. No way."

"It's a negative proof," Thompson said.

"All the stronger for that," said Cavendish. "If we can definitely rule out Jupiter as the origin of our visitor, then that's quite an accomplishment."

"I suppose the next step would be to rule out the other planets."

"Easily done. I should think your computer could crunch through those numbers quickly enough."

Stoner stretched his legs out and slouched back on his chair. He put the steaming coffee cup on his belt buckle and said, "So it's definite—the thing came from outside the solar system. We have the numbers to prove that."

"We will have," Thompson said, "in a few days."

"But that makes things even more puzzling, doesn't it?" said Cavendish.

"How so?"

"Well, if it came from outside the solar system, from another star, it must have taken thousands of years for the blasted thing to reach this far. Millions of years, more likely."

"If it's an unmanned probe . . ."

"Even unmanned"—Cavendish waved his emptied teacup—"a piece of machinery that can stay intact and operate reliably for millennia? For eons? Difficult to believe."

"For *human* machinery."

"What if there's a crew aboard?" Thompson mused. "Our own spacecraft have worked better when astronauts were aboard to repair malfunctions."

"But it's the blasted *time* factor that makes all these arguments so difficult," Cavendish insisted. "If you have a spacecraft traveling from one star to another it would take so many centuries that the crew would have to be prepared to spend its entire life on the ship . . . plus the lives of its children, and grandchildren, and great-grandchildren—dozens of whole generations, don't you see?"

"Not if the ship could fly at the speed of light, or close to it," Stoner said.

"Relativistic effects," Thompson muttered. "Time dilation."

"Not bloody likely," Cavendish countered. "And your own observations show it poking along at a rather sedate speed, actually, more like your Voyager and Mariner probes."

Thompson finished his cup and got to his feet. "Well, one thing's for sure. Whichever way you look at it, the damned thing is impossible."

"But it's there," said Stoner.

"Ahh," Cavendish said with a growing smile. "That's what makes science interesting, isn't it?"

Memorandum
TO: Lt. R. J. Dooley, U. S. Naval Intelligence
FROM: Capt. G. V. Yates, NATO/HQ
SUBJECT: Security clearance, Prof. Roger H. T. Cavendish, FRS, FIAC, OBE, PhD.

1. Prof. Cavendish holds security clearances up to and including TOP SECRET from British Army, Royal Scientific Establishment, and NATO. See attached documentation.
2. Latest security check was concluded 24 Aug 80.
3. Initial security clearance was granted Cavendish 15 Dec 59 after his repatriation from USSR in 1957. He was a POW in Burma, later Manchuria, and then taken into custody by Soviet troops at end of WWII. He remained in USSR *voluntarily* until 1957, when repatriated to UK.
4. British MI suspected Cavendish as a Soviet agent, but repeated checks of his activities have uncovered no suspicious activities. Consequently he has been cleared up to and including TOP SECRET.
5. Conclusion: If Cavendish is a Soviet agent, he is a "deep agent," assigned to do nothing for many years, until he has penetrated to a position of high trust and responsibility. Project JOVE may be that position.

CHAPTER 11

Walking along the gravel path that skirted the long rows of silvery radio telescope antennas, Kirill Markov pulled his fleece hat down over his tingling ears and reflected on how much of the Russian spirit is shaped by the Russian climate.

A melancholy people in a bleak land that suffers a dreary climate, he told himself.

He stopped and surveyed the scene. Endless vistas of flat, snow-covered country, with hardly a hillock to break the monotony. Heavy, dull gray clouds pressing down like the hand of a sullen god. A cold wind moaning constantly, without even a tree to catch it and offer a lighter, cheerier sound.

Why did they have to build this research station out here in the steppes? Why not by the Black Sea, where the commissars have their summer *dachas* and the sun shines once in a while?

He shook his head. Admit it, old boy. If you were getting somewhere with this puzzle they've handed you, you wouldn't mind the scenery or the climate so much.

It was the truth. The radio pulses had him stymied. If they were a language, or even a code, he had not been able to make the slightest dent in it during the months he'd been working on the problem.

Wearily, he turned in his tracks and started trudging back toward his living quarters. The wind tugged at his long overcoat. His feet were freezing.

And the radio pulses were as much a mystery to him as they had been when he had first tackled the problem.

He was walking past the gray cinder block of the administration building when Sonya Vlasov's bright, high voice caught him.

"There you are, Kir! I was wondering where you'd gotten to."

Inwardly he groaned. Sonya had been an easy conquest, if conquest was the correct word to use with someone so willing. Willing? She was demanding. Markov had a notion that their long nights together in bed had something to do with his inability to crack the Jovian puzzle. She was young, frighteningly energetic, athletic and more inventive than a team of Chinese acrobats.

She rushed up and grabbed his arm. "Have you forgotten that the laboratory director has invited you to tea this afternoon?"

It was already getting dark. The lights atop the buildings and along the paths had been switched on. Markov felt cold and utterly bleak deep inside his soul. Incredibly, Sonya was smiling, bouncy and coatless. She wore nothing more than a sweater, loose-fitting slacks and boots.

Her sweater was not loose-fitting, though, and despite himself
Markov felt a tiny glow within. He smiled down at Sonya's
round, happy face.

"Yes, I had quite forgotten about the invitation. Where would
I be without you?"

She laughed. "In bed with one of the other girls. They're all
very jealous of me, you know."

"Ah, my angel of mercy," he said, sliding an arm across her
shoulders. "You are too kind to me. After all, I'm a doddering
old man . . ."

"You are not!"

"Well, middle-aged, then," he said as they headed toward the
wood-frame building where his room was. "There are so many
younger men who are sighing and moaning for a chance to bask
in your smile. Yet you concentrate all your energies on me."

And come to think of it, he added mentally, there are indeed
other women who've been kept away from me by this over-
developed sex maniac.

But Sonya would have none of it. She was single-minded in
her devotion to Markov. And, sure enough, he ended up making
love to her again before he started out for the director's tea. It
came as no surprise to him. As he lay half dozing in her soft,
ample breasts, he found himself trying to count how many times
he had done it over the past two months.

I must be close to a world record for a man approaching fifty
years of age, he marveled.

The director's tea was very private, very quiet, and mercifully
brief. Markov chatted amiably about his studies of oriental languages while the rest of the men and women talked about astronomy and electronics. He didn't understand them and they
didn't understand him. No one spoke about the radio pulses
from Jupiter, because they were supposed to be a secret that
only a half-dozen people in the entire station knew about. And
no one knew who, among the two dozen guests at the tea, might
be reporting conversations back to Moscow.

Markov wasn't hungry by the time the partygoers bade farewell to their host and headed for their own quarters. He trudged
listlessly past the cafeteria building and headed to his room.
Sonya would be there, waiting in bed for him.

Maybe she'll be asleep, Markov hoped. Then he frowned to himself. A fine state of affairs! You're actually afraid of her. It's time you told her that you're a married man and you can't carry on with her any longer.

He thought of the lean, languid blond electronics specialist he had met at the director's tea. Big, sleepy eyes. She'd be more restful, at least.

It was a considerable surprise when he opened the door to his room and found his wife sitting in the chair in front of the electric heater.

"Maria!"

She looked up at him, the usual scowl on her face.

Markov glanced at the bed. It was unmade, but empty.

"What are you doing here?" he asked, closing the door behind him and wondering what had happened to Sonya.

"I've come for a firsthand report on your progress," she said. "My superiors thought that I would like to see my husband after a two-month absence."

Putting on a smile, Markov said, "How thoughtful of them."

He pulled off his heavy coat and hung it on the hook behind the door. Maria's plain black suitcase sat on the floor next to the closet.

The closet! Could Sonya be hiding in the closet?

"You must be tired after such a long trip," he said to his wife. "Would you like some tea? Perhaps dinner?"

"You look tired yourself. There are dark circles under your eyes."

"I've been working very hard."

"Yes, I know."

This must be the way a mouse feels when it's in the paws of a cat, Markov thought. Or the way a prisoner feels when the police take him in.

"I'm afraid I haven't made much progress . . ."

"That depends on how you look at it," Maria said, her voice flat and cold. "The girl who was in your bed seemed quite content with your progress."

"Girl?" His voice squeaked, almost. "Oh, her. She . . . well . . ." He shrugged and grinned sheepishly.

"I hope that you have learned something about the radio signals," Maria said, deadly calm, "in between your sessions in bed."

Markov's grin crumbled. Pulling a wooden chair to sit facing her, he said earnestly, "Maria . . . I don't believe there is anything to be learned from the pulses. We have used computer analyses on them and I have studied them faithfully for months now . . ."

"Faithfully." She snorted.

"Faithfully," he repeated. "There is no hint of a periodicity, or a rhythm, or any of the characteristics that one would expect from a language."

"Are you sure your mind has been clear enough to do your work properly?"

"Have I ever failed you before?"

"You're getting older, but not any wiser."

He slapped a palm on his knee. "That's unfair, Maria Kirtchatovska! I am . . ."

She leveled a blunt forefinger at him and he lapsed into silence. "We must crack this code, Kirill. Do you understand? My superiors will not accept failure."

"But I don't think it *is* a code."

"They do."

Raising his hands to the heavens, Markov demanded, "And if they believe that the Moon is made of green cheese, will they destroy the cosmonauts who bring back rocks?"

She would not move from her chair. To Markov, she looked like a stolid, unyielding mule. Words bounced off her thick hide.

"If it's not a code, it's not a code!" he said, his voice rising. "If it isn't a language how can it be a language?"

Maria's stare bored into him. "So I am to return to Moscow and tell my superiors that my husband has spent two months studying the radio signals and he has concluded that they are completely natural in origin. And when they ask me what kind of studies he did, I can tell them that he spent most of the two months in bed with some oversexed cow who should be sent out to pasture in Siberia."

"No!" Markov snapped. "You wouldn't."

"If you fail, I fail," Maria answered. "And before I let that happen, I'll see your little bitch in hell."

"Maria, you don't understand . . ."

"No, *you* don't understand. I will not accept your word on this. Not when I know you've been playing instead of working. It's my career you're playing with! My life! And your own."

Feeling desperate, he ran a hand through his thinning hair. "Look . . . I have done a serious job with these signals. Honestly I have. Let me show them to Academician Bulacheff. If he agrees with me, will that satisfy you?"

Maria gave him a long, deadly stare, then reached down into the bag at her feet and pulled out a single sheet of handwritten paper.

"Read this," she commanded.

Markov squinted at the letter, patted his pockets until he found his glasses, slipped them on. As he read, his face fell. His hand began to tremble slightly.

Finally he looked back at his wife. "Who . . . who is this man Stoner?"

"An American scientist, an astrophysicist who helped to build the telescope that the Americans placed in orbit earlier this year."

Shakily, Markov made his way to the bed and sank down onto it. "And he thinks there is an artificial spacecraft in the vicinity of Jupiter, causing the radio signals."

Maria said, "Why would he write you such a letter?"

Glancing at the flimsy sheet, Markov answered, "He says he read my book on extraterrestrial languages . . ."

"Your notorious book."

"But . . . do you believe what he says, Maria? Perhaps it's an American trick of some sort."

"Many Americans do not understand the nature of the struggle between communism and capitalism. They believe that the two systems can coexist in peace."

Markov nodded.

"This man Stoner is an idealist. He is also a scientist who wants to be recognized for discovering alien life. That is why he has written to you."

"But why me? Why not the International Astronomical Federation? Or the Soviet Academy of Sciences? Why to me?"

"Who can tell?" Maria replied. "Our agents in America are looking into the matter."

Markov tried to pull himself together. Too much was happening, too quickly.

"Do you still believe," Maria asked, "that the signals are not a language?"

He took a deep breath, then, "They are not a language. At least, they are not any kind of language that *I* can understand."

She reached out and took the letter from his limp hand. Placing it carefully back in her bag, she said, "A few moments ago you expressed a desire to see Academician Bulacheff. Well, he wants to see you, too. Immediately. We go back to Moscow tonight."

. . . at the end of November '67 I got it [a pulsating radio source] on the fast recording. As the chart flowed under the pen I could see that the signal was a series of pulses . . . They were 1⅓ seconds apart . . .

Then Scott and Collins observed the pulsations with another [radio] telescope . . . which eliminated instrumental effects. John Pilkington measured the dispersion of the signal which established that the source was well outside the solar system but inside the galaxy. So were these pulsations man-made, but made by men from another civilization? . . .

We did not really believe that we had picked up signals from another civilization, but obviously the idea had crossed our minds and we had no proof that it was an entirely natural radio emission. It is an interesting problem—if one thinks one may have detected life elsewhere in the universe how does one announce the results responsibly?

S. JOCELYN BELL BURNELL
Speaking at the Eighth Texas Symposium
on Relativistic Astrophysics, 1977,
about her discovery of the pulsars

CHAPTER 12

"It's just too fantastic to be believed!"

"I assure you, Mr. President, it's quite true."

The President got up from the polished mahogany table and walked toward the fireplace. The regular Cabinet meeting had ended in its usual bitter wrangling, and he had gladly left the cold formality of the Cabinet Room for the smaller intimacy of the Roosevelt Room.

Standing by the small bronze bust of Teddy Roosevelt on the mantel above the fireplace, the President looked haggard: tie loosened, collar opened, hair tousled, fists jammed into the pockets of his jacket.

The press secretary watched him worriedly. An old friend and adviser, he knew that the pressures were inexorably grinding the President into despair.

The President looked wistfully at the painting of Teddy the Rough Rider that hung above the sofa. "Things were a lot simpler in his day, weren't they?"

The Defense Secretary shook his gray-maned head. "It only seems so from this distance in time, sir."

"You work so hard to get this job," the President murmured, more to himself than to the others in the room, "and once you've got it, you wonder why you ever tried."

"Somebody's got to do it," the press secretary joked. "They hold an election every four years."

The President smiled weakly at him. Turning to his science adviser, he asked again, "Intelligent life on Jupiter? You're sure of that?"

"No, sir," she answered firmly. "Not totally sure. But it's a strong enough possibility that we should be prepared to face up to it."

With a sigh, the President muttered, "Why does everything have to happen during *my* Administration?"

The Secretary of Defense, a former industrialist, cleared his throat as he always did before delivering an opinion. "Mr. President," he said in his flat Oklahoma twang, "Sally and I don't always see eye to eye on things . . ."

The science adviser glared at him from her seat across the small room. "You can say that again! Joey."

He grinned at her. "All right, I'm a male chauvinist pig . . . *Ms.* Ellington."

"*Dr.* Ellington." She did not grin back.

The President looked pained, but said nothing. So his press secretary chided, "Hey look, there's only the four of us in here, so let's drop the squabbling for a while, huh? This is too important for cheap shots."

"I totally agree," said Defense. "The point I was going to make is that Dr. Ellington and I are convinced that we must turn over the Arecibo radio telescope facility to studying these radio signals."

"Why Arecibo?"

"It's the biggest and most powerful radio facility we have," the science adviser explained. "The biggest radio telescope in the world, as a matter of fact."

"What about the telescope up in orbit?" asked the press secretary.

"That's an optical telescope, like Mount Palomar."

"We need Big Eye, too," Defense added. "In fact, that's how we got the photographs of this thing in orbit around Jupiter."

"If it really is in orbit," muttered the science adviser.

"You think it's artificial?"

She nodded, grim-faced. "Yes, I do. But we don't have enough numbers on its trajectory yet to tell if it's truly in orbit around the planet or merely making an extended flyby. It could be a flyby . . . from beyond the solar system."

The President sank into the chair next to his Defense Secretary. "It's hard to believe, either way." He looked across the table at the press secretary. "Intelligent creatures from another world. Scary, isn't it?"

"Scares hell out of me," Defense said.

"We've got to be absolutely sure about this," said the press secretary. "If word about this leaks out before we're ready to absolutely confirm or deny it . . . there'll be pandemonium."

"I realize that," Defense said. "We're taking every security precaution, I assure you."

But the science adviser said, "We're going to have a peck of trouble with the Arecibo regulars. We can't just walk in there and tell them to pack up and leave for an indefinite period of time. They'd raise the roof."

"Suppose we explained the situation to them and asked for their co-operation . . ."

Defense shook his head. "You've got a lot of academic superstars down there who believe that their freedom of expression comes first and everything else—including the national security —comes afterward. Try to get their co-operation and they'll go running to the *Post*."

"The Pentagon Papers, all over again," said the press secretary.

But the President persisted. "Carl Sagan's one of the people in that group, isn't he? I know Carl. He worked on my election committee. I could explain it to him. He'd want to help us, I know he would."

"Sure! He'd want to run the show," the science adviser said.

"And we can't let that happen," said Defense.

"Why not?"

"He's much too well known. He'd be a terrible security risk. Pulitzer Prize-winning author. Television star. We couldn't let him wander around free if he's going to work on this, and we can't lock him up inside a security compound—his absence would tip off the Russians that we're onto something."

"He's damned friendly with Russian scientists, too, isn't he?" the press secretary asked.

"Don't you think the Russians already know about this?" the President asked. "I mean, they have radio telescopes too, don't they?"

"I don't know if they have anything operating down below six hundred megahertz right now," answered the science adviser. "After all, we stumbled onto the signals only because one of our older facilities was working out at that end of the spectrum."

"And we've got Big Eye," said Defense. "The Reds don't have a comparable telescope in orbit. Ground-based telescopes, no matter how big they are, just can't pick up this thing near Jupiter. We've checked that. You can't see it from the ground, it's too faint to be picked up."

"What about a space probe?" the President suggested. "We could send a probe out there to see if this object is natural or artificial."

The science adviser hiked her eyebrows. Defense made a sour face.

"It would take several years to design, build and launch a suitable probe," the science adviser said. "We simply don't have spacecraft sitting on shelves, waiting to be picked up and used. And it would take almost a year before a probe could reach Jupiter's vicinity, even on a high-thrust boost."

"Besides," Defense said, "we've fired Pioneers and Voyagers past Jupiter for years now and they've never picked up a trace of anything like this."

"Let's get back to the main point," said the press secretary. "No matter what you do, with Arecibo or anything else, this thing has got to be orchestrated carefully. *Very* carefully. The public's got to be prepared for this before we actually release any news."

"Can we keep it from being leaked?" the President asked.

"You're assuming," Defense murmured, "that we can't prevent leaks?"

"Prevent them?" The press secretary laughed. "We can't even slow them down!"

"The Department of Defense . . ."

"Leaks like a sieve."

Defense glowered but did not reply. The science adviser suppressed a giggle.

"We've got to play this game *right*," the press secretary insisted. "We've got to set up the public . . ."

A knock on the door brought him up short. The President's appointments secretary took a single step into the room.

"Excuse me, sir. The delegation from the National Farm Bureau," she said softly.

"Oh . . . yes." The President got up from his chair, smoothed his jacket. "Is the Secretary of Agriculture in there with them?"

"Yes sir."

Sighing, the President turned back to the three at the table. "Work out a plan of action and let me see it. Tonight, if you can."

They stood as the President left the room. Then they dropped back into their chairs.

"Well, what do you think?" Defense asked.

The press secretary grimaced. "The Cabinet won't support him and the Congress spits in his eye every chance it gets. The Senate's got four presidential candidates in it, the Cabinet's got at least two more, the economy's sliding into oblivion, we still have oil troubles, and now he's got Martians coming at him."

"Jovians," corrected the science adviser.

"Whatever. We've got to prepare for the worst. I mean . . . can you imagine what the saucer nuts will do when word of this gets out?"

The science adviser corrected, "You mean the UFO researchers."

"I mean the saucer nuts! And the religious crazies. My god, they committed suicide by the hundreds in Jonestown a few years back over *nothing!* What'll they do when we tell 'em we're going to be invaded by alien monsters?"

"Where's Orson Welles when we really need him?"

"This isn't a joke, Sally."

"What about other nations?" the press secretary asked no one in particular. "Don't we owe it to our allies to give them some advance word on this?"

"NATO's already been clued in," Defense responded. "The Dutch have apparently picked up the radio signals at one of their own facilities."

"Dwingeloo," the science adviser said.

Loosening his tie, the press secretary wondered, "What if we start a big flap about this and it turns out to be a false alarm? Those very same UFO people and religious cults *won't believe us.* They'll think we're covering up."

"They already think we're covering up UFO visitations," said the science adviser.

"Suppose they're right?" Defense asked.

"What?"

"Suppose . . . well, what if this thing really is an alien spacecraft and—and they're hostile? Dangerous?"

The science adviser shook her head crossly at him. "That's exactly what we need around here: paranoia."

URBAN EVANGELIST PREDICTS
"WORLD-SHAKING CHANGE"

Atlanta (UPI)—Rev. Willie Wilson, the self-styled "Urban Evangelist," declared yesterday that a "great and powerful change, an Earth-shaking change" is going to alter the lives of every person on Earth within the next few months.

"Watch the skies," Rev. Wilson told a rapt audience of nearly 1,000 at the Hyatt Regency Hotel. "No one on Earth will be the same after this great and powerful change sweeps over the world."

Rev. Wilson refused to give specifics on the nature of the change, stating only that "Christians and non-Christians alike should prepare their souls for a new world, through prayer and good works."

The evening revival meeting, held in the futuristic atrium of the Hyatt Regency, was part of a nation-spanning "crusade" that Rev. Wilson is making, which will take him to seventeen major American cities over the next six months.

Appearing with Rev. Wilson last night were . . .

CHAPTER 13

Ramsey McDermott swiveled his creaking old leather chair back and forth as he puffed steadily on his pipe, thinking, worrying, trying to plan out the best course of action.

Suppose he's right? the old man asked himself. If it really is extraterrestrial intelligence, there could be a Nobel in it for me. After all, I'm the head of the project. I'm the one who brought Stoner into the observatory. He was just a washed-out astronaut before I asked NASA for him.

The office was dark in the late afternoon. Outside, the sun was already down behind the red brick buildings that lined the Yard.

They'll put a plaque on the building after I'm gone, McDermott told himself. Professor Ramsey McDermott, the discoverer of extraterrestrial life. He pictured the Nobel Prize ceremony, the speech he would give in Stockholm, the interviews with the press. Frowning, he realized that he would have to share the prize with Stoner and Thompson, perhaps one or two others.

Stoner will make trouble, he knew. The man's a born troublemaker.

Maybe it isn't ETI, he thought. It's most likely just some natural object, maybe a new comet or a captured meteor that's been pulled into an orbit around Jupiter.

But what about the radio pulses? How do you account for them? Coincidence? Some influence between this object Stoner's found and Jupiter's radio emissions, like the moon Io affects the radio bursts?

His pipe had gone out. McDermott took it from between his teeth, never noticing the thick clouds of blue-gray smoke that hung in layers through the office, permeating the books, the stacks of papers, the drapes on the window.

It was dark. He switched on the goosenecked desk lamp. And saw the report from Washington again.

Damn that man! He rapped the pipe bowl sharply against the big, dottle-filled ashtray on his desk. The aged, brittle stem snapped.

Double damn him! McDermott snapped to himself. And where the hell is that girl? She should be here by now.

As if in answer, there was a knock on the door. Without waiting for him to answer, Jo opened the door and stepped into Professor McDermott's office.

"You're late," he growled.

"I just got out of class," she replied.

"Oh, you're attending classes these days," he shot back sarcastically.

"When I can."

She seemed completely unflustered. She kept her coat on and her books in her lap as she sat in the chair before his desk. With a disapproving frown, she waved her free hand to push some of the smoke away.

"Having a good time in New Hampshire? I understand you spend every weekend up there with Stoner."

"That's my business," she said.

"I'm making it mine," McDermott snapped. "It's Project JOVE business, you know."

Her back stiffened. "You told me to do what I could to make certain he stays at the house up there without making any more trouble. So I'm doing what I can."

McDermott drummed his fingers on the report resting on his desktop. "Does that include mailing letters overseas for him?"

She hesitated for just a fraction of a second. "What do you mean?"

"Somehow, Stoner got a letter out. To Russia, no less. To some Russian linguist, according to Washington."

"I don't know anything about that," Jo said.

"You're the only one who could have smuggled a letter out for him."

She shook her head stubbornly. "I didn't mail any letters to Russia for him or anyone else. I wouldn't do that."

"You're certain?"

"How does Washington know he sent a letter to this Russian?"

McDermott chuckled. "They don't tell me where their information comes from. I imagine we have spies in the Kremlin, just as they have spies in Washington."

"What's in the letter?"

"Enough to put Stoner into a federal prison for a long, long time." McDermott realized that it was true, as he spoke the words. His heart lightened. With Stoner out of the way . . .

"You wouldn't do that!" she said.

He shrugged. "It's not up to me. It's a Navy problem."

"But . . . you said you need him for the project."

Smiling, McDermott said, "I imagine we can get along without him now. He's been more trouble than he's worth, actually."

"No. You can't."

Her voice was almost pleading. McDermott realized that she was suddenly tense, leaning forward in the chair, her face tight with concern.

"Stoner did it to himself," he said, as he felt his blood stirring, the heat starting to build inside him.

"He wouldn't do anything wrong," she was saying. "This must be some kind of misunderstanding . . ."

But McDermott was barely listening. He heard the tone of her voice, saw the anxiety in her eyes, and realized with an inward shock of discovery that he wanted her for himself. Very much. For himself and no one else.

"There must be something you can do!" Jo begged.

He still had the broken stem of his pipe in his hand. Dropping it into the ashtray, he took another pipe and wordlessly began to fill it, working methodically, silently, watching her watching him, waiting for her to break the stretching silence.

"Couldn't *you* . . . do something? Help him?"

"He's broken the security laws," McDermott said slowly. "He signed a security agreement and then dashed off a letter to Soviet Russia."

"Maybe it's an old letter. Maybe he wrote it before he signed the agreement."

McDermott tamped the tobacco down and put the pipe in his mouth. "It's still a federal crime."

Jo glanced around the room, as if looking for help. "There must be something you can do."

Trembling inside, McDermott heard himself tell her, "I suppose I could tell the Navy that he's too valuable to the project to be sent to jail."

Jo nodded eagerly.

"But why should I? Why should I risk the project's chance of success for him? What's in it for me?"

For several moments she said nothing. McDermott could hear his pulse pounding in his ears.

Finally he could stand it no longer. "If I . . . saved his neck, what would you do?"

Understanding dawned in her eyes. She sat up straighter in the chair. "What would *I* do?"

"For me."

She almost smiled. "What would you want me to do?"

Taking the pipe out of his mouth, still unlit, McDermott said shakily, "Stop seeing him. Spend your time with me instead."

She nodded slowly. "And what do I get out of that?"

He felt confused. "What do you mean . . . ?"

"I want a letter of recommendation from you, to NASA. A letter recommending me for a position in the astronaut training corps."

"You want . . ."

"I'll give you what you want, if you give me what I want."

"And Stoner?"

"He stays with the project. I'll stop seeing him. You write the letter."

Swallowing hard, McDermott answered, "When . . . when the project is finished. I'll write the letter then. We have a lot of work ahead of us, you know."

"You could still send the letter off to NASA. Now. I'll stay with the project until it's finished."

His head was throbbing. "It's not that simple, young lady. If you expect me to . . ."

"I'll do what you want," Jo said. "But first you write that letter."

"I . . . we'll see about that. I have to think about this."

Jo got up from her chair and clamped the books under her arm, against her hip. "Okay, you see about it. When you give me the letter and guarantee that Dr. Stoner will stay with the project, I'll live up to my end of the deal."

She went to the door, turned back to him. "Uh, just so we understand each other . . . I'm not into bondage or S&M, but anything else you want I can give you."

McDermott sat in a hot sweat as she left his office and shut the door firmly behind her.

Markov sat like a guilty schoolboy in the anteroom, waiting, waiting endlessly. Academician Bulacheff's secretary, a portly woman of fifty or more, glared at him now and then. Men shuttled in and out of the academician's office. But no one spoke to Markov.

Outside it was snowing. Markov watched the white flurries paste themselves against the windowpanes. Little by little, Moscow disappeared from sight beneath the snow-filled gusts. Even the spires and walls of the Kremlin became indistinct blurs.

A real blizzard, Markov told himself. It will be a long walk home.

Finally, when he had nearly hypnotized himself into a snow-induced slumber, the secretary's nasal voice rasped, "Kirill Vasilovsk Markov?"

He snapped to full alertness. There was no one else in the anteroom, but still she made a question of his name.

"Yes, that's me," he said.

"Academician Bulacheff will see you now."

Markov got to his feet, a trifle unsteadily, and walked to the plain wooden door of the academician's office.

Bulacheff is the key man, he heard his wife's voice warning him. He is the one you must satisfy. If you can convince him that the signals are not a language, then all may be well. But if he is dissatisfied with your work. . . . Maria had let the sentence dangle, like a noose over Markov's head.

Bulacheff's office was neither spacious nor imposing, but a cheerful gleaming samovar chugged away in one corner of the neat little room. And the academician came up from behind his desk and greeted Markov warmly.

"Kirill Vasilovsk! It was good of you to come in person. I hope you are not caught by the snow on your way home."

Markov smiled and nodded and mumbled polite inanities, thinking, I *had* to come in person, you summoned me. And how can I avoid being caught in the snow, unless we stay here until spring?

"I have read your report," the academician said, returning to his desk. "Most interesting. Most interesting."

He winked at Markov, then reached down to the bottom drawer of his desk and produced a bottle of vodka and two glasses.

"It's not iced," he said apologetically.

Markov grinned at the old man. "Not to worry. I am already chilled quite thoroughly."

Bulacheff gestured his guest to the worn leather sofa at the side of the room. Portraits of Mendeléev, Lobachevski, Oparin and Kapitza hung in gilt above the sofa. The inevitable portrait of Lenin was over the academician's desk. But no contemporary politicians, Markov noted.

He accepted a thimble-sized glass of vodka. Bulacheff toasted, "To understanding."

They both downed their drinks in a single gulp.

As Bulacheff wheeled his swivel chair to refill Markov's glass, the linguist said, "It was good of you to find time for me. I know you must be very busy."

Bulacheff's bald pate gleamed in the light from the panels in the ceiling. "Actually," he said, "I am very glad to see you. I want to discuss this Jupiter business with someone who is not in the Academy, not part of the official apparatus."

"Oh?"

With an almost sheepish smile, Bulacheff eased back in his chair. "It is only too easy to become isolated in a position such as mine. The people I see are all members of the Academy or the government. Sometimes we become too ingrown; we lose sight of the important things because we are so concerned with the immediate problems of the moment."

Holding his refilled glass in front of him, Markov nodded. "I see."

"It is good to discuss this matter of"—Bulacheff inadvertently glanced ceilingward—"of ETI with a man of science, rather than an apparatchik."

Is he looking to the heavens or for microphones in the ceiling, Markov wondered. He said, "It's a matter of grave importance, true enough."

"Yes," Bulacheff agreed. "And the Americans are a jump ahead of us—as usual."

"What do you mean?"

"This man Stoner . . . this idealist who wrote you that letter—do you know who he is?"

Markov shook his head.

"Our embassy in Washington reports that he was one of the astronomers who helped design and build the orbiting telescope that the Americans launched recently: they call it the Big Eye."

"A telescope in orbit? Like a sputnik?"

"Exactly. No doubt the Americans are using it to study Jupiter very closely . . . much more closely than we can, since we have no such equipment in orbit."

Markov stroked his beard with his free hand. "So they have found things that we cannot see."

"Exactly! They have eyes and we are blind."

"That's . . . too bad."

Bulacheff knocked back his vodka and put the glass carefully on his desk. "Science depends on politics. It has always been so. Capitalist or socialist, it makes no difference. We want to study the universe but we must beg for the money from the politicians."

Markov agreed. "Even in the beginnings of science, great men such as Galileo and Kepler had to cast horoscopes for their patrons if they wanted to be supported for their true work."

"Yes. And nowadays we have to invent weapons for them."

Peering ceilingward himself, Markov said, "But that is necessary for the defense of the Motherland."

"Of course," Bulacheff said brusquely. Then he added, "And for the triumph of socialism."

"It's too bad we don't have an orbiting telescope of our own," Markov said.

"It would take ten years to get one into space—nine of them wheedling and begging."

"I wonder . . . is there any way we can get to use the American telescope? Or to see the photographs they have taken?"

Bulacheff fixed him with a beady look. "When they won't even admit publicly that they've discovered something? When they're keeping the entire matter secret?"

"H'mm. Yes. That would be difficult." Markov took half his drink down, felt the vodka burning its way through him.

"If it wouldn't lead to war, I'd be tempted to ask our Cosmonaut Corps to seize the Big Eye," Bulacheff muttered.

Markov almost laughed, but managed to control himself.

"No," Bulacheff said gloomily. "Our only chance is co-operation with the Americans. But with the international situation the way it is, our political leaders will never accept being forced to ask favors from Washington."

"It would be humiliating," Markov agreed.

"But there must be some way to do it!"

Markov looked closely at the bald little man. Frail though he appeared, Bulacheff's voice had iron in it. His eyes were glowing, and not merely from the vodka.

"About my report," Markov began slowly, waiting to be interrupted.

"Yes?"

"I presume you've read it?"

"Thoroughly."

Markov nodded. "If these radio signals from Jupiter are not a language, doesn't that mean that the chances of there being intelligent life there are rather . . . well, nonexistent?"

"I would agree, certainly," Bulacheff said, hunching his shoulders in something approximating a shrug, "except that the Americans are working like fiends on the problem."

"They are?"

Bulacheff began ticking points off on his fingers. Markov noted that they were long, slender, delicate hands: pianist's hands.

"First, your friend Stoner is working on the problem. He has left the American space agency to work for a small, out-of-date radio telescope facility."

Markov began to say, "He is not a friend of . . ."

But Bulacheff went on, "Second, Stoner has influence with the space agency people who run the Big Eye. It seems that they are processing photographs from the orbital telescope and sending them to Stoner, through secure channels."

Markov nodded.

"Third, the entire staff of this radio telescope facility—including your friend Stoner—has been forced to sign new security oaths by the United States Navy . . ."

"*Navy?*"

Bulacheff smirked. "The Americans are very sloppy administrators. Somehow their Navy is in charge of this project."

"I don't understand."

"It makes no difference. The conclusion is that they are working on the Jupiter problem in secrecy. It seems that they have put a code name to their work: Project JOVE. They have told their NATO apparatus about the problem, apparently."

"Maybe they will make a public announcement, once they have proof . . ."

Bulacheff shook his head. "No. They will want to make contact with the aliens. And keep the information from us."

"Then perhaps *we* should announce to the world that we have received their signals, also!"

Again Bulacheff flicked his eyes ceilingward. "That would be against our government's policy."

"But we can't keep it a secret forever," Markov insisted. "And

since the Americans already know, and are ahead of us, it would
be to our advantage to make the whole thing public and force a
worldwide co-operative program."

"I agree, Kirill Vasilovsk," Bulacheff said. "I have considered
that possibility."

Markov nodded eagerly.

"Our ambassador to the United Nations could reveal *our* discovery of the radio signals," Bulacheff said, steepling his fingers,
"and then we would get credit all around the world for discovering intelligent life."

"And we could recommend an international program to study
the signals," Markov added, his pulse racing. "The Americans
would have to go in with us."

"But that doesn't mean the Americans would share their Big
Eye photographs. They could claim that they have never used
the telescope on Jupiter. They could still keep the information
for themselves."

"Oh," said Markov, crestfallen.

"Which is why you are so important to us," Bulacheff went on.

"I am?"

"Of course! The American, Stoner, apparently trusts you
enough to write to you and reveal that he is working on the
problem."

"He never said in so many words . . ."

"Between the lines, Kirill Vasilovsk, between the lines."

"Yes. I see."

"Now you must write back to him. You must gain his further
trust. Perhaps we can arrange for the two of you to meet—in
America, perhaps."

"Me?" Markov gulped with surprise. "Go to America?"

"Suitably escorted, of course. I understand your wife would be
an admirable bodyguard for you."

His heart sank again. "Yes . . . naturally . . ."

"It's only a suggestion. The germ of an idea. But I think it's
important that you correspond with this man Stoner. Write him
a long and friendly letter. Tell him how fascinated you are with
the problem of extraterrestrial languages. Imply much, but reveal nothing."

"I can try . . ."

"We will help you to compose the letter," Bulacheff said cheerfully. "And, naturally, we will make sure that it is exactly correct before we send it overseas."

"Naturally."

"Good!" Bulacheff got to his feet so suddenly that Markov thought he had been stung in the rear. "I knew we could depend on you, Kirill Vasilovsk."

Markov rose from the couch and started toward the door, Bulacheff alongside him.

"It's time we put your name in for nomination to the Academy," Bulacheff said, gesturing grandly. "After all, you are one of the Soviet Union's leading linguists . . . and a very important man to us all."

Markov bobbed his head meekly and took the academician's proffered hand. He could hardly contain himself as he pulled on his coat, out in the anteroom, and pulled his fur hat down over his ears. Not even the glower of the fat secretary bothered him.

Out on the street, it was snowing harder than ever. Nothing was moving. No one else was in sight. The drifts were piling across the building's front steps, head high. But Markov laughed, dug his gloved fingers into the snow and patted a snowball into shape. He threw it at the nearest streetlamp, nearly lost to sight in the swirling storm. The snowball flew unerringly upward through the slanting flakes and hit the lamp. The light winked out.

Startled, Markov glanced around to see if anyone had seen him destroy state property. Then he doubled over with laughter, nearly fell on the snow. Straightening up, he leaned into the wind and started the long trek back to his apartment, a boyish grin on his face, his beard beginning to look like an icicle.

"It's all right, Maria Kirtchatovska," he shouted into the falling snow. "Your fears were groundless. I am an important man. I will be elected to the Academy!"

Up in his warm office, Bulacheff watched Markov disappear into the snowy evening shadows.

"Fool," he muttered. Swiveling his creaking chair away from the frost-crusted window, he poured himself another vodka. "Impressionable fool."

The trouble is, the old man thought to himself, he is a thoroughly likable man. Immature, perhaps, but likable.

Bulacheff sighed and gulped down the vodka. Well, he told himself, if it all works out the way I want it to, Markov will become an academician. If not . . . it's just as well that he likes to play in the snow.

Memorandum
TO: The President   DATE: 7 December
FROM: SecDef   REF: 83-989
SUBJECT: Project JOVE

1. DARPA analysts conclude that moving the entire Arecibo staff out of their facility will cause inevitable security risks. I tend to agree.
2. It may be possible to upgrade the existing radar installation at Kwajalein (in the Pacific Ocean) to meet the requirements of Project JOVE. Kwajalein has a considerable amount of sophisticated electronics gear in place, much of it mothballed, as a result of being the terminal end of our Pacific Missile Test Range.
3. Security at Kwajalein should be much easier than at Arecibo. DOD personnel are already on-station there and capable of maintaining absolute security integrity.
4. The Arecibo radio telescope facility can be used for Project JOVE studies, as needed, by the existing Arecibo staff without revealing the classified elements of JOVE to them.
5. For the above reasons, I strongly recommend that we move Project JOVE to Kwajalein, rather than Arecibo.

CHAPTER 14

"How did you get the letter out?" asked Lieutenant Commander Tuttle. He was standing, in uniform, before the fireplace.

Stoner looked at him for a long moment. The only sound in the room was the crackling of the flames, and the occasional pop of a knot in the firewood. McDermott sat across the coffee table, in the New England rocker. Stoner had the sofa to himself; he was in his sweat suit, they had caught him in the middle of his warm-up exercises, out by the pool.

"I slipped it into a letter I sent to a friend," he answered carefully, "slapped a stamp on it and tossed it in with the reports and other crap that your couriers carry out of here every day."

"You didn't give it to Jo Camerata to mail for you?" McDermott asked, a tense edge to his raspy voice.

Stoner's mind was racing. He made himself shrug. "She might have been the one who took that batch out; I really don't know."

Tuttle's round face was grimly serious. "You realize that this is a security breach of prime magnitude."

Stoner shook his head. "I didn't tell them anything about what we're doing. I merely wrote to a Russian author and asked if he'd heard anything about ETI lately."

"You mentioned Jupiter!" McDermott growled.

"And radio pulses," added Tuttle.

"And a lot of other things," Stoner countered. "If you guys read that letter in its entirety, you'll see that I didn't really tip our hand—*unless* the Russians already know about the Jovian radio pulses, in which case there's no breach of security."

Tuttle gave an exasperated sigh. "You just don't understand the security laws, do you?"

"Or won't," McDermott said.

"Maybe I just don't care," Stoner snapped.

"You could go to Leavenworth for this," Tuttle said.

Feeling the icy calm that always came over him when he got angry, Stoner said, "Fine. Try it. You'll have to put me on trial, and I swear to whatever gods there are that I honestly look forward to having a day in court. At least I'll have a defense attorney; that's more than you guys have allowed me so far."

The little lieutenant commander shifted uneasily on his feet and glanced at McDermott, who said nothing.

"I'm going to get myself a drink," Stoner told them, getting up from the sofa.

"Good idea," Big Mac called after him as he headed for the kitchenette-bar. "Fix me a bloody mary while you're there."

Stoner grumbled to himself, Why can't he want something simple, like a scotch on the rocks? As he searched through the cabinets over the sink for a can of mix, he heard Tuttle call, "Got any orange juice? I'll take it with some ice."

"Sure thing," Stoner said. I work cheap, he added silently.

He could hear the two of them conversing between themselves while he built the drinks. By the time he had all three glasses on a tray, Tuttle and McDermott had a large map spread across the living room carpet and were studying it intently. Stoner looked down at the legend on the map as he put the tray on the coffee table. It said, *Kwajalein Atoll.*

"Don't you guys have families?" Stoner asked, taking his own Jack Daniel's. "I mean, it's Sunday afternoon, five days before Christmas, for god's sake."

"We have work to do," Tuttle said without taking his eyes from the map.

"You want to watch football on television?" McDermott asked derisively.

"I want to see my kids in Palo Alto," Stoner said.

"You'll be lucky if we let you put a phone call through to them on Christmas Eve," McDermott snapped.

Stoner slumped back on the sofa again. "So they're sending you to Kwajalein after all. Good. You don't deserve Arecibo. Puerto Rico's too lush for you bastards."

"There's no call for that kind of language," Tuttle said.

"I've already been deprived of my liberty. Don't try to take away my freedom of speech."

"You've sent classified information to the Soviet Union," Tuttle said, his round face going slightly red. "That's a violation of the security laws. If we wanted to we could slap an espionage charge on you."

"And I told you before, any half-decent lawyer would put your ass in a sling over illegal detention, duress, harassment . . . hell, nobody even read me my rights."

Tuttle glared at him and Stoner realized that the mild profanity bothered the little guy more than the legal position he was in.

McDermott broke up their staring match. "Now, look here, Stoner. You've got to realize that what we're sitting on here is so important that we're not going to allow little legal quibbles to get in our way."

"Try telling that to a judge. Or a jury."

"You won't get in front of a judge," Tuttle said smugly. "You're going to Kwajalein with us and you're going to sit on that island until we're ready to turn you loose."

"Which won't be until Project JOVE is completed," McDermott added. "Listen to me, sonny. You can be either with us or against us, but either way you're going to Kwajalein."

"So what difference does it make?"

"Plenty! If you co-operate with us, work with us, then the Navy's willing to forget any charges of security violation or espionage. Right, Fred?"

Tuttle nodded. "But if you won't co-operate, we'll convene a federal court on Kwajalein, try you there, and keep you in a Navy brig until we're good and ready to transfer you to a federal prison on the mainland."

Stoner took a swallow of Jack Daniel's. "So it's heads you win, tails I lose."

"Exactly," said McDermott.

"Military justice."

"It's legal," Tuttle insisted. "I checked it out."

Stoner laughed. "Legal. Military justice is to justice as military intelligence is to smarts."

Tuttle took it seriously. "Don't you go maligning military intelligence. I worked in Naval Intelligence. Nothing wrong with the smarts there. And we caught you, didn't we?"

"Yeah, I know. You guys are so smart we won the war in Vietnam," Stoner taunted.

"That was *Army* Intelligence! Westmoreland. All he wanted was good news. I know plenty of Army G-2 officers who got pushed further and further out into the boondocks every time they brought in a realistic intelligence report. After enough of them got knocked off by the VC, they started to realize that all Westmoreland wanted was high body counts and optimistic pipe dreams. So that's what they sent in, and they always got rewarded with softer assignments, closer to headquarters, where it was safer."

"And we lost the war."

Tuttle nodded, a bit sullenly. "But that was the Army, not us. Why, if it wasn't for my intelligence background this whole Project JOVE might never have gotten started. When Professor McDermott first told me about the radio pulses I was the one who thought of using Big Eye to search for anything unusual. It was my idea."

McDermott's face went splotchy, but he didn't contradict the lieutenant commander.

Stoner said, "And that's how I got drafted into this game, is it?"

"That's right," Tuttle said. "And you are *in*, for keeps. There's no getting out."

"So are you going to be with us or against us?" McDermott asked.

Stoner looked down at the floor again, at the map spread across the carpet. But his mind's eye was seeing the photographs of Jupiter, the speck of moving light that was the alien space-craft which had invaded the solar system.

Invaded? Stoner was startled at his own use of the term. Then he realized the importance of the question behind it. What is this—thing—doing here? Where did it come from? Why is it here?

Who sent it?

"Well?" McDermott demanded. "What's your answer?"

Instead of replying, Stoner got to his feet and headed for the kitchen. "Get your coats," he said over his shoulder. "I want to show you something."

Puzzled, grumbling, they followed Stoner out to the back door of the house. They pulled on their heavy coats while Stoner slipped into a lined windbreaker.

It was cold outside, but clear and dry. The sun gave no heat, but the bulk of the house kept the wind off the tiny fenced-in area behind the kitchen.

"Hi, Burt," Stoner said to the Navy guard out there. McDermott and Tuttle watched in mystified silence.

Burt was a civilian Navy employee who normally sat in an office in Boston. He was paid double time for standing by the chain link fence that surrounded the house's rear patio. Stoner smiled at him. Burt was fiftyish, portly, with a body that had been strong once but now held more beer than muscle.

"Burt guards the house on Sundays," Stoner explained to

McDermott and Tuttle, "while guys like Dooley and the younger boys take the day off."

"Hey, Dr. Stoner," Burt said, grinning, "I been thinkin' about those boards you broke with your bare hands last weekend. Next time I need some kindlin' broke up, I'll know where to go."

Stoner smiled back at him. "You do that, Burt. You do that."

He pulled himself to a ready stance and forced his body to relax. Tae kwon do is a discipline, Stoner told himself. The true disciple does not seek to fight.

He walked slowly, metering his breathing rate with deliberate care, to the chain link fence, his back to the three other men. Stopping in front of one of the steel posts that anchored the fence to the ground, Stoner gave the fiercest yell he could push out of his lungs and sprang up to kick the very top of the post.

The metal pole bent and twanged like a guitar string. The fence vibrated.

Stoner did it again, screaming savagely, with his left foot this time. And then again. The pole visibly sagged.

"Hey, Dr. Stoner! What the hell you doin'?"

Stoner turned a deadly serious gaze on the guard. "Just practicing, Burt."

"Cheez, for a minute there I thought you was tryin' to knock the fence down!"

Looking straight at Tuttle, Stoner replied, "I could if I wanted to."

"I can see that."

"Imagine what one of those kicks would do to a man's head. Even Dooley's."

McDermott licked his lips, glanced at Tuttle.

"Do you carry a gun, Burt?" Stoner asked.

His hand involuntarily twitched toward the holster underneath his coat.

"Do you think you could get your gun out before I kicked your head in?"

Burt stared at him. Then grinned shakily. "Hey . . . Dr. Stoner, you're kiddin' me, aintcha?"

Stoner closed his eyes momentarily and nodded. "Sure, Burt. I'm kidding." Then he stared into Tuttle's frightened eyes and added, "Any time I want to break out of here, I can. I could pulverize Dooley and two other men with him before they could even react. The only reason I'm here is because I want to be here."

Tuttle began, "I never thought . . ."

But Stoner stopped him with a pointed finger. "I don't like being treated as a prisoner, but I decided the very first day to accept it, because I know—I knew long before *he* did"—he gestured to McDermott—"how important this project is."

"Now, see here, Stoner," Big Mac groused.

Stoner ignored him. "I'm here and I'll stay. So don't try to threaten me. I'm not some little kid who scares easily. Remember that."

For several moments no one said a word. McDermott and Tuttle glanced uneasily at each other. Stoner listened to the wind sighing past the house, the bare trees whispering.

"You've made your point," Tuttle said at last, his eyes on the bent fence post. Then he grinned slightly. "I'm glad you're on our side."

Stoner nodded and started for the kitchen door.

"But we still have to maintain a tight security control on everybody in the project," Tuttle said, following after him.

"I understand that. But don't make any cracks about my not being allowed to phone my kids."

"All right . . . as long as you don't try to smuggle any more letters out of here."

"I won't."

They went into the kitchen and Stoner peeled off his windbreaker. Tuttle and McDermott headed straight for the front door, and the car outside in front of the house, waiting for them. Stoner went with them to the door, looked outside at the driveway that led to the road. No fences there.

Tuttle went to the car and started its engine. McDermott hung back by the doorway, an uncertain scowl on his beefy face.

Finally he turned to Stoner and said, "Don't expect Jo Camerata to come waltzing up here anymore. I've taken her off courier duty."

"You . . . what?"

"I know she took care of that letter for you," McDermott said, his voice a low rumble, "no matter how much either one of you deny it."

"That's no reason to . . ."

McDermott broke into a malicious grin. "Listen, sonny. She's just as happy to be out of this courier routine as she can be. She's gotten everything she can get out of you—which is nothing but trouble. But *I* can get her into the Department of Aerospace Engineering at the university. She wants to be an astronaut, you know."

Stoner wanted to punch that leering, grinning old face. Instead he merely said, "I know."

"So she's after me now. You're out of her game plan."

Tuttle bonked the horn once, lightly. McDermott started toward the car. Over his shoulder, he said to Stoner, "Don't worry. I'll take good care of her."

Stoner stood trapped in the doorway, unable to move, seething.

Memorandum

FROM: V. J. Driscoll, ONM   DATE: 5 January
TO: Lt/Cdr F. G. Tuttle, ONR   FILE: 84-662
SUBJECT: Transfer of   REF: ONM/Log/vjd
         Project JOVE

1. Planning phase of Project JOVE transfer is now complete.
2. Logistic buildup at Kwajalein is under way, preparatory to reception of Project JOVE personnel and equipment by 15 April.
3. Administrative responsibility for Kwajalein and adjoining facilities will be transferred to the Navy by 15 January.
4. Port of debarkation for Project JOVE personnel will be Naval Air Station, South Weymouth, MA. All personnel will be airlifted by MAC in two (2) C-141 transports. MAC will provide a third C-141 or one (1) C-5A, as required, for equipment.
5. It is imperative that all personnel and dependents be prepared to embark no later than 15 April. Facilities for dependents can be made available at South Weymouth NAS for Project JOVE families, if necessary.

CHAPTER 15

Sally Ellington kicked off her sensibly low-heeled shoes, reached across her cluttered desk and picked the phone receiver off its cradle. For a long moment she hesitated. Then, with a glance at the locked door that connected to the empty outer office, she quickly punched out his number on the phone's keyboard.

His voice sounded sleepy, grumpy, when he answered.

"It's me," she said. "Sally."

"At this hour?"

"Be quiet and listen," the President's science adviser commanded. "I've got something that will make your boss the next President."

No reply from the other end. I wonder if he's alone in that waterbed of his? she wondered.

"Well?" he demanded.

"The President's decided to inform the Russians about . . . you know."

"JOVE?" he asked immediately.

"Yes. He's going to use the Hot Line."

"Jesus Christ."

"When that becomes public knowledge, his chances of winning next November are gone."

"I don't know. He . . ."

"I *do* know," Sally Ellington said. "Better than you. He's finished, if and when this news leaks to the press."

"So why are you telling me? If I tell the Secretary about it . . ."

She smiled to herself. "That's your decision to make. I just wanted to be sure you knew."

"I see." His voice faltered momentarily, then, "I appreciate this, Sally. I owe you one."

She nodded, picturing in her mind how he would repay her. In that waterbed.

In Massachusetts during the winter the sun sets by four o'clock. It was nearly six and as black as midnight outside the observatory windows as Jeff Thompson pored over the computer printouts that covered his desk.

Jo Camerata sat alongside him, tracing with her finger a long column of numbers. Thompson could smell a trace of herbal scent in her dark hair. Her fingernail was unpainted, but carefully shaped.

You're a happily married man, Thompson told himself. Then he added, But you're not dead!

"I know the figures look screwy," Jo was saying, "but that's what the computer is spitting out at us. I ran through the program three times, just to be sure, and the numbers came out the same each time."

Thompson could feel the warmth of her body. She was almost rubbing her shoulder against his. Forcing himself to concentrate on the work in front of him, he asked, "And this is the latest run?"

"Yes," she said. "All this column is the data from the latest set of Big Eye photographs."

Thompson frowned at the numbers. It had been years since he'd been faced with a problem in orbital mechanics. Not since he had received his doctorate and gone to work at the observatory under McDermott's direction had he been forced to calculate orbits and trajectories. That's what graduate students were for: they did the dog work.

But this latest batch of numbers churned out by the computer made no sense. It looked so crazy that he had to give it his personal attention.

Thompson shook his head. "You'd better hand this set to Keith. It's more in his line than mine."

Jo moved slightly away from him. "I'm not allowed to go up there anymore. Professor McDermott doesn't want me to see him."

"You're not a courier anymore?"

"No. Mac doesn't even want me to talk to him on the phone."

Pushing his eyeglasses back up over his brows, Thompson gave her a long look. "How do you feel about that? I thought you and Keith were, well . . ."

Jo shook her head. "I'd rather not talk about it, if you don't mind."

"You can't even phone him?"

She made a helpless gesture with her hands. "The phone at the house is tapped. Mac gets a record of all the incoming and outgoing calls."

"Jesus Christ, we might as well be in Russia."

Jo said nothing.

"Well," Thompson said, "I guess somebody else'll have to deliver this can of worms to him."

"Or we could send it over the computer line," Jo said softly. "He's got a terminal up there at the house."

"Yeah, that's right."

"Am I doing something wrong?" Jo asked, looking back at the printouts. "Or is the computer glitching on us?"

"Damned if I know. I'll have to work all night on this to figure out what's wrong," Thompson said.

"I must've made a mistake somewhere." A gloomy note of self-criticism crept into her voice.

"You've been under a lot of pressure."

"That's no excuse."

Thompson pushed his chair away from the desk slightly and straightened up from his usual hunched-over position. "Mac's really leaning on you, huh?"

Jo smiled sadly. "More than you know."

He could feel his blood pressure rising. She looked so helpless, so vulnerable.

"It's a shame Keith dragged you into his crackpot scheme. It wasn't very smart, writing to the Russians."

"He didn't tell them anything he wasn't supposed to say!" she flared.

"That's not what the Navy thinks."

"He's a good man," she insisted. "He wouldn't do anything to hurt anybody."

Thompson grinned at her. "Neither would Chamberlain."

"Who?"

"Neville Chamberlain, the British Prime Minister who caved in to Hitler at Munich."

"Oh," she said. "History."

Suddenly Thompson felt very old.

They pored over the computer runs for another hour, but Thompson found he couldn't concentrate on it. He wanted to work on Jo, instead. Finally, with an enormous effort of will, he pushed his chair away from the desk and stood up.

"Look, kid, you'd better go home. It's going to take the rest of the night for me to figure out where the glitch is."

She looked concerned. "I'm willing to stay here and help you . . ."

"No," he snapped, a bit desperately. "Go on home. Get some sleep. I'm going to phone my wife and tell her to tuck the kids in and keep supper warm for me. I've got three kids, you know."

"Yes. I know."

"Okay. Off you go. See you tomorrow."

She got up from her chair, almost reluctantly, Thompson thought, and went to the door of his cubbyhole office. "I'll check the data recorders downstairs before I go," she said.

"Fine. Good night, Jo."

He stared for a long while at the doorway after she left. Then he phoned home, but the line was busy. Nancy and her goddamned girl friends.

He turned his full attention to the computer printouts, trying to get the vision of Jo out of his mind.

But he heard her call, "Dr. Thompson!"

Looking up from the desk, he saw that she was back at the doorway, her face a mixture of worry and surprise.

"What's wrong?"

"The signals," Jo said, breathless with agitation. "They've stopped!"

"What?"

He bolted from his chair, barked his shin on the corner of the desk and hurried downstairs with her.

The big room was strangely quiet. No one else was there; the night shift wouldn't come on for another hour. The big electronics consoles hummed softly to themselves. The tracing pens were strangely still, inking out dead-straight lines on the graph paper that unrolled slowly beneath them.

Thompson dashed around the cluster of desks in the middle of the room, found a headset and plugged it into the proper console.

He clapped one earphone to the side of his head.

Nothing.

Only the background hiss of the universe, laughing at him. The radio pulses were gone.

This evening I witnessed one of the great political blunders of all time. The President revealed to the Premier of Soviet Russia, over the Hot Line, that we are working on making contact with the alien spacecraft we discovered in the vicinity of Jupiter.

The Premier pretended not to be surprised: said his own scientists are working on the very same thing. The President suggested a joint program, sharing people, information, facilities. The Premier gave a jolly laugh and said he'd like that very much.

He sure as goddamned hell would! And in the meanwhile, any shred of support the President had in Congress is going to bolt the Party when they find out he's giving away our top scientific secrets to the Reds. In the name of peace and brotherhood!

It looks now as if I'll have no choice but to try to wrest the Party's nomination away from him. I've got to take these primaries seriously; it's the only hope for the Party in November.

> Private diary of the Honorable
> WALDEN C. VINCENNES, Secretary of State

CHAPTER 16

Gritting his teeth against the pain, Cardinal Otto von Friederich began the long climb up the marble steps that led to the papal apartment. To the messengers and monsignors proceeding through the halls of the Vatican on the eternal business of Holy Mother Church, the cardinal seemed an austere, aloof symbol of majesty: silent and stately, slowed perhaps by age and arthritis, but the very picture of a Prince of the Church, with his pure white hair, ascetic angular features and swirling red robes.

Cardinal von Friederich knew better. His power within the Vatican was illusory. This new Pope had no time for an old man wedded to the traditions and training of the past. His audiences with the Holy Father were strictly formal nowadays; his days of influence and true power were over.

Silently he prayed the rosary as he climbed the cold marble stairs. The pain grew worse each day. It was a penance, of course, and he knew that God would not send him a Cross that he could not bear. Still, the pain raised a fine sheen of perspiration across his brow.

An elderly monsignor, chalky-white as dust, met the cardinal at the top of the stairs and silently ushered him into a spare, chilly little room.

Cardinal Benedetto was already there, of course, his red cape wrapped around his stocky body. Benedetto always reminded Von Friederich of a Turkish railway porter: squat and swarthy, almost totally bald even though he was nearly twenty years Von Friederich's junior. But he was the Pope's strong right arm these days, the papal Secretary of State, confidant and adviser of His Holiness. While Von Friederich's position as head of the Propaganda Fide, had become little more than a sinecure for a dying old man.

How different it had been in the old days, Von Friederich thought. All my life I have served Italian Popes and battled the Italians dominating the Curia. Now we have a Polish Pope, and the Italians have overwhelmed me at last.

"My Lord Cardinal," Benedetto said in Italian.

Von Friederich inclined his head in the slightest of bows. Even that tiny movement caused him pain.

The room was almost bare of furnishings. A small wooden desk, a few plain chairs. The only light came from the lamp on the desk. Out beyond the windows, the Vatican garden was already draped in the shadows of dusk.

In the gloomy darkness, Von Friederich could see that the walls were covered with frescoes by Titian. Or perhaps Rafael. He never could tell them apart. Vatican wallpaper, he said to himself, keeping his distance from Cardinal Benedetto.

Part of the painting on the wall he was facing—a congregation of saints piously praising God—suddenly swung away, revealing a door cunningly set into the wall. The Pope strode into the room, strong, sturdy, smiling at them both.

The room seemed to brighten. The Holy Father was wearing

white robes, of course. But despite himself, Von Friederich had to admit that it was His Holiness' beaming, energetic features that charged the room with light. It was the open, rugged face of a worker, a common man elevated to greatness, the kind of face that might have been St. Peter's. A fisherman, not an aristocrat. But he rules the aristocrats and the workers alike, Von Friederich knew.

The cardinals knelt and kissed the papal ring. The Pope smiled and motioned for them to seat themselves.

"Come, come," the Pope said in Italian. "No formalities today. We have too much to consider."

Within moments they were deeply into a discussion of the strange radio signals from Jupiter that the American hierarchy had reported to the Vatican only the day before.

"My scientific adviser," said the Pope, "Monsignor Parelli, is beside himself with excitement. He believes this is the most wonderful thing to happen to mankind in two millennia."

"It is a danger," said Von Friederich.

"A danger, my brother?"

Von Friederich's voice had always been high, almost girlish. As a child he had fought many schoolyard battles because of it. Now he struggled to keep it calm, even, logical—and to keep his pain from showing in it.

"When the news of this alien . . . thing . . . reaches the general populace—as it will, sooner or later—they will be stunned and fearful. Does Your Holiness recall the uproar some twenty-five years ago over Sputnik?"

The Pope nodded. "Yes, but that was mainly in the West."

"It will be as nothing compared to the public reaction to news of an alien intelligence in our solar system. Who are they? What are they like? What do they want? *Whom do they worship?*" He hissed the last question in an urgent whisper.

The Pope started to reply, then hesitated and stroked his broad chin thoughtfully.

"I agree, Your Holiness," said Cardinal Benedetto. "This alien presence could be a great danger to the faithful."

The Pope sat back in his chair and tapped his blunt fingertips on his knees.

"It is a test," he said finally.

"A test?"

He nodded. "A test of our faith, my brothers. A test of our courage, our intelligence. But most of all, a test of our faith."

"It could be so," Benedetto quickly agreed.

Von Friederich said nothing, but thought that the Italian was toadying again.

"The Americans have discovered these radio signals and something they believe to be a spaceship, if I understand the information we have received," the Pope said.

Benedetto nodded. "Radio signals from the planet Jupiter, yes. And in space near the planet, an alien . . . artifact."

"Artifact!" The Pope smiled broadly. "An excellent word, Benedetto! A *scientific* word. Noncommittal. Unemotional. Excellent!"

Von Friederich clamped his teeth together.

"I believe," the Pope went on, "that science leads to knowledge and therefore toward the perfection of man's intelligence. This alien *artifact*"—he smiled again—"can help the scientists to learn more about the universe, and therefore to learn more about God's works."

"Ah, I see," said Benedetto. "If we can converse with these alien creatures, we have the opportunity to learn more of God's handiwork, more about His creations."

The Pope nodded to him.

"But Holy Mother Church has the responsibility of protecting her children from error and from danger," Von Friederich said, as strongly as he could manage. "Especially from danger to their immortal souls."

Benedetto turned toward him. "I don't see how . . ."

"This space artifact," Von Friederich said, feeling his voice weaken as he spoke, "will startle many of the faithful. Most of our flock still live in very backward regions of the globe: Latin America, Africa, Asia—even in parts of Europe and North America many Catholics have only a dim knowledge of the modern world. They fear modern science. They cling to their faith for support in their troubled lives."

"Of course," said the Pope.

"And their Church," Von Friederich went on, "has always let them think that we are God's creatures. We and we alone."

"But the Church has never denied the possibility of other creatures elsewhere in the universe," Benedetto said.

"Never formally denied," Von Friederich pointed out. "But Holy Mother Church has never urged her children to prepare themselves for meeting other creatures from space, either."

"Quite true, my friend," murmured the Pope. "Quite true. Even in *Redemptor hominis* I said that man has been given dominion over the visible world by his Creator."

"If the world is suddenly told that there are other intelligent creatures in space, from other worlds, other suns, and that they are in some physical ways superior to us"—Von Friederich closed his eyes to hide the pain—"the faith of many Catholics will be strained to the utmost."

Benedetto nodded reluctantly. "The entire foundation upon which their faith is built could be shaken. It could be the greatest blow to the Church since Luther."

Von Friederich shook his head. "Not Luther. It was Galileo and the scientists who destroyed the authority of the Universal Church. Luther was nothing without them. Rome had dealt with schisms and heresies before the scientists led to the Protestant movement."

"A harsh view of science," the Pope said, smiling.

"Heretics we can convert, given time," Von Friederich said, his voice trembling. "It was the scientists who subverted the Church."

The Pope raised a hand. "We are not here to reopen centuries-old schisms. Science has found this alien artifact. What should Holy Mother Church do about it?"

"Pray that it goes away," said Von Friederich.

"Apparently," said Benedetto, "both the Americans and the Russians are trying to keep the information secret, for the time being."

"Good!"

"They are hinting at the possibility of working together in investigating the artifact," Benedetto went on, "but both of them really want to seize the alien knowledge for themselves, for their own military purposes."

The Pope's face went somber. "Of course. What else would they think of? But how long can they keep this knowledge secret from their own people?"

"Someone is bound to speak up sooner or later," Benedetto agreed.

"We must decide on how to handle the situation when the news is made public," said the Pope.

"We could make the revelation ourselves," Benedetto suggested.

"No!" Von Friederich snapped.

"It would give the Holy Father great prestige," Benedetto argued, "and also show the faithful that our Pope is unafraid."

Von Friederich thought for a moment, then replied, "But if the Americans and Russians are both trying to keep this a secret, wouldn't they deny everything if we tried to make the news public? After all, the Americans have not made a formal announcement of their discovery. We have learned of it through the most circumspect of channels. And the Russians . . . !"

Benedetto said, "The American and Soviet *governments* may wish to keep this a secret. But their scientists do not, I'm certain. And there are many other scientists, in other nations, who could confirm the truth once His Holiness revealed it."

"You are sure of that?" the Pope asked.

"Reasonably sure, Your Holiness."

"Reasonably," Von Friederich sneered.

"But have we decided," the Pope asked softly, "that the time is right to release this news to the public?"

"We must consider this carefully before plunging into a precipitous course of action," Von Friederich said.

The Pope cocked an eyebrow in his direction. "The Propaganda Fide wants a few weeks to think about it?"

"Yes, Your Holiness."

"Or a few months?"

Von Friederich tried to shrug, almost failed.

"We don't have months," Benedetto urged. "We may not even have weeks. We must decide now. Quickly!"

The Pope turned toward him. "My friend, I have learned in my time here that nothing is done very quickly in the Vatican."

"There is one thing that we can do immediately," Benedetto countered. "With your permission, of course, Your Holiness."

"And what is that?"

"The Americans are inviting the Russians and scientists from many other countries to join them in a co-operative research program, to study these signals and attempt to make contact with the alien artifact."

"Yes?"

"So our people in Washington tell me," Benedetto said, a bit smugly, Von Friederich thought.

"What has this to do with us?" the Pope asked.

"We should send a scientist to join this group, if the Americans actually are sincere in their words."

"A scientist from the Church? Now, who . . ."

"We have just the man," Benedetto said, with the air of a magician pulling a rabbit from his hat. "A Dominican lay brother in a monastery in Languedoc. He was a world-renowned cosmologist who received the Nobel Prize for his theories . . ."

Von Friederich interrupted, "A cosmologist who received the Nobel and then retired to a Dominican monastery?"

Benedetto spread his hands in an Italian gesture of regret "He wished to get away from the world. He had a problem with alcohol. There were also other rumors . . . about carnal excesses . . ."

"This man should represent the Vatican?"

"He is much older now," Benedetto said. "The monastic life has purified him."

"Will he be able to face the temptations of the outer world, beyond his monastery's walls?" the Pope wondered.

Smiling, Benedetto answered, "At some scientific research station? I should think so."

"What is his name?"

"Reynaud. Edouard Reynaud."

"I never heard of him," Von Friederich muttered.

"He is a very famous scientist."

"Very well," said the Pope. "Ask his Order for his services. He should come here first, to discuss the matter with you in detail."

"Yes, Your Holiness." Benedetto bowed his head meekly.

Von Friederich gathered his strength and said firmly, "But we will make no public announcements. We must not alarm the faithful."

The Pope nodded. "I agree, my Lord Cardinal. If the Americans and Russians remain silent, we must keep silent, also."

The pain washed over him, but with it Von Friederich felt a

profound sense of relief, almost gratitude. At least I have accomplished that much, he thought. I've stemmed the Italian tide one more time. I've protected Christ's Vicar on Earth from making a fool of himself.

Even through the red haze of his suffering, Von Friederich relished the look of discomfort on Benedetto's swarthy face.

REVIVALISTS, UFO FANS CLASH

SAN DIEGO: A near riot broke out at an outdoor revival meeting in Marineland of the Pacific last night as followers of Urban Evangelist Willie Wilson clashed with UFO fans who had infiltrated Rev. Wilson's meeting.

More than six thousand persons were jammed into the outdoor meeting grounds, police estimate, to hear Rev. Wilson preach his "watch the skies" message. Shortly after he began speaking, an organized band of UFO enthusiasts began heckling, booing and waving protest signs. Several scuffles broke out, but police armed with riot gear quickly quelled the disturbances.

"He's a phony," said Fred W. Weddell, a local UFO expert, of Rev. Wilson. "He's trying to scare everybody with an end of the world sermon. We all know that UFOs are friendly, peaceful."

Rev. Wilson declared, "My message is one of peace and hope. It has nothing to do with UFOs. I'm merely warning people that a Great Change is coming to this world, and we should all be watching the skies for it."

Seventeen persons were injured in the fighting, including two who were hospitalized. Police arrested eight . . .

CHAPTER 17

A storm was coming.

Stoner had lived in New England long enough to know the warnings. The eleven o'clock news on television—two bland men so alike they might have been clones, in their gold blazers, teamed with a carefully coiffed Hispanic woman who traded inane small talk with them—had given a weather forecast of "clear and colder, with an overnight low around zero, winds from the west light and variable."

But now, just past midnight, the wind was moaning and roaring outside the New Hampshire house. A look through the dining room windows showed clouds scudding across the face of the Moon. Trees were swaying and clacking their frozen branches together. The house began to creak like an old wooden ship laboring through heavy seas.

Cavendish, who now shared the house with Stoner, shivered as he stared out the window. "My god, to think that the Puritans faced this kind of weather. They must have been totally unprepared for it."

Stoner laughed to himself. This is the winter that Big Mac was going to save us from. The winter we were going to spend in Puerto Rico.

As he sat at the dining room table, surrounded by Big Eye photographs of Jupiter and computer printouts, Stoner studied the Englishman. Cavendish was smoking a pipe. He wore a sweater beneath his tweed jacket. He turned back from the window and peered from beneath his bushy brows at the photos strewn across the table.

Tapping at the pinpoint of light at the center of one photo, he asked, "You're really quite certain that this thing is from beyond the solar system?"

Stoner said, "Yes."

"Mathematically certain?"

"Check the numbers yourself. It's a tourist, a visitor, from outside this solar system."

"H'mm." Cavendish puffed a cloud of smoke ceilingward. "And the radio pulses have stopped."

Nodding, "It's been nearly a week now. Nothing."

"Just abruptly . . . turned off, eh?"

"That's what Jeff Thompson told me. And now the spacecraft is spiraling out from Jupiter, moving away from the planet."

"Moving away? Really?"

"That's what the numbers from the computer show. It's taken a look at Jupiter, and now it's going away. Maybe it's heading back home."

Cavendish said nothing for a few moments. The pipe smoke smelled pleasant to Stoner, comforting.

"Nothing close enough to us to be a reasonable home for the beast, is there?" the Englishman asked.

Stoner shrugged. "Alpha Centauri's more than four light-years away, but there's no evidence of planets there."

"Quite. Nearest star with planets is Sixty-one Cygni, isn't it?"

"Barnard's Star," Stoner corrected, "if you accept Van de Kamp's work. Not quite six light-years out."

"Really?" Cavendish puffed reflectively for a few moments, clouds of smoke rising slowly to the low, sagging ceiling of the dining room.

Stoner pulled his chair over to the computer terminal, perched on the far end of the dining room table. His fingers played over the keyboard briefly.

"Where's the blasted thing heading?"

"That's what we'd all like to know. The computer's chewing on it now. Seems to be aiming out of the solar system entirely. If we extend its present velocity vector, it'll climb way up above the ecliptic and head back out into deep space."

"You think it's going back home, do you?"

"Or off to another solar system."

"But out of *our* solar system entirely," Cavendish said.

"Right."

"Without visiting us."

Stoner looked up from the keyboard. "We're not that important to it, I guess. It's an alien craft. It entered our solar system, went to the biggest planet it could find, sniffed around, and now it's leaving. Maybe it flew by Saturn before we discovered its presence, I don't know. But whoever sent it probably came from a giant planet, like Jupiter or Saturn, I would guess. They probably can't imagine life existing on a small, hot world like Earth."

"Rather a blow to one's ego, isn't it?" Cavendish murmured.

"What hurts most is that it won't come close enough for us to study in detail."

"Yes. Pity."

With a sigh that he hadn't realized he had in him, Stoner nodded. "No more radio pulses, and our alien visitor is leaving us. Looks like we won't need Kwajalein after all."

"Puzzling."

"Damned frustrating."

Cavendish paced along the dining room table. "Do you always work this late?"

Leaning back in his chair, Stoner answered, "I was hoping the computer could give us an accurate projection of the alien's track tonight, so we could get some kind of fix on where it's heading. But there must be a glitch in the system somewhere. Nothing's coming through."

"Perhaps the machine's gone to sleep?" Cavendish said it with a vague smile.

"It never sleeps."

"Neither do you, apparently."

"You're up kind of late yourself, Professor."

Cavendish's smile crumpled. "Yes, quite. You see, sleep is something of a bad show with me. I dream, you know."

Stoner turned in the heavy dining room chair to follow the old man's pacing.

But Cavendish changed the subject. "So the thing is actually heading out of the solar system." He pointed at the silent computer with the stem of his pipe.

"Looks that way."

"Good. Get rid of it. Godawful nuisance. Something more for the East and West to fight over. Be a blessing if the damned thing would just go away."

Stoner felt surprised. "But we'll never find out where it's from, who sent it, what it's all about."

Cavendish shrugged his frail shoulders. "We already know the important part of it, don't we? We are not alone. It really doesn't matter who made it or where it's from or even why it was sent here. The important fact is that we know now, beyond any shadow of a doubt, that there are other intelligences out there, among the stars. We are not alone in the universe."

"*We* know it," Stoner grumbled, "but the rest of the world doesn't."

"Oh, everyone will, in time. Don't be so impatient. The whole world will find out soon enough."

"Not if Tuttle and Big Mac have their way."

"They won't," Cavendish assured him. "Not for long, at any rate. The news will be out sooner or later."

Stoner sat back and waited for the old man to say more. But Cavendish merely walked to the window and stood staring out at the tempestuous night, puffing clouds of aromatic blue smoke from his pipe. The wind shrieked out there, and from high above came the trembling whine of a distant jetliner.

With a glance at the strangely quiet computer terminal, Stoner got up and headed for the telephone, in the living room.

"I'll be back in a minute," he told Cavendish. "I'm going to call the computer center and find out what the hell's going on with this machine."

"Good," said Cavendish. "In the meanwhile, I think I'll pour myself a brandy. Good night for it."

"Fine. Make one for me, if you don't mind."

"Certainly," Cavendish said.

Jo sat in the little secretary's chair at the main input console of the computer. The glareless fluorescent light panels up in the ceiling gave the huge room a sense of timelessness. There were no windows, no way to tell if it was day or night.

Like a Las Vegas gambling casino, Jo told herself. They want your whole attention devoted to the machines, not to any distractions like sunshine or rain.

The clock on the far wall showed it was well past twelve. Jo knew it was midnight, but a nagging part of her mind warned her that she just might have it all wrong, and it could just as easily be bright noon outside the solid walls of the computer complex.

"Hey, I'm going out for coffee."

Startled, she looked up to see the other graduate student who was working the graveyard shift this week.

"You want any?" He grinned down at her. Pleasant face, young, unlined. He was trying to grow a beard but only a few wisps of blondish hair marred his jawline.

"No, thanks. I brought a lunch." She glanced at the big shoulder bag resting on the floor near her chair.

"Okay. I'll be back in ten–fifteen minutes. Don't open the door for anybody; I've got my key." He dangled the key from its ring. "Too many freaks out there this time of night to take any chances."

"I'll be all right," Jo said.

"Okay."

He pranced off, whistling off-key to himself.

Once he closed the heavy steel door behind him, Jo rose to her feet, stretched her cramped legs and arms and started some deep knee bends. The only sounds in the room were the sixty-cycle hum of the lights, the deeper rumble of the computer's main core and her own rhythmic breathing.

The computer was working on something, a problem that was soaking up a large part of its capacity. It had been humming and blinking to itself without a single line of printout ever since Jo had shown up for her shift, nearly an hour ago.

Maybe it's working on a problem for Keith, she thought as she bent down to sit on her heels. The corners of her lips tugged down. More than two weeks now and he hasn't called, hasn't even sent a message through Dr. Thompson or any of the other people who go up to the house.

He just doesn't care, Jo realized. He doesn't give a damn about me. I was just a convenient lay for him.

The phone rang.

Grunting, she got to her feet and went over to the handset built into the console, next to one of its keyboards.

"Computer center," she said into the phone.

"This is Dr. Stoner," Keith's voice replied. He sounded slightly annoyed. "Who am I speaking to?"

"Keith . . ." She tried to mask the sudden breathlessness of her voice, tried to tell herself it was from the exertion of the exercises.

"Jo? Is that you?"

"Yes."

"You're working at the computer center now?"

She nodded, then realized how foolish it was. "Yes. That's what they've got me doing now. I'm on the swing shift this week."

"How are you?"

"I'm . . ." she hesitated, put her thoughts in order. "I'm all right, Keith. And you?"

"About the same." His voice became guarded, too. "Not much we can say over the phone, is there?"

"No. I suppose the security regulations . . ."

"Yeah, I know."

Suddenly there was nothing she could say.

After a moment's silence, he asked, "How's Big Mac treating you?"

A flash of electricity went through her. Does he know? she wondered.

"I heard from Jeff Thompson that he's written a letter to NASA for you."

She could feel the cold anger in his words. Just as coldly, she replied, "That's right, Keith. He has."

"Good for you," he said acidly. "You're a girl who knows what she wants. I hope you get it."

You ignorant fool! she wanted to scream. You think I'm doing this for myself?

But she answered aloud, "I'm all right, Keith."

"I'll bet you are."

"Why did you call?" she asked woodenly.

She heard him pull in a deep breath before he replied, "I punched in a trajectory problem a couple of hours ago and my terminal's been dead silent ever since. What's going on down there? The problem shouldn't take that long for the computer to work out."

"The machine's been running ever since I came on shift," she said. "Some of those special trajectory problems of yours have built-in subroutines that take a lot of time."

"Well, check it out for me, will you?"

"Certainly," she said. "That's what I'm here for."

She waited for him to answer, to say something to her, anything. Even anger would mean that he cared.

Instead, he merely mouthed, "Thanks."

He doesn't care, she realized. He never cared. Not for an instant. He's more worried about his goddamned computer program than about me.

"You're quite welcome," Jo said.

And hung up.

Stoner heard her voice, icy, as remote as the farthest star: "You're quite welcome."

The phone clicked dead.

The little bitch, he thought to himself. She'll fuck anybody who can help her get what she wants. Well, I hope she's enjoying herself with Big Mac.

He slammed the phone down, feeling the fury seething inside him, knowing that he was raging not at Jo, not even at McDermott, but at himself.

You're quite a man, Stoner, he told himself. You sit here and let them hold you prisoner and tell yourself that your work is more important than personal ties and what you really want to do is kick the fucking door down and go out and grab her and carry her off to your cave.

"Just listen to that wind!"

Stoner jerked away from the phone to see Cavendish standing in the living room doorway, a brandy snifter in each hand.

With a deep, shuddering breath, he brought his raging emotions under control, forced his pounding heart to slow down, smothered the fury he felt burning inside him under a blanket of cold numbness.

"Are you all right?" Cavendish asked, crossing the big room toward him.

Stoner nodded, not trusting himself yet to speak. He accepted the snifter from Cavendish's outstretched hand.

The old man lifted his glass and smiled wanly. "Cheers," he offered.

"Cheers," Stoner said. He sipped at the cognac. It slid down his throat like liquid fire.

Cavendish pulled the rocker up by the crackling fire and sat down with a weary sigh. "Quite a night out there," he said. "Quite a night. You can hear the wind howling in the chimney."

Going over to the easy chair that faced the old man, Stoner asked, "Why can't you sleep?"

"H'mm? What?"

"You said you don't sleep well." It was a safe subject. Stoner could feel the anger damping down inside him, fading away to the hidden corner where it could remain without anyone knowing it was there.

"Bad dreams," Cavendish answered, staring into the bright flames. "I was a prisoner of the Imperial Japanese Army for four years—just about the length of time it takes a photon to travel from Alpha Centauri to Earth."

"Must have been rough," Stoner said.

"Oh, that was only the beginning." A heavy gust of wind rattled branches against the roof and Cavendish glanced up, his eyes haunted. "The Japanese moved us to Manchuria, you see, just in time to allow the Russians to capture us when they finally stepped into the Pacific war."

"The Russians were on our side then."

"They were on Stalin's side. And Stalin decided that any scientist he could lay his hands on—even a young, starved, sick mathematical physicist—was going to stay in the Soviet Union and work for him, whether he wanted to or not."

"They kept you in Russia?"

"In Siberia, actually. You boys had just set off your bloody atomic bomb, and Stalin was in an absolute sweat to catch up."

"I thought they got their nuclear know-how from spies . . ."

"Nonsense! The only real secret about the atomic bomb was that it worked, that you could actually build one and it would explode satisfactorily. You gave that secret away at Hiroshima. Just as the biggest secret revealed by this alien spacecraft is that it exists—it came from somewhere other than Earth."

"How long did they keep you inside Russia?"

"Years. Until Stalin died and his successors tried to ease tensions a bit. Even then, though, it wasn't easy. They put me through hell and back before they let me go."

"How come?"

Cavendish made a wry face. "The bloody KGB took it into their heads that I would make a marvelous espionage agent for them once I got back to England. I was treated to all sorts of brain-laundering techniques—and I do mean all sorts. That's why I dread sleeping."

His hands had started to shake.

"But you didn't break," Stoner said.

"Of course I broke! And I swore to them that I'd be a good Soviet spy for them. It took a lot to convince them, you know. They're very thorough."

Stoner just stared at him, waiting for more.

"Well, once I got home and my head cleared a bit, I went to

British Military Intelligence and told them the entire story. They were delighted. MI told me that I could be a double agent, pretending to work for the Reds but actually working for the Crown."

"Christ Almighty."

"Quite. I didn't want to work for any of them, but I've been doing both ever since. The reason I'm here, actually, is because both the KGB and British MI want me here."

"You're joking!"

"I wish I were. The Russkies have their own people puzzling over the radio pulses, but they don't have a telescope in orbit that can give them data on the spacecraft. I'm supposed to funnel your Big Eye data to them."

"Does the Navy know about this?"

"Your Navy? No. Neither does NATO, I believe. MI are curious about what you chaps are up to, you realize. Your Navy people haven't shared their information fully with their NATO colleagues, as yet."

"Cloak and dagger," Stoner muttered.

"Indeed. In this business a man has no friends, you know. Absolutely none. Anyone could turn out to be your enemy. Anyone could turn out to be an assassin."

"Assassin?" Stoner echoed. "You mean somebody might try to kill you?"

For the first time, Cavendish laughed. It was a thin, harsh, humorless sound. "Not me, dear boy. You. I'm merely a cog in the machine that both sides are working. If there's an assassin lurking in the bush, he's after your head, not mine."

Stoner gaped at him. Slowly, he asked, "Are you trying to warn me, or . . . ?"

The computer terminal suddenly erupted into clattering life. Stoner and Cavendish both bolted from their chairs by the fireplace and rushed into the dining room, where the typing unit was pounding away madly. Line after line of numbers sprouted on the long accordian-folded sheets of paper that passed through the machine's roller.

"What is it?" Cavendish asked, the brandy snifter still in his fingers. "What's it saying?"

"The latest fix on the spacecraft . . ." Stoner yanked the paper up so that he could read the first rows of figures at eye level without stooping over the chattering typewriter.

He gave a low whistle. "No wonder the computer had to chew on the data all night. The damned thing has changed its course."

"What?"

"It's accelerating."

"Can't be!"

"Look at this." Stoner pointed to the numbers. "Here. And here again."

Cavendish snapped impatiently, "It might as well be Sanskrit! I don't know your language!"

"The spacecraft put on a burst of thrust," Stoner explained. "Here, and here."

"It's maneuvering? Changing course?"

"Yes."

"Then there must be a crew on board!"

"Or a damned smart computer."

"But where is it heading? What's its new course?"

With a sinking feeling in the pit of his stomach, Stoner bent over the typewriter. Just as abruptly as it had started a few moments earlier, it stopped.

"Well?"

Stoner stared at the final row of figures. He didn't need to check a reference table. He had memorized that set of numbers weeks earlier, because he had feared, or hoped, or maybe dreamed that they would show up to face him, inevitably.

"Where is the bloody thing heading?" Cavendish demanded.

"Here," Stoner said.

Cavendish's mouth fell open. "Here," he finally managed. "You mean Earth?"

Stoner nodded. "It's finished looking at Jupiter. Now it's heading for Earth."

BOOK TWO

If the light of a thousand suns suddenly arose in the sky, that splendor might be compared to the radiance of the Supreme Spirit.

BHAGAVAD-GITA 11:12

CHAPTER 18

The General Secretary stared gloomily out the window of his limousine at the gray snowy morning.

"You know," he said in a low, heavy voice, "that I am dying."

Georgi Borodinski gasped. "Comrade Secretary! You mustn't say such a thing."

The General Secretary turned awkwardly to face his aide. Both men were wrapped in heavy dark coats and fur hats, despite the limousine's heating system.

With a halfhearted grin, the General Secretary asked, "Why not? It is the truth."

"But still . . ."

"You're afraid the car is bugged. My prospective heirs might get a little overanxious and try to put me out of misery?" He laughed: a dry, rasping sound.

Borodinski said nothing. By the standards of the Kremlin's inner elite he was a youngish man, only slightly past fifty, his receding hair still dark, his flesh still firm. He had risen from the ranks of Party functionaries by steady hard work, unspectacular, uninspired, seemingly unambitious. But he had recognized his one chance for advancement twenty years earlier, and had attached himself with the dogged faithfulness of a loyal serf to the man who was now General Secretary of the Party and President of the Soviet Union.

Now Borodinski stood on the verge of becoming General Secretary himself—if he could survive the struggle that would inevitably follow the death of his master.

"Do you know why we are riding through the cold and snow, instead of staying warm and comfortable in my office?" asked the General Secretary.

"I think I do," Borodinski answered.

Gesturing toward the driver on the other side of the bullet-proof glass partition, the Secretary explained, "A Tartar, from beyond Lake Baykal. He checks the car every day before I step into it. We are safe from eager ears."

"Yes."

"I must live like an ancient Roman Emperor, surrounded by my Palace Guard—all foreigners, barbarians, loyal to me personally and not to anyone or anything else. A fine state of affairs for the leader of a Marxist state, isn't it?"

"Every great leader has enemies, Comrade Secretary. Within as well as without."

The Secretary's heavy brows inched upward. "But if everyone within the Kremlin is a good Marxist, why should I require such protection?"

Borodinski saw where he was heading. "They are not all good Marxists. Even some in the Presidium and the Inner Council have their . . . failings."

The Secretary nodded grimly. "Now then," he said, "about this latest offer from the American President . . ."

Puzzled by the abrupt shift in their conversation, Borodinski blurted, "But what has that to do with . . . ?"

The General Secretary slapped the younger man's knee and laughed heartily. "You don't see it, eh? You still have a few things to learn about the art of ruling."

His laughter turned into a wheezing cough. Borodinski sat still, waves of sadness and fear washing through him. And impatience. But he sat unmoving as his master slowly won his struggle to breathe normally.

"I was saying," the General Secretary resumed, after wiping his lips and chin with a linen handkerchief, "the American President has made what appears to be another generous offer."

Borodinski nodded. "They've invited us to send a team of scientists to their base in the Pacific. Kwajalein Atoll, isn't it?"

"Yes," the Secretary said. "According to all available intelligence, the American offer seems genuine. Their President wants to use this—this alien spaceship—as a symbol to build stronger ties of co-operation between our two nations."

"Despite everything they've done over the past few years?"

"Perhaps *because* of everything they've done over the past few years. They may have finally realized the futility of their so-called 'get tough' policies."

Borodinski considered that possibility for a moment, then asked, "Will you accept their offer?"

Leaning closer to his aide, the Secretary asked, "What would you do?"

It was a test, Borodinski realized, a test to see if he was fit to take over his master's position. He fought down the fear rising in his throat and kept his long-simmering ambition deep within his heart.

"There is strong opposition within the Presidium," he said slowly. "The idea of co-operating with the capitalists can cause bitter resentment among our more conservative comrades."

"The same comrades who insisted that we march into Afghanistan," the Secretary muttered, "without thinking about how difficult it is to march out again."

"They have caused us many difficulties, true," said Borodinski.

"And," the General Secretary pointed out, "there is strong pressure within the Presidium that we accept the American offer."

Borodinski nodded and stroked his pointed, Lenin-style goatee. "I have learned that the United Nations is also interested in the American program. And they will certainly bring the Chinese in with them."

"Then we would be left out in the cold if we refused to co-operate, wouldn't we?"

"But if we do co-operate, it will infuriate some of the most powerful members of the Presidium. Not to mention the Red Army."

The General Secretary gave him a smirking grin. "A nice little problem, isn't it? How would you handle it?"

Borodinski sank into silent thought. The limousine drove on through the snowy gray silence of morning, well beyond the buildings and houses of sprawling Moscow, far beyond the range of rooftop directional microphones and laser snoopers that can record conversations from the vibrations that spoken words make on the windows of a moving automobile.

Finally Borodinski said, "I think we have no alternative but to accept the American offer. Otherwise we will fall behind them and the others. They could obtain enormous amounts of information from this spaceship . . ." He had more to say, but the pleased expression on the General Secretary's face told him it was time to stop talking.

"A good, honest, straightforward decision." The old man patted his knee. "Now allow me to give you a lesson in politics to go with it."

Borodinski sat up a little straighter.

"I am a dying man, comrade. The doctors have confirmed it. Everyone in the Politburo and the Presidium knows it. This is a dangerous time for me—and for you."

Borodinski nodded, not trusting his voice to reply.

The Secretary closed his eyes for a moment. Then, "You pointed out, quite correctly, that if we accept the Americans' offer of co-operation it will infuriate some of our most conservative comrades. It might well enrage them to the point where they might try to—well, hasten my demise."

"They'd never dare!"

"Oh yes they would," the Secretary assured him with a grim smile. "It wouldn't be the first time a ruler in the Kremlin was hurried to his grave. And it hasn't happened only to the Tsars, either."

Borodinski made his face look shocked.

"But, comrade," the Secretary went on, "suppose we prepare a little snare for these hotheads, a little trap to catch them in treasonable activities, eh? Then we can clear the Kremlin of the troublemakers and I can live out my remaining days in peace, knowing that I'm safe from traitors and assassins."

Borodinski stroked his pointed little beard again. "Then the decision to join the Americans in studying the alien spaceship . . ."

"Is the bait for our trap, naturally."

"That's . . . brilliant! Absolutely brilliant! No wonder you have been our leader for all these years."

The Secretary allowed himself a brief smile. "There is something else, as well."

"Yes?"

"If we are to make contact with another race of intelligent creatures, I want it to be in my lifetime. In fact, it would be the crowning achievement of my career if the Soviet Union could make this contact *alone,* without the help of the West."

"But how . . . ?"

"This is what we shall do." The General Secretary leaned

closer to his aide, close enough so that Borodinski could smell the odor of medicine on the old man's breath.

"I am listening," he said.

"We will send a small team of scientists to this island. They will work with the Americans. Among them will be a few of our intelligence people, of course. Links to us. To *me*."

"I see. Of course."

"While the scientists study this spacecraft, we will be preparing one or more of our biggest rocket boosters for flights to meet this alien ship as it approaches us."

"Ahhh, now I see . . ."

"Our scientists on Kwajalein will have the responsibility of keeping us fully informed. If and when the proper moment arrives, we will send cosmonauts to greet the alien ship." He paused, took a deep, wheezing breath. "Or . . ."

"Or?" Borodinski asked.

"Or we will blow the alien out of the sky with a hydrogen bomb missile, if necessary."

Borodinski felt a shock wave go through him.

The General Secretary's face was grave. "That is the one thing that the scientists don't understand. This alien intruder might be hostile. We must be prepared to defend ourselves."

"But . . . it's only one little ship."

"No, comrade." The General Secretary shook his head. "It is only the *first* ship."

"Where?" Markov asked, blinking.

"Kwajalein," said Maria. "It's an island in the middle of the Pacific Ocean, they told me."

"We're being sent there? Why?" Markov glanced around the familiar surroundings of their living room: the bookcases, the comfortable chairs, the old brass reading lamp that he had rescued from his mother's house, the sturdy tree just outside the window.

"First, they send me to the research center out in the middle of the wilderness and now . . . where did you say it is?"

"Kwajalein," Maria repeated firmly. She was still in her uniform, but she held two big paper bags of groceries in her arms. She hadn't even bothered to put them down before telling her husband the news.

"No," Markov protested, his head buzzing. He groped for one of the chairs and sank into it, leaving his wife standing there with the groceries. "I can't go there. I'm not a traveler, Maria Kirtchatovska, you must make them understand that. I want to stay here, at home . . ."

"Ha," she said. It was not a laugh.

He looked up at her.

Stamping the snow off her boots as she walked, Maria headed for the kitchen.

"You want to stay home," she mimicked in a high, singsong voice. "You didn't stay home last night. You weren't even here when I left for the office this morning."

"I wasn't on a tropical island, either," he called after her.

"Where were you?"

"In my office. Working late. I slept on the couch there, rather than walking all the way back here through the snow. The buses stop running after midnight, you know."

"Sleeping on your couch," Maria groused, from the kitchen. "With whom?"

"With a volume of Armenian folk tales that I must translate before the end of the semester!" he snapped. "Your superiors demand weeks of my time, but they don't hire anyone to do my work for me."

She came to the kitchen doorway, a small sack of onions in her hands. "You were with some slut all night. I phoned your office when I got home."

Markov made himself smile at her. "Really, Maria, you can't trap me that easily. I was in the office all night. You did not phone."

She stared at him for a long moment.

"I was really there, Maria," he said. "Alone."

"You expect me to believe you?"

"Of course. Have I ever lied to you, my dear?"

Her face contorted into a frustration that went beyond words. She disappeared back into the kitchen. Markov could hear pantry doors opening, canned goods banging onto the shelves.

She'll break something, he thought.

With a sigh, he got up from the chair and went to the kitchen.
"Kwajalein?" he asked.

She was on tiptoe, shoving jars of pickled beets into the cabinet over the gas range. Over her shoulder, she grunted, "Kwajalein. Yes."

"Here, let me." He squeezed past her in the narrow space between the range and the refrigerator, and took a pair of cans to put away on the topmost shelves.

"Not those!" Maria snatched the cans from him. "They go here."

He watched her put them where she wanted them, then accepted two other cans from her and stacked them neatly on the highest shelf, asking:

"Why do I have to go to Kwajalein? Why can't I stay here at home?"

"Bulacheff specifically asked for you. The Academy is sending an elite team of scientists to join the Americans in studying the alien spaceship."

"Is Bulacheff going too?"

"No."

"I thought not."

"But you are."

Markov leaned his lanky frame against the pantry doors. "But I have nothing to contribute to their studies! Haven't we been through all this once already?"

"The American astronaut, Stoner, will be there."

"Ah. My correspondent."

"Exactly. He knows you, by reputation. That is why Bulacheff picked you to join the others."

"I should never have written that book," Markov muttered.

"You are an internationally recognized expert in extraterrestrial languages . . ."

"Which is to say, nothing," he said.

"And you will be a part of the Soviet team of scientists that is going to Kwajalein to work with the Americans in studying this alien visitor."

Markov shook his head sadly. "All I want, Maria, is to remain here in Moscow. At home. With you."

She eyed him suspiciously. "On that score, you can rest comfortably. I will be going to Kwajalein with you."

"You're going!" He felt shocked.

"Of course. You are far too important to be allowed outside the Soviet Union unprotected."

"Oh, come now, Maria," he said, "are your superiors so frightened that I might defect to the West? I'm not a flighty ballet dancer, you know."

"It's for your own safety."

"Of course."

"Of course!" she snapped. "Don't you think I care about your safety?"

He patted his shirt pockets, searching for a pack of cigarettes. "I think you care about the trouble it would make for you if I defected."

"And all you care about is finding some young slut to pursue!"

He stood up straight. "Maria Kirtchatovska, I told you that I was alone in my office last night."

"Yes, you told me."

He pushed past her and went back to the living room. The cigarettes were on the table beside his favorite chair.

"But you didn't tell me," Maria said, following him like a determined bulldog, "that your little cow-eyed student from the research center has followed you back to Moscow."

"What? Who are you talking about?"

"That Vlasov bitch . . . the one you were sleeping with at the research center."

"Sonya?" Markov felt torn between joy and dread. "She's in Moscow?"

"Look at you!" Maria snarled. "You're having an erection already!"

He shook his head. "Maria, you don't understand. She means nothing to me. She's only a child. An overactive child."

"Who'll pull her pants down anytime you ask her to," Maria said.

Sighing, Markov said, "Maria Kirtchatovska, you know me too well. I can't resist. She throws herself at me. She's lively, and rather good-looking."

And young, Maria added silently. She swung her gaze to the mirror on the wall across the room. She looked at herself: a small, heavy woman with a complexion like bread dough and the face of a potato. In her imagination she pictured her husband with the buxom young beauty she had seen in his bed.

"You won't have to resist her," Maria said, her voice low, venomous. "She'll never be at the university again. She's on her way to a factory in the Ukraine, where she will study tractor repair."

Markov's mouth sagged open. "What have you . . . ?"

"And you're going to Kwajalein, with me," Maria said.

His face turned red. "Woman, you go too far!" he roared, lurching toward her, hand upraised to strike.

But Maria held her ground. "You're too late to do anything about it," she said. "It's already done. And you're not going to be out of my sight for a minute, from now on."

Markov stood there, flushed, perspiration trickling down his neck and into his collar.

"You just . . . sent her away? Ruined her chance for a career in astronomy? Just like that?"

Maria said nothing. She turned and walked slowly back to the kitchen, leaving Markov standing there in the middle of the living room, realizing for the first time the power that his wife held in her hands.

MARSHALL ISLANDS are the easternmost group of islands in Micronesia (*q.v.*) and the eastern district of the United States Trust Territory of the Pacific Islands. Two of the atolls, Kwajalein and Eniwetok, were the scenes of heavy fighting during World War II. Later Bikini and Eniwetok became centres for atomic bomb experiments . . . The islands extend roughly from latitude 3° to 15° N. and from longitude 161° to 172° E. Their land area is 61 sq. mi. and the lagoon area is about 4500 sq. mi. A reef-enclosed lagoon 70 mi. long with an area of 840 sq. mi. makes Kwajalein the largest atoll in the world . . .

Encyclopedia Brittanica
1965 Edition

CHAPTER 19

Keith Stoner sat in the hot, high sun and squinted out across the white sand beach. From here the atoll looked like a classic tropic paradise: graceful palms swaying in the sea breeze; breakers frosting white against the distant reef; the incredibly blue-green lagoon, calm and inviting; crystalline sky dotted with happy puffs of fat cumulus clouds riding the trade wind.

All we need is a wahine in a grass skirt, he said to himself.

But when he turned around and looked inward from the beach, he saw that the modern world had lain its unmistakable hand on Kwajalein. Squat gray cinder block buildings stood scant yards from the beach in a clearing that had been bulldozed where once there had been palms and plums and even an island variety of pine tree.

Further along the narrow flat island was the airstrip, garages and maintenance buildings, machine shops clanging in the hot sunshine, jeeps and trucks buzzing along the only road—a crushed coral track that led from the docks at the northern end of the island to the living compound at the south.

Above it all loomed the radio telescope antennas, six of them, a half-dozen huge dishes of metal and mesh that all pointed toward one invisible spot in the sky: the approaching spacecraft.

"Beachcombing?"

Stoner turned to see Jo Camerata walking toward him, shoeless in the sand, wearing cutoff jeans that showed her long legs well and a skimpy halter top. She was already tanned to a deep olive brown.

In the few days since they had arrived on the island, Stoner had managed to avoid her. But you knew you'd have to see her sooner or later, he told himself.

"Sort of," he answered guardedly.

She smiled. "You're dressed for it, all right."

He was in an old pair of jogging shorts and a light shirt that hung loosely, unbuttoned, its sleeves rolled up above the elbow. The Navy's repeated warnings about infection and jungle rot had convinced Stoner that he'd keep his socks and shoes on at all times.

"How are you?" he asked.

For a moment she didn't reply. Then, "Do you really want to know, Keith?"

He saw something unfathomable in those deep eyes of hers. "Big Mac treating you well?" he asked.

Her mouth went tight.

"You're sleeping with him now," Stoner said flatly. "Everybody knows it."

Nodding slowly, she said, "He treats me better than you did."

"Than I did?" He felt genuine surprise. "What'd I ever do to you?"

"Nothing. Not a damned thing," Jo said, her eyes blazing now. "You treated me like Kleenex: use it and throw it away."

"That's not fair, goddammit!"

"But it's true, Keith."

"So you just walked off and attached yourself to McDermott. Got yourself a better deal."

"You're damned right I did. And I got a better deal for you, too."

"What's that supposed to mean?"

She started to reply, but instead turned her back to him. He grabbed her by the shoulder and spun her around to face him.

"What're you talking about?" he demanded. "What better deal?"

He had thought she was crying, but she was dry-eyed, in full control of herself.

"What better deal?" Jo repeated. "I left you alone so you could devote all your attention to your work. To your pictures of Jupiter and your computer runs. That's all you ever wanted, wasn't it? A few sanitary conveniences and no personal ties to bother you."

He took a staggering step backward, away from her. "Jesus Christ, you sound like Doris."

"Doris? Your ex-wife?"

He nodded.

Jo's shoulders slumped. The fire disappeared from her eyes.

"I didn't walk out on you, Keith," she said softly. "I was never part of your life. You never let me be part of you."

He turned away from her, scanned the horizon and the breakers along the reef, pulling his emotions back under control. Leave her alone, he told himself. She's too young to get involved with you; you're in no position to get involved with her.

"Look, Jo," he said, facing her again, "this is a damned small island and we're going to see each other every day, just about. Let's just call a truce and forget about what's already happened. Okay?"

"Sure," she said, her voice strained. "Water under the bridge and all that."

"Yeah."

"Okay," Jo said, lifting her chin to stand as tall as she could. "I was just taking a walk around the beach, to see what the place looks like. See you."

She strode off, leaving him standing there alone. With a shrug, Stoner started walking up the beach in the opposite direction.

Only after several minutes had passed, and she had looked

over her shoulder three times to make certain he wasn't anywhere in sight, did Jo allow herself to cry.

Stoner walked steadily up the beach, cursing himself for a fool
but not knowing what else he could have done.

He saw Jeff Thompson sitting on the sand, his back against
the bole of a sturdy, slanting palm tree. Jeff scrambled to his
feet as Stoner approached.

"How do you like our tropical paradise?" Jeff asked, by way of
greeting.

"I was just thinking," Stoner replied, burying his thoughts of
Jo, "how many times I dreamed of coming to an island like this,
when I was a kid."

"Well, here we are."

"Yeah. We sure are." Stoner took a deep breath of salt air.
"Your family decide to come with you?"

"No," Thompson said. "Gloria doesn't want to pull the kids out
of school. I agree with that. So I'm on my own for a couple of
months."

"Maybe we'll be back home before June."

"Fat chance."

"Yeah. I know."

"The Russian plane's due in this afternoon."

"How many are they sending?"

"About twenty, from what I hear. Where are they going to put
everybody?"

"Dorms. Houses. Trailers. We've got room for them, I think,
unless they all want to stick together, by themselves."

"And there's another couple of planeloads due in tomorrow,"
Thompson added. "One from NATO and one from the UN that's
supposed to represent Third World scientists."

Scuffing at the sand under his shoes, Stoner grumbled, "This
place isn't a research station—it's a damned political circus. Next
thing you know they'll be bringing in the Queen of England and
the Mormon Tabernacle Choir."

"Only on Sundays . . ."

"ATTENTION. ATTENTION," blared the island-spanning
network of public address loudspeakers. Thompson and Stoner
looked up at the horn set on the bole of the palm tree.

"THE RUSSIAN DELEGATION IS NOW ESTIMATED TO ARRIVE AT SIXTEEN-THIRTY HOURS. ORIENTATION BRIEFING FOR THE RUSSIAN DELEGATION HAS BEEN RESCHEDULED TO TWENTY-ONE HUNDRED HOURS, AFTER THE EVENING MEAL."

The metallic, booming voice stopped as suddenly as it had started, making Stoner feel momentarily as if a hole had been left in the air around him. Then the breeze gusted and a gull screamed and the nearby palms sighed. The island went back to normal.

"They're late," Thompson said.

"They must be flying a Russian plane," Stoner muttered, "with a dependable Soviet crew."

Markov studied the island intently as the plane circled at altitude.

Maria was sitting on the aisle seat beside him, her hands clutching the armrests with white-knuckled anxiety. The flight had been far from restful. First, they had to circle a huge springtime storm over the Urals. Then they made an extra fueling stop near Lake Baykal—where they were coolly informed that one of the engines was malfunctioning and would have to be repaired or replaced.

That did little to build one's confidence for the long flight across the Pacific Ocean. Nor did the fact that they were kept locked inside the plane for six hours, with nothing to look at but the sight of Mongol mechanics peering puzzledly into the innards of the engine nacelle.

But now at last they were circling over the tiny sliver of an island, with its black gouge of an airstrip, the way a dog circles his sleeping mat before finally settling down for a snooze.

Markov paid scant attention to the glorious cloudscape that was turning the western horizon into a molten palette of reds and oranges. He studied the island.

There wasn't much to see. A cluster of buildings at one end. The airstrip. More buildings on the other side of the airstrip. A single road. Some radio telescope antennas.

The other islands scattered along the oval-shaped coral reef seemed empty, abandoned. White beaches and lush green foliage. All of them tiny, barely a few city blocks long, Markov judged. The main island was bigger, but had been almost totally denuded of trees to make room for the buildings and the airstrip.

He reached down under the seat for his satchel.

"What are you doing?" Maria groused.

"Looking for the binoculars."

"What do you expect to see? Dancing girls in grass skirts?"

Markov sighed. He had given up that particular fantasy when the KGB briefing officer had informed them that the Americans had turned Kwajalein into a military base more than twenty years earlier.

"No, of course not," he muttered.

"Those antennas"—his wife pointed, her other hand still clutching the seat arm in a death grip—"were once radars, to observe the re-entry of test missiles fired from California."

"Yes, so they told us."

"They have been adapted to observe the alien spaceship," she said.

"Umm," muttered Markov as he put the binoculars to his eyes and adjusted the focus.

There was no sign of natives at all. No one gathered at the airstrip to welcome them. No dark-hued girls with garlands of flowers to drape around their necks and kiss them on both cheeks. Nothing down there but efficient machines and businesslike Americans and that peculiarly American artifact—house trailers.

He pictured Sonya Vlasov's face in his mind's eye and wondered what she was doing now, in Kharkov, in a tractor factory. How she would have loved to come here! Markov realized. There must be something I can do to help her, some way I can get Maria to remove the blot she's placed on her record.

He glanced back at his wife as the plane lurched into its final approach. The landing gear went down, filling the cabin with a rushing, roaring sound that startled the old man drowsing across the aisle from them into a wide-eyed, frightened awakening.

She says that she will not let me out of her sight for a moment, Markov thought. Very well. I will be the perfect husband. I will charm her as she's never been charmed before.

But the look on Maria's face did nothing to encourage him. She was staring straight ahead, stolidly refusing to show fear as the plane shuddered and slewed through the gusting cross winds on its approach to the airstrip. Waves rushed by outside the window.

Markov remembered those furious few moments back in their apartment, the triumphant look on Maria's face when she announced Sonya's fall from favor, her loss of her student's status, her transfer to a factory.

And he remembered the stark hatred he felt in his own heart. It won't be easy to woo her, he told himself. But it must be done; that girl shouldn't suffer on my account.

A blur of palm fronds startled Markov and then the plane's wheels screeched on the cement runway, bounced sickeningly, hit again and rolled the length of the airstrip. The engines roared with thrust reversers out and all flaps extended full.

As the plane slowed and trundled off the runway, heading toward the single building of the airport's terminal, the color began to come back to Maria's cheeks.

Turning to Markov, she whispered, "You remember the American who wrote to you, Stoner?"

He nodded.

"You must find him and befriend him. He trusts you."

"And I am to betray his trust. Is that it?"

Maria scowled at him, her old self again. "You are to do what is necessary, whatever that may be."

Markov sighed and knew he would do what she told him to. That's a surer way of wooing her than plying her with kisses, he realized.

YUKON TERRITORY

George Umaniak stowed his rifle under the blankets in the back of the skimobile. Even though he had not even seen a caribou, the white policemen would give him a hassle if they discovered he had been out with a hunting gun.

The wind was picking up, coming down in a cold moaning sigh from the frozen mountains. The sky was dark again, and the wind spoke of ghosts and the dance of the dead. George pulled up the hood of his parka, shivering.

The damned skimobile was slow to start. He twisted the ignition key hard, several times, but the motor refused to catch. George swore to himself. It couldn't be the battery, he had checked it just the day before.

A flicker of light across the growing darkness caught at the corner of his eye. George looked up and saw the aurora shimmering over the mountains. Green, palest pink, ghostly yellow, the Northern Lights danced over the mountaintops in rhythm with the moaning wind.

George swallowed hard and finally got the motor to cough itself to life. He opened the throttle all the way and raced homeward. This was no night to be out in the cold and dark.

CHAPTER 20

The lecture hall was about half filled. It had originally been a movie theater for the military personnel of Kwajalein, and Stoner found himself hoping they would show films in it again. But this evening it was a lecture hall, a gathering place, a social focus for the scientists and technicians of Project JOVE.

Nearly a hundred and fifty men and women sat uncomfortably on the government-issue metal folding chairs. Jeff Thompson sat

next to Stoner, in one of the rearmost rows. Jo Camerata was nowhere in sight. Big Mac and Tuttle were down in the front row,
within one step and a hop of the speaker's podium.

The buzzing of scores of conversations died away as McDermott climbed heavily up onto the little platform at the front of
the hall. Cavendish stepped spryly up alongside him, carrying
his own chair. He opened it and sat down behind McDermott,
who leaned ponderously on the shaky little podium. An older
Russian came up alongside Cavendish and took the chair that
had already been placed there.

"Good evening, ladies and gentlemen." Big Mac's rasping lec-
ture-hall voice was met by a shrill scream of feedback from the
microphone.

He glared at the audio technician sitting off to one side of the
room behind a deskful of black boxes, while everyone else
winced at the loudspeakers set into the rafters of the hall's
wooden ceiling.

"Mac doesn't need a microphone, for god's sake," Stoner muttered. Thompson grinned and nodded.

McDermott used the microphone anyway, which amplified his
voice into a booming, echoing thunder that rattled the walls of
the building. He introduced Academician Zworkin, the astronomer who headed the Russian team. The old man—gray thinning hair, grayer pallor to his face, rumpled gray suit despite the
heat—got slowly to his feet and came to the podium. He pulled
the goosenecked microphone down to his own level.

"Thank you, dear Professor McDermott," he said in a high,
thin, singsong voice. His English was quite good: the accent was
from Oxford.

Addressing the seated crowd, Zworkin said, "Although I have
attended two of the SETI conferences over recent years, I am
far from being an expert on extraterrestrial intelligence. But
then, who is?"

A polite murmur of laughter rippled through the audience.

"My own field of specialization is planetary astronomy. I am
not an astrophysicist or an astrochemist. I am, if such a word is
possible, an astro-geologist. I am not quite sure what I am doing
here, among you, except that I was too old and slow to avoid
being picked for this job."

The audience laughed once again, but Stoner realized, He's warning us not to expect any great ideas out of him. He's beyond his depth here and he wants to get back home as soon as possible.

Zworkin then began introducing each of the fifteen Russian scientists. All but one of them were men, although several of them were accompanied by their wives. Who were pointedly not introduced.

A lanky, gangly Russian stood up, looking slightly flustered and boyish despite his scraggly, graying beard. Zworkin introduced him as Professor Kirill Markov, of the University of Moscow, a linguist.

He's the one I wrote to! Stoner realized. I've got to talk with him.

The introductions finished, McDermott took over the podium again.

"We're going to be working together on this project for some months," he said in the tones of a high school football coach. "I'd like to ask Dr. Cavendish to summarize where we stand right now."

Cavendish smiled his way to the podium.

"Right," he said, like a ritual throat-clearing. "I haven't prepared any slides or graphs . . . thought that we'd all be digging into the details quickly enough." He hesitated a moment, as if gathering his thoughts. "The, ah . . . *object* that entered the solar system last summer and engaged in a rather lengthy flyby of Jupiter, is now approaching Earth. It has been accelerating as it comes toward us, and our current projection is that it will reach its nearest distance to Earth on or close to fifth July."

"The acceleration," one of the Russians asked, "is this normal —I mean, natural?"

"Quite. In essence, the object is falling freely as it comes closer to the Sun, you see, and the solar gravitational pull is accelerating it. No, it has not shown any signs of life or purpose since it left Jupiter's vicinity and altered its course to head our way."

"Then it is inert now?"

"Dead as a rock, as far as we can tell," Cavendish said. "It's just coasting along."

"What size is it?"

"Any data about its shape?"

"Surface brightness?"

Cavendish held up both his long-fingered hands to stop the questions from coming faster than he could answer them.

"Well, it's rather larger than a breadbox . . ."

The Americans in the audience laughed. The Russians exchanged puzzled glances with each other.

"Actually," Cavendish went on, "we don't know very much as yet about its true size, mainly because we haven't a firm fix on its intrinsic brightness. If it's made of highly reflective material, then it must be rather small—on the order of a hundred meters or less."

"What is the maximum size it could be?"

Cavendish hiked his eyebrows and searched through the audience for help. "Anyone care to make an educated guess?"

Stoner called out, "It can't be more than a few hundred meters across, at most. From the mass measurements we made during the Jupiter encounter, it must be very small, with negligible mass—about what you would expect if you put three or four Salyut or Skylab space stations together."

Zworkin turned in his chair. "Then it is large for a spacecraft."

"But tiny in comparison to an asteroid or even a very minor meteor," Stoner said.

"I see."

Cavendish tapped the microphone and all eyes focused back on him. "The object is still too far out for accurate radar measurement of its size, although within the next few weeks it should get close enough for a go at it."

"Why not use the Goldstone or Haystack radars?" someone asked.

"Why not Arecibo?"

McDermott got to his feet and said from where he stood, "Security. Our governments have agreed to keep this project as quiet as possible, to protect the people from undue shock and panic."

"We can track it with the Landau facility," Zworkin said, his voice barely audible without the microphone.

"Actually," Cavendish broke in, trying to regain control of the discussion, "since the object is rushing toward us, all we need do is wait for a few weeks and we should be able to snap its photograph with Brownie cameras."

"One question on my mind," said a woman—not one of the Russians—from her chair, "is this: how do we go about making contact with it?"

"By radio, I should think," Cavendish answered.

"What about lasers?"

"What wavelength should be used for the contact attempt?"

Cavendish shrugged. "As many as we can, I suppose. We really have no idea of which wavelengths it communicates in."

"If any."

Stoner rose to his feet and said, "We ought to try to physically intercept it—go out and meet it, rendezvous with it, board it."

"I suppose we could consider that, of course."

But McDermott bellowed, "Out of the question! It'd take months to prepare a manned space shot, years, and this thing will whiz past us before we'd be ready. Besides . . ."

"If we pushed hard," Stoner countered, "we could set up a Space Shuttle launch in time."

"And what would we use for the upper stages," McDermott taunted, "a slingshot?"

"If we have to."

"Actually," Cavendish stepped in, "I suppose we should attempt radio contact first, don't you think?"

Markov stood up, his slightly reddish face set in a puckish grin. He glanced back at Stoner as if he recognized him.

"I am not a physical scientist," he said, turning toward the podium. "However, in the question of communicating with the spacecraft, may I make a suggestion?"

"Yes, certainly," said Cavendish.

"If you have made tape transcriptions of the radio signals issued from Jupiter during the spacecraft's encounter with that planet, perhaps it would be useful to play these recordings back to the spacecraft as it approaches the Earth."

McDermott scowled. Cavendish knitted his shaggy brows together. "Play back the radio pulses from Jupiter?"

"Yes," said Markov. "That would immediately tell the alien that we observed the radio pulses that he caused. It would immediately be recognizable to him as an artificial signal from our world."

"H'mm. Striking."

"What makes you think it's a *him?*" a woman's voice called out.

"Shouldn't we be more cautious?" Jeff Thompson said, getting to his feet beside Stoner. "I mean, maybe we ought to wait for *it* to signal us before we start bombarding *it* with radio waves or laser beams. It might not like being bathed in electromagnetic energy."

"If we wait too long," Cavendish countered, "it just might sail right past us and leave the solar system entirely, just as Professor McDermott said."

"That's why I think we should try to make physical contact with it," Stoner said, still on his feet. "If it's unmanned we could even try to capture it and bring it into an orbit around the earth."

"Absolutely not!" McDermott snapped.

"Why so?" asked Cavendish.

"Too risky. Too many unknowns. It's one thing to make radio contact, we've got the equipment and personnel for that. We are *not* going to play space pirates—boarding and seizing an extra-terrestrial spacecraft. If they want to put that thing in orbit around Earth, they'll do it themselves."

"So what'll happen," Stoner said, his voice rising, "is that we'll spend the next few months trying to get an answer out of it, and it'll sail right on past us and out of the solar system forever. Why wave bye-bye to it when we might be able to get our hands on it?"

"It might not *want* to be captured," somebody said.

Cavendish, leaning his elbows on the rickety podium, responded, "That's assuming there's a crew aboard, isn't it?"

"Or a smart computer."

"Damned smart computer, to take the bird across interstellar distances."

"We have no authority," McDermott insisted, hunching his shoulders like a football player about to make body contact, "to attempt to intercept the spacecraft."

"Then get the authority," Stoner insisted, "before it's too late and the thing sails right on past us."

"We should try to establish radio contact first," Zworkin said. "If there *is* a crew aboard . . ."

"Of course," Stoner agreed. "But let's start making the necessary plans for a rendezvous with the bird."

McDermott's face was getting splotchy with anger. "Do you have any idea of the magnitude of such a task?"

Stoner let himself grin at Big Mac. "As the only experienced astronaut in this group, yes, I think I do."

"We don't have time to play space cadet!"

"You don't have time for anything else. If that spacecraft just zips past us without our learning anything from it . . ."

"We'll make radio contact," McDermott said.

"And what happens if it doesn't respond? What if we don't hit the right communications frequency and it just ignores us?"

Zworkin stood up and made a little bow toward McDermott, almost apologetically. "I believe the young man is correct," he said, his singsong voice barely carrying back to the row where Stoner stood.

McDermott started to reply, but the Russian went on, "We should, of course, be preparing to meet this alien craft in space and, if it is at all feasible, to bring it back to Earth for careful scrutiny. I will recommend such a course of action to the Soviet Academy. Perhaps the Soviet Union can make rocket boosters and cosmonauts available, even if the United States cannot."

McDermott looked as if he was choking, but he managed to say, "I understand. And I will recommend to the White House that NASA be alerted to the possibilities of such a mission."

Stoner resumed his seat, but not before receiving a venomous glare from Big Mac.

You've won the first battle, Stoner said to himself. But it's going to be a long, dirty war.

OFFICE OF

SENATOR WILLIAM PROXMIRE

WISCONSIN

For Release After 6:30 A.M. Thursday, February 16, 1978

Senator William Proxmire (D-Wis) said Thursday, "I am giving my Golden Fleece of the Month award for February to the National Aeronautics and Space Administration, which, riding the wave of popular enthusiasm for 'Star Wars' and 'Close Encounters of the Third Kind,' is proposing to spend $14 to $15 million over the next seven years to try to find intelligent life in outer space. In my view, this project should be postponed for a few million light years."

The Golden Fleece of the Month Award is given for the biggest, most ironic or most ridiculous example of wasteful spending for the month. Proxmire is Chairman of the Senate Banking, Housing and Urban Affairs Committee and of the Senate Appropriations Subcommittee, which has jurisdiction over NASA funds.

"NASA is proposing to pay $2 million this year and $14 to $15 million over the next seven years to Pasadena, California's, Jet Propulsion Lab to conduct 'an all-sky, all-frequency search for radio signals from intelligent extra-terrestrial life.' But this is only the foot in the door. Under the heading of 'broad objectives' the Jet Propulsion Lab proposal indicates that the purpose of the study is to:

Build an observational and technological framework on which future, more sensitive SETI (Search for Extra-Terrestrial Intelligence) programs can be based.

"What this tells me is that while the public is intrigued by the outer space phenomena, the Space Agency is so mesmerized that it is attempting to translate the momentum into a multi-million dollar, long-range program of questionable searches for intelligence beyond our solar system.

"What's wrong with the program? Like so many other big spending projects, this is a low priority program which at this time constitutes a luxury which the country can ill afford.

"First, while theoretically possible, there is now not a scintilla of evidence that life beyond our own solar system exists. Yet NASA officials indicate that the study is predicated on the assumption that intelligent extraterrestrial beings are out there trying to communicate with scientists here on Earth. If NASA has its way, this spending will go forward at a time when people here on Earth—Arabs and Israelis, Greeks and Turks, the United States and the Soviet Union, to name a few—are having a great difficulty in communicating with each other.

"Second, what if from some place, somewhere a radio message had been sent? The Earth is four and one-half billion years old. Some solar systems are 10 to 15 billion years old. If we intercept messages sent from them, they could have been sent not only before Columbus discovered America or the birth of Christ, but before the Earth itself existed. The overwhelming odds are that such civilizations, even if they once existed, are now dead and gone.

"Third, NASA didn't even select the least expensive way to do it. A less expensive, more narrowly focused SETI proposal from the Ames Research Center (cost $6.5 million over 7 years) was rejected in favor of the $14 to $15 million Jet Propulsion Lab project. However, to add insult to injury NASA has told my office that what it may do is to plug in the Ames project in the fiscal year 1980 budget so that both projects would be operating at the same time.

"At a time when the country is faced with a $61 billion budget deficit, the attempt to detect radio waves from solar systems should be postponed until right after the federal budget is balanced and income and social security taxes are reduced to zero."

CHAPTER 21

Edouard Reynaud sipped at his fourth brandy while he reclined as far back in his seat as the chair would go. It seemed to him that he'd been inside this chartered airplane forever: Rome, Amsterdam, New York, San Francisco, Honolulu and now—would it ever stop? Was this purgatory, perhaps? A millennium or two of being locked inside an aluminum canister, able to do nothing except eat, sleep and eliminate?

It's like being a baby again, he thought to himself, drowsy from the brandy. A flying metal nursery, that's what they've put us in. And the stewards are the nursemaids.

He was fighting off sleep. He knew it would come if he relaxed, and with it would come the bad dreams, the guilt dreams, unless he had the proper level of alcohol in his blood. So he drank brandy after brandy, calling for a fresh one as soon as he finished the one in his hand.

The young blond angel in the chair beside him slept innocently, his mouth slightly open, his breath easing in and out of him as calmly as the ebb and flow of the tides.

Reynaud suppressed a desire to touch his sweet face, stroke his beardless cheek.

Instead, he turned to the window and looked out at the dark, starry sky. He recognized Orion, the Bull, the Dogs. Yes, everything is in its place, as usual, he saw. Deep in that infinite sky, he knew, new stars were being born and old ones torn apart by titanic explosions. Galaxies whirled out there in the darkness and quasars burned with a fierceness that no human mind could comprehend.

"How long," Reynaud whispered to himself, "will you keep your secrets? If God set you in place, when did He do the job? And how?"

It did not occur to him to ask why. That was the province of the theologians. Reynaud was a cosmologist.

He saw his own reflection in the glass of the airplane's window, and he frowned at it. A fat, round face atop a fat, round body. Sagging jowls and baggy eyes, bloodshot and failing. A man who sought refuge in the monastic life when the world became too much for him to bear, and still managed to stay fat, and drunk, still managed to lapse into homosexuality now and then, despite all the controls and the punishments the Abbot could wield over him.

Reynaud smiled bitterly at his memory of the Abbot's face, when that stern master of the monastery was told that the Pope himself wanted Reynaud sent to him.

"What His Holiness wants with *you* is beyond my comprehension," said the Abbot, his hawklike visage grim with self-control, his piercing eyes ablaze. "If the Vatican had seen fit to ask my opinion in this matter, you would spend the remainder of your days cleaning the stables, which is what you deserve."

Reynaud bobbed his head in agreement.

But the Vatican had asked for him, for Reynaud, the famous cosmologist, the Nobel laureate. What they are getting, he told his reflection in the plane's window, is Reynaud the drunkard, the pervert, the ruins of the man they believe they are getting.

The boy beside him stirred, sighed softly, opened his sky-blue eyes.

"Did you sleep well?" Reynaud asked in French.

He answered in some Germanic tongue, and Reynaud remembered that he had gotten aboard in Amsterdam.

With a shake of his head, Reynaud asked, "Do you speak English, perhaps?"

"Yes." The boy smiled. Feeling old and very, very tired, Reynaud smiled back at him.

"Hans Schmidt is my name. I am from the University of Leiden."

With a slight nod of his head, Reynaud replied, "Edouard Reynaud. I have no university affiliation, but I was . . ."

"Edouard Reynaud!" Schmidt's eyes went round. "I've read your books!"

Feeling ancient and foolish in his shabby black suit and unshaven jowls, Reynaud shrugged. "They were written long ago. They are all outdated now."

"Yes, of course," Schmidt answered with the unconscious cruelty of youth, "but they were classics in their field. We had to read them in undergraduate classes."

"You are an astronomer?"

Schmidt's enthusiasm turned sour. "I was," he said, growing gloomy. "Now I am a prisoner."

"So are we all," said Reynaud. "But don't worry, the plane will land soon enough on Kwajalein and then we can walk in the sunlight."

"You don't understand," the young man said. "All the others on this plane—astronomers and astrophysicists from all over Europe—they volunteered for this assignment. They are happy to be going to Kwajalein, to study the alien signals."

"You are not?"

Schmidt shook his head slowly. "I *discovered* the radio signals. But I'll never get credit for it."

Reynaud made a sympathetic noise.

"I was working for Professor Voorne at the big dish in Dwingeloo, last summer. I picked up the signals before the Americans or anyone else did," Schmidt explained, his voice going almost sulky. "We checked on their dates; I had the signals before they did."

"Then you should get the credit," Reynaud said.

"Fat chance! Voorne is so slow and conservative that your grandmother could run circles around him. He refused to let me send a note in to the astrophysics journal until we had triple-checked everything. By that time the NATO bureaucrats came around and put secrecy stamps on every piece of paper I had. They wouldn't let me publish anything, not one word."

"Too bad," said Reynaud.

"And now they've exiled me to this blasted little island. I don't want to go. They forced me to! I have my girl in Leiden; we were going to be engaged in another few weeks. But the government said either I go to Kwajalein or I go into the Army and get sent to Kwajalein anyway."

Reynaud shook his head.

"It's the Americans," Schmidt muttered. "They're behind all this. They want to get all the credit for themselves and make sure that I don't get any."

Reynaud pursed his lips, then replied, "Don't you think that the matter of finding an intelligent extraterrestrial race is the really important thing?"

"Sure! That's why the Americans want all the credit for the discovery."

"Well . . . I've been ordered to Kwajalein, too. I had no desire to go, but my superiors have sent me anyway. That's why I'm on this plane, just as you are. But I don't think it's an American plot, really."

Schmidt said nothing.

"I've been sent on this mission by the Holy Father himself," Reynaud added.

"The Pope?"

"Yes."

"Why is he interested in astronomy?"

Reynaud chuckled, bitterly. "He isn't. Nor are the cardinals that surround him. They are merely interested in preserving their power, and keeping the truth from the people."

Schmidt stared at him in disbelief. "You are a priest and you say such things?"

"A priest? Me? Oh no! Not a priest. I'm not even a monk, really. I've taken no vows."

Confused, Schmidt said, "I thought . . . we had heard that you had retired to a monastery . . ."

"Yes. Yes, I had. But His Holiness has brought me out of retirement. Here I am in the world again—and it's a very different world from the one I left, years ago."

The two men talked as the night faded from the sky and the sun rose over the endless gray waters of the Pacific. The other passengers slowly stirred out of their sleep, stretching cramped muscles, yawning, groaning, lining up at the plane's lavatories.

Stewards started moving along the aisle, helping people get rid of their blankets and pillows. Over Schmidt's shoulder, Reynaud noticed that the stewards were all young men. Eventually they brought little plastic trays of breakfast. Reynaud couldn't bear to look at the stuff once it was set before him: it was gray and dead, as plastic as the receptacles on which it was served.

The pilot came on the intercom and cheerfully announced that in a few hours' time they would be landing at Kwajalein.

"If I can find it," he added with a chuckle.

Reynaud shuddered a little. He looked over at Schmidt, who had eaten every scrap of food on his tray and closed his eyes to sleep. With a sad shake of his head, Reynaud turned to stare out at the featureless gray expanse of ocean so far below them, wishing that he could sleep without dreaming.

He awoke with a cold, gasping start as the plane thumped and banged.

"Landing gear," said Schmidt, now wide awake. "I was going to wake you . . ."

Reynaud thanked him and looked out the window. A ring of islets showed green and white against the sea.

The plane circled the largest island of the group and finally landed with a thump that seemed more like a controlled crash than a true touchdown. But Reynaud was grateful for small miracles: purgatory was over and he could enter paradise.

The scientists were ushered off the plane and into the blindingly hot sunlight of the equatorial island. The airport seemed to be filled with Americans, many of them in military khakis, the rest in open-necked shirts and shorts.

Smiling, efficient, broad-shouldered young men led the scientists across the crushed coral rock rampway and into a cement block building. It was air-conditioned to the point of chilblains. Americans, Reynaud thought. Always so extravagant. Papers were examined, luggage picked up. Reynaud let himself be bundled into a jeep with Schmidt and another man.

"Your luggage'll be on th' truck," said their driver, an energetic-looking sailor. He put Reynaud on the seat beside him; the other two had to crawl into the rear seats.

As he gunned the jeep's motor to roaring life, the sailor asked, "You a Catholic priest, sir?"

"No," Reynaud replied in English. "I am a lay brother of the Order of St. Dominic." The Order of Thomas Aquinas, he added silently. And of Torquemada.

The jeep lurched into motion. "Oh. I was wonderin', with your black suit and all," the driver yelled over the motor's howl. "We got a chaplain on the island but he ain't Catholic. They fly the Catholic padre in on Sundays from Jaluit to hear confessions and say Mass."

"You are a Catholic?" Reynaud asked, clutching the edge of his seat as the jeep barreled along the dusty road.

"Ah, well, sometimes, yeah," the sailor stammered. "You know how it is."

Reynaud said nothing, but thought, I know exactly how it is.

After a few terrifying minutes of racing past featureless blurs of cement block buildings, the driver pulled the jeep over to the side of the road in a grinding, squealing, skidding stop.

"Kwajalein Hilton," he announced.

Reynaud saw a three-story gray drab building.

"Bachelor Officers Quarters," the sailor explained as a swirl of coral dust drifted past the jeep. "BOQ is the way most people say it. Not for you, Father . . ." He tugged at Reynaud's sleeve and said to Schmidt and the other scientist, "You two guys are gonna be stayin' in here."

They climbed out of the jeep as Reynaud remained in his seat.

"Yer luggage'll catch up with you in a couple minutes." The sailor put the jeep in gear and left them standing in a spray of dust. "You rate special, Father. You got a whole trailer to yerself."

"I'm not a priest," Reynaud said. "You should call me Brother."

The driver gave an embarrassed little laugh. "Sounds kinda funny. But if that's the way you want it . . . okay, Brother, here we are."

He skidded the jeep to a stop and pointed grandly to a house trailer, one of a dozen standing in a row on the sandy soil, gleaming metal under the hot sun.

"All for you, Fa . . . eh, Brother."

The sailor came into the trailer with Reynaud, showed him the sink and the refrigerator, the narrow, cotlike beds, the built-in cabinets, the toilet.

"By Kwaj standards, this is the Ritz."

Reynaud nodded and mumbled his thanks. The sailor grinned and turned on the air conditioner.

"Linens are in here." He opened a closet door. "I can make your bed for you."

"Oh no, please. I can do it for myself."

"Well, you got privacy and runnin' water. What more can you ask for? See you Sunday, at Mass."

Reynaud nodded absently and the sailor left, shutting the flimsy metal door behind him carefully. It felt as if a small, playful puppy had just gone away. Reynaud stood there, feeling bewildered, listening to the air conditioner rattle and groan and fill the trailer with a clammy, morguelike chill.

Exiled, he thought to himself. That's what young Schmidt said, and he's right. We've all been exiled to this horrible place. I sought the peace and protection of the monastery and the Pope himself pulled me away from it, exiled me here in this wretched island. Whatever becomes of me is their fault, not my own.

Stoner stalked out of the air-conditioned chill of the administration building, into the enfolding warmth of the setting sun. It was muggy, but the heat felt good after the artificial dryness of the air inside—and McDermott's stubborn obstructionism.

Go take a long walk, Stoner commanded himself, seething. Find an empty spot on the beach and do an hour's worth of exercising—before you punch out Big Mac's stupid face.

McDermott was dragging his feet about the rendezvous mission. He had not yet sent his recommendation to Washington, and wouldn't allow anyone else to make such a recommendation. Stoner had spent an hour arguing with the old man, to no avail.

Why won't he go for it? Stoner asked himself for the twentieth time. What's wrong with him that he can't . . . ?

Then he saw Jo, coming down the "company town's" only street from the computer center, heading toward him.

"Hi, Keith," she said brightly as she approached him. "How're y . . . ?" She saw the thundercloud expression on his face. "Wow! What's got you pissed?"

"Your pal McDermott," Stoner growled.

Jo's own face stiffened with anger. "My pal, huh? What's he doing now?"

"The same old crap—delaying until it's too late to do what needs to be done."

She eyed him tauntingly. "I think it's the heat. It's got old Mac down. Literally."

Ignoring her implication, he muttered, "I'd like to put him down. Literally."

"He's still not going for the rendezvous flight?" Jo asked.

"He won't even sign a memo about it."

"Well, it *is* a long shot," she said.

"We're here to make contact with an intelligent extraterrestrial visitor, and you talk about long shots?"

"You take everything so seriously," Jo said, reaching up to tap a fingertip against the end of his nose. "Relax. Loosen up. We're here, we might as well enjoy it."

He brushed her hand away as he would swipe at an annoying insect. "We're here to make contact with that spacecraft."

"I know that."

"How's it going to look if we let the damned thing get away from us?"

"We won't," Jo said.

"You've got it all figured out, do you?"

"No." She shook her head. "But I know you. You'll figure it out, one way or another. You'll make Mac look good doing it, too."

"And it won't hurt your career, either, will it?"

"Why do you think I'm here?"

"Because Mac brought you with him," Stoner snapped.

For an instant she looked sad, betrayed. "If you only knew," she said softly.

"You'll have to tell me about it sometime. Or better yet, put it into your résumé. It'll impress the hell out of NASA."

"Keith, you can be a real sonofabitch when you want to be, you know that?"

"It's the heat. It's got me down."

"Go to hell."

"Don't tell me you haven't already rewritten your résumé. I know the way your ambitious little brain works."

"You think so?"

"Sure. I can see it now, right up on the top of the page, where you list your accomplishments: 'Research assistant, Project JOVE. Worked with elite international research team, in top-priority program to establish first contact with intelligent extra-terrestrial life form.'"

With a satisfied smile, Jo said, "Sounds terrific. How many girls can include that in their *curriculum vitae?*"

"I thought you wanted to be called women, not girls."

"I can say girls," Jo answered. "You have to call us women."

"Yeah," he said tightly. "Figures."

Her face serious, Jo asked, "Keith, you're not still sore at me, are you?"

"Are you still sleeping with Big Mac?"

"Oh, Christ! You'll never figure it out, will you?"

"I've already figured you out, Jo."

Her fists clenched in frustration, she said, "I don't give a damn about Mac! Don't you understand that?"

"Of course I understand that," he said, icy calm, frigid with anger. "That's what makes it so goddamned rotten."

She started to reply, hesitated, let her hands drop to her sides. Without another word, Jo brushed past him and continued on her way toward the administration building.

Toward McDermott, Stoner told himself, as he stood alone in the middle of the dusty street and watched her walk away from him.

> Grandfather, I send my voice to You.
> Grandfather, I send my voice to You.
> With all the universe I send my voice to You.
> That I may live.
>
> *Wiwanyag Washipi*: The Sun Dance
> of the Oglala Sioux

CHAPTER 22

Jo shivered in the darkness. As she unhooked her bra and slid her panties down her long legs, she asked McDermott, "Why do you keep it so cold in here?"

From the bed, his bullfrog's voice croaked, "So that you'll have to huddle close to me to stay warm."

She was glad that he kept the lights off and the drapes pulled tightly across the trailer's windows. He couldn't see the expression on her face. The damned bunk's not big enough for a fatass like him by himself, Jo grumbled silently, let alone the two of us.

Still, she padded over to the bunk, pulled the covers aside and squirmed onto the few inches of tough rubbery mattress beside Big Mac. This is ruining my back, Jo thought.

"And how's my sweet young thing this evening?" McDermott asked, reaching for her breast.

The same line, the same approach, as predictable as sunrise. But McDermott's own rising was beyond prediction. He needed lots of Jo's help to raise an erection. And many times nothing she did could help him.

Jo worked on him calmly, dispassionately, a graduate student working on an experiment in order to get a good grade from the professor. She could feel the tensions easing out of McDermott's body as she massaged and fondled him.

"You're doing fine," she cooed. "Big, strong daddy is going to fill me up, aren't you?"

McDermott was moaning softly, lying on his back, arms at his sides. Bending over him, Jo whispered:

"That's a good boy . . . You're getting big and strong for me . . ."

Finally she straddled him, rocking back and forth until he came. When she stretched out beside him again, he was whimpering. Tears wet his face.

"What's the matter?" Jo whispered, genuinely surprised. "Are you all right?"

"They want to take it away from me," McDermott snuffled. "It's *my* project, I'm in charge, but they want to go and turn it into some kind of space cadet circus."

"Nobody's going to take it away from you," she soothed. "You're the director of the entire project."

"It's that Stoner." His voice was high and quavering, like a little boy's. "He's after me all the time. He wants to fly out there and meet the alien spacecraft."

"Even if he does"—she stroked his chest—"you'll still be head of the project. So what if he flies off into space . . ."

She felt his whole body shudder. "Go out and meet it? Touch it? Suppose it's carrying disease germs? Suppose it's some kind of slimy, horrible . . . *thing?*"

"No, no. It won't be. Everything will turn out all right. You'll see. It'll be all right."

"It could be evil . . . dangerous. It's alien . . . not like us."

"There, there. It'll all work out. Nobody's going to hurt you. Try to relax and get some sleep."

It seemed like hours, but finally Big Mac was snoring peacefully, his white-haired chest rising and falling in calm rhythm. Jo slipped gratefully out of the bunk, glanced toward the shower stall. It'd wake him up, she knew. Pulling on her shorts and blouse, she decided to take a dip in the lagoon before returning to her own room at the hotel.

"But it's a good idea," Markov was saying to his wife. "A necessary idea!"

It was dark outside as they sat in the front room of their little bungalow. The Americans had given married couples each a tiny cement house of their own. Maria had spent their first two hours in it searching for hidden microphones.

They sat with two trays of precooked dinners—soggy American vegetables and thin slices of unidentifiable meat—resting on their laps. Markov's was almost untouched.

"A good idea," Maria mumbled, her mouth stuffed with a buttered soft white roll.

"Yes," Markov replied.

His wife glared at him from her upholstered chair. "Technically, perhaps it is a good idea. But not politically."

"Politically?"

Maria finished the roll and butter. As usual, she seemed both annoyed and disappointed with her husband.

"Don't you understand why the Americans brought up this idea of meeting the alien spacecraft?"

"To capture it and bring it close to Earth for study," said Markov.

"And who would make this thrilling capture?"

Markov shrugged. "Stoner is a former astronaut. I suppose he would want to be in on it . . ."

"Exactly! An *American* astronaut."

"But we're all working on this together, aren't we?"

"Hah! There is together and together."

Markov glanced down at his tray and decided that he couldn't face another bite of the bland food. Maybe she's right, he thought. Certainly we can't trust the Americans to feed us.

Maria continued, "All through this project the Americans have tried every trick they know to keep the knowledge of this alien spacecraft to themselves."

"So have we," Markov protested weakly.

Maria ignored him. "Now the one astronaut they have on their team suggests that we go out into space and bring the alien ship into orbit around the Earth."

"But it's a good idea!" Markov insisted.

"And how will they do this thing?" she retorted. "With the American Space Shuttle, and American launching facilities, and American astronauts."

"They will share the information with us."

"How do we know that? How do we know they will share *all* the information with us that they obtain?"

"Zworkin feels the idea has merit."

"Zworkin!" Maria almost spat. "That Jew! He's probably in league with the capitalists."

"Maria!"

"It's true," she insisted. "Our task is to make certain that if anyone reaches this spaceship it will be Soviet cosmonauts. We cannot allow the Americans to steal this alien spaceship for themselves. And we cannot allow the Soviet Union to be betrayed by naïve scientists and unconscious traitors."

Feeling pitifully weak in the blast of his wife's hot fervor, Markov said weakly, "I've already told Zworkin that I will serve on the committee that will examine Stoner's suggestion."

"H'mph. And have you befriended Stoner himself, as you were ordered to do?"

Ordered? Markov's brows went up. Now she is giving me orders? To his wife, he replied, "I have met him twice; both times in groups with other people. We have said hello to each other, nothing more."

"Nothing more," she repeated sullenly.

"But Zworkin has accepted me for the committee, so I should see a good deal of Stoner in the near future."

Maria's scowl eased slightly. "See to it that any rocket adventures we enter into are done by Soviet cosmonauts."

With a sad shake of his head, Markov got up from his chair and headed for the kitchen with his unfinished tray.

"Where are you going?" Maria called after him.

"Out for a walk. I'm not sleepy yet." Even though there were twin beds in the bungalow's one bedroom, the thought of sleeping in the same room with Maria was becoming unbearable to Markov.

"Don't wake me up when you come in," she growled.

Once outside, in the sighing night breeze and the friendly whisper of the palms, Markov could breathe again. She overpowers me, he knew. It's a battle for survival between us, and she's winning it.

He threaded his way through the little cluster of bungalows and made it to the beach, glowing white in the moonlight. He took off his shoes to stroll in the sand. It was still warm from the day's sun. The water lapped gently a dozen meters away. Out in the night, along the invisible reef, he could hear the surf breathing like a restless sea god.

Markov stood alone on the sand and stared out at the moonwashed night. How long before the ocean wears away these islands? How long before Maria and I tear each other apart?

He laughed out loud. How dramatic you are! Tear each other apart! She'd snap you like a twig, but you couldn't even muss her hair, no matter how hard you tried.

He thought again of those few moments in their apartment, when Maria had gloatingly told him how she had destroyed Sonya Vlasov's life. Even then, Markov said to himself, even in full fury, you knew better than to try to fight her.

Something made him look back up the beach and he saw a woman walking toward him. An apparition. Aphrodite, come out of the sea, tall, long-legged, with the slim waist and full bosom of a goddess. A white blouse, ghostly in the moonlight, was tied around her middle. Shorts clung lovingly to her hips.

Markov stared as she calmly approached him, smiled to him and said in English, "Good evening."

His heart spun around. He was instantly, hopelessly, in love.

"A good evening to you, beautiful lady. I have been waiting for you all my life."

She laughed. "You're one of the Russians, aren't you?"

"Does it show?"

"I've seen you with the other Russian scientists," Jo said.

"And why have I not seen you? Have I been blind, or have you kept yourself invisible, goddess that you are?"

"Goddess? Wow!"

"Aphrodite, goddess of love and beauty. I am your humble servant, Kirill Vasilovsk Markov, ready to follow you across deserts and mountains."

Jo laughed. "I'm afraid I'm not Aphrodite. My name is Jo Camerata, and I'm an American. But there *is* some Greek blood in my ancestry, come to think of it."

"You see?" Markov said. "The goddess exists in you."

Jo laughed.

"And what is such a lovely young lady doing in this romantic setting, all alone? Are there no handsome young men to escort you?"

With a shake of her head, she replied, "No. No young men."

"That is sad."

"Yes . . ." She smiled again. "But you're here."

"Ah, the moonlight must be playing tricks on your eyes, fair one. I am neither young nor handsome."

"I can see perfectly well," Jo said. "I came here for a swim. Would you like to go in with me?"

"Swimming? Now? At night?"

"Sure. The water's warm."

"Intriguing."

"Wouldn't you like to try it?"

"But I have no swimsuit."

She laughed. "Neither do I. We can skinnydip. Nobody else is around."

"My English . . ." Markov couldn't believe she was saying what he thought she was saying. "You mean—in the nude?"

"Sure. Just leave your clothes here and wade in."

She stripped quickly and ran for the water. Markov fumbled with his clothes, his eyes on the glowing curves of her naked body. Finally he stepped cautiously into the bath-warm water. It felt good, relaxing, inviting.

"Tell me," he called to her as he waded in up to his chest, "were you going to go swimming all alone?"

"Yes, but it's always safer to go with somebody else," Jo answered. "Especially at night. The sharks come into the lagoon at night."

"Sharks?" Suddenly the water felt cold and dangerous to Markov.

Hideki Takamura prowled the plunging deck of the catcher boat, bundled into his hooded sweater and windbreaker. It was late in the season to be searching for whales, and if a plane or ship from the International Commission saw them, Japan would be reprimanded and embarrassed before the entire world. At least the meddling fools from Greenpeace had sailed homeward, he knew. That was something to be thankful for.

The season's catch had been poor, so even though the Commission had ordered all the whaling fleets home, they still plowed through the heavy Antarctic seas as the nights grew longer, hoping to find a few straggling whales to fill their half-empty holds.

The clouds overhead parted as if pulled away by the hands of a giant. Takamura looked up at the coldly glittering stars.

And his breath caught in his throat. The sky was shimmering with light: veils of eerie fluorescence streamed across the heavens, red, green, violet—the lights of the gods, dancing across the sky.

Stark fear clutched Takamura's heart. All the long years of schooling and scientific training on which he prided himself vanished from his mind. This is an evil omen, he knew. An evil omen . . .

CHAPTER 23

The day was slowly dying.

Stoner had eaten dinner with Jeff Thompson at one of Kwajalein's three government-owned restaurants. The food was cheap and about as appetizing as its price would indicate. It was still bright daylight outside when he finished, so he returned to his office and went over the latest batch of photographs from Big Eye.

Even in the orbital telescope's best magnification the approaching spacecraft looked like nothing more than a featureless blob of light, a tiny smudge on the picture, a whitish thumbprint set against the sharp, unchanging patterns and endless blackness of eternity.

By the time he left his office the sun was throwing spectacular swaths of red and orange across the tropical sky. Stoner walked alone down the main street, past the cinder block government buildings, heading in the general direction of the Officers' Club.

He wondered where Jo might be, what she was doing, and an image of her in bed with McDermott filled his mind. He tried to shut it away, to forget it, to think of something else instead. He quickened his pace toward the Officers' Club; he knew he needed company, conversation, something to erase those pictures from his mind.

"Ah, Stoner!" Cavendish was standing at the doorway of the club with a lanky, flaxen-haired, sullen-faced young man.

"I want you to meet Hans Schmidt, of the Netherlands Radio Observatory at Dwingeloo."

Stoner put his hand out automatically. Schmidt's grip was lukewarm.

"Dwingeloo," Stoner said, his memory tweaked. "I saw a report a few days ago that said Dwingeloo picked up the radio pulses from Jupiter last summer."

"That was my work," Schmidt said in British English. "But it was classified secret by NATO."

The young man was slightly taller than Stoner, youthfully thin. But his face was still soft with baby fat. The forehead was high, the eyes a bit puffy, the lips set into a pout. He'll be bald before he's thirty, Stoner thought, but he'll still look like a kid.

"Welcome to the club," Stoner replied. "My work got stamped secret, too."

"Quite," said Cavendish, laying a hand on each man's back and gently urging them into the Officers' Club. "Schmidt here may actually have priority on discovering the radio pulses, you know. When did your group first pick them up?"

"It wasn't my group," Stoner said. "I was just hired on as a consultant. You want to talk to Jeff Thompson about that."

They went to the crowded bar and ordered. Cavendish had a

brandy, Stoner a scotch and water, Schmidt a Heineken's. The club was noisy, smoky, the best and only bar on the island. After fifteen minutes of talk, Stoner agreed that Schmidt had probably recognized the strange nature of the radio pulses earlier than Thompson had.

"So you'll get the recognition," Cavendish said, "once all this comes out into the open."

That seemed to make Schmidt even more morose. "By the time all this comes out into the open I'll be an old man."

"Oh come now, you still have a ways to go, you know."

Schmidt drained the last of his beer and looked as if he wanted to cry.

"They've pushed you around, haven't they?" Stoner said.

He nodded slowly. "I was to be engaged. . . . Now who knows how long I'll be here?"

"Me too. They've been shoving all of us around like a pack of animals. You know how I celebrated Christmas? They let me make a phone call to my kids. One call. Like a prison inmate."

"Couldn't they fly your girl out here?" Cavendish asked.

"They wouldn't let her come. And she wouldn't do it, anyway. I asked her, but she said no. I can't blame her . . . to leave her home and family and go to the end of the Earth." He shook his head sorrowfully.

"Damned bad show," Cavendish murmured.

"First, they destroy my thesis with their secrecy laws," Schmidt went on, staring into his glass, "and now they exile me to this island. If I had murdered someone I would be treated better than this. If I became a terrorist and captured a train or threatened to blow up an airliner they would treat me better than this."

Stoner said grimly, "But you're not a terrorist. You're a scientist. They know they can kick us around and all we'll do is beg for another chance to do our work."

"There is one thing," Cavendish said slowly.

"What?" Schmidt asked.

"A thousand years from now, when human history is written, your name will go down as the first man to make contact with an intelligent extraterrestrial race."

Stoner put his drink to his lips, saying silently to himself, No.

Schmidt may have discovered the radio pulses, but I am going to be the first man to make actual contact with that alien. Or I'll die trying.

Schmidt's little-boy pout deepened. "What makes you think there will be a human race to write its own history a thousand years from now? Or even a hundred years from now?"

"Well, of course . . ."

"Suppose," Schmidt went on, "that this spacecraft is an invader, the first scout for an alien invasion fleet that will wipe us out? How will my name be written then?"

"That's rather farfetched, don't you think?"

Stoner, in the middle of another swallow of his scotch, sputtered laughter into the drink. "Here we are," he said, blinking tears from his eyes, "sitting on a godforsaken atoll in the middle of the Pacific, waiting for an alien spacecraft to get close enough for us to study it in detail, and you're talking about something being farfetched? This whole business is farfetched!"

"H'm. Quite. But still, I don't believe that an intelligent species goes batting about the universe with rape and pillage on its mind, do you? That's strictly funny-book stuff."

"Who knows?" Stoner said. "Can't plot a trend with only one data point."

Cavendish smiled, a bit uneasily. "Datum, dear boy. Datum is the singular of the word."

"I stand corrected."

The old man put his empty glass on the bar. "Getting rather late for me. I believe I'll toddle off." He pulled a balled-up dollar bill from his pocket and left it on the bar. "Good night."

And just that abruptly he left Stoner and Schmidt standing at the bar. Stoner felt awkward with the younger man, who seemed content to plunge into solitary gloom.

Cavendish has stuck me with baby-sitting this kid, Stoner realized suddenly. That dirty old man!

He scanned the club, seeking a friendly face. The big room was filled with smoke and men. Noisy, drinking, laughing men who waved cigarettes and cigars at each other, playing cards, telling stories and clustering around the few women who were present. Kwajalein's normal complement of military and civilian technicians had been tripled by the influx of Project JOVE's scientists and staff, but the ratio of men to women was still huge.

The local merchants vote in favor of the alien, Stoner thought. The bartender isn't worried about being invaded. Not as long as the tips keep coming.

He spotted Markov sitting at a table across the smoky room, surrounded by a mixed crew of Americans, Europeans and Russians. They seemed to be enjoying themselves.

I ought to get to know Markov better, Stoner told himself.

Glancing back at Schmidt, who was staring morosely into his second glass of beer, Stoner said, "Come on, let's join that gang over there."

Wordlessly the Dutch astronomer followed him.

". . . so she then informs me," Markov was saying, his eyes bright and both hands toying with a tumbler of vodka, "that she wishes to go for a midnight swim."

Stoner pulled an empty chair from the next table and joined the circle. Schmidt remained standing behind him.

With barely a blink of a hello, Markov went on, "Obviously she is an American, and quite good-looking. When I told her I had no swimsuit, she introduced me to a new American word: 'skinnydipping.'"

It struck everyone as funny and they all laughed. Except Schmidt. Stoner wondered who the Russian was talking about.

"Naturally, when she explained what 'skinnydipping' means, I joined her with enthusiasm!"

They roared.

"Then, once we were in the water, she tells me that the lagoon is filled with sharks, especially at night."

"That's true," said one of the Americans.

"Moray eels, too."

"But, she added, we would be perfectly safe as long as we stayed in the shallow water. The only sharks we would bump into would be little ones."

Looking up, Stoner saw that Schmidt hadn't yet cracked a smile. Hopeless case, he thought.

"What did you do?"

Markov shrugged elaborately. "What could I do? Faced with

the dilemma of meeting a shark or leaving her in the lagoon alone and unprotected, I did the correct thing." He paused dramatically. "I ran up onto the beach as fast as I could and started putting my clothes on!"

Stoner laughed with the rest of them. But suddenly it struck him that the Russian might be talking about Jo.

"She called to me from the water, 'Don't be afraid! These little sharks don't bother anyone!' I called back, 'You are wrong. They do bother someone. Me!'"

One of the Russians said, in heavily accented English, "A man has much more to lose to a shark than a woman."

"It was quite an experience," Markov went on. "She came right out of the water behind me and started to berate me for my cowardice. Have you ever been castigated by an angry young woman who happens to be naked and dripping wet, under a tropical moon? Nerve-racking!"

He took a long pull on his vodka.

"So you went home full of sand and water," someone said.

"I would have preferred to go to her quarters—to wash up, if nothing else," Markov explained. "But she is living in the hotel with the rest of the single women, and it is impossible to get past those guards after midnight."

"Too bad."

Markov sighed. "I have my hopes. The Post Exchange sells shark repellant, I hear."

"There are swimming pools, you know," someone said. "Here at the Officers' Club, at the hotel and another one at the BOQ."

"Yes, I understand. But you see, it isn't actually the swimming that interests me."

The rest of them roared with laughter, but Stoner thought, Jesus Christ, I'll bet it is Jo he's talking about. Sounds like her kind of stunt. He realized he didn't like the idea of the Russian making jokes about her, but at least Markov didn't identify her by name. Probably he doesn't even know her name.

The men swapped stories for another hour or so, then the group around the table started to break up. As he got up from his chair, Stoner saw that Schmidt had already disappeared. He frowned, wondering how long ago the youngster had walked off.

"Dr. Stoner," Markov said to him.

"You tell a good story," Stoner said.

Markov shrugged modestly and they started out toward the door.

"I never got the chance to tell you how much I appreciated your kind letter to me."

"You wrote a good book."

"Thank you," Markov said, his voice so low that Stoner could barely hear it over the hubbub of the club. "But you must understand that your letter revealed to our government that you were working on the radio pulses from Jupiter."

"I know. That's why I wrote it. I figured, if you didn't know about the pulses the letter wouldn't mean anything to you. But if you did know about them, well . . . we should be working together on this, not in competition with each other."

They reached the door and stepped through, into the quiet of the night. "I was afraid that you would be arrested by your security police, once they found out about the letter."

"I was. Do you think I'd be here if they hadn't forced me to come?"

In dead earnest Markov replied, "Of course you would be here. You would steal a submarine and sneak in here under cover of darkness if there were no other way to get in. This is the only place for a man like you, and don't try to hide that obvious fact, especially from yourself."

Stoner stopped in his tracks, under the streetlamp outside the club's entrance, and stared at Markov. After a moment, he admitted, "You're right. Dammit, you're right."

Markov broke into a boyish grin.

"But how did a linguist get dragged into this? Don't tell me my letter got you into trouble?"

"No, not at all. If anything, it enhanced my stature among the guardians of the people's safety." He started walking slowly along the street, and Stoner followed alongside him. "No, I have been bitten by the same bug that has infected you." Markov raised his eyes to the starry sky. "I want to *know!*"

Nodding reluctantly, Stoner said, "Yeah. If there's only one Project JOVE, then this is the place where we have to be."

"Of course. Knowledge is the important thing, the only thing that lasts. Discovery—ahh, that is the thrill. Better than women, I tell you."

"Better than *some* women," Stoner corrected.

Markov threw his head back and roared laughter. "Yes, yes! I agree! Better than some."

Glancing at the luminous digits of his wristwatch, Stoner asked, "Want to come over to the radar center? They're going to try to make contact with the bird tonight."

"Make contact?"

"Bounce a radar beam off it," Stoner explained.

"But it's still father away than Mars, isn't it?"

"Yeah, but the radar guys think they might be able to get a signal bounced off it. They're itching to try."

"I will go with you," Markov said, nodding eagerly. "I've never seen this done before."

"Neither has anybody else," Stoner said. "And we might not see it done tonight. The damned thing *is* a helluva long way off."

The two men walked side by side down the empty street, through the warm, humid darkness, oblivious to the scent of flowers and salt spray on the air.

Academician Bulacheff sat uneasily in the stiff-backed chair. Borodinski's desk was raised on a little dais, so that visitors had to look up at him. It was an old trick, but Borodinski carried it off well. He had greeted the academician brusquely, waved him to the chair in front of the desk and then bent his balding, neatly bearded head to the paperwork on his desk.

It's true, Bulacheff said to himself. The General Secretary is dying and we're going to have to put up with this young pup. I wonder if he's deliberately trying to make himself look like Lenin?

As if he could read minds, Borodinski looked up at precisely that moment.

He smiled paternally. "I'm sorry to have kept you waiting, Academician Bulacheff, but the press of urgent business has been almost overwhelming these days."

Bulacheff hesitated a moment, then asked, "The Comrade Secretary? He is well?"

"Oh yes, quite well." Borodinski's smile waned. "But extremely . . . busy. You must excuse him."

"I had expected to see him personally. We have always discussed this matter between ourselves, face to face . . ."

"For security reasons, I know. But our friend has asked me to meet with you today."

"I see." Bulacheff wondered how far he could trust this younger man.

"The reports coming from Kwajalein indicate that it may be desirable to send a team of cosmonauts to meet the alien spacecraft," Borodinski said. "Are preparations being made toward this end?"

He knows, Bulacheff realized. No sense trying to stall him off. "The appropriate departments of the Academy are keeping track of the spacecraft and preparing the necessary navigational plans for a rendezvous mission."

"Good."

"It is not within our jurisdiction, however, to force the Army to allocate the necessary rockets and cosmonauts."

"I understand." Borodinski nodded. "These steps are being taken, I assure you. What we need from you, for now, is continuously updated tracking information for an interception flight."

"Interception?"

"If the spacecraft is hostile, or about to fall into unfriendly hands . . ."

"You would destroy it?"

Borodinski flicked both hands upward. "Poof! With an H-bomb. Didn't our friend tell you of that possibility?"

"He mentioned it once, yes, but . . ."

"Then you understand that we need the necessary tracking data. Only your long-range radio telescopes have the power to provide such data, I'm told. The Army's anti-missile radars haven't the required range."

"Of course."

Borodinski smiled pleasantly and fingered his trim little beard.

"Comrade . . ." Bulacheff began, then hesitated.

"Yes?"

"There . . . have been rumors . . . of arrests, interrogations. Is the General Secretary safe and well?"

The younger man's eyes narrowed and the slightly smug smile left his lips. "Comrade Academician, I assure you that the General Secretary is safe, and well, and most vitally interested in this alien visitor. As for rumors of . . . changes within the Kremlin—don't let that bother you. It does not concern you, I promise."

Still, Bulacheff felt an old familiar weight pressing against his heart.

Rising from behind his desk, Borodinski said, "All you have to worry about, my dear Academician, is the tracking data we require."

"For making rendezvous with the spacecraft."

"Or for intercepting it with a missile." Borodinski pointed a forefinger toward the scientist. "We will either board that spacecraft or blow it out of the sky."

Cavendish was having the nightmare again. The tropical weather seemed to leach all the energy out of his frail body, and he had been going to bed earlier and earlier each night since he'd arrived on Kwajalein. But his sleep was far from restful.

They were standing over him again with their needles and the lights. He was very small and he had been very wicked to resist them. They were giants and to resist them was not only foolish, but wicked. He could see the gold in their teeth when they smiled and he wanted to run, but his body was frozen and the needles were sinking into his flesh and he could feel the burning juices as they all bent closer over him . . .

He sat up in bed, shivering with cold sweat. His head throbbed. The muscles of his neck were so taut he could barely turn his head.

Alone in his single room in the Bachelor Officers Quarters, Cavendish pulled on his faded old robe, stuck his slippers on his bony feet and took a towel and a bar of soap from the rack by the room's sink. He flap-flapped down the bare wooden hallway floor to the washroom.

It was empty at this hour of the night. He got into a shower stall and stood under the taps for several minutes. The water was only lukewarm, more frustrating than relaxing.

Back in his room, he stared at the rumpled, sweaty bed for long moments, then found himself pulling on an old shirt and a pair of slacks. He felt utterly weary; his eyes wanted to close. But mechanically he donned his only pair of sandals, buckled them across the instep and walked out of the BOQ like a sleep-walker, into the late night darkness.

He went directly to the bungalow where the Markovs lived, went up the cement steps and opened the front door without knocking.

Maria sat on the rattan sofa in the front room, an open suit-case beside her. Its innards were filled with knobs and dials. It hummed faintly, and a single red light glowered in it like an angry evil eye.

Maria's face was an anxious mixture of awe, disbelief and fear.

"Dr. Cavendish?" she whispered, as if afraid of waking him.

"Yes," he said. Somewhere deep inside him Cavendish wondered who this woman was and what she wanted of him. Only one lamp was lit in the room, over by her, next to the open suit-case filled with electronic equipment.

"Sit down," Maria said.

Cavendish took the easy chair and crossed his ankles. He folded his hands in his lap and stared ahead blankly.

Maria licked her lips anxiously. She knew Kirill would be coming back soon; it had taken her hours to get the equipment to summon Cavendish—partly because she had been afraid to dial the power setting high enough, she realized now.

"You will remember nothing of this meeting tonight, will you?" she asked, her voice trembling slightly.

"Not a thing," he said calmly.

"The reflexes are still there, even after all these years," she marveled. "I was only a young girl when I first met you, Dr. Cavendish. You don't remember me at all, do you? It was at a place called Berezovo."

"The . . . hospital . . ."

"Yes, yes. You were a difficult patient. But you won't be difficult now, will you? You won't force me to . . . to do what they did . . . in the hospital."

"I won't be difficult."

"You will be very co-operative, won't you?"

"Co-operative."

Maria sighed with relief. "Now then . . . about this American, Stoner."

"My orders were to find out how much he knew and then, if possible, to eliminate him."

"You did not follow those orders."

"I sent out the necessary information. Eliminating him proved impossible. We were constantly guarded."

"Is that the only reason?"

Cavendish licked his lips. "I felt the orders were foolish. Why eliminate him when we can use what he knows, what he discovers?"

"You did well, Dr. Cavendish."

His hands unclenched, his eyes brimmed with tears. "I want to do well. I really want to. Honestly I do."

Maria felt her stomach wrenching within her. She closed her eyes to blot out the sight of the weeping old man.

It was well past midnight but neither Stoner nor Markov had left the electronics building. Outside, on a clear sweep of denuded, treeless land, two giant antennas pointed up into the windswept night.

Stoner and Markov hunched over the back of the radar technician who sat at the main console. All three of their faces were reflected dimly in the faint green glow of the circular screen that dominated the console's front panel. Other men and women had left their tasks and were crowding around them.

"It's a blip, all right," the technician muttered. "Damned weak, though."

The screen sparkled and scintillated almost as if it were alive. Concentric circles of hairline-thin yellow made a sort of bull's-eye against the screen's sickly green background. High in the upper right quadrant of the outermost circle, a flickering orange dot glowed faintly.

"Can you center it?" Stoner asked.

The technician checked a clipboard hanging beside the screen. "Not yet. Still some satellite traffic in the way. You'll get scatter off them and lose the bogey you want."

"Is that *it?*" Markov whispered, staring fixedly at the screen.

"That's it," said Stoner.

The little group behind them seemed to sigh collectively. Markov tugged at his beard and saw his own reflection in the screen's smooth glass: baggy-eyed, purse-lipped, nervous, awed, afraid.

"What do you have for a velocity vector?" Stoner asked the technician. To Markov, the American seemed calm, intensely calm, as if he was holding himself together for fear that if he let go for one single instant he would explode.

Wordlessly, the technician touched a set of buttons on the keyboard before him. Numbers and letter symbols sprang up on the screen next to the glittering orange blip.

"Where's a computer terminal?" Stoner snapped. "I can't tell if that's within our prediction envelope . . ."

"There's a terminal right over there, sir," said one of the women technicians. She pointed to an empty desk with a computer screen and keyboard atop it.

Stoner slid into the chair and punched up the proper code. The screen flashed a long set of equations momentarily, then replaced it with a shorter list of alphanumerics. Stoner swiveled his chair to peer at the radar screen and its list.

"Zap!" he yelled. "Right on the money! That's our bird, all right."

Markov looked at the featureless blob of light on the radar screen and then back at Stoner's satisfied grin. They were all smiling now, as if they had just witnessed a birth. All Markov saw was a featureless flicker of light and some numbers.

"What's your frequency again?" Stoner asked the radar operator.

Markov let his attention wander as the two of them plunged into a discussion that was more numbers than any human language. He tried to get the significance straight in his mind. They had sent out a radar beam from the antennas outside this building, more than an hour ago. The beam had gone deep into space, reached the approaching spacecraft and been reflected back to the same antennas. That little gleam of light on the radar screen represented the alien spacecraft.

Later, when they stopped congratulating themselves and realized lamely that no one could find a bottle of champagne at this hour of the night, the triumphant little group broke up. Two of the technicians remained at their posts; the others headed homeward.

As they walked through the night, Markov asked Stoner, "What do we know now that we didn't know before?"

The American shrugged. "Nothing. Not a damned thing. Except that it's there, where we thought it would be."

"Then why the excitement?"

"Because we've locked onto the bird," Stoner said as they passed a row of darkened house trailers. "We've got a new way of examining it, like a new pair of eyes focused on it. Precisely calibrated eyes, too. Now we can get the other radars locked onto it—the big dishes at Roi-Namur, for instance. Goldstone and Haystack, back in the States. Even Arecibo. They'll look at it in different frequencies—different wavelengths."

"And what will that tell us?"

Stoner waved a hand in the night air. "Length, size . . . maybe the bird's mass, if we're clever enough. Put the radar measurements together with optical photos and maybe we can start to get some idea of what it's made of—its material and shape."

Markov nodded. "And when do we attempt to signal it?"

"I don't know. That's your end of the game. Big Mac will make that decision. But—in a way, we've already signaled it."

"The radar beam?"

Nodding, Stoner said, "If there's any kind of intelligence aboard that spacecraft—either a live crew or a smart computer —they'll have sensors aboard that will tell them we've bounced a radar beam off them. They'll know we've spotted them."

Markov looked up toward the stars.

"If they don't want to make contact with us," Stoner went on, "they'll start to maneuver away from us."

Or if they are hostile, Markov thought, they will take some other form of action.

ULTRA TOP SECRET

Memorandum

TO: The President   DATE: 18 April
FROM: R. A. McDermott, Director,
      Project JOVE   REF: K/JOVE 84-011
CC: S. Ellington, OSTP
SUBJECT: First contact

1. This is to confirm my telephone message to the effect
that we have successfully established radar contact with
the subject object.

2. In response to suggestions raised by a minority of
Project JOVE participants, I respectfully request a
study by NASA and/or other appropriate Federal agen-
cies as to the feasibility and desirability of launching a
manned rendezvous mission to same, presumably at or
near the time of the object's closest approach to the
Earth.

3. It is my considered opinion, however, that the ease of
establishing electromagnetic contact and the difficulties
inherent in any manned rendezvous mission must miti-
gate against the latter and in favor of the former.

4. A manned rendezvous mission would be extremely
costly in funds and personnel, expecially if it fails.

ULTRA TOP SECRET

CHAPTER 24

The Lincoln sped through the dark Nevada night, arrowing
along I-15, across the flat salt desert. On every horizon craggy
mountains loomed pale and silent in the cold silver light of the
crescent Moon.

"It's gonna peak," Charles Grodon was saying. "We can't keep
kidding the people along much longer."

Willie Wilson sat slumped, eyes closed, chin on chest, in the velour rear seat of the Lincoln. Beside him sat his brother and manager, Bobby. Grodon was on the jump seat, facing them.

"Come on, Charlie," whispered Bobby. "He's wiped out."

Bobby was three years younger than his brother, several inches shorter, twenty pounds heavier. Where Willie was blond and intense, Bobby was a pleasant-faced, freckled redhead. They joked about being twins.

"We're all tired," Grodon answered. "Battin' around the country, working our butts off. I just don't wanta see it all go down the drain."

Grodon was wire-thin, sharp-featured, with nervous hands that were never still. He drummed his fingers on the razor-sharp creases of his pinstriped trousers. He toyed with the buttons of his vest. He rubbed at his nose.

"We got the biggest crowd Vegas ever seen," Bobby said, keeping his voice low to avoid disturbing his brother. "National TV coverage on all three network news shows. *Time* magazine sniffing around. What more do you want?"

"We gotta give them something more than 'Watch the Skies,'" Grodon said. "Willie's got to take the next step, tell them something they haven't heard before. Otherwise they're gonna get tired of it and stay away."

"We're booked solid in Washington and Anaheim," Bobby pointed out.

"Lemme tell you something," Grodon said, jabbing a finger toward Bobby. "First big national promo campaign I worked on was for Mark Spitz . . ."

"Oh, the swimmer?"

"Yeah. We made Mark Spitz a household name. Everybody knew who he was, how he won seven gold medals in the Olympics. He was on every TV show there was. He was on posters. Wheaties boxes. Milk cartons. You name it. And six months later nobody knew who the fuck he was."

Bobby's round face pulled into a frown.

"Because," Grodon explained, "the big schmuck had nothing to offer. He was a terrific swimmer, so what? He couldn't sing. He couldn't act. He couldn't even read a joke off the cue cards.

All he could do was take off his clothes, jump in the fuckin' water and swim like a dolphin."

"I don't see . . ."

Grodon leaned forward on the jump seat until he was nearly touching noses with Bobby. "The thing is this—it's easy to get attention. We've done that. Willie's got everybody watching him, waiting for his Big Event. 'Watch the Skies,' he's telling 'em. So they're watching. But they ain't seeing anything. *Nothing's happening.*"

"It will."

"Yeah?"

"If Willie says it will, it will."

Grodon made a sour face. "Come on, Bobby. This is me, Charlie the Jew. Remember? Willie might believe all this crap he's spouting but we can't go off the deep end with him, for Chrissakes. Somebody's gotta keep his head screwed on straight."

"It'll happen," Bobby repeated stubbornly. "If Willie says it's going to happen, it'll happen."

"When?"

"When it happens."

"It better be soon. Damn' soon. Because if something spectacular doesn't happen soon, all those big crowds and those media people are gonna disappear . . . like that." He snapped his fingers.

"It's going to happen," Willie said.

Both men turned toward him.

"It's going to happen," Willie repeated. "I know it will, just as sure as I know my heart's beating. I don't know what it's going to be, or when it'll come . . ."

"It better be soon," Grodon muttered.

"Don't worry so much, Charlie. It'll happen soon enough. Whenever the Lord decides it to be, that'll be soon enough."

"The Lord don't have to worry about gate receipts."

Willie laughed and called to the driver, "Hey, Nick, pull over, will ya? I gotta take a leak."

The Lincoln slowed smoothly and pulled over onto the shoulder of the broad, empty highway.

Willie ducked out the rear door, shivering in the sudden desert chill. The nearest cover was a straggling bush a dozen yards from the car, but the whole moonlit plateau was empty this late at night. Nothing but the moaning, cutting wind and the distant glittering stars.

Willie unzipped his fly and urinated onto the desert ground. He imagined his piss soaking into the porous sand so quickly that it didn't even leave a momentary puddle.

As he zipped up again and rebuttoned his jacket he glanced up at the sky.

"Jesus Christ Almighty," he whispered, goggling. Then he shouted it. "Jesus Christ Almighty! Look! *Look!*"

Bobby bounced out of the car in an instant while his brother danced and yelled and pointed upward. Grodon climbed out after him. Then the driver. They all stared up.

Eeerie green and pink flickers of light were playing across the sky, glowing fingers of radiance that danced and shimmered among the stars.

"Wh . . . what is it?" the driver asked, his voice hollow.

"It's coming!" Willie howled. "I told you it's coming and it's coming!"

Bobby stood open-mouthed, staring at the display.

"It's just the Northern Lights," Grodon said. "It happens sometimes this far south. Must be sunspots or something causing 'em."

"It's a sign," Willie insisted. "It's a sign!"

Grodon shook his head. "Too bad you can't arrange to have 'em on during the rally in Washington."

Willie laughed. "Who knows? The Lord works in mysterious ways."

Bobby stood rooted to the ground beside the car, slack-jawed, gaping, awed by what he saw and by his brother's ability to predict that it would happen.

Jo woke early. The Kwajalein sun streamed into her room, even though she had tacked a blanket over the window. Bright sunlight etched the edges of the window and made the thin blanket glow like molten metal.

She had insisted on having her own room at the hotel, with

the other single women in the group. McDermott had groused at first, but as long as she spent part of the night with him, he seemed satisfied. He didn't want sex, Jo quickly realized, as much as a sense of ownership.

She rose, showered, dressed quickly while mentally debating whether she wanted to take the free breakfast at the dingy government mess hall or buy something slightly better at one of the island's three restaurants. With a shrug, she decided to skip breakfast altogether.

I can make tea at the office, she told herself as she finished combing her hair. She put on her lipstick, nodded to herself in the dresser's time-fogged mirror and went to the window to take down the useless blanket.

She saw Stoner striding along the street, heading for the mess hall, his face set in its usual impersonal scowl. Always in his own world, Jo thought, with no time for anyone else.

With a shake of her head, she turned away from the window, found her purse and headed for the computer complex.

The computer building was constructed around a massive IBM facility. The big, boxy computer consoles—each of them larger than a full-sized refrigerator—stood in long rows inside a central well that rose three stories high. Offices surrounded this well, which the workers called the Pit. Balconies ran along its four sides.

Jo had wangled a private office on the second floor, overlooking the balcony and the Pit. It was little more than a cubbyhole; the walls were bare and painted a ghastly institutional green. The desk was a strictly functional metal affair, dented and dulled from long use. The swivel chair squeaked and tipped over if you leaned too far back on it, according to the warning of the sailor who delivered the furniture to the room. The file cabinets rattled. But the computer terminal atop the desk was sparkling new and worked perfectly. For Jo, that was enough.

Her electric teakettle was just starting to whistle when Markov appeared at the open doorway and tapped on its wooden frame.

She turned, kettle in one hand. "Oh! Hi!"

He blinked at her. "My swimming instructor. So this is where you hide during the daytime."

"I'm not hiding, I'm working," Jo said. Motioning him into the office with her free hand, she asked, "Do you want some tea?"

Markov smiled and nodded as he took one of the two metal-and-plastic chairs that stood against the bare office wall.

Jo took a plastic cup and an extra tea bag from the bottom file cabinet drawer and poured tea for Markov. She set the cup amidst the computer sheets and typing paper littering her desk.

"I don't have any milk or sugar," she apologized.

"This will be fine," said Markov.

She sat on the other chair, beside him, close enough for him to smell the fragrance of her skin, the shampoo she had used on her hair.

Clearing his throat, Markov announced, "I am here on official business."

"Not for another swimming lesson?" Jo teased.

He broke into a grin. "Perhaps later."

"Okay."

He seemed flustered, like a young boy going out on his first date. "Yes. The, ah . . . the radio astronomers are going to begin beaming messages to the spacecraft this morning, as soon as it rises above the horizon."

"I know," Jo said.

"Several different kinds of messages will be sent, on a variety of frequencies."

"Will they try laser beams, too?"

Markov said, "Stoner has requested a very powerful laser system from an observatory in Hawaii. It will be sent here within a week or two."

So he's getting his way on the laser, Jo thought. I figured he would.

"They have also decided," Markov went on, "to follow my suggestion of transmitting the Jupiter pulses we recorded back at the spacecraft."

"That's a great idea," Jo said.

"Really?" He beamed.

"Of course. A really terrific idea."

He reached for the tea, took one scalding sip, then said, "Well, I'm afraid that we're going to need a good deal of computer time to translate the tapes we have back into signals that the radio telescopes can transmit. They sent me to find someone in the computer services group who could help us with the problem."

"These are audio tapes?" Jo asked. "Didn't Dr. Thompson bring the original computer analyses of the tapes when we moved here?"

"Yes, I have spoken with Thompson about this. He says he has both."

With a slight toss of her head, Jo said, "Then it's no problem. We just need a little time to check out the computer tapes and make sure they're compatible with the machine language we're using here. Filling in the requisition forms will take more time than doing the job itself."

Markov gave a relieved sigh. "How soon . . . ?"

"How quickly do you need it done? Everything I'm working on here right now is pretty routine. I could get to work on this today and have it for you tomorrow."

"Wonderful!"

She grinned at him. "After all, we're old swimming partners, aren't we?"

His face reddened. "I . . . you must accept my apologies for that evening. We Russians are not noted for our swimming abilities, you know."

"No need to apologize," Jo said.

He was certain that she could hear his heart thumping in his chest. "Jo . . . dearest lady, I would fight dragons for you."

"On land."

"Uh, yes . . . perferably on land."

"You're very sweet, Dr. Markov," she said.

"Kirill."

"Kirill. If I run into any dragons, I'll let you know."

He took her hand in both of his and kissed it. "I love you madly, dear lady."

"Oh no," Jo said, her face turning grave. "You shouldn't think that."

He gave a helpless shrug. "It's much too late for such advice. I love you. Totally."

Very seriously, Jo said to him, "If we had met a year ago . . . or even six months ago . . ."

"I know, I know," he said, gazing soulfully into her eyes. "Professor McDermott has his claim on you. But surely you can't be serious about him."

"I'm not." Jo's voice was so low that he could barely hear her.

"Then you can be serious about me!" Markov said, trying to make her smile.

She didn't answer. Her whole body seemed to droop.

Taking her chin gently in one hand, Markov raised her face so that he could look into those marvelous eyes once again.

"There is someone else," he realized.

Still she remained silent.

"Someone who does not return your love," the Russian went on. "Or . . . perhaps he does not even know you love him?"

For some unfathomable reason, Jo knew she could trust this gentle, boyish man. She nodded slowly.

Markov sighed wistfully. "He is a fortunate man, whoever he is," he said softly. "And a fool."

Reynaud was trudging along the beach, his bare feet sloshing in the gently lapping waves, his black trousers rolled up to expose his chubby knees, his shirt clinging wetly to his back.

He blinked against the afternoon sunlight. A body lay sprawled on the sand up ahead, half in the water.

Reynaud ran, puffing, to the body. It was Hans Schmidt.

"Hello," said the young Dutch astronomer, squinting up at Reynaud. "What are you running for?"

With a final gasp of exhaustion, Reynaud sank to his knees beside the lad. "I thought you were unconscious, or dead, laying here like this."

Schmidt was still stretched out flat, his blond head on the sand, his shirt open and stirring slightly in the breeze, his trousers and sandaled feet in the water.

"I'm not dead," he said, grinning crookedly. "I'm not even unconscious."

"Then why . . . ?" Reynaud made a gesture.

"Why not? What else is there for me to do?" Schmidt raised

the hand he had been holding at his side. There was a brownish cigarette smoldering between his fingers.

"Isn't there any work for you to do? You're an astronomer, after all."

Schmidt took a long drag on the cigarette. "I wasn't sent here to work. I'm in exile. This is a prison. I've been sent here for knowing too much."

"But surely . . ."

Offering the cigarette to Reynaud, the young man went on, "But it's not a bad prison, as prisons go. The scenery is lovely. And they have some very good grass. Here, try it. The sailors sell it cheap; they fly it in from the Philippines."

Reynaud stared at the joint. "That's marijuana?"

Laughing, Schmidt propped himself up on one elbow, sand sticking to his damp hair. "I forgot. Your generation is into alcohol, isn't it? You'd be afraid to try pot."

"Well . . ." Reynaud watched as his hand reached out for the joint. He put it to his lips and inhaled deeply. And coughed.

Schmidt collapsed back on the sand with laughter.

"It . . . it's been many years," Reynaud croaked, eyes tearing, "since I've been able to smoke anything."

He handed the joint back to Schmidt, who puffed on it contentedly.

"Don't stare at me so disapprovingly," the young astronomer said. "I know I could be helping them out. Those Americans and the Russians. They're so busy, so industrious. But why should I help them? I *discovered* the damned signals. If it weren't for me they'd all be home with their families and friends. I'd be home with my Katrina. We'd be making plans for our wedding. I'd be getting laid. Instead, I'm here and she's probably screwing with somebody else."

Reynaud plopped down on his backside and stretched his stumpy legs out in front of him. "I know how you feel. This thing has uprooted all of us."

"The hell you know," Schmidt grumbled. "What do you know about wanting to get laid?"

With a bitter laugh, Reynaud reached for the joint again and took a deep drag on it. This time he didn't cough.

"Every time one of those Americans looks at me," Schmidt

muttered, "I can feel the hostility, the anger. They blame me for making them come here, to this island."

"Nonsense. Most of them are glad to be here. This is an exciting project for them."

"Not for me," said Schmidt.

"Or me, either." Reynaud shaded his eyes and looked out across the lagoon. Not a sail, not a sign of life clear out to the horizon. They might have been marooned, as far as the eye could tell.

"You're bored too?"

With a shrug, Reynaud answered, "There's nothing for a retired cosmologist to do here."

"Invent new theories!" Schmidt said. "That's what cosmologists are for, isn't it?"

"Perhaps. But I'm so badly out of date . . . I feel like a fossil, a mummy that's just been exhumed after thousands of years in the dark."

"What'd you do to get sent out here? Rape a nun?"

Reynaud looked down at the golden angel's face. "Hardly."

They shared the joint until there wasn't enough left to hold without scorching their fingers. Schmidt carelessly flicked it into the lagoon.

"Plenty more where that came from," he said, his voice lazy, relaxed.

Reynaud's head was spinning. Shakily, he climbed to his feet. "I think I'd better be getting back . . ."

"Stay here. Maybe the damned spaceship will drop right into the lagoon and then we can all go home."

"It's still more than fifty million kilometers away."

"All right then!" Schmidt suddenly hiked himself up to a sitting position. "Let's go meet the damned thing halfway."

"What do you mean?"

With a knowing grin, "In my room . . . I've got some pills that can take you right out to the stars, *zoom!* Just like that. Bought them from one of the civilians who runs the Post Exchange."

"No, I don't think . . ."

But Schmidt struggled to his feet and grabbed Reynaud by

one arm. "Come on, I'll show you. Nothing to be afraid of. Better than alcohol. Come on with me."

Reynaud let the young man drag him up the beach, toward the BOQ.

So if it is possible to communicate, we think we know what the first communications will be about: They will be about the one thing the two civilizations are guaranteed to share in common, and that is science.

CARL SAGAN
Murmurs of Earth: The Voyager Interstellar Record
Random House
1978

CHAPTER 25

Stoner paced back and forth across the hot, stuffy control center, threading his way around the jumble of chairs and standing men and women. A dozen technicians sat at their humming electronics consoles, headsets clamped over their ears, eyes riveted to their green-glowing screens.

The room was dark except for the glow from the screens and the lighted buttons on the console keyboards. There were too many people standing around, radiating heat and anticipation, overpowering the rumbling air conditioners.

Stoner prowled ceaselessly, like a caged jungle cat, scowling at the backs of the seated technicians and the shimmering numbers on their readout screens.

The outside door opened and a painful spear of sunlight lanced into the room. Everyone flinched and squirmed. Vampires, thought Stoner. We're like a pack of goddamned vampires, hiding from the light of day.

It was Markov. He closed the door quickly and tiptoed, in his gangly, loose-jointed way, to Stoner's side.

"Anything?" he whispered.

"Zilch," Stoner said. "It's been damned near six hours and no reaction from them at all."

Markov peered at the nearest screen. "I don't know whether to be happy or sad."

"Sad," snapped Stoner.

The Russian shrugged. "I have a message for you from the photo lab. They have received the latest high-resolution photographs from Greenbelt."

Stoner pulled his attention from the screens. "From Big Eye? Did they take a look at them? How do they look?"

"They said . . . not good."

What did you expect? Stoner asked himself. Nothing is going right. Not a goddamned thing.

"I'd better go over and take a look at them."

Markov said, "They told me that the photos still don't show anything except a blur. It looks almost like the head of a comet."

"Christ! Don't say that around McDermott. That's all he'll need to renege on the rendezvous mission."

Dr. Marvin Chartris leaned back in his padded swivel chair and looked through the heavily barred window of his ground floor office. Outside on the scruffy, patchy lawn of the museum, a pair of dogs were enthusiastically humping, tongues lolling out of their toothy mouths, while a dozen children stood around watching.

Ah, springtime in Manhattan, thought Dr. Chartris.

His phone rang.

Chartris glanced out the open office door. As usual, his secretary was nowhere in sight. He had once replied to a visitor's question as to how many people worked at the museum, "About a third of the staff." His secretary was among the majority.

With a sigh, he picked up the phone. "Planetarium," he said.

"Marv," crackled the voice on the other end, "this is Harry Hartunian."

"Hello, Harry. How's everything in San Diego?"

"Great. Getting good crowds. How about you?"

"Almost breaking even."

"Been mugged lately? I hear New York's worse in good weather."

"When do we get good weather?" Chartris countered.

Hartunian chuckled. "Hey, Marv, you got any information about unusual sunspot activity? Or solar flares? I been trying to get Kitt Peak Observatory to tell me what's going on, but they won't say a word."

"You too?"

"Whattaya mean, me too?"

Chartris shifted in his chair, squirming like a precocious schoolboy who was being ignored by the teacher.

"I've been getting calls from all over the map," he explained, "since last Tuesday. Everybody's seeing aurorae . . ."

"Yeah. There was a big display here last night."

"As far as I know, there's no unusual solar activity. I've checked Kitt Peak, the Smithsonian, even some friends at NASA. No solar flares, not even much in the way of sunspots right at the moment."

"Then what the hell caused last night's aurora? We don't get the Northern Lights down here—I mean, it just doesn't happen here!"

Scratching his head, Chartris said, "Darned if I know, Harry. But you're not the only one who's got them. Denver, Salt Lake City, even Las Vegas saw them during this past week. Through the neon."

"You seen it in New York?"

"Are you kidding? We're lucky when we see the full Moon around here."

Hartunian didn't laugh. "What's going on, Marv? Any ideas?"

"Not the slightest. Whatever it is, it's extremely unusual."

"Unusual? It's damned scary!"

The conference room in the computer building was too small to accommodate the entire Project JOVE staff, and Ramsey McDermott liked it that way. He wanted only the top echelon people, not the flunkies.

"Keep the peons at their work," he muttered to himself as he walked the few steps down the corridor from his office to the conference room.

McDermott had taken the most spacious office on the ground floor of the computer building for his own. It was the most impressive and comfortable office on the island, except for that of the Navy captain who commanded the military staff. Captain Youngblood had a larger office, but it was in the old military administration building, with its leaky window air conditioners and the airstrip right outside. Lieutenant Commander Tuttle had a broom closet next door to his captain's office.

But McDermott had the central air conditioning and restful quiet of the computer building. His office befitted the project director, a respected senior scientist who reported straight to the White House, who was in line for a Nobel Prize, if everything worked out well.

He always made certain to arrive late enough for these weekly staff leaders' conferences so that everyone else was already present: Zworkin and his two top aides, plus their linguist, Markov; Cavendish, representing NATO; the three rotating dark-skinned types from the UN; the three Chinese, who had yet to utter their first word at these conferences; Reynaud, the Vatican's representative; and Thompson, representing McDermott's own group from the United States, with two of his aides.

One of them was Stoner.

McDermott frowned at Stoner's presence. The man was a troublemaker and had been from the start. He was always insisting on planning for a manned space flight to meet the approaching spacecraft.

He wants to take the leadership of this project away from me, McDermott knew. Well, that's something he'll never do. I've got his girl and I'm top dog on this project . . . and I'm going to stay on top! Of both of them!

He was chuckling to himself as he strode into the conference room and went to the head of the table. He pulled his pipe, lighter, tobacco, reamer, pipe cleaners from various pockets of his suit and spread them on the table before him, then sat down and acknowledged his staff leaders' hellos with a single nod of his head. He was the only man to wear a suit or even a jacket; the others were all as unkempt as beachcombers. Even the Russians were in short-sleeved shirts.

That's why I'm at the head of the table, McDermott told himself. I know how to maintain my dignity.

He looked over the table. "Where's Dr. Reynaud?"

No one seemed to know.

McDermott glared at his secretary, a middle-aged Navy civilian employee, sitting in the corner to his left with her tape recorder ready.

"He knew about the meeting," she said apologetically.

"Phone his quarters," McDermott commanded. "Find him." Turning back to the group, "We'll have to start without him."

The secretary clicked the tape recorder on, then scurried from the room.

"Well," McDermott rumbled, "where do we stand?"

The others around the table glanced at each other, wondering who should start first.

Markov tugged at his beard, then said, "We began beaming a variety of radio messages to the spacecraft this morning . . ."

"Yes," Zworkin took over. "I have a slide that shows the types of messages broadcast and the frequencies we are using." He touched a button set into the side of the table at his seat, and a list appeared on the projection screen at the back wall of the room.

"There's been no response," McDermott said.

"Not yet," replied Zworkin. "It has been only a few hours, however."

"We've got the laser system coming in from Maui," Jeff Thompson said.

"What frequency is it?"

"Infrared . . . one-point-six microns."

"Then it's not a CO_2 laser."

"No. Neodymium."

Stoner asked, "Can't we use the laser as a radar, as well as a communications channel? That could give us really high-resolution data about the bird."

"We'd need a high-resolution receiving system," Thompson said.

"Which costs time and money," McDermott added.

"But they have the receiving system at Maui, don't they, Jeff?" Stoner countered. "They've been using that laser to track satellites."

A born troublemaker, McDermott repeated to himself. Aloud, he said, "We're getting good information about its shape and size from the radar returns, aren't we?"

Thompson glanced at Zworkin, sitting across the table from him.

"Go ahead," said the Russian, gesturing with both hands.

The sandy-haired Thompson pushed his chair back slightly and fingered the projector control buttons at the table's edge.

"Just like Keith said," he started, "we've been using the communications frequencies as radars, too: monitoring the echoes we get off the spacecraft. The results we're getting are . . . well, puzzling."

A new slide appeared on the screen. It showed an oval shape, rather like an egg. Inside it was an elongated oval, like a fat cigar.

"What the hell is that?" McDermott grumbled.

"Our visitor," answered Thompson. "At the lowest frequencies the thing looks like a fuzzy, irregular egg shape. There's some evidence that the shape pulsates, but that might be just equipment anomalies. We're checking that. At any rate, the pulsations —if that's what they are—don't come on any regular basis. I think the chances are that they're just noise in our equipment."

"But it is fuzzy, not solid," said Cavendish.

"That's right."

"Like a gas cloud," McDermott said.

"A plasma cloud," Thompson corrected. "An ionized gas that reflects low-frequency radar."

"How large is the cloud?"

"Oh, about a hundred meters, hundred-twenty. On the order on a football field's length."

"And the thing inside it?"

"That gives a pretty solid reflection on the higher frequencies. It's twenty meters by five. Reflection spectrum like metal, from the preliminary analysis, or like highly metallic rock. It's pretty smooth, apparently."

"Looks like a comet to me," McDermott rumbled.

"No tail," answered Thompson.

"How do the Big Eye pictures look?"

Thompson turned to Stoner.

"Could you douse the overhead lights, please?" Stoner called, loudly enough for the technician in the next room, who baby-sat the automated slide projector, to hear.

He's always got to be different, McDermott groused to himself.

Stoner flicked on a slide that showed a faint fuzzy blob against a black background. He got up from his chair and walked to the ceiling-high screen.

"Not much structure is visible . . ."

"It looks like a damned comet," McDermott repeated, loudly, in the darkness.

Stoner's jaw clenched, then he went on, "There's an old astronomer's trick—Jeff, will you hit the button for my next slide, please?"

The same photograph appeared on the screen, but this time in negative. The sky background was now a grayish white, the fuzzy blob a dark gray.

"Here in this negative print you can see some structure within the cloud," Stoner said. "In particular, if you squint a little, you can make out the cigar-shaped object that the radar has picked up."

"What is the cloud?" Zworkin asked.

Stoner said, "So far, spectral analysis has given us nothing more than a reflected solar spectrum. Whatever that cloud is composed of, it's reflecting sunlight almost like a perfect mirror."

"A fuzzy, pulsating mirror," Cavendish mused.

Stoner made his way back to his seat, tapped his projector control button again. The screen went blank and the overhead fluorescent panels went on again.

"It is an enigma," Zworkin said.

"It's a comet," insisted McDermott.

"Too small . . ."

"A cometary fragment," said Big Mac. "We're sitting here thinking we're looking at an alien spacecraft and all the time it's just a chunk off a comet."

Markov shook his head. "I cannot believe that."

"Look at it!" McDermott thundered. "It's a ball of gas surrounding a chunk of metallic rock."

"It doesn't behave like a comet," Stoner said. "There's no

coma, no tail. It's much too small. It doesn't have the spectrum of a comet."

"It's an anomalous chunk that was spit off by a bigger comet," said McDermott. "Remember Kohoutek, back in seventy-three? Supposed to be 'the comet of the century,' and it never developed into much of anything. This thing is just a chunk of rock with some gas around it. We're on the trail of a red herring."

Zworkin glanced puzzledly at Markov, who explained in Russian what a red herring was.

"I do not agree," Zworkin said at last. "But even if you are correct, Professor McDermott, we must still study this object very carefully. Even if it is a natural body, it can still tell us much about the nature of the solar system."

"Hard to justify spending this kind of talent and money on a little cometary fragment," McDermott replied.

"It's not a comet!" Stoner snapped. "No comet ever outgassed a cloud that reflects sunlight like a polished mirror. No comet ever changed course after flying past Jupiter—not that abruptly."

McDermott shrugged. "The course change was probably the result of some outgassing—the thing burped a little gas, which caused a jet action and set it on a course toward us. We all jumped at the conclusion that it was *purposefully* aiming at us."

"Ockham's razor," Thompson muttered to himself.

"It's not actually coming that close to Earth," McDermott went on. "It'll pass us about four times farther out than the Moon's orbit, won't it, Stoner? Am I right?"

"If it doesn't change course again."

"What, and land on the White House lawn? Want to make any bets on that?"

"What about the radio pulses from Jupiter? What caused them?"

"Coincidence," McDermott said easily. "The Jovian radio signals were a natural phenomenon, and when you looked in that direction with Big Eye you discovered this bitty hunk of a comet and got all flustered about extraterrestrial spacecraft."

Stoner slumped back in his seat and glared at the old man.

McDermott looked around the table, daring anyone to challenge his conclusions.

"All right, then," he said. "I'll tell you what we'll do. It seems to me that it's too early to report to Washington that this object is natural in origin. We just might be wrong about that, and Project JOVE would be stopped in its tracks."

Markov tapped his fingertips on the tabletop. "If there is even the slightest chance that this object is indeed a visitor from another civilization, we would be criminally negligent to abandon this project. Even if the chance is microscopically small, why disband, when in another few weeks, another few months at most, we will definitely *know*, one way or the other? Why not continue to study the object with every means at our disposal, on the chance that it *is* an intelligent visitor, and that it *will* respond to our signals? If we abandon this work now, the thing may pass us by and we will lose our one chance to make contact with an intelligent extraterrestrial civilization. That would be criminal!"

McDermott picked up his pipe, toyed with it. "I'm willing to give it another few weeks. If it's intelligent, if it's alive, it'll respond to our signals in some way. But if it isn't, there's no sense indulging in wishful thinking." He focused his gaze directly on Stoner. "Or planning."

So that's what he's after, Stoner realized, his mouth compressing into a hard thin line, his insides turning to ice. The old bastard wants to shoot down the rendezvous mission.

Looking around the table at the others' faces, alternately glum or reluctantly nodding agreement, Stoner saw that McDermott had accomplished his goal. They'll let him get away with it. Rather than have him recommend shutting down the whole project, they'll go along with dropping the space flight mission.

Too angry to trust himself to answer Big Mac, Stoner sat in smoldering silence as the meeting adjourned.

Cavendish walked past him, patted him on the shoulder and murmured, "Too bad, old man."

"Why didn't you say something?" Stoner demanded, getting to his feet.

Cavendish shook his head. "Your McDermott is determined to stop the rendezvous mission."

"It would have helped if you'd spoken up."

"Quite . . ." Cavendish seemed confused for a moment, disoriented. "I . . . really, I haven't been feeling too well lately. I'm sorry . . ."

Stoner saw that his face was gaunt, eyes hollow.

"Are you sick?" he asked.

Cavendish half smiled. "I really don't know."

"You ought to see a doctor."

"Yes," he said vaguely. "Quite." And he left Stoner standing there as he wandered out of the conference room.

Markov was by the doorway, a frown on his long face. "Professor McDermott is wrong," he said as Stoner came up to him. "We must be prepared to send a cosmonaut to inspect this spacecraft. It is *not* a natural object. I feel this in my bones."

"Feelings don't count in this business," Stoner said. "Evidence does."

"But why is McDermott so stubborn about this?"

"Because he knows if there's a manned space mission, I'll be the logical choice as the man to go. And he hates my guts."

"That is no reason."

"It is for him," Stoner said.

"We must not let him get away with that. We must be daring. Revolutionary!"

Stoner leaned against the doorjamb, feeling suddenly tired, worn down. "What do you mean?" he asked.

Markov said, "We must bypass McDermott and start our own space program."

With a laugh, Stoner asked, "And how do we do that?"

"I'm not sure," Markov answered honestly. "But we can begin with the two of us, and recruit others. We will create a revolutionary underground movement."

He was serious, behind his bantering tone, Stoner could see. "We'll need somebody from computing to keep us up to date on the spacecraft's track," he said.

Markov smiled. "I have just the person. An American, Jo Camerata."

"Jo?" Stoner looked sharply at the Russian. "No, she wouldn't work with me."

"Ah, but she would with me," Markov said.

A sudden rush of anger surged through Stoner. Surprised at his own reaction, he fought it down.

Finally he managed to say, "Okay. You work with her."

Markov studied the American's face intently. "So you are the one."

"One what?" Stoner asked tightly.

"You care for her."

"No." He shook his head.

"Then why do you look as if someone has just stabbed a knife into your liver?"

"Look, Markov . . ."

"Kirill."

"Okay, Kirill—Jo and I had something going months ago. But it's all over now. Dead."

"And yet you have the power to hurt each other deeply."

"Each other? She's feeling hurt?"

Markov nodded gravely.

"Because of me?"

"Apparently so."

Stoner tried to assess this new piece of data, but it didn't seem to fit inside his head. "I don't understand it," he muttered.

"Neither do I," said Markov, with a heavy sigh. "I am madly in love with her, you know, but I can see that it will do me no good. I think perhaps you are madly in love with her too, but you haven't admitted it to yourself."

Stoner said nothing. His brain seemed to be short-circuited: no output.

"Well"—Markov made a rueful smile—"I will ask her to join our revolutionary underground. At least it gives me a legitimate reason to speak with her."

He left Stoner standing in the doorway, puzzled, doubtful, wondering.

The Search for Extra-Terrestrial Intelligence (SETI) is an idea whose time has come. A decade or so ago only a handful of scientists were active in this area; actual searches were almost non-existent and few people had heard of SETI. But today hundreds of scientists are actively involved, a dozen radio observatories around the world are carrying out actual searches, and much serious thinking is being devoted to SETI. . . .

The earth is mankind's cradle and although we are a very young, emerging civilization and still in our cradle, we are now adolescent enough to look beyond that cradle and acquire a cosmic perspective. Only by achieving a true view of ourselves as we relate to the planets and stars of our galaxy and the universe beyond can we attain maturity. SETI is a first step toward the growing up of mankind. . . .

ROBERT S. DIXON AND JOHN KRAUS
Editors, *Cosmic Search*
Vol. 1, No. 1
January 1979

CHAPTER 26

Jo was going down the stairs from her office to the main floor of the computer building when she saw Dr. Cavendish standing listlessly at the bottom of the stairwell.

With a shock, she realized that he looked older than he had when they had first arrived at the island, only a few weeks earlier. His body was gaunt, the clothes hung on his frame limply. His face was deeply etched with sleeplessness, his eyes were dark and sunken.

"Dr. Cavendish, are you all right?" she asked him.

He blinked and peered at her. "Ah, yes . . . Miss . . ." His voice trailed off.

"Camerata. Jo Camerata. I'm with the computing section here."

"Oh, yes, of course," Cavendish said. "How stupid of me not to recognize you."

"Is there something I can do for you?"

He shook his head slightly. "I've just come out from the weekly meeting with Professor McDermott, and I was gathering my strength before going out into the hot sun again."

"It *is* more comfortable in here," Jo agreed.

"It's not true about mad dogs and Englishmen, you know. I hate the heat. I think it's affecting my health, actually."

"Isn't your office air-conditioned?"

"Oh yes. They've wedged me into a splendid little nook over in the electronics building. Brand-new air conditioner sitting in the window, puts frost on my tea when I turn it all the way up. But it's the getting there that's bothersome. I'll have to walk half a mile in that sun . . ."

Thinking swiftly, Jo said, "Why don't you work in my office for the next hour or so, until the sun goes down a bit and the afternoon breeze cools things off outside?"

"In your office? Oh, I couldn't. All my papers and things . . ."

Jo took him by the arm and started walking slowly up the steps with him. "The data you're working on is in the central computer, isn't it? You can use my terminal and work just as easily here as at your own desk."

"I never thought of that."

She smiled at him. "You're accustomed to working with paper. My generation is accustomed to working with electronics. Anything you need can be called up on the computer terminal's readout screen."

"Yes, but I'll be dispossessing you of your own office."

"I can work anywhere," Jo said as they climbed the stairs. "Don't worry about it. You'll be a lot more comfortable here."

"It's awfully good of you," Cavendish said.

They reached her office. Jo sat the old man down at her desk and showed him how to summon up his own work on the computer terminal.

"Marvelous," Cavendish said, smiling.

"I even have a teakettle here, if you don't mind drinking American tea."

His smile lost a notch. "From tea bags?"

Jo nodded. "If you need anything, I'll be down on the main computer floor, in the Pit."

"The Pit?"

"That's what the programmers call the central well of the building: the Pit."

Cavendish's shaggy brows rose. "Is there a Pendulum also?"

"A pendulum? Like on a clock?"

"Edgar Allan Poe's story, 'The Pit and the Pendulum.'"

With a shake of her head, Jo admitted, "I don't think . . . oh, wait, wasn't there a Vincent Price movie by that name?"

American education, Cavendish thought sadly.

After a few more words, Jo left him and headed back downstairs, feeling like a good daughter. Cavendish played delightedly with the computer for a few minutes, but then the headache came back with blinding force and he nearly collapsed on the desk.

It was nearly midnight in Washington. The offices in the West Wing of the White House were still lit. The national monuments were aglow, even though the downtown streets were empty. Don't go out at night, tourists were told, and they stayed in their hotels until the sunrise drove the pimps and muggers off the streets.

NASA's sleek, modern headquarters building was almost entirely dark. Only a few office lights still burned. One of them was the office of the Deputy Director for Manned Space Flight, Dr. Kenneth Burghar.

Jerry White pushed that door open without knocking and grinned down at his boss, who was sitting at his desk, awash in paperwork.

"Christ, I thought I was the only kook in this outfit who burned the midnight oil," White said cheerfully.

"Budget cuts," Burghar muttered. "OMB wants to slice another twenty million from the budget."

White's grin turned sour. "Here, take my left arm. I need the right one to sign my unemployment checks."

"It isn't funny, Jer."

"I wish to Christ it was," White said fervently.

Burghar pushed his chair away from the desk slightly, leaned back and rubbed his eyes. His tie was gone, his shirt sleeves rolled up. The remains of a slice of pizza decorated one corner of the desk, next to a half-empty paper cup of black coffee.

"What are you doing here at this hour?" he asked White.

"Same as you," White replied, plopping down on the plastic couch along the side wall of the office, "trying to do the work of the guys who've already been laid off."

"Sometimes I wonder if it's worth it. If they don't give a shit over at Budget and on the Hill, why the hell do we knock ourselves out?"

"Because we're dedicated, committed men."

"We ought to be committed—to a funny farm."

White shrugged. "Maybe."

"You didn't come in here to discuss fiscal policy, did you?"

"No, I didn't." White pulled a one-page memorandum from his jacket pocket and handed it over to his boss.

"What's this?"

"From the Office of Science and Technology Policy: Sally Ellington and those West Wing geniuses must be puffing pot again."

Burghar scanned the memorandum. "A manned mission that goes four times farther than the Moon's orbit? What the hell is this all about?"

"Search me. The White House wants a quickie study on the problem and a report, right away."

Burghar huffed. "Thank god they don't want hardware. It'd take ten years."

"Ken, I don't even have the people to do a paper study! Where'm I going to find the manpower to . . . ?"

"Person power," Burghar corrected wearily. "Affirmative action, remember? And when the memorandum comes from the White House, you *find* the persons."

"But what's it for? All they say is a manned rendezvous mission with an unspecified target."

Burghar shrugged. "They're being secretive. Probably it's for some military operation."

"It's just another goddamned idiot study that'll go into their files and gather dust. Why the hell should we do it?"

"What can I say?"

White leaned closer to his boss. "Ken . . . there's one thing. I've been hearing rumbles about some kind of alien spacecraft that's been spotted in deep space. Could this be it?"

Burghar ran a hand through his scant hair. "Go ask OSTP. They won't tell me anything, but maybe they'll like you because your tennis game is better."

"Sure. And Sally Ellington's hot for my body." White didn't grin. "Seriously, Ken, what kind of a half-ass study can I get done without the manpower? And what's the point of it? We don't have the hardware to send a manned mission four times farther than the Moon!"

"We sure as hell don't. So do the usual kind of half-ass study and give them the report they want, when they want it. Don't get flustered about it."

"It's not an alien spacecraft, huh?"

"Oh crap," Burghar moaned. "Next thing you'll be seeing flying saucers out the window."

"Okay, okay . . . I'll put Sally baby's request into the old paper mill, with all deliberate speed."

"Good. Do that. And learn to say personnel, not manpower. Save me a lecture, will ya?"

Cavendish picked listlessly at his dinner, finally gave it up. The headaches came in waves, unpredictably, and nothing seemed to help them. He had staggered from Jo's office to the medical center and spent nearly two hours being tested and examined by a young Navy medic.

"Migraines are often caused by emotional stress," the earnest young man had said with the look of a funeral director on his tanned face. "Perhaps you're working too hard."

Cavendish accepted his prescription, wadded it into a tight little ball and threw it in the first trash receptacle he found outside the medical building.

Useless, he knew.

Now he stood on the front steps of the island's best restaurant (the scientists had rated it at only minus one star) and decided to take a walk on the beach. His headache was gone, for the moment, but the memory of it had triggered an old fear in him that coursed through every nerve of his body.

The sun was touching the horizon, a fat ball of molten red. The sky was glowing copper, with a few long streamers of gold and purple clouds hanging in the west.

Cavendish felt bone-tired. His whole body ached. His eyes burned from lack of sleep. Yet something made him walk along the beach that circled the island. He walked slowly, like a man searching for a specific spot even though he doesn't know where that spot might be. The sun sank out of sight and the shadows of evening covered the world.

All the way past the docks he walked, like a sentry, like an automaton, and down around the ocean side of the island, where the reef came close and the surf boomed out of the twilight.

Someone was sitting under the trees that fringed the beach. Waiting for him.

"Good evening," said Maria Markova.

"Yes," Cavendish answered.

Maria's suitcase of electronic gear was at her feet, opened, its tiny light gleaming red in the shadows.

"Report."

Without hesitation, Cavendish began, "The meeting was attended by Professor McDermott, Academician Zworkin, Dr. Thompson . . ."

Nearly an hour later, they were both sitting on the sand. Maria rested her back against a tree; Cavendish sat cross-legged, straight-backed. It was too dark to see the pain in his eyes.

". . . and he suggested that I see a psychologist," the Englishman finished.

Maria sat in silence for a while, thinking. "Anything else?" she asked.

"No . . . except for Schmidt."

"Schmidt? The Dutchman?"

"Yes. There are rumors circulating around the island that he is becoming a drug addict. Certainly he has been useless as far as real work is concerned."

"Tell me about Schmidt; everything you know about him."

Cavendish did.

"This young man could be useful," Maria said when he had finished. "Befriend him. Play on his animosity toward the Americans. Be certain to make him believe that it is Stoner who is stealing the glory from him."

"Stoner?"

Nodding in the darkness, Maria said, "Stoner. He is the one who must be stopped. And Schmidt may be the way to stop him."

"I . . . don't understand," Cavendish said.

"It is not necessary for you to understand. Only to obey."

"Yes."

"Very well," Maria said. "You have done well. You may go now."

"Yes," Cavendish dutifully answered. He got slowly to his feet, and as he stepped out from under the shadows of the trees, into the pale moonlight, Maria could see for the first time the anguish that twisted the old man's face into a hideous death's mask.

Her breath caught. Cursing herself for a weakling, she dismissed Cavendish almost angrily. Painfully, stiffly, he walked away without another word.

Maria's hands were shaking as she turned off her machine and snapped shut the lid of its suitcase. It felt heavier than ever as she carried it back to her bungalow.

The rustic little briefing room was jammed with news-men. Even though no TV cameras were allowed, photog-raphers clicked and whirred away as the press secretary strode up to the podium.

"Okay," he said, adjusting the microphone with one hand. "Here's today's statement:

"The President had breakfast with the Reverend Wil-lie Wilson, the Urban Evangelist, this morning. Rever-end Wilson's evangelical mission is sponsoring an out-door rally at RFK Stadium next Tuesday evening, and Reverend Wilson invited the President to attend. The President reluctantly declined, due to the press of other business. . . ."

"Like the way the primaries are going," a reporter *sotto voce*'d loudly enough for the whole room to titter.

The press secretary frowned, then returned to his statement: "The President congratulated Reverend Wil-son on his fine work for inner city people. Reverend Wilson's now famous 'Watch the Skies' message was not —repeat, *not*—discussed."

The press secretary looked up at the reporters and photographers.

"That's it?"

"That's it. This isn't a press conference; I'm not going to answer any questions. Copies of the statement will be available in about ten minutes."

CHAPTER 27

Stoner and Markov were eating together in the mess hall when Schmidt sauntered in.

"A sad case," Markov muttered, spooning soup past his beard.

"What do you mean?" Stoner asked.

"Haven't you heard? Schmidt spends his days puffing on narcotics instead of working."

Stoner stared at the young astronomer, who was getting into line in front of the steam counter.

"Narcotics? You mean pot?"

"Marijuana, other things. I understand there is quite a market here for tranquilizers, amphetamines." Markov shook his head in stern disapproval.

"So that's why he's been no damned use to anybody since he got here," Stoner said, his mouth tightening. "Maybe we should have him busted."

"Busted?"

"Thrown in jail. What he's doing is illegal."

"It is?" Markov looked surprised. "I thought the drug culture was an integral part of the decadent capitalist society."

"It may be," Stoner replied, his eyes still on Schmidt, "but that doesn't mean it's legal."

"The hypocrisies of capitalism."

Stoner looked at the Russian. He was grinning.

Turning back to Schmidt, he saw that the young astronomer had filled his tray, walked as far as the cash register, spoke a few flustered words to the native Marshallese woman working as cashier, then—red-faced—left the tray where it was and walked quickly out of the mess hall.

"What's he doing?" Stoner wondered.

Markov shrugged. "He's probably spent all his money on drugs and forgot that he didn't have anything in his pockets to pay for his dinner."

Edouard Reynaud was sitting at the writing desk in his trailer, trying to compose a dignified letter to Cardinal Benedetto on the latest progress of Project JOVE.

He let the pen drop from his fingers, then rubbed his eyes. The words kept blurring. His head still buzzed from whatever he had taken that afternoon with Schmidt. Besides, he hated writing. Equations are so elegant and direct, he thought. Words are slippery and full of pitfalls.

Looking up, he saw that it was fully night outside. The little desk lamp was the only illumination in his trailer.

"I'll miss dinner," he mumbled to himself. The food on this miserable island made it easier to avoid the sin of gluttony.

A knocking rattled the trailer. Reynaud got up and went to the flimsy metal door. Opening it, he saw Hans Schmidt standing on the step, droopy-eyed, worried.

"I don't have any more money," Schmidt said.

Reynaud blinked with surprise. "What?"

Schmidt seemed to be weaving slightly, even though his feet didn't move. "Money. They took all my money. I can't buy a meal."

Remembering the mosquitoes that could keep a man awake all night, Reynaud stepped outside and shut the trailer door firmly. "You mean you've spent all your money, and now you have nothing left for food?"

Schmidt insisted stubbornly, "They took it all. They didn't leave me any for myself."

"Come and have dinner with me," Reynaud said, reaching for the young man's arm. "You've had enough of a high for one day. You must sober up before you hurt yourself."

Schmidt laughed. "Come over to my place. I have some good grass."

"No, no." Reynaud tugged at his arm. "Come and get some food into you."

"I thought you were my friend."

Looking up at that angelic face with its golden frame of hair, Reynaud took his hand away from Schmidt and said carefully, "I *am* your friend. More of a friend than those who are selling you these drugs."

Schmidt backed away, stumbling slightly on the sandy ground. "You're just like all the rest of them! Go away! Get away from me! Leave me alone. I know who my *real* friends are."

Reynaud stood in front of his trailer as Schmidt lurched off into the night. It would be so easy to go with him, to use the drugs to seduce him. But with a resolute shake of his head the cosmologist turned in the opposite direction, toward his dinner.

I can't help him, Reynaud told himself. I can only make things worse for him.

Jo Camerata sat glumly at the bar in the Officers' Club, an unfinished daiquiri in front of her. It was early in the evening, the club was quiet and almost empty. McDermott was probably wondering where she was, but she just didn't have the heart to spend another evening with the old man.

She slipped off the barstool and headed for the ladies' room. The trio of Navy officers at the end of the bar smiled and called to her. She smiled back but kept on going.

Once inside the ladies' room the smile vanished from her face. Jo sat in front of the cosmetics mirror and took a long look at herself. You'd better start spending more time sleeping, girl, or you'll look like forty before you're twenty-five.

When she came out and surveyed the club again she was suddenly filled wth boredom. The same guys making the same jokes, she thought, and thinking with their balls. She went to the door and stepped out onto the dimly lit street, heading for the hotel where the single women were quartered.

"Mind if I walk you home?"

She turned and saw, in the dimness of a distant streetlamp, that it was Jeff Thompson.

"Oh, hello, Dr. Thompson."

"Calling it a night so soon?" Thompson asked, falling in beside her.

"I'm tired," Jo said.

"Yeah. Me too."

"Have you been working all this time?"

"I dropped over to the comm center, to see if our visitor has decided to say anything to us yet."

"Nothing?"

"Not a peep."

"Maybe it's trying to decipher our messages, just like we tried to decipher the radio pulses from Jupiter."

Thompson shook his head. "I just wish it was all over and done with. I'd sure like to be back home."

"Your wife will be coming out here soon, won't she?"

Thompson shrugged. "Now the kids are complaining that

they don't want to miss the summer with their friends. It's hard to uproot a family."

Jo said nothing. They walked along the empty street side by side for several paces in silence.

Then Thompson asked, "How's Big Mac?"

She almost laughed. "He's old."

He reached out and took her hand. "Jo, I never thought that . . ."

But she wouldn't let him finish. "You know, Dr. Thompson, you're the kind that would hate himself the next morning."

"You think so?"

"Yes." She stepped closer and kissed him, swiftly, on the cheek. "That's the way you are, and it's a shame. You would have been so much better for me."

Then she turned and walked quickly down the street, toward the hotel, leaving Thompson standing there alone, smiling foolishly, wondering whether he ought to be proud of his self-control or mortified at his lack of courage.

He jammed his hands into the pockets of his slacks and walked slowly toward the BOQ, determined to call his wife despite the hour and the cost.

Markov and Stoner left the mess hall together, and saw Jo striding alone down the street.

"Ah, our fellow revolutionary," Markov said. He hurried down the stairs and called out to her, "Jo! Miss Camerata!"

She turned and saw the two of them loping up toward her like a pair of eager teen-agers.

"Hi," Jo said to them both.

Stoner felt suddenly awkward with Markov beside him. "Hello . . ."

But the Russian took her hand, kissed it and said, "And a good evening to you, my lovely lady. Your beauty outshines the stars."

Jo giggled. Stoner felt his face go slightly red.

Tucking her arm under his own, Markov said, "Tonight we must make a request of your knowledge, your skill, your bravery."

Keeping her voice light, Jo asked, "What are you talking about?"

"We need you to do some bootleg work for us," Stoner said.

"What do you mean?"

As they strolled slowly down the street, Stoner began explaining his plans to her. Jo looked back and forth from him to Markov and back to Stoner again.

"Sure," she said, "the computer stores all the tracking data from the radars. I could start a rendezvous program easily enough. But I thought that McDermott had put . . ."

"That thing isn't a comet," Stoner blurted. "It's not a natural object at all. It's an artifact."

"Professor McDermott is being too narrow-minded," Markov added. "We must prevent him from ruining the entire purpose of this project."

"He's afraid of it," Jo said. "Mac *wants* it to be a natural object because he's scared of what it might really be."

Stoner shook his head. "He doesn't have that much imagination."

"Now, listen," Jo insisted, "I know what goes on in his head . . ."

"I'll bet you do."

Before she could reply, Markov stepped between them. "Jo, dearest lady, I said that we needed your courage as well as your skill. And we do. This tracking data must be prepared without Professor McDermott knowing of it."

"It's important," Stoner said, dropping his argument with her. "Vital."

Jo said nothing.

"Will you help us?" Stoner asked.

"So you can fly up to this thing and meet it," she said.

He nodded. "That's right. You want to be an astronaut someday? Help us make contact with this bird and they'll be hiring astronauts by the thousands."

"Sure," Jo said. "It'll be a great opportunity for me. If Mac doesn't toss us all in the slammer first."

Stoner raised his hands in a gesture that said, *It's all up to you.*

"Why a manned rendezvous mission?" Jo asked. "Why not an automated probe, like the kind that landed on Mars and Venus?"

Stoner answered quickly, "Because it takes years to build such probes. And they're *dumb*. They're just preprogrammed machines that do exactly what they've been programmed to do and not one damned thing more. How do you design a machine to examine something we've never seen before? That we know almost nothing about?"

"The object would be gone from the solar system before the committee discussions were finished," Markov pointed out.

"But we do have manned spacecraft," Stoner went on urgently. "NASA has its Space Shuttle. The Russians have their Soyuzes. I think there's even a launch facility out on Johnston Island, not that far from here."

"We also have our Salyut space station in orbit continuously with two cosmonauts aboard it. They can be sent to . . ."

"No," Stoner snapped. "I'm the man who goes."

Markov replied, "I realize that you would like to be the one to go, but . . ."

"No buts. We need somebody who knows what to look for. You can't program a cosmonaut with everything he needs to know. You can't turn a rocket jock into an astrophysicist, not in a couple of months. I'm the logical man for this mission. If you send anybody else, it'd be just as stupid as sending an automated probe with its limited programming."

Tugging at his beard, Markov said, "Your logic is unassailable. Certainly you have all the knowledge of what we are doing here. Perhaps we can get you boosted up in a Soviet rocket, with one of our cosmonauts as your companion."

Stoner nodded. "That would be fine by me."

Jo said, "But if you go . . . it's going to be a kind of hurry-up, makeshift mission, isn't it?"

"That's right," Stoner said. "If Big Mac had planned on a manned rendezvous mission from the beginning, things would be a lot easier for us."

She shook her head. "It sounds awfully chancy."

They were passing under a streetlight, and Stoner could see real concern on her face.

He smiled at her. "Don't worry. Driving a car in Boston is a lot more dangerous."

Jo nodded, but she didn't look convinced.

"You don't believe me?"

Jo thought a moment as the three of them walked down the

dimly lit street, past house trailers and the dull, graceless cement block office buildings.

"Does it really matter what I think? You've made up your mind that you're going off into space to greet our visitor."

"I've got to go," Stoner said. "I've got to."

Markov broke in, "We will need someone else to help us with our little revolution."

"Someone else?" asked Stoner.

"Yes. Someone with enough stature to override Professor McDermott's objections once he finds out what we are doing."

Jo suggested, "What about your head man, Zworkin?"

"Not him," Markov said. "He is too old and cautious to outshout McDermott. I was thinking of the cosmologist, Reynaud."

"The monk?"

"Yes. He has a direct line to the Vatican, which can be politically very useful."

"The Vatican? What political clout does the Vatican have?"

Markov laughed softly. "Our lamented Josef Stalin once asked the same question—and found the answer, much to his chagrin."

"Reynaud looks like a cream puff to me," Stoner said. "He won't have the guts to fight Big Mac. What about Cavendish?"

"He's sick," Jo said.

"But he's with NATO, and he's pretty well connected higher up, as well, from what I've heard."

"I don't think he would be the man for us," Markov said slowly.

"And he's sick," Jo repeated. "He's really in trouble, physically."

"I could still talk to him," Stoner said.

Markov objected, "But you must not approach him, Keith. You are too well known to be opposed to your Big Mac."

"Then how . . . ?"

"I'll talk to him," Jo said. "But I don't think it'll do any good."

"And I will approach Reynaud," Markov said.

They were strolling past the bungalows now. Far down the street, Stoner could see another couple walking slowly toward the beach.

"Ah, there's a light in my window," Markov said. "My darling wife must be waiting up for me."

They walked him to his bungalow.

"Would you care to come in for a nightcap?" Markov asked.

Jo glanced at Stoner, who shook his head. She declined also.

"Very well, then." Suddenly Markov gripped Stoner's right hand in both of his. Looking straight into the American's eyes, Markov said, "There are enormous forces working against us."

"I know," Stoner said.

"More than you realize," the Russian insisted.

Stoner nodded slowly. "It doesn't matter."

"Yes. We will fight the good fight. Together. Against them all!"

"Damned right."

"Keith . . . I am proud to be your friend."

"And I'm proud to be yours, Kirill. We'll beat the bastards, you'll see."

"Yes. Of course." Markov turned to Jo, took her hand, put it to his lips. "And you, dear lady. Any man would gladly face the firing squad for you."

"You're very sweet," Jo said, grinning, "but much too dramatic."

"Ah yes, I know. It's our national curse. We Russians are an emotional people. We feel things deeply." He seemed slightly flustered, embarrassed. With a forced little laugh, Markov said, "Well, good night. Perhaps tomorrow our visitor will answer our signals and we won't need to start a revolution, after all."

"Good night," Stoner said.

Markov trotted up the cement steps and entered his house. Stoner walked slowly with Jo back toward the hotel.

"He's a funny guy," Stoner said. "I like him."

"I do too."

"Do you really think Reynaud would be any help to us?"

"More than Cavendish," she answered. "That poor guy ought to be in the hospital."

"But you'll talk to him about helping us, won't you? It's important."

"More important than his health?"

He looked down at her, walking along beside him. "Of course it's more important than his health! It's more important than anything else . . ."

"For you, Keith," Jo said. "It's important to you. This is your dream, your obsession."

For a moment he didn't reply. Then, softly, "No, you're wrong, Jo. It's my *life*."

CHAPTER 28

The Officers' Club bar was quiet, cool, shadowy. It was not yet six o'clock, but the place was slowly filling up with the after-work, before-dinner crowd. Stoner sat glumly in a corner booth, his back to the wall.

Markov sauntered in, his head pivoting as he blinked and waited for his eyes to adjust after the burning glare of the street outside. He spotted Stoner at last and came over to the booth.

"Better get yourself a drink first," Stoner told him. "There's no table service until after six."

Markov went to the bar, quickly negotiated a vodka-tonic and hurried back to the booth.

"How was your meeting with Professor McDermott?" he asked as he slid in across the table from Stoner.

Stoner pointed to the two empty beer glasses in front of him and the nearly empty condition of the third.

"That bad?" Markov asked.

"Kirill, we're in the hands of fanatics," Stoner said. "Big Mac is a paranoid and Tuttle is a religious nut."

Markov took a sip of his drink. "Tell me about it."

Stoner began to explain.

Maria Markova sat in the cushioned chair in the front room of her bungalow. On her lap was a letter from Moscow, just in on the weekly flight from the U.S.S.R. She held an oblong black object in her hands, about the size and shape of a pocket calculator.

The letter was handwritten in a neat, tight Russian script and signed, "Affectionately, Cousin Anna." Cousin Anna was nonexistent. The pocket calculator was a cryptographic computer, and Maria was using it to decode her latest orders from Moscow.

The message was brutally simple: Prevent the Americans from mounting a rendezvous flight to meet the visitor. Use all necessary means available.

Maria cleared the computer's little glowering red readout symbols and got heavily to her feet. She burned the letter in the kitchen sink, then went into the bedroom and put the computer back into its fitting inside the electronics suitcase.

Use all necessary means available.

That meant Cavendish. He was her only tool, her only weapon. She sat on the bed next to the suitcase. The mattress sagged and squeaked under her.

Cavendish. She closed her eyes, but still saw the look of agony on the old man's wretched face. And that was merely when she had been asking him for information. Now she had to *use* him somehow, and if he resisted, she would have to punish him.

Maria shuddered.

Behavioral psychology began with Pavlov's work on dogs, Maria had learned. Western psychologists developed this into the principle of positive reinforcement: reward the subject when he does the correct thing, and withhold the reward when he fails to do the correct thing. It was a weakling's approach to the problem, requiring enormous amounts of time and patience, for little return.

Maria's superiors had long ago discovered that the reverse principle works better, more surely. Punish the subject for failure, and only when he obeys you absolutely do you withhold the punishment. It was the same principle that Pavlov had discovered, actually. But by manipulating the punishment instead of the reward, you got better results, more quickly. The long-term effect on the subject was deleterious, of course, but that could not be helped.

Maria fingered the control knobs on her suitcase of electronic gear. The microelectrodes had been implanted in Cavendish's brain many years earlier, but they still worked, and they were so small that they had escaped detection all these years.

Western psychologists would have put the electrodes into the brain's pleasure center, to reward Cavendish for good behavior with a jolt of pure electronic rapture. The surgeons in Moscow, however, knew better. Maria could cause a variety of effects in Cavendish's brain, ranging from sleeplessness to agony.

If he refuses to help me, she thought, with mounting apprehension, I'll have to torture him.

Markov gulped down his second vodka-tonic and put the glass precisely on the ring it had left on the Formica table when he'd picked it up.

"As a revolutionary," he told Stoner, "I would say that we have hit a stone wall."

"That's your considered opinion, is it?"

Sighing unhappily, "Yes."

Stoner slid out of the booth, walked unsteadily to the bar and got two more beers and two vodka-tonics.

"You are anticipating a long siege," Markov said as Stoner put the glasses on their table.

"A true revolutionary must be prepared for long sieges," Stoner answered gravely. "And for stone walls."

"We have enough of those," said Markov.

"In a good cause there are no failures, only delays."

Markov raised his glass. "To the revolution."

"We will gain the inevitable triumph," Stoner quoted Roosevelt, "so help us God."

"Do you have any plans for dinner?" Markov asked once the glass left his lips.

Stoner slowly shook his head.

"Do you foresee eating a meal sometime this evening?"

"I guess so. No hurry."

"Of course."

"Were you successful in rousing our good friar, Brother Reynaud?" Stoner asked.

"If I had good news about that, would I be drinking here with you in this lugubrious mood?"

"Lugubrious? You *are* a linguist, aren't you?"

"At times," Markov said.

"Lugubrious." Stoner turned the word over in his mind. "Now is the winter of our discontent . . ."

Markov raised his glass halfheartedly. "Our revolution is not going well, I'm afraid."

"Well, the American Revolution didn't start off too smartly, either, friend. We're in our Valley Forge period, right now."

Markov's face brightened a bit. "That's right. You were a revolutionary nation, too."

"Were? We *are* a revolutionary nation," said Stoner. "We invented the telephone, didn't we? Wasn't that a revolution? And the airplane, the computer, the Mickey Mouse wristwatch—that was a *real* revolution, my friend."

"I thought *we* invented the telephone," Markov said, scratching at his beard. "I'm sure I read that in *Pravda* once."

"Okay, you can have the telephone. But we invented TV dinners."

"A true revolution."

"And bubble gum."

They drank to bubble gum.

Jo pushed her castered chair away from the computer console and glanced up at the big clock on the wall of the Pit. It was slightly past six.

"I've had it," she told the programmer sitting next to her. "Nine hours with no break except for a lousy sandwich."

"And nothing to show for it but chipped nails," the programmer said.

She grinned at her. It's in a good cause, she said to herself. All the extra calculations of the spacecraft's projected track, they're more work but they're necessary for the rendezvous mission. If it comes off.

To the programmer, she said, "Listen, if they're not paying you overtime you shouldn't work overtime. Working through lunch hour was enough."

"I just do what I'm told," she said, getting up from her chair and heading for the ladies' room.

A few minutes later Jo went out into the hot sunshine. She decided to stop off at the Officers' Club before facing dinner.

As soon as her eyes adjusted to the club's dimness she saw Stoner and Markov over in the corner booth. Actually, she heard them before she saw them.

"To the glorious October Revolution and all the revolutionary peoples of the world!" Markov was shouting. "I toast you all, wherever you are!"

Stoner looked up as Jo walked over to their booth. She asked, "Is this a private celebration, or can anybody join?"

Markov answered instantly, "Come! Sit down! Join our funeral."

"Funeral?" Jo slid into the booth beside the Russian.

Stoner lifted his glass an inch from the tabletop and saluted her with it.

"We are celebrating the Fourth of July a few months early." His words were slightly slurred. "I think."

"But why call it a funeral?"

"Russian melancholy."

"Then there is the glorious November Revolution," Markov said, blithely ignoring their words. "Ah, my friends, that was the turning point. When the immortal Lenin appeared at the train station in Petrograd, the world changed."

An unhappy-looking Marshallese waitress, solid and square as a sack of cement, came to their table. "More drinks?" she asked.

Jo ordered a piña colada. Markov had gone to straight vodka on ice. Stoner stayed with beer.

When the drinks came, Stoner said, "I think we ought to toast the United States Marine Corps: the brave men who wrested this island from its fanatical Japanese defenders in nineteen forty-something."

Looking from one of them to the other, Jo asked, "What's going on here?"

"You really want to know?" Stoner replied.

"Yes!"

"Don't ask."

For an instant, Jo looked as if she was going to be angry. But then she laughed, shook her head and picked up her frosted goblet. "Okay," she said. "If that's the way you want to play it. But at least tell me what we're drinking to."

"To revolution!" Markov shouted.

"The Copernican Revolution," said Stoner.

"The Revolution of Nineteen-Five," Markov countered.

"Whatever."

They drank.

"What we need," Markov said, slapping his emptied glass down, "is an orchestra. We should be playing Tchaikovsky's 'Eighteen-twelve Overture.'"

"Not revolutionary enough," Stoner argued. "How about 'Stars and Stripes Forever'?"

"Counterrevolutionary!"

"It is not!"

"What about 'Me and Bobby McGee'?" Jo suggested.

They both stared at her blankly.

"Janis Joplin," she explained. "She was a revolutionary singer in the . . . oh, forget it!"

Stoner hunched over the table and the other two leaned toward him. "There's got to be some way," he said quietly, "of getting Big Mac to agree to a rendezvous mission. We've got to find a way."

"True revolutionaries are not discouraged by the stubborn opposition of reactionary elements," Markov said with perfect diction. Then he burped.

"We've got to find a way," Stoner repeated.

"Or make one," said Jo.

"Perhaps when they shine the laser on the alien," Markov mused, "that will tickle him to react."

"Him," Jo said. "You still think of the alien as a male."

"It," Stoner compromised. "What did you mean, 'Make one'?"

"Huh?"

"I said we've got to find a way to get Big Mac off his ass, and you said, 'Or make one.' What d'you have in mind?"

Jo blinked at him. "Nothing. I was just . . . talking."

But Stoner's mind was churning through the alcoholic haze. "Suppose . . . Kirill, listen . . . suppose we started to get a response from one of the radio telescopes. Nothing definite . . . just a few clicks and scratches . . ."

Markov looked at him blearily. "You are suggesting that we fake such a response?"

Stoner waved one hand slowly in the air. "Let's say we . . . improve on the return signal a little. Just a teeny little bit."

"Very dangerous," Markov said, shaking his head. "Very unscientific."

"Yeah. I suppose."

"But would it work?" the Russian went on. "Could you fool your Big Hamburger?"

"If we had somebody at the radio telescope who knew how to do the trick," Stoner said.

"And," Markov added with an upraised finger, "if he knew how to keep his mouth shut."

A slow smile spread across Jo's face. "What about Dr. Thompson? I think maybe I could get on his good side."

Maria Markova was sitting on her bed, drumming her stubby fingers on the lid of the suitcase. Kirill will be out for hours, she knew. As long as there is a bar open or a pretty girl to chase, he will be busy.

That gave her the better part of the night to interrogate Cavendish. She had to find some way to use the Englishman to stop the Americans, to prevent Stoner from going through with his plan to rendezvous with the alien spacecraft.

Stoner, she thought. It all focuses on him. If I can put him out of the way, I will have accomplished my assignment.

Jaw clenched, she unsnapped the locks on the suitcase and opened its lid. The unit was powered by its own tiny radio-isotope source, and the baleful red light that showed it was working glared back at her.

Maria reached for the transmitter knob and turned it to beam out a hotter, more painful signal. But the face she visualized as she sent the agony on its way was not Cavendish's. It was her husband's.

WASHINGTON (DC) HAS BECOME FOCAL POINT
FOR FEDERAL CRACKDOWN ON MANUFACTURE
AND DISTRIBUTION OF PHENCYCLIDINE (PCP):
FEDERAL AGENTS HAVE UNCOVERED 10 PCP LAB-
ORATORIES AND SEIZED MANUFACTURED MATE-
RIALS WITH STREET VALUE OF ABOUT $2 MIL-
LION SINCE JAN/78; SPECIAL AGENT DAVID
CANADAY INDICATES MORE PCP HAS BEEN UN-
COVERED IN DC THAN IN ANY OTHER US CITY;
NOTES PCP ABUSE IS CONCENTRATED ON EAST
COAST (M).

THREE LOS ANGELES TIMES ARTICLES DISCUSS
EFFECTS OF THE USE OF SYNTHESIZED DRUG
PCP, COMMONLY REFERRED TO AS "ANGEL
DUST," ON USERS, HEALTH AND LAW ENFORCE-
MENT PERSONNEL, AND CHEMICAL COMPANIES;
PCP CAUSES UNUSUAL BODY STRENGTH AND IM-
MUNITY TO PAIN. OFTEN ACCOMPANIED BY BI-
ZARRE AND VIOLENT BEHAVIOR, MAKING IT DIF-
FICULT FOR POLICE TO USE TRADITIONAL
RESTRAINT METHODS; HEALTH OFFICIALS HAVE
NOT ESTABLISHED STANDARD REGIMEN OF
TREATMENT BECAUSE VERY LITTLE IS KNOWN
OF HOW PCP WORKS; PCP IS INEXPENSIVE
AND MADE FROM LEGALLY AVAILABLE CHEMI-
CALS . . .

CHAPTER 29

Reynaud sat on the edge of Schmidt's bed, tense as a crackle of
electricity, staring at the young astronomer.

For more than an hour now, Schmidt had been sitting on the

floor in a corner of his room in the BOQ, arms hanging slackly
from his shoulders, hands limp on the bare wooden flooring, eyes
glazed and staring at nothing.

He looked dead, except for the rapid, panting rise and fall of
his chest and the puffing, almost wheezing breath from his open
mouth.

Reynaud had tried to talk to the youngster, tried cold water,
even slapped his face. Schmidt just sat there and stared, glassy-
eyed.

If I call for medical help they'll lock him up, Reynaud
thought. God knows where he's gotten the drugs. What if he
doesn't pull out of this? What if he dies?

For the hundredth time, Reynaud got up and went as far as
the door. Perhaps there is a doctor who would treat him without
letting the authorities know, he told himself.

But his hand refused to turn the doorknob.

As he turned back toward the astronomer, Schmidt's hands
slowly clenched into white-knuckled fists.

"I can see it," he said, his voice hoarse from the dryness of his
throat.

Thank God, Reynaud thought. He's coming out of it.

"It's coming," Schmidt croaked. "Oh, Jesus God, it's coming
right at me! It's coming!"

He scrambled to his feet. Reynaud went toward him, feeling
small and helpless next to the youngster.

"It's coming at me!" Schmidt screamed. "The colors . . ." He
flung an arm across his eyes. "The *pain!*"

"No, no, you'll be all right," Reynaud said, reaching for the
younger man's other hand.

But Schmidt flung him backward with a wild sweep of his
arm. Reynaud hit the bed with the back of his legs and tumbled
across it, landing with a painful thump on the floor on the other
side.

"I can't stand it!" Schmidt screamed.

He lifted the entire bed completely off the floor, raising it over
his head. Reynaud knew he was going to die. He couldn't move.
For a terrifying instant Schmidt loomed over him like an Aztec
priest ready to rip the heart out of his chest.

Then the young man, face twisted into an agonized mask of
primeval fury, swung around and threw the bed as easily as a

child throws a stick. The metal frame crashed against the wall, splintering the dresser and chair, smashing the plasterboard like a bomb.

Schmidt raced for the door, flung it open and disappeared down the hallway, leaving Reynaud on the floor, white-faced with pain and shock, one arm twisted under his body grotesquely.

"It will never work," Markov was saying.

"Sure it will," Stoner insisted.

They were still at their booth in the Officers' Club, drinking coffee now. Stoner's head thundered. Markov looked bleary, gloomy, exhausted.

Jo had gone to the cafeteria before it had closed and brought them back soggy sandwiches. Now, sitting beside Stoner, she said:

"I think it could work. Dr. Thompson would help us, I'm sure."

Markov shook his head, just once; the obvious pain made him stop and close his eyes.

"You're worried that too many people have to be in on it," Stoner said.

"Yes," Markov agreed, eyes still closed. "A faked message from our visitor would require the three of us, Thompson and at least two or three of the radio telescope technicians. Besides, don't you think that men such as Zworkin and Cavendish are clever enough to recognize a faked message after a bit of study?"

"That's where you come in, old friend," said Stoner. "Your job is to create a message that'll keep them puzzled long enough for us to get the rendezvous mission going."

Markov opened his eyes and smiled sadly at them. "I see. It all depends on me."

"A lot of it does."

"Will you try?" Jo asked him.

The Russian pursed his lips, then smiled at her. "For you, beautiful one, I would dare anything. Why not? It will be a challenge. And if we are truly revolutionaries, we must take some risks, mustn't we?"

Despite his own headache, Stoner saw that Markov was

humoring them both. The Russian had no faith in the desperate
scheme. But he raised his coffee cup to Markov.

"To our revolution," Stoner toasted.

Markov clicked his cup against Stoner's. Jo added hers, saying,
"To us."

Through a red wash of agony, Cavendish saw them bring
Reynaud into the infirmary: two husky young sailors carried the
stretcher with the fat little priest resting on it like a small
beached whale in a black suit. Cavendish's own pain made his
vision blur; he couldn't tell if Reynaud was conscious or not.

"What . . . happened to him?" Cavendish's voice was weak,
hollow.

The efficient middle-aged nurse who had been watching over
him clucked her tongue. "Never you mind him. You just lay back
there and rest."

Cavendish felt too weak to do anything else. But the pain was
getting worse, not better. It had been a mistake to come to the
hospital when the pain had started. Now he was trapped in here,
and the waves of torture were racking his whole body, despite
the analgesics the doctors had pumped into him.

He knew where he had to be, what he had to do. He was
being disobedient, and they were punishing him for it. As they
should. He had been a fool to disobey. But now this American
nurse was hovering over his narrow infirmary bed and he was
too weak to fight his way past her.

If she would just go away for a minute or two, Cavendish
thought. Just long enough to let me slip away.

The young doctor who had given him the injection stepped
into the little curtained alcove.

"How's he doing?" he asked the nurse.

"Restless."

Turning to Cavendish, the doctor put on a professional smile.
"Still feeling some discomfort?"

Discomfort? Cavendish thought. Why can't they say the word
pain?

"I'm . . . I feel somewhat better," he lied, knowing that the
doctor expected such an answer.

"Good. You just try to relax. Migraines don't last forever."

"The . . . man they just brought in," Cavendish managed to gasp out. "Was that . . . Dr. Reynaud?"

The doctor nodded. "Yes. Fell down and broke his arm."

"It's busy tonight," the nurse said. "Some nights you just sit here, bored to death. But tonight's busy."

"And it's not even payday," the doctor said.

Cavendish let his head sink back onto the pillow and ground his teeth together to keep from crying out with the pain. The doctor left, but the nurse went no further than the end of the curtains framing Cavendish's bed.

A terrific clatter and roar of shouting voices suddenly erupted from somewhere beyond the curtains.

"For Chrissake, hold him down!"

"Gimme a hand!"

"Orderly! Nurse! Come on, quick . . ."

And over it all, the screaming, screeching voice of a . . . what? Cavendish couldn't tell if it was a man or a woman. Or a beast.

The nurse disappeared. Cavendish could make out the sounds of struggle, fighting. Bodies flailing and thumping against walls and floor. A pair of burly orderlies raced past his curtained bed. Then the same doctor who had treated him.

"Hold him, hold him!"

Every muscle in his body fluttering from the effort, Cavendish slowly, excruciatingly, pulled himself up to a sitting position. They hadn't taken his clothes off, just his shoes. Getting to his feet nearly made him faint. Reaching down to pick up his shoes was an agony of effort.

And through it all, the melee out in the hallway continued.

In his stocking feet, Cavendish stepped to the edge of the curtains and peered out into the hall. A tangle of bodies thrashed on the floor by the hospital's main entrance, orderlies and nurses struggling to hold down a single young blond man who battled them all with rabid, insane ferocity.

One doctor, armed with a hypodermic, was trying to plant his knees on the young man's chest. Another—the doctor who had treated Cavendish—was attempting to stick a needle into one of his thrashing legs.

Good Lord, Cavendish thought with a shock of sudden recognition, that must be young Schmidt! But it was hard to tell; the man's face was contorted into that of a wild animal.

Cavendish gaped, almost forgetting his own pain, for several moments. Then he slipped away down the hall, heading for the hospital's rear entrance, carrying his shoes in one hand like a husband sneaking home to his angry wife after staying away too long.

Jo was holding his arm as Stoner came out of the Officers' Club. Markov stood on his other side, beneath the naked light bulbs that illuminated the club's sign. Thousands of insects buzzed and hovered around the lights, trying in their mindless, instinctual way to understand its mystery.

The lights went out abruptly.

"I had no idea it was so late," Stoner said. "We closed the joint."

"It's midnight," Jo said. "They close at midnight."

Stoner took a deep breath of sea air. It was cool and seemed to cut through the fog in his head.

"Well, my fellow revolutionaries," he heard himself say, "what do you think our chances are?"

"We can do it," Jo answered immediately.

Markov's reply was slower, "I will need a few days to create a suitably confusing set of signals."

"But what chances of success do we have?"

The Russian tugged at his beard. "Practically zero," he admitted. Then, with a boyish grin, "But the difference between zero and *practically* zero is the margin of all successful revolutions."

"We're all crazy, you know," Stoner said.

"Not crazy. Drunk, certainly. But not crazy."

"We can do it," Jo repeated, grasping Stoner's arm more tightly. "Big Mac isn't that smart; he'll fall for it. He'll probably have a heart attack, but he'll fall for it."

"That's a fringe benefit I hadn't thought about," Stoner said grimly.

"I'll talk to Dr. Thompson about it first thing tomorrow morning," Jo said.

"Thompson," Stoner echoed.

Nodding, she said, "He's the key to this whole plan. We've got to get him to go along with us."

"He won't do it," Stoner said.

Jo answered, "I think I can talk him into it."

He looked at her for a long moment, then walked down the three wooden steps from the club's doorway to the coral-cement paving of the sidewalk.

"Skip it," he said.

"What?"

Turning back to face Jo and Markov, Stoner said, "Forget the whole idea. I'm not going through with it."

Markov's face fell. "But it was your idea!"

"I know. But it's no good. Forget about it," he said.

Stepping down to his side, Jo said, "Keith, if you're worried about Jeff and me . . ."

"I'm not worried about anything," he snapped. "But I'm not going to fake data. That's a scheme that only a drunk would even think of."

And, abruptly, he turned and walked off toward the BOQ. Jo stood at the base of the steps and watched him disappear up the shadowy street.

Markov went to her. "I never believed he would go through with it," he said gently. "It was merely wild talk, to get over his disappointment about Professor McDermott's intransigence."

But Jo said, "No. That's not the real reason. He won't tell us his real reason. He won't even admit it to himself."

Markov put a hand lightly on her shoulder. "Dear child, I know how you must feel."

"How could you?"

"I know what a broken heart feels like."

Jo shook her head. "And I thought mine was shatterproof."

"None of them are," Markov said. "The best you can hope for is some quick-setting cement to put the pieces back together again."

With a rueful grin, Jo said, "Quick-setting cement? And here I thought you were a romantic."

Markov put his arm around her shoulders and started walking her along the street. "Come, I will escort you to the hotel."

Jo let him lead her. She only turned once to look down the street in the direction Stoner had taken.

In the darkness of her bedroom, the baleful red light of the electronics unit stared at Maria like a devil's unwinking evil eye.

He's an old man, she told herself. I can't keep it on maximum power for long; he'll collapse and die on me.

She was about to turn the power dial down when she heard a strange shuffling, dragging sound outside the window. Looking out toward the street, she saw Cavendish moving like a zombie, up the porch steps, to her front door.

Maria glanced at her wristwatch. The luminous dial was fuzzy, the hands indistinct. With an impatient huff, she leaned across the bed and turned the power dial down to minimum. The eyes are getting worse, she thought as she got to her feet. I will need stronger lenses soon.

Smoothing her dress, she went into the living room and unlocked the front door to admit Cavendish. He was standing there obediently, like a dog or a stolid cow, waiting to be allowed to enter.

Maria kept the lights off. She didn't want to see the Englishman's face. He went to a chair, collapsed into it with a soul-wrenching sigh.

"Your shoes," Maria saw in the dim light from the street. "Why are you holding your shoes?"

"I was in the infirmary," he answered.

"Why there?"

Slowly, Cavendish began to tell her what had happened to him, how he had tried to outwit his just punishment by going to the American hospital.

"How did you get away?" Maria asked.

He told her about the hubbub with Schmidt.

"Everyone knows he's been popping drugs," Cavendish said in his flat, machinelike tone, "but apparently he's taken a serious overdose of something very powerful. He was like a madman. A berserker."

A berserker. The phrase caught in Maria's mind. A berserker.

Certain narcotics can turn an ordinary young astronomer into a mindless fighting machine.

In the darkness, she smiled. Now I know how to stop Stoner, she thought. And it won't even hurt Cavendish. For some strange reason, she felt relieved by that thought.

> **God elevated the forehead of Man and ordered him to contemplate the Stars.**
>
> OVID

CHAPTER 30

The rally began at eight, but the powerful lights of RFK Stadium were already blazing when the first eager people arrived to begin filling up the huge oval.

Willie Wilson wiped a bead of nervous perspiration from his upper lip as he saw the seats filling up under the still-bright early evening sky of Washington.

"I told you it'd be a sellout," his brother Bobby said, smiling. "We'll be turning 'em away at the gates in another half hour."

By the time the warm-up bands and singers and guest stars had prepared the huge, sellout throng, it was fully night, even though no one could see the sky through the overpowering glare of the stadium lights.

Willie's entrance was carefully, dramatically staged. All the stadium lights were to go out except for the single spot that would pick him up as he stepped out of the entrance ramp and onto the turf. Then the spot would follow him as he walked—magnificently alone—the length of the runway and up the steps to the platform where the microphone stood waiting for him.

No matter how many audiences he spoke to, no matter how many times he delivered his message to the people, Willie still felt that sick, fluttery queasiness in his gut the last few seconds before he went out.

Behind him, he could hear Bobby crowing to Charlie Grodon, "I told you it'd be a sellout crowd, didn't I?"

"This time," Charlie agreed reluctantly. "But what about Anaheim? From what I hear the tickets ain't moving so fast out there."

Willie shut their voices out of his mind. They were not important. Nothing was important except convincing that crowd out there that his message was worth listening to.

He stood poised tensely as a young bronco about to be let out of its chute as the ex-singer turned prosyletizer raised her voice in praise of him. Willie felt the clammy sweat oozing from his pores as she shouted into the microphone:

". . . THE MAN YOU'VE ALL BEEN WAITING TO SEE," the loudspeakers bellowed, "WITH THE MESSAGE YOU'VE ALL BEEN WAITING TO HEAR—THE URBAN EVANGELIST HIMSELF, *WILLIE WILSON!*"

The combined bands struck up a fanfare, the lights faded and died, and the crowd roared.

Then choked into silence.

In the lone spotlight, Willie halted in the middle of a loping, athletic stride.

Silence. As if the whole stadium had disappeared. As if he'd been whisked away into the darkness of interplanetary space.

Confused, bewildered, scared, Willie halted with the spotlight still dazzling his eyes. He could see nothing in the overpowering glare of that single light.

But he heard gasps. Voices. Groans.

"Look!"

"My God, what can it be?"

"Up there, look at the sky! *Look at the sky!*"

Willie tried to shade his eyes but it did no good. There were screams now, strangled cries of . . . what? Fear? Awe? Terror?

He took a couple of fast strides forward and the spotlight stayed where it was. Even the light's operator had frozen.

Willie looked up and saw it. Flickering in the sky. The message.

The stadium was coming alive with sounds now. People were cursing, hollering, moving, jamming toward the exits, pulsing with the animal fear of a mindless mob.

Willie raced for the platform. Even in the darkness his steps were unfaltering. He banged his shin on the first stair, gritted his teeth and made his way to the top of the platform.

The mob was a living, breathing, mindless organism out there in the darkness. He could hear whimpers and screams and the bellowing of animal rage.

His hands clutched the slim rod of the microphone.

"LISTEN TO ME," he shouted, and his voice was amplified a millionfold throughout the vast stadium.

"LISTEN TO ME! HEAR MY VOICE! THE WORD OF GOD IS HERE AMONG US. FALL TO YOUR KNEES!"

The clamor in the flickering darkness faltered, took in a collective breath. Willie thundered:

"FALL TO YOUR KNEES! HEED THE WORD OF GOD. THIS IS THE SIGN THAT WE HAVE ALL BEEN WAITING FOR. DO NOT BE AFRAID. THERE IS NOTHING TO FEAR."

He hesitated, face raised to the lights in the sky. They pulsed and flickered like a living presence. The spotlight suddenly jerked into motion, caught him in its radiant circle.

"I TOLD YOU TO WATCH THE SKY. NOW LOOK AT IT! SEE THE HANDIWORK OF THE LORD GOD ALMIGHTY! THIS IS NOT A TIME FOR FEAR. IT'S A MOMENT OF TRIUMPH! TO YOUR KNEES AND PRAY. GIVE THANKS. GOD IS SPEAKING TO US IN A VOICE OF FIRE, BUT IT'S A LOVING VOICE. IT'S THE VOICE OF LIFE ETERNAL. WITNESS THE BEAUTY OF IT, THE KINGDOM AND POWER AND GLORY OF OUR LORD AND SAVIOR JESUS CHRIST, OF GOD THE FATHER AND THE SON AND THE HOLY SPIRIT, FOR EVER AND EVER . . ."

The newspapers next morning said that Willie spoke for three straight hours, never faltering once nor leaving that lone circle of light. His voice alone averted a panic that might have crushed thousands in a terrified stampede for the stadium exits.

Jo said good night to Markov at the hotel's entrance, and even stepped into the foyer, where the sleepy guard sat with his chin on his chest.

With an unhappy shake of her head, she pushed the door open again and stepped back outside. Markov was already well down the street; no sense calling to him. Jo walked across the street, slipped between cement block buildings and headed for the beach.

She wasn't surprised when she saw Stoner there, walking stolidly alone down the silvery-white sand. He looked up as she approached, and he didn't seem surprised either.

"Hello, Keith."

He almost smiled at her. "Well, you said we were two of a kind. Here we are."

She fell into step alongside him and they walked on the warm sand, beneath the tall, stately palms that rustled softly in the breeze. Jo stopped for a moment to take off her shoes. Stoner sniffed at the warm sea breeze, heavy with the scent of flowers. The surf murmured off in the darkness, endlessly.

Walking alongside him again, Jo asked, "What's your real reason for backing away from our little scheme?"

"I told you," he answered in the darkness. "I won't be party to falsifying data. It sounded good when I was drunk, but now I'm sober."

"That's the reason?"

"Yes."

"The only reason?"

He stopped and turned toward her. "What do you want me to say: that I don't want to do it because I don't want you cuddling up to Thompson?"

"Yes, Keith, that's exactly what I want you to say."

"It would make a difference to you?"

"I love you, Keith."

For a moment, he said nothing. Then, "Does McDermott know?"

"Of course he knows. Why do you think he made me go with him? To take me away from you. Makes him feel macho."

"And why did you go with him?"

"To make sure that you'd be allowed to come here with us, and not be sent to prison."

"They wouldn't send me to prison," he said. But his voice was lower, softer.

"McDermott said they would."

"And that's why you've been sleeping with him."

"Yes. And to get what I want out of him, too," she answered.

His shoulders slumped. "Jesus Christ, Jo. You're right, we *are* two of a kind."

"I've known it all along. And now all you really want is to go flying off into space again, isn't it?"

He shrugged and resumed walking along the beach.

"Everything you've done," Jo said, "all the mountains you've moved . . . it's really only for the chance to fly out and meet this alien spacecraft."

"So I'm a single-minded fanatic," he muttered.

"You're a human being, Keith. You scare me sometimes, but you're human. If only you'd act like one more often . . ."

"I scare you?"

"This single-mindedness of yours. This drive to fly away from everything, away from everyone . . ."

He put his arms around her. "I don't want to fly away from you, Jo. I really don't."

She let him pull her close and leaned against his strong, sure body and felt all the anger, all the doubts, all the fears wash away like dead fallen leaves swept off in a cleansing torrent.

He tilted her chin up and kissed her, lightly, and she clung to him, eyes closed.

Their lips parted. "You're so beautiful, Jo. So impossibly beautiful . . ."

But as she opened her eyes and looked up at him she saw the sky. "Keith . . . what is it?"

He turned his gaze upward and she felt him tense for an instant. He let go of her and spun around, head flung back, staring, mouth agape, arms spread outward to balance him as he turned again and again and again, gazing raptly at the bright flickering sky.

"What is it, Keith?" Jo repeated, staring herself at the glowing curtains of light that streamed across the heavens from horizon to horizon.

He laughed. "What is it? Take a look! It's our revolution! It's the biggest cosmic joke of them all! Look at it! Just look at it!"

The whole sky was alight with blazing veils of color, shimmering reds and greens and palest yellows, curtains of light that shifted magically across the heavens, dimming the stars, scattering their reflections in the calm waters of the lagoon.

Jo felt the breath suck out of her. It was awesome, frightening, overpoweringly beautiful.

"The Northern Lights!" Stoner was laughing, spinning around like a little boy on the sand, drinking in the wonder of it. "Or maybe the Southern Lights. Who cares? If they're shining here, this close to the equator, they must be shining everywhere. All over the planet! Got to be. Look at them! Aren't they magnificent?"

She ran to him. "The Northern Lights? But why . . . ?"

Sliding an arm around her, "It's our visitor, Jo. Don't you see? He rattled the magnetosphere of Jupiter and now he's doing the same thing to Earth's magnetic field. It's his answer, his signal to us! *Magnificent!*"

The planet turns. The line dividing night from day races across seas and continents. And as darkness touched the abodes of humanity:

Along the broad avenues and narrow alleyways of Peking, millions of startled citizens stare up at the sky, watching the fire dragons dance across the heavens. With single mind, they rush toward the Forbidden City, thronging in the ancient square, seeking an answer, an explanation, word from their leaders that will expel the dragons and ease the fears that clutch their hearts.

In Tehran the muezzins climb hurriedly to their minaret balconies to proclaim the glory of Allah, the All-Wise, the All-Compassionate. Men fall to their faces in prayer, casting fearful glances up at the fire-lit sky. Women huddle together and weep. The end of the world is very near, they know.

In Warsaw and Cape Town, in Dublin and Dakar, in Buenos Aires and Nova Scotia, the sky blazes and the people gape and cry out and pray to their gods or their scientists for some saving word, some hope, something to take away the fear that turns blood to ice.

And the lights in the sky dance, everywhere, all across the nighttime of Earth.

BOOK
THREE

O Lord, I love the beauty of Thy house,
and the place where Thy glory dwelleth . . .

THE TWENTY-FIFTH PSALM

CHAPTER 31

Since his arrival on Kwajalein, Stoner had worked at a desk in an open office area on the top floor of one of the oldest buildings on the island.

Seventeen men and women whose jobs were deemed not important enough to rate private offices shared this area, which they affectionately called the Swamp. Their desks were jammed together like an old-fashioned newspaper city room. It was almost as noisy as a newspaper office, too. No matter how carefully one tried to avoid irking one's neighbors, phones rang, computer terminals clacked, voices echoed off the low corrugated ceiling and the bare cement block walls. And when the sun pounded on the low metal roof, not all the air conditioning on the island could make the Swamp bearable.

Rain was hammering on the roof as Stoner stood in front of his desk, watching the President's televised speech on the viewscreen that normally served the computer. A tropical squall yowled outside their windows, but no one in the Swamp paid any attention to it.

Everyone in the room watched in dead silence as the President spoke. Slowly, carefully, the President told the people about the spacecraft, patiently explaining that it presented no threat to anyone on Earth. No threat. He kept repeating that. It was an opportunity, a marvelous, unexpected revelation that the human race is not alone in the universe. It is not a threat to us.

But the President looked frightened. And very, very weary.

Stoner listened, watched, waited. He sensed every nerve in his body stretching taut, every muscle aching with strain as he literally tried to *pull* the words he wanted to hear from the President's televised image.

And then the words came: "This morning I issued a directive for a joint American-Soviet space mission, to fly out toward this extraterrestrial spacecraft and examine it firsthand. We will go out to meet this alien visitor."

The breath sighed out of Stoner. His knees trembled. We're

going to do it, he told himself, still too tense to smile or say anything. We're going to do it. *I'm* going to do it.

He barely heard the President go on to announce:

"I have therefore decided to devote my entire personal effort to achieving the international co-operation and understanding necessary to allow us to make effective contact with the alien spacecraft and to garner maximum benefit from that contact. Since this will be such a heavy responsibility upon me personally, and upon my aides and advisers, I have decided—reluctantly—not to seek re-election to the presidency."

Somebody in the steaming hot room yelped. Stoner barely paid attention.

"I will not accept my party's nomination for re-election, and I will not campaign for any candidate this year. My full energies must—and will—be devoted to leading the international effort to learn as much as we can from this alien visitor."

A few ragged cheers came from the others watching the screen.

"Maybe now we'll get some decent food," one of the men wisecracked.

"Or get my window fixed," said a woman, regarding the leak that trickled down the wall from the windowsill.

The tension snapped. Even Stoner grinned as he sat back at his desk and resumed his interrupted task: scanning the spectral analyses of the approaching spacecraft.

The rain ended almost as abruptly as it had begun. The afternoon brightened and the Swamp heated up to its usual mugginess. People began drifting away from their desks, finding reasons for going across to the computer building, or the radio telescope installations, or anywhere that might be cooler and drier.

"I worked through lunch," said one technician as he passed Stoner's desk. "I'm entitled to leave a little early."

Stoner barely glanced up at him. The man started down the stairs with two buddies trailing close behind him. He had made the excuse within Stoner's earshot, as if he now regarded Stoner as the man who made decisions.

As they disappeared down the echoing metal steps, Jo Camerata came in. She looked around for a moment, then went to Stoner's desk and perched on the edge of it, her long bare legs crossed, hair pulled back and pinned up off her neck.

"How can you work in this heat?" she asked. "It's unbearable."

"I didn't notice," Stoner said.

"Didn't notice? You're sweating like a horse. Your shirt is soaked."

He glanced down and picked at his shirt front, plastered against his chest.

"Must be my Zen training. Mind over matter."

Jo tapped her own shirt front. "Well, *this* matter is going out to the beach for a dip before dinner. Want to come with me?"

He smiled at her. "I've got work to do, Jo."

"It can wait. Come on, you can come to work early tomorrow. That's what I do. I get in before seven."

Stoner gave her a skeptical glance.

"Well . . ." Jo broke into a grin. "Would you believe, before eight?"

"Sometimes."

She leaned toward him. "I can't tempt you? I know some very nice empty beaches, where nobody goes."

"Jo, we've only got a few weeks to get everything ready."

"You work too hard. At the wrong things."

He could smell the fragrance of her scent. Leaning back in his chair, away from her, he offered, "Look—I really have an awful lot to do here. Can I meet you for dinner? Around seven?"

"I have to go swimming alone?" Jo made a pout.

"It's a rough life," Stoner said.

"You're a difficult man, Keith Stoner," Jo said, getting to her feet.

Looking up at her, he replied seriously, "I'm not trying to be difficult, Jo. Honestly."

"Oh, I know! I just wish that you'd put your own needs a little higher up on your list of priorities."

He didn't answer. She glanced around, saw that the Swamp was practically empty, leaned down swiftly and kissed him on the lips. Before Stoner could react she was on her way to the stairs, grinning.

He grinned back at her. Then he swung right back to his work. His smile disappeared as he returned to the spectral analyses, almost alone in the steamy room.

Outside in the sun-dazzled street, at least there was a sea breeze to moderate the drenching heat. Jo took a deep breath and, instead of heading for the beach, started walking back toward the computer building.

Halfway there she met Markov, coming up the street in the opposite direction.

"Ah, my heartbroken friend. How are you this afternoon?"

Despite herself, Jo laughed. "Still heartbroken. And you?"

"The same."

She stood in the hot sunlight, gazed at the squat, windowless computer building, then turned her attention to the Russian. He was smiling at her, boyishly polite and expectant.

Just because Keith's a fanatic about this is no reason for me to be, too, Jo thought. I've got my own life to lead.

"Can you paddle a canoe?" Jo asked Markov.

He blinked. "I beg your pardon. Sometimes my grasp of your euphemisms . . ."

"A dugout canoe," Jo said. "There's lots of them on the beach, up past the airstrip. We could paddle out across the lagoon and find a nice private island, all to ourselves."

Markov's face lit up. "And no sharks?"

"No sharks."

"Show me where these canoes are," Markov said, offering his arm. "I will power you through the water like a dolphin!"

The Swamp was empty, except for Stoner, when Jeff Thompson and Lieutenant Commander Tuttle came in. Tuttle looked around, a puzzled frown on his snub-nosed, sunburned face.

"Why isn't the air conditioning on?" he asked.

"It is," Stoner said.

Tuttle was in his khakis, but the short-sleeved shirt was already darkening with perspiration.

"We've got to get you out of here," the lieutenant commander said. "How can you work in this soup?"

"Dedication."

"Now you know why he can drink so much beer without getting fat," Thompson said, yanking his shirt out from the waistband of his shorts.

Stoner turned off this computer screen and leaned back in his creaking chair. His back felt wet.

"What brings you up here?" he asked Tuttle.

Thompson answered, "You saw the President's speech?"

"Stood at attention all the way through it."

Tuttle pulled a wheeled chair from the next desk and sat down. He's so little, Stoner thought. I always thought Jeff was small, but Tuttle looks like a kid beside Jeff.

"Professor McDermott received orders from Washington just before the speech was broadcast," Tuttle said.

"About the rendezvous mission?" Stoner asked.

"Right. Our people in Washington are talking with the Russian embassy. I expect Professor Zworkin will be getting orders from Moscow before the day's over."

"So it's going to happen."

Thompson nodded gravely. "You're going out to meet our visitor. In a Russian ship, it looks like."

"Big Mac must be overjoyed," Stoner muttered.

"Professor McDermott . . ." Tuttle glanced at Thompson, then continued, "Professor McDermott is in a sort of state of shock. I don't think we can depend on him to make any effective decisions for the time being."

"He's sick?"

Thompson said, "He needs a rest."

"Dr. Thompson is taking over McDermott's administrative duties. He and Professor Zworkin will be coequals on Project JOVE for the time being."

"I see. Good luck, Jeff."

"And you," Tuttle went on, "will take over the planning for the rendezvous mission."

Stoner nodded.

"We'll have to move you out of here, into a better office . . ."

"How about Big Mac's office?" Stoner suggested, straight-faced.

Tuttle's jaw dropped open.

"He's kidding," Thompson said quickly. "He can take the office next to mine. We'll find someplace else for the people in it."

"Okay," said Tuttle.

Stoner said, "I want Professor Markov to work with me."

"Markov?"

"He's the linguist," Thompson said.

"That's right," said Stoner. "He's got a more open mind about alien thought processes than the others around here. And he can help me get along with the Russians I'll have to work with."

"Alien thought processes?" Tuttle repeated.

"Language, psychology, call it whatever you want. But the fact is that we'll be going out to meet something, or somebody, that has no point in common with any language or race or culture on Earth."

"You don't think that thing has people on it, do you?" Tuttle's eyes were widening.

"I doubt it," Stoner admitted. "If it's come all the way from another star, another solar system, it would have to be gigantic to hold a crew. Even one man would need all sorts of supplies, fuels, life support equipment . . ."

"How could they keep a crew alive for thousands of years?" Thompson asked.

"Freeze 'em," said Stoner. "Then thaw them out and revive them automatically when they come close to their destination."

"Their destination?" Tuttle asked in a hollow tiny voice. "You think they're coming here deliberately?"

Stoner shook his head. "No. I don't see how they could have picked out our planet over interstellar distances, any more than we could find theirs."

"But they're here. They found us."

"True enough."

"They could have aimed for a star like their own," Thompson suggested. "A nice, stable, G-type yellow star."

"If they themselves came from a G-type star."

"Chances are that they did."

"Maybe. But look at how that spacecraft behaved when it entered our solar system," Stoner pointed out. "First, it headed for the biggest planet in the system, the one with the strongest magnetic field wrapped around it."

"Hey, that's right!"

"And after swinging around it for a while, they took off for the inner planet with the strongest magnetic field."

"Earth," whispered Tuttle.

"So *that's* what they're looking for," Thompson said. "They must come from a world that's got a good-sized magnetosphere, and they figure that only worlds shielded by strong magnetic fields can support life on them."

"Could be," said Stoner. "Sounds logical."

"But is it a manned ship or is it automated?" Tuttle demanded. "Does it have a crew aboard or not?"

"My guess is that it's not manned," Stoner said. "Why send a crew on a one-way mission into the unknown? It's obvious they're just sniffing around, looking for signs of life."

"We've been broadcasting radio and television out into space for more than seventy-five years," Thompson said. "They could have picked up our broadcasts from dozens of light-years away."

Stoner chuckled. "Somehow I don't see an interstellar mission being sent out on the strength of 'I Love Lucy.'"

"You never know." Thompson grinned back. "Maybe there's an intersteller FCC that wants us to stop polluting the ether."

"Now, that makes sense," Stoner agreed.

"But if they do have a crew aboard," Thompson mused, growing more serious, "think of the technology they must have to keep people alive and functioning over interstellar times and distances."

"It can't be!" Tuttle blurted. "It's got to be unmanned. It's *got* to be!"

"Is it very painful?" Cavendish asked.

Hans Schmidt's eyes looked heavy, sleepy, rather than pained. He turned his head slightly on the pillow and gazed out the hospital window.

"Can you hear me? Am I bothering you? I'll go away if you like," said Cavendish.

"No, it's all right," Schmidt said. "I . . . it's just that I don't know what to say."

Schmidt could not understand the suffering that had turned Cavendish's face into a bone-tight mask of tension. To the young astronomer, the Englishman was merely an old man with red, sleepless eyes and a nervous tic in his cheek.

"You've had a bad time of it," Cavendish said, his voice strained, harsh.

"It's my own fault," said Schmidt.

"Hardly," Cavendish made himself say. "Someone sold you the drugs. An American, I'll wager."

"Several Americans."

"You see?"

Schmidt's eyes closed. Drowsily, he said, "You're the only one who's come to visit me, other than Dr. Reynaud. He's just down the hall. I broke his arm, you know."

"It's a minor fracture, actually," Cavendish said, "and Reynaud's told everyone that he did it himself, falling over your bed."

Schmidt shook his head slowly. "I demolished the room. They told me about it. I have no memory of it."

"It's not your fault," Cavendish insisted. "You mustn't blame yourself."

"Who, then?"

Cavendish started to reply, but the words wouldn't come out. He got up from the little wooden chair on which he was perched, walked stiffly, painfully, to the window and looked out. Perspiration beaded his brow.

They're making you do this, a part of his mind shouted silently at him. They're forcing you to do it. But you can fight against them. You don't have to obey.

His breath caught. He gasped with pain.

"I can't," he muttered.

"What did you say?" Schmidt asked from his bed.

Turning back to face the astronomer, Cavendish could feel his legs shaking beneath him, his stomach wrenching with the pain.

"It . . . it's not your fault," he repeated, and the pain eased a little. "The Americans . . . they forced you to come here, pulled you away from your home, your studies . . ."

"My girl, too."

"Yes. You see?" It was easier if he just kept talking; the pain faded while he spoke to Schmidt. "You can't blame yourself for what happened. It's the bloody Yanks who've called the tune all along."

Schmidt agreed with a nod, "I could have been home and happy. I never touched anything stronger than pot in my whole life until I came here."

Woodenly, like a marionette jerked along by invisible strings, Cavendish stepped back to the chair beside Schmidt's bed. Instead of sitting in it, he leaned both bony hands on the chair's back.

A wave of pain washed over him and his knees nearly gave way.

"Stoner!" he blurted.

"What?"

Looking toward the young astronomer through pain-reddened eyes, Cavendish said, "It's Stoner who's at the bottom of all this."

"Stoner? The American?"

"Yes . . ." Taking a deep, shuddering breath, Cavendish went on, "We'd all be home now if it weren't for him. McDermott wanted to finish the project and send us all home, but Stoner insisted on pressing on."

"He wants to get all the credit, doesn't he?" Schmidt said, the old sullen pout returning to his lips.

"Yes." It was more of a whimper than a word.

Schmidt finally noticed the old man's pain. "What's wrong? Are you ill?"

"Headaches," Cavendish grated out. "I . . . get headaches."

"Shall I call a doctor?"

"No. No, I'll be all right." Cavendish fished in the pockets of his trousers and pulled out a small plastic bottle. "They gave me pain-killers. Quite good, actually."

Schmidt had propped himself up in the bed on one elbow. "They won't let me have anything for the pain," he said. "Nothing stronger than aspirin."

Holding the bottle in front of the youngster, Cavendish repeated, "These are quite good. Non-narcotic. Non-habit-forming."

"Really?"

"Yes," the old man lied.

"It gets worse at night," Schmidt said. "The pain."

Straightening up, Cavendish said, "Perhaps it would be all right if I let you have a few of these . . ."

Schmidt nodded as Cavendish unscrewed the cap and shook out four pills into his trembling palm.

"You're sure you can spare them?" Schmidt asked.

"I . . . can get more . . ."

Schmidt accepted the ovate yellow capsules, held them in his hand and looked down at them.

Cavendish's whole body was on fire. "Try one," he croaked. "It . . . will keep the pain . . . away."

Schmidt hesitated only a moment, then took the cup of water next to his bed in one hand and popped a capsule into his mouth with the other. He drank and swallowed.

Within a few moments he was leaning back on the bed, glassy-eyed.

Cavendish, twitching as if electric currents were being applied to his nerve centers, came over to the bed and whispered into Schmidt's ear:

"It's all Stoner's fault. If you can get up from this bed and find Stoner, you can go home again and be happy. Stoner wants to hurt you. Stoner wants to kill you. You've got to stop him before he kills you."

Cavendish's eyes widened at the words pouring from his lips. It was as if someone else were speaking, using Cavendish's mouth as a transmitter, a machine totally disconnected from his own control.

Terrified at what was happening, he jerked away from the bed. A glance out the window told him that it was still late afternoon outside. Cavendish shambled out of Schmidt's room, heading away from the hospital as fast as he could. He never noticed that out in the peaceful lagoon an outrigger canoe with two people in it abruptly capsized.

CLOSE ENCOUNTERS

Billed as the "UFO Event of the Year" . . . UFO '79 offered the same old cliches to an audience long familiar with the pros and cons of ufology. . . .

Walter H. Andrus, international director of the Mutual UFO Network . . . told [us] that four types of aliens are looking in on us: dwarflike humanoids, human-appearing beings comparable in size to ourselves, animallike creatures, and robots. . . .

Alan Holt, astrophysicist training supervisor at NASA . . . described the interaction between magnetic and electrical fields and the theory of space-time curvature as it relates to gravitational propulsion. . . .

To sum up UFO '79: All the papers presented seemed to cry out for the scientific community to accept UFOs. Yet despite the efforts of people like Holt, rational scientific inquiry had clearly taken a backseat to promotion by those UFO groupies who sell the notions of visitations by alien beings.

HARRY LEBELSON
Omni magazine
April 1980

CHAPTER 32

They were already soaked from the first time the outrigger had overturned. Markov paddled furiously, battering the water with uneven, choppy strokes, while Jo sat up in the bow and tried not to laugh.

"Watch out now," she warned, "we're getting into another channel between islands . . ."

Before she could finish the sentence the current caught the canoe and it started to tilt over. Markov watched helplessly as the outrigger pontoon swung up over his head and the two of them were dumped again into the bath-warm water.

He stood waist-deep in the water and felt his pockets. If anything's lost, it's lost forever, he knew. Then he remembered his wristwatch. It was dripping water and the crystal was fogged over, but the sweep-second hand still seemed to be moving.

"Come on, help me right it," Jo called.

With a heavy sigh, Markov grabbed the pontoon struts and pushed the canoe right side up again. It was full of water. Laughing, Jo motioned for him to tilt the canoe enough to let most of the water out.

"I thought," Markov said, grunting with the effort, "that these boats could not turn over. Isn't that what the outrigger is for?"

Jo just laughed. He helped to push her back into the canoe, making certain to get a good handful of her backside in the process. Firm yet tender, he appraised.

Still grinning at him, Jo stuck out a hand. "Come on, climb back in."

Markov surveyed the distance to the empty beach nearest them. "No thank you, I'll walk. It's safer."

"Walk?"

"Wade. In fact, I will propel you to a safe harbor."

"I thought you were afraid of sharks."

He looked down into the perfectly clear water. "If I see a shark coming, I'm sure I can outrun him to the beach."

He got behind the canoe and started pushing it through the water like an oversized child's toy.

Jo clutched the gunwales and beamed at him. "My hero! Just like Humphrey Bogart in 'The African Queen.'"

"Who?" Markov asked, sloshing through the thigh-deep water.

She gaped at him. "You never heard of Humphrey Bogart?"

"Wasn't he Vice-president of the United States?"

As he nudged the outrigger up onto the beach, the sky darkened and unloaded another shower. Jo hopped out of the boat and helped him push it safely up on the sand. Then they ran for the cover of the trees up the beach and collapsed on the sand, wet, laughing, breathless.

"I don't believe that I was meant for the outdoor life," Markov observed.

"Whatever makes you say that?" Jo countered.

"I am a civilized man. That means I belong in a city, not out in this wilderness."

"Moscow?"

He nodded. "Yes. Moscow would look very good to me right now. Providing you were there to share it with me, of course, dear one."

"What's it like?" Jo asked. "I've never been there."

"It is a city," Markov answered, shrugging. "Not as beautiful as Paris, nor as large as London. Not as crowded as Tokyo. The sun shines there for two whole minutes each year. Everyone rushes outdoors to witness the phenomenon. Then it gets cloudy again and it snows for the rest of the year."

She laughed. "You love it, don't you?"

Watching the rain gusting across the lagoon, Markov answered, "I suppose I do. I was born there. I imagine I will die there. My father died fifty kilometers to the west of Moscow, helping to hold off the Nazi invaders in nineteen forty-one. His father died in the civil war that followed the Revolution."

Jo bent over slightly and touched his cheek with her outstretched hand. "But you'll live a long and peaceful life, won't you?"

He actually blushed. "I have every intention of doing so," he said, trying to recover his composure.

They waited as the shower drifted across the island and headed off to the west. The sun came out from behind the scudding clouds, hot and bright. In minutes the beach was dry again.

Markov squinted at the sky. "Our clothes would dry faster if we spread them on the sand."

Nodding, Jo teased, "Then we could go skinnydipping again."

"I think I've been in the water enough for one afternoon," Markov said.

Jo thought it over for a few moments. "Maybe we'd just better let the sun dry us off, without stripping."

With a nod, Markov answered, "The better part of valor."

Jo smiled at him, then said, "I just hope we can get back to Kwaj before it gets dark."

It was midnight in Washington.

Despite the tension he felt, Willie Wilson smiled easily and leaned back on the couch. The hotel suite was well furnished; the management had given him its very best, top floor and top prices.

"You're not from the insurance company?" Willie asked, spreading his arms across the back of the couch.

The young man sitting on the chair facing him smiled. "No, sir, I'm not. I'm with the Department of Justice."

"Justice?" Willie glanced at his brother, who stood uneasily by the empty, unused bar, an almost scared look on his ruddy face.

"Yes, sir," said the young man. He was neatly dressed in a conservative gray suit and quiet maroon tie. He looks like a lawyer, Willie thought.

"What do you want with me?" Willie asked him.

"We want to prevent a tragedy from happening," the young man said.

"We?"

"The Department. The Attorney General. The White House."

Willie gave a low whistle. "Heavy stuff."

The young man nodded.

"What tragedy are you worrying about?" Willie asked.

"The panic you've been spreading."

"Panic? I don't deal in panic. I'm just a simple minister spreading the Word of the Lord."

"Sir, you are frightening people. What happened at RFK Stadium could have been a colossal tragedy. It was only avoided by the narrowest of margins."

"By *his* quick thinking!" Bobby snapped, jabbing a finger toward his brother.

"It was the Lord's doing, not mine," Willie said softly, still smiling.

"Reverend Wilson, you are frightening people. It was bad enough when you were just telling them to watch the skies. But now—with these lights in the sky every night . . ."

"That's the message we've been waiting for," Willie said.

"People are scared! They think the end of the world is coming."

"I never said that."

"But that's what people believe you're saying," the young man said earnestly. "All over the country."

"I'm just a simple minister of the Lord . . ."

"You've become a powerful national figure, Reverend Wilson. And you've got to show some responsibility for that power."

"What do you mean, responsibility?" Bobby asked.

"You've got to cool it."

"What?"

"You've got to stop scaring people. You've got to tell them that the lights in the sky have nothing to do with God or the end of the world."

"I can't do that," Willie said flatly.

"You'll have to."

"Or else what?" Bobby asked.

The young man turned slightly in his chair to face Bobby. "Or else the federal government will get very tough with you."

Willie's smile never faded. He said, "I've met with the President, you know."

"Yes, sir, I know. He sent me here, Reverend. He asked me to remind you of the tremendous responsibility you hold in your hands."

"The President did?"

"That's right, sir. He could have sent someone from IRS. Or from FCC."

Willie's smile became a shade tighter, just a little forced.

"In other words," Bobby grumbled, "we play ball or the government shuts us off from television and goes through our books with a hundred auditors."

"What do you mean, play ball?"

"Where is your next big rally, Reverend Wilson?"

"Anaheim."

The young man nodded. "Yes. We've already been in contact with the stadium management there."

"What right do you have . . . ?"

"It's very simple, Reverend. A panic at one of your rallies could kill hundreds of people. Maybe thousands. None of us wants that to happen. Right?"

Willie nodded slowly.

The young man took a deep breath. "Then what you have to tell your followers is that the lights in the sky are completely natural, that they're caused by the spacecraft that's approaching us, and that there is no supernatural meaning behind the lights whatsoever. You must disassociate the lights in the sky from the voice of God."

"But that's not possible," Willie said.

"Yes, it is. You'll have to say it."

Willie glanced up at his brother, then looked back at the man from the Justice Department. "You're interfering with the Lord's work."

"You work for the Lord, sir. I work for the Attorney General." He hesitated, then added, "And we all work for the IRS."

It was sunset before Stoner emerged from his office building. He stood at the entrance for a moment and looked out through the fringe of palms across the street toward the flaming sky. Then he turned and headed for the Post Exchange.

An hour later, showered, dressed in clean slacks and pullover shirt, he walked from the BOQ to the hotel, only to find that Jo wasn't there. With a shrug, he went to the computer building, then to the Officers' Club. She wasn't in either place.

Where the hell could she be? he wondered. The clock behind the club bar showed it was well past seven. She said she was going for a swim; if anything had happened to her the whole island would be buzzing with it.

He made his way past the hardy group of regulars who lined the bar and sat wearily in the same corner booth he and Markov had used before.

She couldn't have forgotten, he knew. She just decided not to show up. Cold anger seeped through him. She's probably with McDermott.

No matter where Cavendish walked, no matter how far he decided to go or which direction he decided to go in, his feet kept returning him to the hospital.

It was dusk now, and as he leaned against the bole of a palm across the tennis courts from the hospital's blocky shape, he could see lights going on in the windows.

I've got no will of my own, he whimpered deep within himself. They're controlling me, making me walk and talk like some bloody animated doll.

He sagged against the tree. The pain wasn't so bad at the moment, but nothing could make it go away altogether. Only obedience to their commands alleviated the agony.

"Damned clever of them," he muttered to himself. "If they devoted as much effort to bettering their blasted economy as they do to controlling people's minds, they wouldn't need their blasted KGB."

The pain wasn't so bad now. Maybe I could get some food down, he thought. Or sleep! He leaned his head back and closed his eyes. Sleep. What a luxury that would be.

Cavendish never saw Schmidt raise his window, lean out over its edge and drop the two floors to the sandy soil at the base of the hospital wall. The young man was fully dressed, his eyes glittered wildly, and in his buttoned shirt pocket were only two of the capsules that Cavendish had given him a few hours earlier.

Markov felt like a sailor returning home from a shipwreck. He was stiff-kneed with muscle strain, sticky with salt and sand, and sunburned painfully on his face and high forehead.

Every muscle ached. He had rowed the damnable outrigger canoe for hours while Jo sat grinning at him. If it hadn't been for the brightness of the aurorae and the lights from the buildings on Kwajalein, Markov knew they would have drifted out to sea in the nighttime darkness and perished in the watery wilderness.

Now he clumped up the front stairs of his own little bungalow, crossed the uneven cement porch and pushed through the front door. It was not yet nine o'clock but it felt like four in the morning to Markov. Maria will be surprised to see me home so early, he thought.

She was not in the front room. He shrugged, and the movement under his shirt made him realize that his neck and shoulders were also sunburned.

With a sigh that looked forward to nothing more than collapsing face down on his bed, he opened the bedroom door.

Maria gaped at him, startled, shocked. The suitcase on her bed beside her was filled with strange electronic controls. A tiny glowing screen was flickering with a jagged trace of light, like an EKG.

But it was the expression on her face that stunned Markov. Guilt, anger, fear were all there. Her mouth was open but no sound issued from it. Her eyes stared at him and he could see all the way into her soul through them. She looked the way Lucifer must have looked when he realized that God had opened the pits of hell for him.

"What are you doing?" Markov bellowed. "What is this?"

All pain forgotten, he advanced on his wife. She got up from the bed, backed away from him, confusion and shame written across her face.

Markov looked from his wife to the suitcase of electronic gear. He grabbed the suitcase and raised it over his head.

"Don't!" Maria screamed, and leaped at him.

He hurled the suitcase against the nearest wall. It split in two under the impact of the cement.

"You don't know what you're doing!" Maria screeched, clawing at him.

He pushed her away and she bounced onto the bed. Markov stepped over to the electronic equipment. One baleful red light was still on. In a cold fury he smashed his sandaled foot against it. Glass shattered and plastic buckled. Again and again he stomped the suitcase until nothing was left but unrecognizable shards of glass and circuit boards.

Maria was round-eyed. "You . . . you've destroyed a vital piece of state property."

"Be silent, woman," he growled, "and be grateful that I don't do the same to you. I don't know what that equipment was for, but it was for no good, I can see that much."

Staring at the smashed equipment, Maria broke into sobs. "They'll kill us both, Kirill. They'll kill us both."

"Then let them!" Markov snapped. "Perhaps we'd be better off dead."

I reject as worthless all attempts to calculate from theoretical principles the frequency of occurrence of intelligent life forms in the universe. Our ignorance of the chemical processes by which life arose on earth makes such calculations meaningless. Depending on the details of the chemistry, life may be abundant in the universe, or it may be rare, or it may not exist at all outside our own planet. Nevertheless, there are good scientific reasons to pursue the search for evidence of intelligence with some hope for a successful outcome. . . . The societies whose activities we are most likely to observe are those which have expanded, for whatever good or bad reasons, to the maximum extent permitted by the laws of physics.

Now comes my main point. Given plenty of time, there are few limits to what a technological society can do. Take first the question of colonization. . . .

FREEMAN DYSON
Disturbing the Universe
Harper & Row
1979

CHAPTER 33

Stoner sat alone in the corner booth, feet up on the opposite bench, a half-empty bottle of champagne sitting in a plastic bucket on the table.

Some big night, he said to himself. You sure are having a wild time, old buddy.

The club was filling up with the after-dinner crowd. Somebody had put blaring disco music on the stereo, and people had to shout to hear themselves over it. A few people came over to Stoner's table from time to time, but he quickly and firmly shooed them away.

Maybe I ought to go over to McDermott's trailer and see if she's really there, Stoner thought. But what if she is? Then what do you do? Drag her off by the hair of her head?

He yanked the bottle from its icy water and poured his plastic glass full. The champagne looked pretty flat. California stuff, he guessed, peering at the label. Christ, not even that: New York State. He dunked the bottle back into its bucket so hard that some of the ice water splashed on him. Blinking, Stoner swung his feet to the floor.

Hell, I can't even get drunk when I want to.

The front door of the club banged open so hard that the crash made everyone jump. Stoner saw Schmidt standing framed in the doorway, shoulders hunched and head lowered as if he were going to ram a wall.

For a moment all conversations stopped. The disco music blared inanely on, and Schmidt's heavy, open-mouthed breathing seemed to match the music's thumping beat.

Stoner turned back to his champagne. The club filled with talk again. People moved, laughed, drank. But Schmidt, burning eyes fixed on Stoner, pushed his way past the crowd at the bar, heading for the corner booth.

"It's all your fault," he said to Stoner.

Stoner looked up at him.

"You can sit there and drink champagne," Schmidt said, his words only slightly slurred, "and keep us here in this godforsaken hole."

"What are you talking about?" Stoner asked.

"Sure, you drink champagne and wait for the Nobel Prize while the rest of us rot away!" the young astronomer said, his voice rising.

"Sit down," Stoner said, "and stop making a fool of yourself."

"I'll show you who's a fool!" Schmidt shouted.

He grabbed Stoner by the shirt and yanked him out of the booth as easily as a child lifts a toy. Stoner felt his shin scrape against the table's edge and then he was completely off his feet and thrown to the floor.

Everything in the club stopped. Even the music.

"Champagne!" Schmidt screamed, slapping the bottle and its plastic bucket off the table.

"What the hell's wrong with you?" Stoner bawled, scrambling back to his feet. No one in the club moved, they all stood frozen, wide-eyed, watching the two of them.

Turning on him, Schmidt roared, "It's all your fault!" and leaped at Stoner, grabbing him by the throat. His thumbs were like steel against Stoner's windpipe. Stoner gagged, couldn't breathe.

Instinctively, Stoner locked his hands together and swung both arms hard inside Schmidt's wrists, ripping the younger man's hands away from his throat.

"You're crazy," he croaked raggedly.

But Schmidt, his eyes afire, screamed back, "You want to steal everything from me."

Out of the corner of his eye, Stoner saw the club door swing open again and Jo stepped in, hair still glistening wet. Her mouth dropped open as she saw the two men confronting each other.

Schmidt swung at Stoner and he saw the punch coming but he was too surprised and slow to avoid it. The Dutchman's heavy fist caught him on the cheek and spun him around. He crashed into the booth's table and sprawled over it. Schmidt was on him before Stoner could turn over, both knees on his back, pounding his head and shoulders with bunched fists.

"Your fault! Your fault!" Schmidt screamed with each blow.

Stoner felt himself starting to black out and knew that Schmidt would go on pounding him to death while all the rest of them watched. By the time they got past their shock it would be too late to help. With raw animal instinct he jammed one foot against the back of the bench and pushed the two of them off the table. They fell heavily to the floor and he broke free of Schmidt's insane grip.

For an instant the two men crawled away from each other. Stoner saw the younger man's eyes. He's crazy! Schmidt's hair was matted over his face, eyes dilated, mouth hanging open, gasping for breath, snarling at him. Stoner could taste blood in his own mouth and every muscle of his body throbbed with pain.

He'll kill me! Stoner's mind shrieked at him. He'll kill me if I let him.

Schmidt scrambled to his feet as Stoner did. Stoner backed away a short step, and felt the heel of his shoe touch the champagne bottle. The floor was wet where he stood.

Focus, Stoner heard his old instructor hiss at him. Focus your strength and speed.

Snarling, Schmidt rushed. Stoner sidestepped, kicked at his kneecap and sent him sprawling across the slippery mess on the floor.

Schmidt got up immediately, as if he couldn't feel the pain, as if there were no pain. His face had somehow been gashed along one cheek and blood dripped down his neck, into his collar. White showed all around his eyes and his lips were pulled back to bare his teeth.

Again Schmidt leaped. Stoner tried to avoid him again, but the younger man's outflung arm caught him neck high and they both went slamming against the club wall. Stoner pushed Schmidt away and tried to get to his feet. Schmidt grabbed the empty champagne bottle and hefted it like a club.

Backing away, knees bent, hands out defensively, Stoner heard his instructor's voice again: The martial arts are not a game! You are not trying to score points, you are trying to save your life!

Schmidt advanced toward him, brandishing the bottle. A low growl came from his throat. Stoner watched the young man's feet as he came closer, forcing himself to concentrate on what he must do, calming his breathing rate, putting his body in balance.

Nobody's going to lift a finger to help, he saw with a strangely detached part of his mind. They either figure this is a private grudge or they're scared of getting hurt.

Schmidt swung the bottle in a wild overhand sweep. Stoner ducked under it and leaned all his weight into a punch to Schmidt's diaphragm. Then he grabbed him and spun him into the wall.

Schmidt turned and swung again wildly but Stoner blocked it with a forearm and kicked him through the partition between booths. The wood splintered and screeched as the young astronomer's body shattered it.

Stoner stood over Schmidt's prostrate body and let the breath sigh out of him. He saw Jo still standing at the doorway and now Reynaud was beside her, insanely dressed in gray Navy pajamas, with his arm in a light sling. The others in the club were edging toward him now, timidly approaching.

But Schmidt started climbing slowly to his feet, the bottle still firmly in his hand, a grisly smile on his bleeding face. Everyone froze into stillness.

Jesus Christ! Stoner gaped. He's like Frankenstein's monster. Nothing stops him.

Schmidt giggled like a schoolboy pulling the wings off a fly and came at Stoner again.

Stoner buried the fear and pain he felt and did what had to be done. Block, kick, punch to the side of the head. Schmidt sagged to his knees. Stoner grasped the wrist of his right hand, yanked the arm out full length and kicked Schmidt's ribs. The bottle fell from his hand. Ribs cracked audibly. Stoner chopped a vicious knife-edge blow to Schmidt's neck and he went down on his face.

The crowd surged in closer.

"Don't get near him!" Stoner panted. "He's crazy."

And Schmidt slowly climbed back to his feet. The crowd gasped and backed away. His ribs must be broken from that kick, Stoner knew. What in hell is going to stop him?

His face set in a hideous death's-head rictus, Schmidt charged again at Stoner, who met him with a front kick to the abdomen and a hammer blow to the shoulder. Schmidt's collarbone cracked.

Break him down, Stoner told himself. Go for the bones. Chop him down like a fucking tree.

It seemed like an eternity. Stoner worked automatically blank-minded, remorselessly, until Schmidt lay inert on the wooden floor, as still as death.

Reynaud pushed his way through the onlookers with his one good arm, Jo trailing behind him.

"You've killed him!" Reynaud cried, sinking to his knees beside Schmidt's prostrate form.

"I don't . . . think so," Stoner panted. "Hope not. I couldn't . . . he went . . . berserk . . ."

Jo was staring at him. "You're hurt."

"I'm okay," he said. "Get an ambulance . . . for the kid. I had to hit him . . . pretty hard."

"But you . . ."

The adrenaline was wearing away and every muscle in Stoner's body was starting to scream.

"Just get me back to my room," he mumbled, heading for the door. "I just want to lie down."

But there were four uniformed shore patrolmen at the door. Stoner collapsed into their arms.

Cavendish woke up slowly, blinking and struggling to clear the fog of sleep from his brain. He shivered with cold. For long moments he had no recollection of why he was sitting slumped against the bole of a big palm tree, legs folded painfully under him, across the tennis courts from the island's hospital.

Gradually he remembered. He remembered Schmidt and the wild untrue words he had poured into the young man's ear. Shame burned through him. They're controlling me, he told himself. They've stolen my soul.

He looked out across the tennis courts. It was dark and no one was in sight. Leaning against the tree, he pulled himself up to his feet.

His legs were afire with pins and needles, but his head felt clear. The pain is gone! His hands flew to his face, his scalp, as if they had a will of their own, probing, searching, trying to find from touch if he were deluding himself and the pain was really lurking in there somewhere, hiding, waiting to come back in even more terrifying force.

"It's gone," Cavendish whispered shakily to the night shadows. "Truly gone . . . as completely as if someone had turned off a switch."

A switch. "Quite," he said to himself. "A switch that they can turn on again just as easily, whenever they decide they want more from me."

He pulled his trembling hands away from his head. Despite their tremor, inwardly he felt quite calm. His mind was his own again—at least for a little while.

And with a clarity that comes only when all distracting thoughts have been burned away, Cavendish at last realized what he had to do.

The only person who makes slavery possible, he had once read somewhere, is the slave himself.

And with that brilliant, blazing clarity of vision that had suddenly been granted him, Cavendish saw how he could end his own slavery.

"I know what you want," he muttered through clenched teeth, "but you can't make me do it. I'm a man, not one of your bloody trained dogs."

Very deliberately, he turned his back on the hospital and threaded his way past the trees, through the buildings, across the main street and through the clustered buildings on the other side. The ocean side. It took only a few minutes to span the width of the island and stand on the ocean beach.

The surf boomed closer here. The sea stretched out under gleaming skies. Beyond the scudding clouds the aurorae flickered and laughed at him.

I know what you are, and what's causing you, Cavendish said silently to the dancing lights. That's enough. I won't get to meet you in person, but that's all right. I've had enough for one lifetime.

The ocean surged at his feet, alive, breathing.

Cavendish smiled sadly into the dark waters. "Sophocles long ago heard it," he quoted. "And it brought into his mind the turbid ebb and flow of human misery."

There were strong currents in that remorseless ocean, currents that would sweep a man away from land, currents that harbored the planet's most efficient carnivores.

Cavendish stood at the water's edge for only a moment. No thoughts of his past life paraded through his mind. He thought only of the future, a bleak, grim future of pain and slavery to unknown, unknowable masters.

With a crooked smile he muttered, "But while I have the strength, I can end all that."

He waded into the sea, into the warm engulfing amniotic fluid that would erase his pain forever. Straight into the waves he walked, up to his knees, up to his hips, his shoulders, oblivious to what waited out there hungrily, oblivious to the lights in the sky that made the night brilliant with eerie glowing fire. Sure enough, the current seized him and soon he disappeared from the land.

Even through his acoustically insulated helmet, the pilot was getting a headache from the helicopter's rattling, roaring engine. Below him was nothing but empty gray ocean. At his side, the crewman scanned the choppy sea with binoculars.

"How th' fuck they expect us to find a guy in th' fuckin' water without a fuckin' dye marker?" the pilot hollered over the chopper's cacophony.

The crewman put the binoculars in his lap and rubbed his bloodshot eyes. "Orders," he yelled back.

"Fuck! The dumb sonofabitch went out swimmin' at night and got pulled under. He's fuckin' shark food by now."

"I know that," the crewman hollered, "and you know that, and even the commander knows that. But the regs say we gotta put out a search."

"Fuckin' regulations. Waste of fuckin' time."

But when the precise second came for his radio check-in, the pilot's harsh voice changed to a smoothly professional, "J-five-oh-four to Kwajalein control. Position six-niner-alpha. No joy."

He clicked off the radio and resumed, "Another three fuckin' hours we gotta spend fuckin' around up here! Fuckin' dumb Englishman."

CHAPTER 34

Stoner sat stiffly in the uncomfortable wooden chair in Tuttle's small office. Every part of his body ached horribly. His head buzzed from the hours of questioning. And the rattling drone of the air conditioner in the lieutenant commander's one window was giving Stoner a headache.

Two other officers sat facing Stoner, while Tuttle leaned back in his swivel chair, behind his metal desk. The other two were from Base Security: a young black lieutenant junior grade and a grizzled, ruddy-faced guy who looked much too old to be merely a full lieutenant.

"But why did he attack you?" the j.g. asked for the hundredth time.

Stoner started to shake his head, but the pain made him wince instead. "I told you before," he replied, "I don't know."

"He said something about it being your fault," the older officer chimed in. "What was he talking about?"

Around the same bush again, Stoner thought, giving them the same answers he had given dozens of times already: I don't know, I don't know, I don't know.

But in his mind he saw again Schmidt's crazed face, felt the insane inhuman strength of the man, the total mindlessness of his attack. And Stoner realized, It wasn't an accident. It couldn't have been just blind chance. He was out to get me. He wanted to kill me.

"Where could he have gotten the drugs?" asked the lieutenant.

His black junior said, "We got the report on what he was on: PCP. Angel dust. Enough to stoke a regiment."

"Where could he have gotten that?" Tuttle asked, his round face a picture of concern.

Stoner laughed. "You guys aren't serious, are you? This island's a floating junk paradise. Take a walk down the street any night, there's enough pot in the air to fly you home."

"Angel dust is a lot more serious than marijuana," the older lieutenant said sternly.

"There's a lot of pill popping going on around here," Stoner said. "You guys must be aware of that."

"But not angel dust," the black lieutenant said.

Stoner shrugged and lapsed into silence.

"What reason would Schmidt have for attacking you?" Tuttle asked.

"None that I know of," said Stoner.

"You'd never argued over anything before?"

"We'd hardly ever talked to each other before," Stoner said.

Their questions continued and Stoner continued to fend them

off with ignorance, but inwardly he began to realize: Schmidt came after me for a reason, and not just because he was bombed out of his skull. He wanted *me*. He wanted to put me out of the way. Why? Because somebody told him that's the surest way to end this project and get everybody sent home again.

Tuttle called in an aide and had sandwiches brought in. The questioning continued as they ate.

Finally Stoner stood up. "Look . . . we've been over the same ground now dozens of times. I've told you everything I know—which isn't much, I admit. But I've got work to do and I don't see any point in going on with these questions."

Tuttle said, "This is a serious matter, you know."

Feeling every muscle in his body groaning, Stoner answered, "I know. I'm the guy that got jumped on. But if you people put some effort into finding out where Schmidt got the drugs, you might get somewhere. I've told you everything I know."

He turned and went to the door. No one stopped him, so he left the office, went outside into the painfully bright sunlight and walked toward the building that housed the Swamp.

Then he remembered that his office had been moved to the computer building. Head still buzzing, his insides churning, Stoner went to his new office.

He was sliding cardboard boxes full of photographs into the empty bookshelves of the new office when Markov rapped once on the open door and came into the room, grinning, hands behind his back.

"You are coming up in the world, Comrade Stoner. Congratulations."

Wiping sweat from his forehead, Stoner said, "Thanks. It *is* more luxurious than the Swamp."

"Do you think this new office is a reward for your intellectual abilities," Markov asked, "or for your prowess as a fighter?"

Stoner's insides went cold. "That's not funny, Kirill. I might have killed that kid."

"Yes, I know." Markov's own face was somber. "But I am glad that it's him in the hospital today, and not you."

"How is he? Have you heard . . . ?"

"He'll be all right. He is young and healthy. His bones will knit quickly."

Stoner dropped down into his desk chair. "They woke me up at eight this morning and brought me down to Tuttle's office. I've been answering questions all goddamned day."

Markov remained standing, hands still behind his back, nodding sympathetically.

"What're you hiding behind your back?" Stoner finally asked.

"Oh." Markov suddenly looked almost embarrassed. "It's nothing. A gift of sorts. For your new office."

"A gift?"

"A symbol, really. Emblematic of the problem that has brought us together and led to our friendship. A symbol that is truly representative of where we are and what we are faced with."

"What are you talking about?" Stoner asked, intrigued despite himself.

Markov was warming up, more like his cheerful self. "I had thought of bringing you champagne and caviar, to celebrate your new office. But what good are they? Merely food for the belly. I bring you a lasting gift for the mind. Besides, I couldn't afford to buy champagne and caviar."

Stoner sat up straighter and placed both his hands on the polished surface of his broad, empty desk. "Okay, I'm bracing myself for this terrific symbol."

With a flourish, Markov produced from behind his back a large, brown, shaggy coconut.

Stoner stared, then laughed.

"No, no, no!" Markov said, his face almost serious. "It is truly a symbol, as I said. It is symbolic of this island, isn't it? And if you try to open it, you'll find that—and this is an American idiom, I believe—it is a tough nut to crack!"

Stoner raised his hands in mock surrender. "You're right, friend. When you're right, you're right."

"A tautology," Markov replied. "Another thing about this symbol: it is a world traveler. The coconut can float across the entire Pacific Ocean, I am told, and germinate on shores far from its place of origin."

"Like our visitor," Stoner realized, his grin dissolving.

"Exactly."

"You're a deep thinker," Stoner said. He took the coconut from Markov's hands and placed it on his bare desktop, next to the telephone. "I'll keep it here, to remind me of what we're up against."

"Good. One more symbolism: Once you *have* cracked open a coconut, it contains milk and meat to sustain life."

"But the trick is to crack it open."

"Not easy."

"Unless you have the proper tools . . . and the skill."

Markov nodded.

"Thanks, Kirill," Stoner said. "You've cheered me up. It's been a pretty somber day."

"Yes. They still haven't found Cavendish, you know."

"Cavendish?" Stoner tensed.

Blinking, Markov asked, "You haven't heard?"

"Heard what?"

"Dr. Cavendish has disappeared. They presume he has drowned. There is no trace of him on the island, and the Navy has sent out search patrols . . ."

Stoner sagged back in his chair. As if to reinforce Markov's revelation, a helicopter thundered by; the building vibrated to the roar of its engines.

"Cavendish," Stoner repeated. "My god . . ."

Markov tugged at his beard. "Are you all right? Your face has gone white."

Looking up at the Russian, Stoner said, "Cavendish was an agent . . . a spy . . ."

"No," Markov said.

"He told me himself. A double agent. He worked for your side, the KGB—but he really was working for British Intelligence."

Markov's mouth dropped open in a silent gasp of amazement.

"He told me himself," Stoner repeated. "Both sides were leaning on him."

"And now he's disappeared," Markov whispered. "Dead, no doubt."

Stoner mused aloud, "Schmidt tries to kill me last night, and Cavendish disappears. The same night." He looked up at Markov. "Kirill, what does it add up to?"

The Russian just stared back at him, wordlessly.

"Do you think your people are out to prevent me from making the rendezvous flight?"

"I . . ." Markov hesitated. "I think perhaps that might be true," he said, his voice barely audible.

"Jesus Christ."

Markov shook himself, like a man trying to throw off a bad dream. "Let me check into it. Let me see what I can learn." He got to his feet.

But Stoner put out a restraining hand. "Maybe you ought to stay out of it, Kirill. You could get yourself into real trouble if you put yourself in the middle of this."

"I am already in the middle of this," Markov said with iron in his voice. "They have tried to kill my friend."

"And they've already killed Cavendish."

"Perhaps so."

Stoner stood up and came around the desk. "Stay out of it, Kirill. Don't get yourself in trouble."

Markov laughed. "We are all in trouble, my friend. Every last one of us."

Into the hot afternoon sunshine Markov strode, unblinking, unseeing. Down the main street, his back to the radio telescope antennas, past squat blockhouse office buildings, past the BOQ, the hotel, the trailer park. He turned into the area where the bungalows stood and marched straight to his own house.

"Maria Kirtchatovska!" he bellowed as he slammed the front door shut behind him.

She came out of the kitchen, a sizzling saucepan in one hand. "What are you doing home?"

"Put that down and come here," Markov said, pointing to the sofa.

She scowled at him, but went back into the kitchen and reappeared a moment later, wiping her hands on a towel.

"I was making dinner for us," she said.

"Sit down."

"I haven't told anyone about your temper tantrum last night . . ."

"Dr. Cavendish is dead," Markov snapped, feeling fury racing along his veins. "Drowned, most likely."

She sat heavily on the sofa. "Drowned?"

Still standing, Markov added, "And young Schmidt went berserk with a drug overdose last night and tried to kill Stoner. Do you see any connection between these two events?"

Maria looked away from him without answering.

Looming over her, Markov said, "That . . . machine you were using last night. It had something to do with Cavendish, didn't it? Or was it Schmidt?"

"Kir, we agreed long ago that there are certain parts of my work that we would never discuss."

He was tempted to raise his hand and slap her. "That agreement is finished. I should have ended it when you ruined that young student's life. Now you've murdered Cavendish, haven't you?"

"No!"

"Don't lie to me, Maria Kirtchatovska! The man was a KGB informant and now he is dead. You killed him, with that infernal machine."

She shook her head stubbornly. "The device was a communications system, a sort of radio . . ."

"Nonsense! You communicate with Moscow by those silly letters you send each week in the supply plane. I know that much. Somehow your machine killed Cavendish."

"It couldn't have . . ."

"I saw the look on your face when I caught you at it! You weren't communicating anything except pain and death! Don't try to deny it."

"Kirill, I . . ." Maria ran a hand through her short-cropped hair, suddenly agitated, tearful. "What could I do? I have to follow my orders. What else could I do?"

"Murder. Torture. You've been involved in it all along, haven't you? All these years."

She was crying, tears leaking down her broad cheeks. "No. Not until now. And I didn't want to. I had to. It was the only way to survive . . ."

"And all these years I closed my eyes to it. I *knew* that all the whispered stories were true, but I kept telling myself, 'Not my Maria. She wouldn't do such things. She's only in the cryptographic section. She's not involved in arrests and interrogations and assassinations . . .'"

"I'm not!" she wailed. "Not until this . . . this . . . *thing* came upon us."

"You never had anyone arrested? You were never involved in interrogations? Murders?"

"No! Not directly."

He threw up his hands and paced across the room. "Pah! Not directly. Your hands are clean—almost. Disgusting. Disgusting! To think that I've lived with you all these years and kept my eyes closed."

Her chin went up. "I've kept my eyes closed to your adventures. If you . . ."

"My adventures!" He wheeled around to face her. "I was making *love*, woman! I was seeking beauty and kindness and joy! I wasn't giving electric shock treatments to some poor wretch in the basement of a prison hospital."

"I never . . ." Maria's voice faded away into sobs.

"It's over," Markov said sternly. "Do you hear me? It's ended. Finished. I won't share my life with a torturer and murderess."

"What do you mean?"

"Either you leave the KGB or you leave me. Take your choice."

Her eyes went wide. "I can't resign! They don't allow it."

"Retire, resign, transfer to another job. Otherwise I'll never live with you again. Never! I couldn't!"

"But, Kir, if you try to leave me there'll be questions, an investigation . . ."

"Tell them you've thrown me out because of my escapades. They'll believe that."

"I don't want to leave you," she said. "I don't want you to leave me."

"Then you must quit your job."

"I can't . . ."

He went to the sofa and sat beside her. She had stopped crying, but the tears had left fat streaks down her face.

"Is it true that you didn't want to do what you did? That they forced you into it?"

"They ordered me and I obeyed," she said. "I had no choice."

"They ordered you to do what? To kill Stoner?"

She gave a little gasp of surprise. "Not . . . they want to prevent Stoner from flying the rendezvous mission. They want him stopped—any way possible."

"But our government is co-operating with the Americans on this!" Markov said. "Zworkin, Academician Bulacheff, the General Secretary himself . . ."

Maria shook her head stubbornly. "I only know what my orders are. They want Stoner stopped."

Markov sighed. "Maria . . . how can I live with someone who . . . who follows such orders? It's impossible!"

"It's as much your fault as mine," she said. "I never wanted to get involved in all this."

Markov shook his head in misery. "What are we to do, Maria? What are we to do?"

Spoke privately with our lame-duck President this afternoon, after the regular Cabinet meeting. I must confess he seems stronger, surer of himself, now that he's removed the burdens of running for re-election from his rounded shoulders.

The Party is in an uproar, of course. The organization people are terrified that he's just handed the election to the opposition. I've tried to point out to them that he's created such a fluid situation that no one has a preferred position. It all depends on what we do from here on in—that's all that counts now.

If our scientists make real contact with this alien spaceship, whatever it is, and it all turns out well and beneficial for the world, then the President will be a saint and his halo will cast a very favorable light on whoever's running for our Party.

If it's benign, I can head the Party's ticket in November and win easily. But if the alien is trouble, then all bets are off.

> Private diary of the Honorable
> WALDEN C. VINCENNES, Secretary
> of State

CHAPTER 35

Jo sat staring at her computer terminal's readout screen. The numbers and letters glowing at her were meaningless; her mind couldn't concentrate on them. She got up from her desk and walked out onto the balcony outside her office. Down in the Pit the computer hummed and winked its lights in intricate patterns, too fast for any human to understand.

With a shake of her head, she stepped back into her office, grabbed her worn leather shoulder bag from the desk and headed downstairs.

She stopped in the rest room first, pushed a comb through her thick hair and checked her face. Then she marched straight to Stoner's new office.

The door was open. He was on the phone, his back to her. She waited just inside the doorway.

"Sure," Stoner was saying. "I can take all the physical checkups they want right here at the base hospital. If NASA wants their own people to run the tests then NASA can fly them out here. Right? Good. Okay. Thanks again. See you."

He turned his chair around to hang up the phone and saw Jo standing there.

A flicker of uncertainty crossed his face. "Hello, Jo."

"Hi." She stepped further into the office. It was still bare, new-looking. Voices echoed slightly off the freshly painted walls. Half the bookshelves were empty, the rest held stacks of photographs and a few thick looseleaf notebooks. Three unopened cardboard boxes rested on the carpeted floor beside the steel file cabinets. The desk was steel also, but its top was painted to look like walnut. It also was bare, except for the telephone and an incongruous coconut.

"Have a seat," Stoner said, without getting up from his chair.

Jo took the nearest chair, chrome and plastic, cold and uncomfortable.

"You're all right?" she asked.

He nodded slowly. "Bruised and aching, but okay. I checked the hospital a half hour ago; Schmidt's in stable condition. No lung punctures, just some broken bones. He'll mend."

Clenching her hands on her lap, "I feel terrible about it."

He said nothing.

"I mean . . . if I hadn't been late for our dinner date," Jo explained, "you wouldn't have been at the club and Schmidt wouldn't have found you."

His face took on that grim, almost angry look that shut everyone else out. "He'd have found me, no matter where I was. It's a small island, and he was looking specifically for me."

"But why? What made him?"

"Where were you?" Stoner asked.

Jo's heart quickened within her. He cares! It matters to him!

"I was stuck halfway across the lagoon," she said, the beginnings of a smile curving her lips. "Markov and I took a canoe trip."

"Kirill?"

Nodding, "We borrowed an outrigger and neither one of us could keep it from tipping over. You should have seen us! Soaked."

"Kirill's in love with you," Stoner said, without hostility.

"Like Cyrano was in love with Roxane," she replied. "I'm perfectly safe with him."

"Unless you both get eaten by sharks."

"We made it back okay." She felt her smile fade into an apologetic look. "But I was late. By the time I got to the club . . ."

"It's not your fault," Stoner said quickly. "You mustn't think that. Somebody pumped Schmidt to the gills with angel dust and sent him out to get me."

"Who would do that?"

He shook his head. "I don't know. Maybe the Russians."

"The Russians? Do our Navy people . . . ?"

"I haven't told them a word, and I don't want you to, either." Stoner leaned across his desk, eyes fastened on hers. "If they start cloak-and-daggering each other, you can kiss this rendezvous mission good-by."

"But if somebody tried to kill you . . ." Jo's voice trailed off.

With a shrug, he answered, "I think they just wanted to knock me around so I wouldn't be ready for the trip to Russia and the flight. Somebody doesn't want an American to make the rendezvous mission."

"The Russians," she murmured.

"Not the Russian scientists," Stoner pointed out. "Probably not the Russian Government, either. I think it's just an element within their government. The hardliners. The KGB, most likely."

Jo sagged back in the chair, her insides going hollow. "Then you're in real danger."

"Maybe. Kirill's checking it out for me."

"You've got to tell the Navy!" she urged. "Tuttle and the others, they've got to know about it so they can protect you."

"No," he said firmly. "They'll fuck up the rendezvous mission once they start clomping around."

"Better that than getting you killed."

"Jo, I told you once that this is my life. I meant that, quite literally. Let me handle this my way."

"And get killed."

"I'll take that risk," he said.

"Keith . . ." But what can I say? she asked herself silently. That desk is between us. His work, his obsession. It's more important to him than life itself. More important to him than I am.

"Besides," he was saying, trying to make it sound less grim, "it was probably Cavendish's doing. I don't think his disappearance on the same night was a coincidence."

She nodded slowly. "There are a lot of rumors going around about Dr. Cavendish."

Stoner nodded back. "Yeah, I guess there are."

"Was he really an agent for the Russians?"

"Back in New England he told me he was a double agent. I'm not sure that he knew which side he was really working for, now."

"He was awfully sick."

"Maybe. Maybe he was faking that."

"Do you think any of the other scientists are working as intelligence agents for their governments?" Jo asked.

Stoner's brows rose. "I don't know. I never thought about it. Some would, I suppose."

"Professor McDermott would," she said, very deliberately.

Stoner gave a bitter bark of a laugh. "Big Mac? Some spy he'd make, with that mouth of his."

"He's sneakier than you think," Jo said.

He gave her a long, searching look. "Yeah, I'll bet he is."

"His health isn't very good," Jo went on. "Ever since the aurorae started, he's been a wreck."

"So I've heard. I haven't seen him for more than a week."

"Neither have I," she said pointedly.

He hesitated, then said evenly, "That's good."

For long moments neither of them said anything. Jo waited for Stoner to speak, to come out from behind his desk and reach toward her, touch her, do something to show that he cared for her. Instead, he merely sat there, looking uncertain, uncomfortable.

"I heard," she broke the silence at last, "that you're in charge of picking the personnel to go to Russia with you."

"Yes, that's right."

"I want to go. I've checked the personnel requirements, and you can carry me as a computer analyst. There's an opening."

He drummed his fingers on the bare desktop for a moment. "Jo . . . if there's any danger in this trip for me, it might catch any other Americans traveling with me."

Her chin went up a notch. "Do you think you're the only one around here who can be a hero?"

He almost grinned. "I'm no hero, Jo. I'm a madman. I know that."

She couldn't help smiling at him. "Keith, I told you a long time ago that we're two of a kind. I want to go, just as much as you do."

"You really do?"

"Like you said—it'll look good on my résumé."

"Yeah," he replied. It was nearly a sigh. "Okay, I'll put you down for our computer analyst. Better get over to the hospital for the physical checkup."

She got to her feet. "Thanks, Keith."

"You're crazy, you know."

"I know," she said. "Just like you."

He stood up too, but wouldn't come out from behind his desk. Jo went to the door and left his office, with him standing there watching her go.

"Jesus Christ, willya look at that!"

The TV newsman frowned at the helicopter pilot. "Keep a decent mouth," he said, more into his lip microphone than across the whining roar of the turbine engine.

"We won't be on the air for another twelve minutes," the pilot shot back, still staring down at the mammoth throngs streaming into Anaheim Stadium. As far as the eye could see, along the freeways stretching back toward Los Angeles and out beyond Disneyland, solid masses of cars inched along bumper to bumper.

"Where'd they get all the gas?" the pilot wondered.

The TV reporter lifted his tinted eyeglasses and rubbed at the bridge of his nose. "Look," he said to the pilot, "keep a decent mouth anyway, will ya? All we need is for a wrong word to sneak out on the air and we'll have all of *them* screaming for our scalps." He pointed downward, toward the cars.

The pilot shook his helmeted head. "I never seen a crowd like that. Where they gonna put them all?"

The reporter heard it as an awed whisper in his headset earphones. Turning in his seat, safety harness cutting into his fleshy shoulder, he looked across the early evening sky for the camera copter. It was skittering along the Orange Freeway, taping the incredible traffic for the eleven o'clock news.

The reporter reached forward to click the radio dial to the frequency that connected him with the camera ship.

"Harry, this is Jack. Can you hear me?"

"Yeah, Jack."

"How's the equipment?"

"Everything's A-okay here. Fine."

"Good. Now remember, in the middle of Wilson's spiel they're gonna douse all the lights so everybody can see the aurora. That's the shot I want—the stadium lit by the Lights from the Sky."

"I know. I'll get it."

"You sure?"

"I got the low light level snooperscope. Don't worry about a thing. It'll come out terrific."

"It better," the reporter said.

The stadium literally pulsed with the immense crowd. It was like a vast supernatural beast, breathing and murmuring in the gathering twilight. Row upon row, tier upon tier, the crowd filled every seat, jammed the cement stairways so that vendors couldn't get through to hawk their wares, stood shoulder to shoulder on the ramps behind the seats and down on the field surrounding the speaker's platform.

Off at one end of the huge oval, the mammoth scoreboard used for baseball games proclaimed in fluorescent lights, HOME OF THE ANGELS. A gigantic letter A, its apex circled by a glowing halo, stood out against the darkening sky.

Outside the stadium, still more thousands milled around the parking areas. Portable TV sets flickered on the tailgates of station wagons. Families picnicked amid the carbon monoxide fumes.

The night deepened and the activities began. The many-throated crowd roared and laughed and sang as it was prompted to by evangelists, guitar players, rock groups and politicians who followed each other up onto the makeshift wooden platform at the center of the field.

A former astronaut who had become deeply involved in studies of extrasensory and paranormal experiences came to the microphone and proclaimed, "This alien ambassador is bringing us our chance to join the brotherhood of the galaxies."

The crowd sighed with awe.

An evangelist, red-faced in the spotlight, exhorted the crowd, "This message from the Lord is a warning that we must mend our ways, atone for our sins and surrender our willful hearts to Christ Jesus, our God and our Savior."

Thousands fell to their knees, shouting praises and screaming for forgiveness.

"Let those who have scoffed at us," bellowed a noted UFOl-ogist, "come forward and admit that they were wrong! We are not alone, and we never have been!"

The crowd roared its approval.

Finally, after more hymns and clapping in time to a Gospel choir, after a deafening medley from an overamplified rock group, after full darkness had shrouded the brilliantly lit stadium, the loudspeakers solemnly proclaimed:

"Ladies and gentlemen, the man whose voice cried out in the wilderness, the harbinger of the Great Days to Come, the Urban Evangelist himself—WILLIE WILSON!"

Like a huge animal with a hundred thousand voices the crowd surged to its feet and bellowed as Willie Wilson, slim and lithe in a sky-blue denim suit, loped down the cleared path through the crowd on the field and up the wooden steps to the microphone.

I can't do it, he said to himself as he reached for the microphone. Feeling the power of the crowd around him, the fervent anticipation that electrified the air, he shook his head and told himself, I can't disappoint them. I can't let the government interfere with the Word of the Lord.

He raised both arms and turned slowly in the circle of light, soaking in the crowd's roaring approval. The bellow shook the ground.

High overhead, unnoticed in the glare of the stadium lights, the two TV helicopters circled endlessly, photographing the dramatic moment while the news reporter spoke his impromptu commentary into his microphone.

"Thank you all and God bless you, each and every single one of you," Willie shouted into the microphone, pulling it off its slender stand so that he could turn full circle and be seen by every part of the throng.

The crowd quieted, resumed its seats. Those on the field surrounding the platform remained standing, though.

"My message is a simple one," Willie began. "God loves you. Each and every single individual one of you. God knows each of you personally, individually, knows what's in your heart and in your mind. And He loves you. Each one of you. Despite your shortcomings. Despite your failures. The Lord God Jesus Christ loves *you*"—Willie pointed into the crowd—"and you, and you, and each and every one of you."

They murmured and sighed. A few scattered "Amens" rippled through the night.

"And because God loves us," Willie continued, "He has put a sign in the sky, to remind us of who He is and who we are . . . a sign that is at the same time a warning and a herald . . . a sign that is unmistakable." He paused dramatically, and a part of his mind told him that the IRS would be on his back within twenty-four hours.

"Look to the sky!" Willie proclaimed. "And see the glory of the Lord!"

Every light in the stadium winked off on cue and the crowd

gazed up into the sky. Not a sound from them. Moments ticked by in eerie silence as the huge throng stared into the darkness and the shimmering glow of the aurora slowly became visible to them.

They moaned. They gasped. They sobbed. Willie himself, watching the display from the platform, could feel the hairs on the back of his neck standing on end.

Don't drag it out too long, he reminded himself. Catch them right at the peak . . .

In that unnatural silence Willie heard a strange whining drone, the *whicker-whicker-whicker* of helicopter rotors. Turning toward the sound, he saw the blinking running lights of a low-flying chopper as it made a pass over the stadium.

"It's them!" somebody screamed.

"They're here!"

"They've come! They've come!"

The vast animal of the crowd surged and panicked. Before Willie understood what was happening, a human wave broke across the stadium. People shrieked and screamed and ran.

"No, wait!" Willie shouted into the microphone. "It's nothing to be afraid of . . ."

But the animal was mindless with terror. People were being trampled at the jammed exits. Others jumped from ledges to get away. The wave of terrified beasts broke across the wooden platform, swarmed over it; the platform swayed, sagged, groaned and collapsed into a sea of screaming, trampling, bloody panic.

And beneath it all, among the splintered planks and thundering, stampeding feet, Willie Wilson lay inert as maddened people tripped over his prostrate form and went down on top of him.

WILSON, 126 OTHERS KILLED IN PANIC

ANAHEIM: Rev. Willie Wilson was among 127 persons killed last night when panic swept the overcrowded Anaheim Stadium. More than 3,000 were injured.

Rev. Wilson, the Urban Evangelist, was the featured speaker in the mammoth outdoor revival rally. Police said that the stadium was filled well beyond legal capacity for the meeting that brought together many of the nation's leading fundamentalists, UFOlogists, researchers in the occult and religionists of more orthodox faiths.

The panic was apparently triggered, according to police, when a television camera helicopter swooped low over the stadium, causing some to believe that an alien UFO was about to land. The huge crowd panicked and thousands were trampled in the rush for the exits.

Rev. Wilson, who repeatedly associated the aurorae caused by the alien spacecraft now approaching the Earth with a message from God, was born . . .

CHAPTER 36

Markov sat in moody silence on the darkened porch of the bungalow. A mosquito whined near his ear but he paid no attention to it.

Go ahead and drink my blood, he said silently. You won't be the only one.

The front door creaked slightly as Maria opened it. She came out and sat on the other end of the wicker couch, as far from Markov as she could get.

"Well?" he asked.

For several seconds she made no reply. Then she said flatly, "I have sent my report to Moscow. I told them that Cavendish committed suicide and I then destroyed the apparatus to avoid any possibility that the Americans might discover it."

"Did you tell them that you wish to retire from the service?"

"Certainly not!"

"Did you ask for a transfer to a branch that doesn't get involved in these hideous things?"

"Kir," she said, "I've told you a thousand times, our branch normally does not deal with undercover agents and interrogations. It's only this . . . this alien *thing* that's forced us into this situation."

"I want you out of the KGB, Maria Kirtchatovska," Markov said. "I want you to be the wife of a university professor and nothing more."

She turned toward him and in the dim light from the window he could see the stubborn expression on her face. "You'd enjoy that, wouldn't you? I sit home and collect a retirement pension while you spend each night with a different college girl. A wonderful life! For you."

"Do you believe that torturing people and killing them is such a good way to live?"

"I never did anything like that!"

He slapped his hands against his thighs and got to his feet. "Maria, you are lying. Lying to me, and even lying to yourself. If you can live with what you've been doing, so be it. But *I* can't live with it. I can not live with it!"

"You've been living with it for nearly twenty years," she countered.

Looking down at her, he said, "Yes, I've been keeping my eyes closed for twenty years. Now they are open."

"What do you want of me?" Maria asked. Her voice was different, no longer hard and stubborn, almost openly pleading.

"I told you what I want."

"I *can't* retire," she said. "They'd never allow it. Don't you realize what's happening these days? With the General Secretary ailing and the Presidium going through earthquakes?"

"The only other thing I can do is divorce you," Markov said.

"Divorce? After all these years?"

"I can't live with what you're doing," he said. "I know you're trying to prevent Stoner from getting to fly on the rendezvous mission. The man is my friend, Maria. If you harm him, you put yourself against me."

She sighed heavily. "Kir, you're going to end up teaching school in some prison town in the Gulag."

Markov nodded in the darkness. Glancing out at the shimmering sky, he said slowly, so softly that he could barely hear it himself, "There is one other possibility."

"What other possibility?"

"I could stay with the Americans . . . ask for asylum."

He heard her gasp with shock. "Defect? Leave Russia forever? Turn your back on your own people, your own nation?"

"I don't want to do that, but . . ."

"They'd kill you, Kirill Vasilovsk." Maria's voice was metal-hard, as matter-of-fact as an automatic pistol. "I'd kill you myself before I'd let you do that to us."

When Stoner looked up from the work on his desk he saw that out beyond his window it was night. Even through the panes, though, the shimmering, beckoning lights made the sky dance.

He glanced at his wristwatch, then on impulse reached for the phone. It took a few minutes to track her down through the island's central switchboard, but finally he heard Jo's voice:

"Hello?"

"It's Keith Stoner, Jo."

"Oh. Hello, Keith."

Suddenly he felt schoolboy awkward. "Um . . . have you had your dinner yet?"

"An hour ago."

"Oh."

"Are you still at your office?"

"Yeah. There's a lot to do . . ."

"And you haven't had anything to eat since lunch?"

"No."

She said, "Well, you'd better get down to Pete's place. He's the only one who stays open after nine. I'll meet you there."

"But you said you've already eaten."

She hesitated only a second. "I'll have some dessert with you. Okay?"

"Sure. Fine."

An hour later, as they left the seedy like restaurant, Jo said: "Remind me to stick to Jell-O next time."

"The cake was no good?" he asked.

"It must have been left here by the Japs after World War Two, it was so stale."

He laughed.

Automatically they walked across the empty street, between buildings, heading for the beach. They walked side by side, not touching, but close enough for Stoner to feel the warmth of her. Jo was wearing a dress, a light sleeveless flowered frock that caught the warm, scented sea breeze.

"Keith . . . answer a question for me?"

"If I can," he said.

"Why is this rendezvous misson so important to you? I mean, why do *you* have to make the flight?"

He looked down at her. "Christ, Jo, you ought to understand that. You'd feel the same way, wouldn't you?"

"I *do* feel the same way," she said earnestly. "But I don't understand why. What's driving us? Why do you have to go? Why do I want to go?"

He thought about it as they stepped clear of the buildings and out under the trees that fringed the beach. The sand lay white and warm, the surf murmured distantly to them.

Finally, Stoner answered, "It's my career, Jo. The path I've chosen. The work I do."

"No," she said. "There's more to it than that. It's not a job, it's . . . it's a drive. A fierceness to get into space and leave everything else behind."

"I've got nothing to keep me here," he said. Then, before she could reply, he added, "Except you."

Jo put a hand on his arm. "But even . . . no, Keith, that's not true. You still want to go out there and meet this alien visitor, no matter what, don't you?"

"Of course."

"Why? Why does it have to be you, personally?"

"Because I want to *know*," he said with quiet ferocity. "That's what every scientist wants—to know, to discover, to be the first to uncover a new piece of knowledge, a new chunk of territory."

"But you could learn that even if somebody else goes on the mission," she said.

"Not the same! I want to touch it with my own hands, see it with my own eyes. Like a caveman, Jo. Like Doubting Thomas from the Bible. I've got to see it for myself. That's the bang of it. The drive."

She stared up at his face as they walked along the beach. The sky was lit by the aurora, gleaming, dancing, calling.

"Think about all the people you know," Stoner said to her. "How many of them realize that the atoms of their bodies were created inside distant stars? We're all stardust, every one of us. Every atom of your body, Jo, was built up inside a star, eons ago. We're part of the universe, kid. It's inescapable."

She laughed softly. "There's a poet inside you, somewhere."

"Maybe," he admitted. "But there's a practical side to all this, too. Down here, I'm just another astrophysicist. An overtrained specialist in a field that's filled with men and women who're better trained, younger and brighter than I am. I'm only a mediocre scientist, at best."

"Now you're being modest."

"I know my limitations. I'll never get close to a Nobel Prize or a fat fellowship. I'll plug along and teach at some second-rate university in total obscurity."

"Unless . . ."

"Unless the space program opens up again." He jabbed a thumb skyward. "I'm good up there. I can lead a team of engineers and scientists. I know both ends of the job and I'm not afraid of living inside a pressure suit at zero gravity."

"I don't think I'd be afraid, either."

Grinning, "No, I don't think you would, Jo. It's our milieu, or ecological niche. That's where my career lies, and maybe yours, too. That's where we can make the best contributions to the human race's storehouse of knowledge."

"And that's where the alien is."

"Yes. Like a godsend. We can't let him pass us by without making contact with him."

"Or her," Jo kidded.

"It," he said.

Jo laughed and suddenly kicked off her sandals. "Come on, take those shoes off, Keith Stoner. Break down and have fun for once in your life."

He frowned at her. "I have fun . . ."

"You call chopping boards with your hands *fun?*" And she dashed away from him, down along the beach, bare feet splashing in the lapping waves.

Stoner watched her for a few moments, then bent down and yanked off his shoes and socks, nearly tumbling onto the sand as he hopped on one foot to finish the job. Then he raced after her, under the glowing sky.

He splashed along the waters of the lagoon, laughing as he caught up with her. Grabbing her by the wrist, Stoner hauled her along at his pace until she shrieked with breathless laughter and they both collapsed onto the shining sand.

"Keith, you're not fair," she panted. "Your legs . . . are so much longer . . ."

"Oh, jeez, you make me feel like a kid again, Jo. You make me forget everything else and want to play."

He raised himself up on one elbow and lifted her head toward him. Jo wound her arms around his neck and felt his hands caressing her, warm, strong hands against her bare skin. She could hear the pulsing beat of the distant surf against the reef, but it was quickly lost in the thunder of her own heart. Eagerly they pulled their clothes off and she pressed her naked body against his, wanting him, wanting all of him inside her. She clutched his hair and stifled the scream of ecstasy inside her by pressing her lips against his.

Then they lay side by side, spent, watching the shimmering curtains of pastel lights that flickered across the sky while the warm, tideless waves of the calm lagoon lapped at their feet.

Jo turned her head on the sand and saw Keith staring a million miles off into that sky.

He forgot everything else for such a little while, she thought sadly. Such a little while.

"And why is the General Secretary not present?" asked the Minister of Industrial Production.

Borodinski, seated at the head of the long, polished table, replied, "He is indisposed. He asked me to preside over this meeting in his place."

They glanced at each other uneasily. Of the sixteen places around the table, five were conspicuously empty. Their usual occupants would never see the inside of the Kremlin again.

Borodinski introduced Academician Bulacheff, sitting at the very foot of the table, and opened the discussion on the topic of the alien spacecraft.

"Then we are going through with this scheme of sending cosmonauts to greet the alien?" asked the Foreign Minister.

"It is the General Secretary's plan," Borodinski said.

"But with an American astronaut aboard *our* Soyuz?" grumbled the Minister of Internal Security. He sat close to the head of the table, but the chairs on either side of him were empty.

"Yes," said Borodinski.

"He'll be able to spy on our launch facilities, our rocket boosters—everything!"

"He is no spy," said Bulacheff, his voice surprisingly strong. "He is a scientist, not a hoodlum."

Dead silence fell over the conference room. Borodinski barely suppressed a laugh. The academician is too new to these meetings to show the proper respect for our chief pesticide, he thought. Then he reflected, Or he is old enough so that he doesn't care about running the risks, perhaps? This alien visitor must be very important to him.

The Security Minister glared at Bulacheff, then leaned back in his chair and slowly put a long, filtered cigarette to his lips.

"We will fly out to meet the spacecraft," Borodinski said firmly, "and the American will be aboard our

Soyuz. Every precaution will be taken, of course, to see to it that he does not gain any information that we do not wish him to have."

General Rashmenko grinned heartily at them all. "Not to worry. Our missiles can blow the alien out of the sky—and the American with it. All I have to do is make one phone call."

CHAPTER 37

The Minister of Internal Security held the wine glass up to the light from the chandelier. The deep red liquid glowed within the crystal goblet. Slowly, cautiously, he took an experimental sip of the wine.

With a smack of his lips he put the goblet down on the damask tablecloth and pronounced, "Excellent. Truly excellent!"

His host, across the table from him, beamed with satisfaction. "It's from our comrades in Hungary. They call it 'The Blood of the Bull.'"

The Minister laughed. "A dramatic people, the Hungarians."

"But they make good wine," said his host, nodding to the servant standing behind the Minister.

The servant began ladling a stew of freshly caught rabbit into the Minister's china plate. The Minister was a small, bald man, with the tiny, delicate hands of a watchmaker. But his face was heavy, almost gross, with thick lips, a bulbous nose and narrow deepset eyes that were often impossible to fathom.

His host, the director of one of Internal Security's biggest bureaus, was by contrast an elegant figure: tall, suavely handsome with silver hair and an aristocratic, almost ascetic face, soft-spoken, with the polished manners of a born gentleman.

By the time dessert was served, the Minister was in a relaxed, almost happy mood.

"Ah, Vasilli Ilyitch, it's difficult to believe that this magnificent home is actually in Moscow, here, today, now. I always feel as if

I've been transported to some other time, when life was more gracious, easier."

"Before the Revolution, Comrade Minister?" the bureaucrat asked mildly, a slight smile touching his lips.

The Minister's look suddenly turned cold.

"Or perhaps," the bureaucrat continued, "you are experiencing a premonition, a view into the future, when true communism rules the world and all the peoples everywhere can live in peace and luxury."

"That's better," the Minister said sourly. "Your sense of humor will get you in trouble some day, Vasilli."

His smile broadened. "I always thought that it was my sense of luxury that will someday be my downfall."

Now the Minister grinned. "Come now, my old friend! Life is grim enough without us becoming morose."

"True enough! Come with me into the library. I have a cognac there that will interest you."

An hour later, the Minister was relaxed in a deep leather chair, snifter in one hand, cigar in the other, his face scowling.

"To talk to me like that," he was muttering. "That academic pipsqueak. That . . . that . . . *schoolteacher!*"

"Academician Bulacheff?" his host asked.

"Bulacheff," the Minister snapped. "In front of the others, too."

"But the General Secretary did not attend the meeting."

"He's at death's door. Borodinski sat in his chair."

"H'mm. Borodinski."

"Yes, I know what you're thinking," the Minister said.

His host became quite serious. "You, comrade, have the power of life or death over Borodinski. You realize that, don't you?"

"I wouldn't state it quite that way."

"But it is true, nevertheless. Borodinski wants you on his side. If you agree, he is safe. If you join the others . . ."

"There aren't that many others to join," the Minister pointed out. "Borodinski's being very thorough."

"What will you do?"

The Minister puffed for a moment on his cigar, then, "What can I do, except go along with him? I have no desire to see the struggle deepen. We are safe. Borodinski won't interfere with us."

"You're certain?"

The Minister smiled, but there was nothing pleasant to it. "You needn't worry, my dear friend. Borodinski is clever enough to avoid a fight with me, if I don't oppose him. I will keep the ministry, and you can keep your fine house, and servants, and wine cellar."

"And you," the bureaucrat added in a whisper.

"Yes, and me too."

The bureaucrat smiled boyishly and took another sip of his cognac.

"But the alien," the Minister said. "That's another matter. I will *not* have Americans snooping around Tyuratam, not without teaching them all a lesson."

"But Americans saw Tyuratam years ago, during the joint Soyuz-Apollo operation."

"That was then. This is now. I won't have Bulacheff or even Borodinski going over my head in matters of internal security."

"But what can you do? The Americans are already on their way here."

"Yes, I know. I can't stop them from arriving in Tyuratam. But I can prevent them from achieving their goal. They will never make contact with that alien spacecraft. I will see to that, and Borodinski will know that I did it, and he will be powerless to oppose me."

His host let out a long, low sigh. "You play for very high stakes."

"Borodinski must understand that I will not oppose him, but he must not oppose me, either. This matter of the alien spacecraft and the American astronaut is a good way to teach him that lesson. Practically painless for him, but obvious."

"Yes, I see. But how will you go about . . . eh, teaching him this lesson?"

The Minister took a long gulp of cognac, put down his emptied glass and said harshly, "How? Kill the American astronaut, of course. What could be simpler?"

Stoner spent his last afternoon on Kwajalein in a round of meetings with Thompson, Tuttle, the Russians, the full conference room of group leaders. Then, suddenly, he was back in his office alone.

He stood at his desk and surveyed the room. As impersonal as a telephone booth. One by one he opened the drawers of his desk. There was nothing in them that he needed, nothing that he wanted to take with him, nothing that was *his*.

Then his eyes lit on the absurd coconut resting beside the telephone. He broke into a slow grin.

"You," he said to the shaggy brown lopsided sphere, "are going on a long, long journey."

"I know it."

Startled, he looked up and saw Jo leaning against the doorjamb.

His grin turned to embarrassment. "Uh . . . I've taken to talking to coconuts. Sign of nervousness, I guess."

"You don't look nervous to me," Jo said, stepping into the office. She was wearing her usual cutoffs and half-unbuttoned blouse. Her skin was a deep olive brown. A quizzical smile touched the corners of her mouth.

"Iron self-control," Stoner muttered.

"Are you all packed?" she asked.

"Just about. What about you? You're not going aboard the plane in those clothes, are you?"

"Of course not," she said. "I just thought I'd take one final stroll along the beach before dinner. Plenty of time to change and catch the plane."

He nodded. "Well, I'm sure not going to miss the food here."

She reached out for his arm. "Come on, take a walk with me. Let's say good-by to the island together."

They walked barefoot, arm in arm, along the wave-lapped beach, toes digging into the warm sand, long shadows thrown ahead of them in the red glow of the dying day.

Out beyond the lagoon and the tiny fringe of islands rimming it, the sun was sinking into the ocean, turning the whole world the color of molten gold. Birds crossed the cloud-streaked sky, calling, calling.

"Our last sunset on Kwajalein," Jo said, clasping Stoner's arm in both of hers.

"We never got much of a chance to enjoy this beauty, did we?" he asked.

"There's a lot we've never had a chance to do," she replied. "A lot of living."

"I know."

"When this is over, Keith, when our lives settle down into something more ordinary . . ."

"Will they?"

"They've got to," she said. "Don't you think so?"

"I don't know. The alien changes everything so much . . . who can tell what's going to happen?"

She turned and put her arms around him and leaned her cheek against his shoulder. "Keith, please don't go through with it. I'm scared of this rocket mission."

He breathed in the scent of her hair. "Scared? You? I thought you wanted to be an astronaut."

"I wouldn't be afraid if I was going," she said. "But I'm scared to death for you."

He laughed, but she could feel his body tense. "Reynaud thinks the Russians are out to kill me."

"You see?" Jo pulled away slightly and looked into his eyes. "I'm not the only one."

"I've talked to Kirill about it. It's nonsense."

"Did he say it was?"

"Sort of."

"What do you mean, sort of? Did he laugh it off or take it seriously?"

Stoner waggled a hand. "Kind of in between."

"Keith, you *are* in danger from them. I can feel it."

"I'm going to be a guest of the Russian Government. We all will be. They wouldn't dare do anything."

"You're being stubborn," she said. "And stupid."

"Kirill's going to look out for me."

She raised her hands to the heavens. "Some bodyguard. He can't even paddle a canoe!"

Stoner laughed.

"Don't do it, Keith. Please. Let the Russians send their own cosmonauts to rendezvous with the alien. Stay on the ground with the rest of us."

"No," he said.

"Keith, I'm scared for you! I'm frightened!"

"I know you are," he said, "but it doesn't matter. I'm a heartless sonofabitch, okay? But this is more important to me than anything else. It's my *life*. Can you understand that? More important to me than my kids, than you, than anything or anyone else. I've got to do it. I *need* to do it. I'd walk through fire to get to it."

Jo said nothing. Her chin fell. She stared down at the sand at their feet.

"Am I wrong to feel this way? Am I some kind of a monster?"

"Yes," she answered softly. "You know you're putting yourself in danger. But you turn your back on every human emotion, every human need. The only thing you want is to go out there and make this flight, even though you know they're going to kill you over it."

"What can I say?" he wondered. "So I'm a monster, after all."

"Not a monster, Keith," she replied. "A machine. An automated, self-programmed machine. I saw the way you battered Schmidt. He was an animal, but you were a machine. An inhuman, tireless, unemotional machine. Nothing can stand in your way. You drive over every obstacle, anything that gets in your way. Mac, Schmidt, the whole goddamned Navy . . . even your own children. None of us can hold you back."

"That's what you think of me?" Stoner's voice was a strangled whisper. His insides felt cold and empty.

"That's what you are, Keith," Jo said, struggling to keep her own voice calm, untrembling.

For a long moment he said nothing. Then, "Okay. We'd better get back. I still have some packing to do."

"Right. Me too."

They walked in cold silence and Stoner left her at the entrance to the hotel. Jo watched him stride away, stiff with pride or anger or pain, and she realized that he did have emotions and vulnerabilities.

But he doesn't care about me, she also realized. There's no way that I can make him care about me.

Then she hurried inside, ran upstairs to her room and shut the door tightly behind her.

There can be little reasonable doubt that, ultimately, we will come into contact with races more intelligent than our own. That contact may be one-way, through the discovery of ruins or artifacts; it may be two-way, over radio or laser circuits; it may even be face to face. But it will occur, and it may be the most devastating event in the history of mankind. The rash assertion that "God created man in His own image" is ticking like a time bomb at the foundations of many faiths . . .

ARTHUR C. CLARKE
Voices from the Sky
Harper & Row
1965

CHAPTER 38

The Ilyushin jet transport was noisy and uncomfortable despite the fact that only two dozen passengers rode in its cavernous cabin.

Stoner sat up front, staring out a window at the endless expanse of steppe: nothing but grass, as far as the eye could see. Not a tree, not a town, not even a village. This must be what the American plains looked like before the farmers covered it with corn and wheat, he thought.

The plane rode smoothly enough at this high altitude. If only the seats weren't so crammed together, Stoner complained silently. The only rough part of the flight had been when they'd crossed the Roof of the World, passing close enough to Everest to see its lofty snow-plumed peak, then across craggy Tibet and the wild Altai Mountains. Stoner imagined that far off in the distance he could see Afghanistan, where the hill tribesmen still fought for the independence, as they had fought against the armies of Alexander the Great.

Across the cramped aisle from Stoner, Professor Zworkin

snored fitfully. The others were scattered around the long cabin. Jo had taken a seat far in the rear, he knew.

His stomach rumbled. Food service aboard the flight was non-existent. They had been fed once when the jet had landed at Vladivostok, and then once again, many hours later, at the refueling stop near Tashkent. Neither time had any of the passengers been allowed to step off the plane.

They had crossed the wild hill country where Kazakh horsemen still dressed in furs and conical felt hats and rode stubby ponies after their herds of sheep and goats. Now the grassland, the eternal steppe, with the city of Baikanur coming up and beyond it, the rocket-launching base of Tyuratam.

Stoner sensed someone leaning over him and turned in his seat. It was Markov, an odd little half-smile on his bearded face.

"We enter the country the same way our revered Lenin did, in 1917," Markov said, nearly shouting to be heard over the thundering vibration of the jet engines.

"Lenin flew in?"

Markov lowered his lanky body into the seat next to Stoner's. "No, the Germans sent him into Mother Russia in a sealed train. No stops, no one allowed on or off until it reached Petrograd. We fly in from the other direction, in a sealed airplane."

Stoner tapped the window with a fingernail. "It's a big country out there, your Mother Russia."

"Oh, this isn't Russia," Markov corrected. "It's Kazakhstan, a Federated Republic, part of the Soviet Union. But not Russia. These people are Asians . . . Mongols. Russia is another thousand kilometers to the west, on the other side of the Ural Mountains."

"But it's part of your country."

Nodding, "Yes, just as Puerto Rico is part of the United States."

Stoner looked out the window again. "Pretty damned big. And it looks untouched . . . raw."

"Much of the Soviet Union is still virgin land," Markov said. "It was Khrushchev's dream to cultivate such lands, make them yield rich harvests."

"What happened?"

Markov's grin turned sardonic. "He was outvoted . . . while his back was turned."

"Oh."

"They allowed him a peaceful retirement, though. He died of natural causes. Very unusual for a Russian leader. A sign of our growing civilization."

Stoner asked, "Are you laughing or crying, Kirill?"

With a shrug, Markov said, "Some of both, my friend. Some of both. I feel like a life-sentence prisoner returning to jail after a brief escape. It's hateful, but it's home."

"I should've talked you into staying at Kwajalein," Stoner said, lowering his voice even though the drone of the engines made it impossible to hear anything a few feet away.

"No, no," Markov protested. "This is where I belong. This is where I should be."

Stoner searched the Russian's face. "You really believe that?"

Markov closed his ice-blue eyes and nodded gravely. "I have talked about it at some length with Maria. We are going to try to work things out between us. She will put in for a transfer to a . . . a less demanding job." His boyish grin returned. "If I can make *her* more human, easier to live with, perhaps there is hope for the rest of the Russians as well."

Stoner sensed there was much more going on in Markov's marriage than the Russian was willing to talk about.

"In the meantime," Markov went on, "all of us here will act as your bodyguard. You are part of us, and we are part of you. You will get to fly into space, never fear."

"That's all I ask," Stoner said.

Markov's face grew serious. "I know there has been talk about a Russian plot against you."

"Kirill, I never thought that you or anyone among us . . ."

"Not to worry," he said, raising a hand to silence Stoner. "I will be in communication with Academician Bulacheff the instant we land at Tyuratam. This project will go through without interference, I promise you."

"Okay," Stoner said. "Fine."

"We are not pawns in some international power game," Markov muttered darkly. "The government will treat us—all of us—with some respect."

"Do you really think you can change the system that much, Kirill?"

Shaking his head slightly, Markov said, "It isn't necessary to change the system, as much as it is to get the bureaucrats to *return* to the system, to use it honestly and fairly. The Russian people are a good, hard-working people. They have suffered much, endured much. We must return to the true principles of Marx and Lenin. We must return to the road that leads inevitably to a truly just and happy society."

"That's a big job," Stoner said.

"Yes, but I have help," Markov said. "Our alien is going to help me."

"How?"

With an absentminded tug at his beard, Markov said, "Look at what the alien has already accomplished. Not merely for me, but for you as well. America and Russia are co-operating—in a limited way, to be sure, but co-operating in the midst of confrontations on almost every other front."

Stoner countered, "Then why wouldn't they let us off this airplane? They're co-operating so well that they're afraid we'd steal something if we set foot on their ground."

"Do you realize how great a strain it is on our national paranoia to allow Americans to come to our premier rocket base? And two Chinese scientists?"

"I suppose so, but . . ."

"Our alien visitor has already forced all the governments of the world to change their habits of thought."

"An inch," said Stoner.

"Perhaps only a centimeter," Markov granted, "but still it is a change. They can never think again of our world as the whole universe. They are being forced to work together to find out who this alien visitor is. Never again can we think of other human beings, other human nations or races, as being truly alien. Our visitor from space is forcing us to accept the truth that all humans are brothers."

"Jesus Christ," Stoner muttered. "Scratch a Russian and he bleeds philosophy."

"Yes," said Markov. "And pious philosophy, at that. But mark my words, dear friend. This alien will bring us all closer together."

"I hope you're right, Kirill."

"It has already done so! It has made friends of us, hasn't it?"

Stoner nodded.

"It has been a good friendship, Keith." Markov's eyes got watery. "I am proud to have you for a friend, Keith Stoner. You are a good man. If necessary, I would lay down my life for you."

For several moments, Stoner didn't know what to say. "Hey, Kirill, I feel the same way about you. But this isn't the end of our friendship, it's only the beginning."

"I hope so." Markov sighed. "But once we land, neither my life nor yours will be completely under our own control. Events will catch us up and carry us on their shoulders. And, certainly, I may never get the chance to leave Russia again, to see you or any other foreigners."

The realization caught Stoner by surprise. He heard himself answer, "And I might never come back from the rendezvous mission."

"Ah," Markov said, "I hadn't even thought about that possibility."

Stoner took a deep breath.

"There is one thing I can promise you, though," Markov said before Stoner could think of anything.

"What's that?"

"You will get to go on the rendezvous mission. No one will stop you from going. That I promise."

Stoner nodded and smiled and told himself, He means what he's saying, but he's got no way of keeping that promise.

Markov nodded back, eyes misting again, and wordlessly got up to head back for his own seat.

Turning back to the window to watch the endless empty steppe, Stoner soon drifted off to sleep. He was jolted out of the doze by the plane's sudden lurching and the loud banging noise of the landing gear being lowered. The plane shuddered and banked hard over until the grassy ground seemed to tilt upward to meet them.

It sounded as if a gale was blowing through the cabin. As he pulled his seat belt tighter, Stoner saw that Zworkin, across the aisle, was very much awake now and clutching the arms of his chair with white-knuckled terror.

Then the plane straightened out, lurching and bumping

through the early evening twilight as the pilot lined it up for the final approach to the airfield. Stoner looked out the window and his jaw dropped open.

Tyuratam.

It was like the skyline of Manhattan, except that these were not buildings, but gantry towers. Steel spiderworks for holding and launching rockets. Miles of them! Stoner saw, gaping. One after another, a whole city full of rocket-launching towers. It made Cape Canaveral look like a flimsy suburban development, modest in scale and temporary in endurance. This was built to last. Like Pittsburgh, like Gary, like the acres upon acres of factories in major industrial centers, Tyuratam was a solid, ongoing, workaday complex of giant buildings, vast machines, hardworking people.

Their business was launching rockets. Their industry was astronautics. The place was a port, like fabled Basra of the *Arabian Nights,* like modern Marseille or New York or Shanghai. Ships sailed out of this port on long, bellowing tongues of flame, heading for destinations in space, bringing back new riches of knowledge.

And someday, Stoner knew, they'll bring back energy, and raw materials, and they'll start building factories up there in orbit.

But for now they probed the uncharted seas of space for knowledge, for safe harbors where satellites could orbit and relay information back to Earth.

The plane edged lower. Stoner could see spotlights blooming around one launch pad, where a tall silvery rocket stood locked in the steel embrace of a gantry tower.

That's a Soyuz launcher, he realized. That's the bird I'm going to fly on.

He did not notice, far off on the other side of the vast complex of towers and rockets, two other boosters standing side by side. They were painted a dull military olive-gray, and were topped by blunt-nosed warheads of megaton death.

CHAPTER 39

Stoner sat hunched over the gray sheet of paper, ball-point pen hesitating in midair. So far he had written:

Mr. Douglas Stoner
28 Rainbow Way
Palo Alto, CA 94302
Dear Son:

How are you? If you've been following the news at all, I guess you know by now that I'm in Russia, about to take off on a space mission to meet the alien spacecraft—if that's possible. The Russians have made us very comfortable here. They put us up in a kind of barracks—sort of like a dormitory. We each have a small room to ourselves. Not that I spend much time in it.

For the past few weeks I've been working very hard with the Russian cosmonauts and launch team. You should have seen them trying to fit me into one of their pressure suits! I'm taller and slimmer than most of the cosmonauts and they had to do some fast custom tailoring to fit me. And their medical people have been all over me; you might think I was the alien the way they've been checking me out!

Everyone here has been very good to us although we are restricted to this barracks building and the few other buildings where we do our work. The Russians don't like us roaming around. I suppose we would be equally careful with foreign visitors at Kennedy SFC in Florida.

There are eleven other foreign scientists here, in addition to

He put the pen down. What difference does that make? he asked himself. Doug wouldn't be interested in it.

Stoner pushed his chair back and stretched his arms over his head.

What the hell is Doug interested in? he wondered. He realized that he didn't know his own son; the boy was a stranger to him. And his younger daughter he knew even less.

With a snort of self-disgust he slammed the pen down on the wooden desk, got up and headed for the door. He walked slowly down the narrow hallway. All the other doors were closed. It was not late; dinner had ended less than an hour earlier.

But tomorrow's the big day, Stoner told himself. The final countdown. The launch.

Everything seemed unnaturally quiet. His previous launches, in America, had been livelier, busier. There were constant meetings, press conferences, get-togethers even late at night, news photographers poking their cameras at you.

Not here, he realized. No reporters. No photographers.

He went downstairs to the common room, where they ate their meals. One of the Chinese physicists was sitting in the leather chair in the corner, under the wall lamp, reading a book in Russian. Stoner nodded to him and the Chinese smiled back politely. His interpreter was gone and they could not converse.

Stoner looked over the round table in the middle of the room, scanned the mostly empty bookshelves, prowled restlessly toward the door of the kitchen and pushed it open.

Markov was bending over in front of the open refrigerator, peering into it.

"You had two helpings of dessert," Stoner said.

Markov straightened up. "So? Spying on me? Well, I can't help it. When I'm nervous, I eat. I must keep up my blood sugar, you know."

"It was damned good baklava," Stoner admitted. "At least the cooking here is first-rate."

"Do you want some? That is, if there's any left?"

"No." Stoner shook his head. "When *I'm* nervous I can't eat."

Markov looked at him. "You, nervous? You look so calm, so relaxed."

"I've got the jumps inside."

With a disappointed sigh Markov closed the refrigerator. "It's all gone," he said. "Strange, I could have sworn there was some left."

"Like Captain Queeg's strawberries," Stoner said.

"Who?"

"Never mind."

They drifted back into the common room. The Chinese physicist had left, but one of the Russians had taken the leather chair and turned on the radio on the bookshelf. Classical piano music filled the room.

"Is that Tchaikovsky?" Stoner asked.

Markov gave him a stern professorial glance. "That," he said firmly, "is Beethoven. The 'Pathétique Sonata.'"

Stoner refused to be cowed. "Tchaikovsky wrote a Pathétique too, didn't he?"

"A symphony. It requires at least a hundred musicians and almost an hour's time. Really, Keith, for a civilized man . . ."

"I just thought a Russian station would play only Russian composers."

Markov began to reply, then realized that his leg was being pulled. He laughed.

"Come on," Stoner said. "Let's see if we can find some coffee."

"Aren't you supposed to refrain from stimulants tonight?" Markov asked. "I thought the medical . . ."

Stoner raised a finger to silence him. "That muscular fellow sitting in the corner is one of your medical team," he said in a pleasant lighthearted tone. The Russian paid no attention to them. "He's going to stick a needle in me the size of the Alaska Pipeline, right at eleven o'clock. But until then, I'll eat and drink what I want."

"I have vodka in my room," Markov said.

"That's going too far. Coffee won't blur me tomorrow. Vodka could."

They went back into the kitchen and Stoner started a pot of coffee brewing. The strains of Beethoven filtered through the kitchen door.

"I have been thinking," Markov said as he sat at the kitchen table, chin in hand, "about a British philosopher—Haldane."

"J. B. S. Haldane? He was a biologist, wasn't he?"

"A geneticist, I believe. And a Marxist. He was a member of the British Communist Party in the nineteen-thirties."

"So?"

"He once said, 'The universe is not only stranger than we imagine; it is stranger than we *can* imagine.'"

Stoner frowned, turned to the coffeepot perking on the stove, then looked back at Markov.

"Don't you see what it means?" the Russian asked. "You're going to risk your life tomorrow and fly off to this alien spacecraft. But suppose, when you reach it . . ."

"*If* we reach it," Stoner heard himself mutter. It surprised him.

"If and when you reach it," Markov granted, "suppose it's

something beyond human comprehension? Suppose you can't make head or tail of it?"

Stoner took a potholder and pulled the coffeepot off the stove. He stepped over to the table and poured coffee into the two strangely delicate china cups that seemed to be the only kind the kitchen stocked. Beethoven's Pathétique flowed into its second movement.

"Do you hear that?" Stoner asked, gesturing with the steaming coffeepot.

"The music? Yes, of course."

"A human being created that. A human mind. Other human minds have played it, recorded it, broadcast it over the air so that we can hear it. We're listening to the thoughts of a German musician who's been dead for more than a century and a half."

"What has that to do with the alien?" Markov asked.

"An alien mind built that spacecraft . . ."

"A mind we may not be able to comprehend," said the Russian.

"But that spacecraft follows the same laws of physics that we *do* comprehend. It moves through space just like any spacecraft that we ourselves have built."

"And sets off the Northern Lights all around the planet."

"Using electromagnetic techniques that we don't understand— yet. But we'll learn. We have the ability to understand."

"I wonder if we do."

Stoner put the coffeepot down on the table.

"Don't you see, Kirill? We do. We *do!* Why do you think I want to go out there? So I can be overawed by something I can't fathom? So I can worship the goddamned aliens? Hell no! I want to see, to learn, to *understand.*"

"And if you can't? If it's beyond comprehension?"

Stoner shook his head stubbornly. "There is nothing in the universe that we can't understand—given time enough to study it."

"That is your belief."

"That is my religion. The same religion as Einstein: 'The eternal mystery of the universe is its comprehensibility.'"

Markov grinned at him. "Americans are optimists by nature."

"Not by nature," Stoner corrected. "By virtue of historical fact. The optimists always win in the long run."

"Well, my optimistic friend, I hope you are right. I hope that this alien is friendly and helpful. I wouldn't want to have to bow down to someone who isn't even human."

They walked back into the common room, coffee cups in hand. The Russian medical technician sitting in the corner looked up at them, pointed to his wristwatch and said something to Markov.

"He wants to remind you that you get your shot at eleven."

Stoner made a smile for the technician. "Tell him I appreciate his sadistic concern and I'd like to take his needle and stick it up his fat ass."

The technician smiled and nodded as Markov spoke to him in Russian.

Beethoven ended and the little oblong radio on the bookshelf started playing chamber music: gentle, civilized strings, abstract, mathematical.

"Bach, isn't it?" Stoner asked, taking one of the leather chairs that flanked the room's only couch.

Markov sighed. "Vivaldi."

The outside door banged open and Jo stamped into the room, making annoyed brushing motions across her arms.

"Mosquitoes," she said. "Big as jet fighters."

"One of the joys of the countryside," Markov said.

Jo wore jeans and a light sweater. She ran a hand through her hair as she complained, "They have those damned floodlights all around the building. You can't see the sky at all, and they won't let you walk past the lighted area."

"But look on the positive side," Markov suggested. "The floodlights attract the mosquitoes."

She laughed, despite herself, and came over toward the sofa. "I don't think I'll be able to sleep tonight. Too keyed up."

"Would you like some coffee?" Stoner asked.

"That'd just make it worse."

"A glass of hot tea, perhaps?" Markov offered. "Or some vodka."

"No alcohol. I've got to keep my head clear for tomorrow,

even if they won't let me actually get my hands on any of the hardware."

"Perhaps we could get our medical friend here to give you the shot he's going to give Stoner. It puts you into a deep, relaxing sleep and then lets you wake up the next morning clear as a mountain lake."

"So they claim," Stoner put it.

"No thanks," Jo said. Looking at the technician, she asked, "Does he understand English?"

"No," Markov said. "Only Russian."

"Where's he from?"

Markov asked the technician, who smiled hugely for her, revealing a picket fence of stainless steel inlays, and answered with a long string of heartfelt words.

"He comes from a little village near Leningrad," Markov translated, "the most beautiful little village in all of Russia. He would love to show you how beautiful it is, especially in the springtime."

Jo smiled back at him, asking, "He's really a Russian, then? Not a Ukrainian or a Georgian or a Kazakh."

Markov glanced at the overweight, red-haired, fair-skinned medical technician. "He is quite Russian, I guarantee it. But why this interest in our federated nationalities?"

Turning back to Markov and Stoner, Jo answered, "I've been talking with some of the people around here—you know, guards, clerks, ordinary people."

"Not astronomers or linguists," Markov murmured.

Ignoring him, Jo went on, "A lot of the Russians here are kind of worried about the Kazakhs, and other non-Russian ethnic groups."

"Worried?" Stoner asked.

"The tide of Islam," Markov said in a bored tone. "Ever since Iran and Afghanistan, the major topic of gossip is the possibility of a native uprising. It's quite impossible, you know."

"An uprising," Jo said. "But what about sabotage? Suppose the people who used Schmidt use some Kazakh technician to tamper with the rocket booster tomorrow?"

Markov shook his head and raised his hands toward the ceiling. "No, no, no! Impossible. That's one thing that our security people have checked quite thoroughly. No one but Russian nationals has been allowed near the boosters. That, I promise you."

"Am I safe from all the Russian nationals?" Stoner asked.

For an instant, Markov did not answer. Then, one hand stroking his beard, he said very seriously, "Yes, you are. I am certain of it."

The two men looked at each other, eye to eye, for a long wordless moment.

"I think I would like some of that tea," Jo said, breaking their wordless deadlock.

"Allow me." Markov was instantly heading for the kitchen. "I will make you a glass of tea that will soothe your nerves and invigorate your spirit. Not like that dreadful sludge they call coffee. Phah! How can anyone drink that stuff regularly?"

Stoner laughed as Markov went through the kitchen door. He's leaving the two of us alone, he realized. Jo sat on the couch next to the shuttered window. The Russian technician stayed at his chair in the corner. Stoner went over and sat next to Jo.

"My last night on Earth," he said. Then he added, "For a week or so."

"Aren't you nervous?"

"Hell yes."

"You don't look it. You look perfectly calm."

"On the outside. Inside, everything's twitching. If you took an x-ray picture of me, it'd come out blurred, unless you used a stop-action shutter on the camera lens."

Jo laughed softly.

"I always get nervous before a flight, especially the last few minutes before lift-off. My heart rate goes way up."

"That's understandable," she said. Her face grew somber. "You can still back out of it, you know. The Russians have cosmonauts in reserve who . . ."

"I know," he said.

"You're not afraid of them trying to—to stop you?"

"Kirill's been watching over me like a St. Bernard."

"That's not enough . . ."

"And so have you," he added. "I've been watching you poking around, getting mosquito bites while you're checking out everybody around here."

She looked surprised. "I haven't . . . well, the two of us aren't enough of a bodyguard for you."

He reached out and clasped the back of her neck. "I appreciate it, Jo. I understand what you're doing and I appreciate it, really I do."

"Sure you do."

"I do. I hope you understand why I'm being so stubborn about all this."

Nodding, she answered, "Yes, I do understand, Keith. That's what frightens me. I'd be doing exactly the same thing, in your place. But I hate the fact that you're doing it, you're taking the chances with your life."

"That's the way it is," he said softly.

"And there's no changing it," she replied. "I know."

Markov came back into the room, holding a steaming glass of tea in each hand. The glasses were set into silvered holders. He hiked his eyebrows at the sight of Stoner and Jo side by side on the couch.

"Star-crossed lovers," he sighed. "How I envy you."

Stoner pulled his hand away from Jo and she reached for the handle of the glass that Markov offered her.

"Thank you, Kirill."

"For you, beautiful one, I would conquer China so that you would be assured of the best tea whenever you desired it."

She grinned at his flattery.

As Stoner sipped at his cooling coffee, the medical technician studied his wristwatch, hauled himself out of his chair and clicked off the little radio. The three of them watched him lumber back into the tiny office on the other side of the common room. Through the office window they could see him unlocking a medicine cabinet.

"Your hour has come," Markov said solemnly.

Stoner glanced at Jo. She was watching the technician as he removed a black plastic case from the cabinet.

"Nobody's been able to substitute poison for the tranquilizer they're going to give me," Stoner heard himself say.

Jo flicked her dark, anxious eyes to him. "I've been checking the cabinet all day. They've kept it locked."

Markov frowned but said nothing.

The four of them went up to Stoner's room, the technician in the lead. Stoner sat in his creaking desk chair and rolled up his shirt sleeve while Markov and Jo hovered beside him.

With elaborate care the technician fitted the syringe together and tested it. Stoner stared down at the unfinished letter to his son. Hastily, he scrawled:

I've got to go now. You'll probably see the flight on TV. I hope to see you and Elly soon. Please write, and ask your sister to write, too. I love you both very much.

He signed his name, folded the letter and stuffed it into the envelope he had already addressed. Handing it to Markov, he asked, "Would you mail this for me, Kirill?"

Markov nodded.

The technician came up, swabbed Stoner's bare arm just above the elbow. Markov turned his head. So did Stoner. He felt the faintest prick of the needle, and then the technician was pressing a cotton swab on his arm.

"It's all finished," Jo said.

"Christ, I hate needles," Stoner muttered.

The technician smiled at them, his smile growing especially big for Jo, and then left. Stoner got to his feet, tested his legs.

"Nothing. No effect at all."

"It will hit you soon enough," Markov said. "You had better get into bed."

"Yeah, I guess so."

Markov toyed with his beard. "Keith . . . tomorrow you will be surrounded by others, technicians, doctors . . . you know."

Stoner nodded. Markov grabbed him by the shoulders and embraced him. Stoner pounded the Russian's back with both hands and got the same treatment in return.

"Good night," Markov said, pulling himself away. "Good luck, my friend."

"Good night, Kirill."

Markov hurriedly left the room. Stoner turned. Jo was still standing there, between him and the bed.

Stoner put out a hand to push the door shut, missed it, staggered a few steps.

"Whoa . . . !" The room swayed.

"Here, let me help you," Jo said.

"I can manage." He gripped the open door, clung to it for a

moment to steady himself, then pushed against it. It swung shut and he swung around to face her.

"That must've been some shot he gave you," Jo said. Her voice sounded far, far away.

"Kid stuff," Stoner said. He tried to snap his fingers, but it didn't work.

Somehow she was holding him, propping him up, walking him toward the bed. An infinite distance. Endless.

"My last night on Earth," Stoner mumbled. "I want to spend it with you."

"Sure you do," she said.

He was falling, gliding slowly, effortlessly, weightlessly toward the bed that stretched out so invitingly, so far below him.

"My last night on Earth," he repeated as he bounced on the squeaking, sagging mattress.

"Yes, I know."

She was beside him and he held her close. She felt warm and the scent of springtime flowers buzzed through his brain.

"We are stardust," he told her.

Her voice was a distant purr in his ear. "You told me that our last night on Kwajalein."

"A million years ago. Yes, I remember."

"Close your eyes, Keith. Sleep."

"I want to make love with you, Jo. I want you to make love with me."

Her soft laughter was like windchimes. He couldn't hear the sadness in it. "Keith, you're going to be unconscious in another minute."

"No, I'm not. I'm going to . . ." The words faded away as his eyes closed.

Jo sat next to him for long moments, watching his face relax into deep, untroubled sleep. She kissed him lightly, and he smiled.

"Say you love me, Keith," she whispered to his sleeping form. "Tell me just once that you love me."

But he lay there sound asleep, smiling.

Jo got to her feet, straightened her clothes, and went to the door. With one final look at him sleeping peacefully on the bed, she opened the door and left his room.

"Harry, come on! You're missing Walter!"

"Walter? I thought he retired."

"He's on for this. Hurry!"

"Hold on. Hold on. Here I am. Turn up the sound."

"I swear you're getting deaf. I swear it."

"If you'd shut for a minute, maybe I could hear the darned TV!"

"Don't yell at me, Harry! First time Walter's on all year and you have to start an argument."

"Just turn up the sound and sit down."

". . . and for that story, we switch to Roger Mudd, in Moscow."

"It's three A.M. here in Moscow, Walter, and the city is asleep. But the lights in the Kremlin offices where the upcoming space shot is being monitored are burning intensely . . ."

"Is that happening now, Harry?"

"Cantcha see? It says, 'Live by Satellite.'"

". . . and in the Russian cosmodrome of Tyuratam, final preparations for the rocket's lift-off are being made in the glow of floodlamps . . ."

"Is that a real Russian rocket?"

"Sure it is."

"Gee, it looks just like one of ours."

CHAPTER 40

Maria Kirtchatovska Markova watched the sky slowly brighten with dawn as she lay wide awake beside her husband's sprawled, sleeping form.

Even with his beard and his hair turning silver, when he slept he looked like a baby: his face was unlined, except for the smile crinkles around the corners of his eyes, his mouth was open slightly, his breathing deep and regular.

Her eyes burned with sleeplessness. All night long she had lain in bed, rigid with tension, worrying about the future. The American was doomed, she knew that. He was nothing more than a pawn in the power struggle taking place within the Kremlin. But if Stoner was a pawn, Maria herself—and Kirill— were even less. They could both be swept away with the brush of a careless hand.

I must protect him, she knew. I must protect us both.

Slowly, carefully, she lifted the bedcovers enough to slip out of bed. The floor felt cold to her feet, but she barely noticed it. She went to the window, felt the summer sunlight warm on her face.

"Maria?" Markov's sleep-fogged voice called.

She didn't answer.

"What are you doing?"

Turning, she saw that he was sitting up in the bed. His faded green nightshirt was twisted ludicrously around his torso, but the sight brought no laughter to Maria's lips.

"I'm watching the sunrise," she said. "It's quite beautiful."

Markov reached for a cigarette from the pack on the bedside table.

"What's wrong?" he asked, lighting it. "Why are you up at this ungodly hour?"

She shrugged. There was no sense talking to him about it. He would only get angry and climb up on his high horse and make silly pronouncements.

Markov got out of bed and came to the window beside her.

"You haven't slept all night, have you? You eyes are all red."

"They launch the rocket this morning," she said.

"Yes." Markov puffed on the cigarette and gazed out the window. From this side of the building the launching pad couldn't be seen.

"Strange to think," he went on, "that Stoner will be safer once he's in space than he's been on the ground."

Maria said nothing.

Her husband mused, "At least there are no assassins in outer space."

She still said nothing.

He looked down at her, his eyes searching. "Maria Kirtcha-tovska, he *will* be safe in that rocket, won't he?"

"Yes," she answered automatically. "Of course."

Taking her by the shoulders, Markov said in a near whisper, "Maria, he is my friend. I don't want any harm to come to him."

"There's nothing I can do to harm him," she said.

"But you can help him."

"No, I can't."

"Is he still in danger, Maria?"

She pulled away from him.

But he grabbed her again, harder. "Maria! If there's any chance at all for us to live together, you must be honest with me. Is he still in danger?"

"It's not in our hands, Kirill," she said, trying to avoid his eyes. "There's nothing we can do about it."

"About what?" His voice was becoming frantic.

"I don't know!" she said, pleading. "The decisions that are being made—Kirill, we shouldn't even be *thinking* about it! It doesn't concern us!"

"Yes, it does!" His voice was so intense it cut through her. "If you let them kill Stoner you're also letting them kill us."

"Kir, I can't . . ."

"What are they going to do?" he demanded.

"I don't know."

"But they are going to do something?"

"There are . . . factions, at the very highest levels of authority."

"You must find out what they plan to do, Maria. Before we let him get into that rocket!"

"It won't be the rocket," she said. "That much I know. They don't want the rocket launch to fail, not in front of worldwide television coverage."

"Then what?"

"How can I know, Kir? If I even hinted at trying to find out, it could mean . . . I can't do it, Kir. I can't."

He circled his arms around her and held her close. Instead of bellowing, his voice became gentle, almost passionate. "You must, Maria. It's the only hope for us, for all of us. You must find out what they plan to do to him. And quickly."

Their voices woke Jo. She couldn't make out words through the thin walls separating the second-floor rooms, but she could tell from the rhythms of the voices that it was Russian being spoken. Heatedly.

Jo showered and dressed quickly. It wasn't until she stood in front of the foggy mirror over her sink to put on lipstick that she realized her hands were trembling.

She was the first downstairs in the common room. The cook and her helper—both pale-skinned Russians, wives of technicians—had already set the table for breakfast and filled the kitchen with the steamy aroma of hot cereal, eggs, ham and the thin, limp local equivalent of crepes.

Markov came downstairs, looking as tense as a bowstring pulled taut, followed by his dumpy, sour-faced wife. Jo realized it was their voices that had awakened her. In a few minutes the two Chinese scientists came down, then Zworkin and two of his aides. No one spoke much. Anxiety crackled through the air like high-voltage electricity.

Jo couldn't eat. She sipped at a cup of coffee as the team from the launch complex pulled up outside in their van. A half-dozen technicians in white coveralls clumped into the common room, spoke a few words in Russian with Zworkin, then headed upstairs.

Jo followed after them. As she climbed the stairs she realized that Markov was just behind her.

"My hands are shaking," she said to him.

"Yes," he replied. Nothing more.

Stoner was out in the hallway, also in coveralls that the Russians had furnished. The technical team surrounded him like a phalanx of bodyguards, like an escort of white-robed priests.

"I'm to go with him," Markov muttered, pushing his way past Jo.

"Kirill!" Stoner said with a happy grin. "Good morning. Will you kindly tell these guys that I'm ready to go? What're we standing around here for? Let's get the show on the road."

Markov spoke in Russian and the technicians laughed and nodded to one another. They started for the stairs. Jo started to move aside for them, then saw that Zworkin and all the others had clustered at the bottom of the steps, craning their necks upward.

The farewell committee, she thought.

Stoner stopped as he came next to her. "So long, kid. Thanks for everything."

She froze, unable to move her hands, pinned against the wall by the crowd of technicians.

"Good luck, Keith," she managed to whisper.

He leaned over, kissed her lightly. "I'll be back," he whispered.

Then he was gone, clattering down the stairs in his flight boots, Markov slightly ahead of him, the technicians following behind.

Jo stood there, suddenly alone in the upstairs hallway, and thought:

At least he's on his way. They won't try anything now. If they did, it would kill the cosmonaut who's going up with him.

It was nearly midnight in Washington, but the Oval Office was brightly lit and filled with the President's advisers.

"How long before lift-off?" asked the press secretary.

"Less than two hours now," the science adviser answered. She was sitting rigidly upright on one of the straight-backed chairs that had been brought in from the secretary's office.

"When do we start praying?" cracked Senator Jay. He was working on his third scotch of the evening.

"I started an hour ago," the President said from behind his desk.

Their eyes were all riveted on the TV screen built into the wall of the Oval Office. It displayed the picture being relayed out of Tyuratam without the interruptions of the networks' commercial coverage. The President could, at the touch of a button on his desk, switch on commentary from any network he chose, or from the NASA analysts who were monitoring the broadcast from the basement offices under the West Wing. At the moment, the CBS News commentary was being shown, printed on a smaller screen beneath the big picture. The President kept the sound off.

Walden C. Vincennes, tanned and handsome in his flowing, leonine gray hair, somehow had managed to get the old Kennedy rocker for himself and place it to the right of the President's desk.

"If they pull this off, Mr. President," he said, his rich baritone cutting through the other conversations buzzing around the room, "your stock will go up incredibly high."

"Perhaps," said the President. "We'll see."

The press secretary focused his attention on the two of them, even though he was sitting all the way across the room, wedged into the couch between Senator Jay and General Hofstader.

Vincennes smiled like a movie star. "You know, Mr. President, if all this goes well, the people might demand that you reconsider your decision not to run again."

The President shook his head. "I doubt it."

"There could be a draft at the convention."

"No."

"I've heard . . . talk."

It seemed to take an effort for the President to pull his eyes from the TV screen. "Walden, *if* we make contact with this alien spaceship, and *if* it's not hostile, and *if* there's a lot to be gained from the contact—don't you think I'll have my hands full, between now and November? How could I campaign for re-election and do justice to all that?"

Vincennes put on a thoughtful look. His smile faded by degrees, but the press secretary thought his eyes looked even happier than they had when he'd been smiling.

"I suppose you're right," Vincennes said.

"And if this doesn't go well," the President went on, "if that young man dies or the alien turns out to be hostile or some form of monster . . . then I'm finished anyway."

"That's true. But I'm sure it will all go well."

The press secretary laughed to himself. Vincennes is angling for the Chief's endorsement as the party's candidate. I'll be damned! He really wants to run for it! Then he thought, more seriously, I ought to have a long talk with him about it. He'll need an experienced staff, after all.

In California it was 9 P.M. and all the prime-time television shows had been pre-empted for the live coverage of the space shot.

Doug and Elly Stoner sat in their grandparents' living room, watching the TV set. Their mother was out with friends. Their grandparents flanked them on the long sectional sofa as Walter Cronkite explained:

"This will be the most difficult and complex manned space mission ever attempted, demanding as it does that the astronaut-cosmonaut team fly four times deeper into space than any human being has ever gone before."

Cronkite was sitting at a curved command console of a desk. Behind him a four-color chart showed the position of the Earth, the Moon and the alien spacecraft.

"Already, a team of Russian cosmonauts aboard the Soviet space station *Salyut Six* has assembled three modules rocketed up from Tyuratam over the past two weeks."

Pictures of the space modules appeared behind Cronkite's ear, replacing the chart. The modules were silvery cylinders with bent-wing panels of solar energy cells jutting out from each side. Each module bore the red letters CCCP stenciled on its side.

"These modules contain the air-recycling equipment, food and water for the two-week-long space mission," Cronkite went on, "as well as the scientific apparatus with which the American astronaut and Russian cosmonaut will study the alien spacecraft, and—if everything goes *very* well—make a rendezvous in space with this visitor from a distant solar system."

Doug fidgeted nervously on the sofa, wishing for a beer. His sister shot him a stern glance, then returned her attention to the television screen.

"Piloting the Soyuz spacecraft will be Major Nikolai Federenko, a veteran of three earlier Soviet space missions. The scientist-astronaut will be Dr. Keith Stoner, of the United States' National Aeronautics and Space Administration—NASA. Dr. Stoner . . ."

For some ridiculous reason, tears sprang up in Doug's eyes. He kept his face rigidly staring forward, toward the blurring TV screen, and felt thankful that the living room was too dark for his grandparents or his sister to see him.

Markov had no children and his only sibling—an older sister— had married and moved off to an industrial city in the Caucasus while Kirill was still in college. So the emotional swirl of walking Stoner through the long morning caught him unaware.

As the American's translator, Markov went every step of the way with Stoner as they entered the launch control building, sat down for the final physical checkup (a simple blood test and EKG) and then went downstairs to suit up.

"It's like a bridegroom putting on his tuxedo," Stoner said as a pair of white-smocked technicians helped him climb into the bulky, cumbersome pressure suit.

Markov sat on a bench and leaned his back against a metal locker. "More like a knight putting on his armor," he observed.

Next they went out to a minibus and drove to the launching pad. With four other technicians crowding into the rickety elevator cab, they rode to the top of the launch tower. Stoner looked to Markov as if some puffy white headless monster had almost completely swallowed him. Markov felt jittery, almost sick to his stomach, as if he had forgotten something vital, as if something terribly wrong was about to happen.

But these are all good, hardworking men. They have devoted their lives to our space programs. They wouldn't deliberately sabotage their own work. They couldn't!

Yet he felt far from reassured. It only takes one rotten apple, whispered a coiled cobra inside his brain.

The elevator opened onto a cramped enclosure teeming with technicians in the inevitable white coveralls. A featureless tube of smooth gray walls led out of the enclosure, ending at the hatch of the Soyuz spacecraft.

Stoner turned toward his friend. "This is as far as you go, Kirill. Launch crew only from here on."

Markov saw that the cosmonaut, Major Federenko, was already partway down the access tube, waiting, his pressure suit zipped up and his fishbowl helmet under his arm.

"It's okay," Stoner said. "Federenko speaks English pretty well. I won't get lost."

Markov forced a smile. "Good luck, Keith. *Vaya con Dios.*"

Stoner grinned at him. "*Et cum spirito tuo,* old friend. I'll see you when I get back."

Markov stood there feeling empty and terribly sad as Stoner clumped down the tube toward the cosmonaut.

"Hello, Nikolai," he heard Stoner say. "Looks like a good day for flying."

"Yes, yes," Federenko replied in a deep bass voice that echoed off the tube walls. "Good day. Very good day."

Like two young knights sallying out for adventure, Markov thought. Then he realized why he was so sad. And leaving me behind.

He went back down the elevator and was driven in the minibus back to the launch control building. Maria was waiting for him as he stepped down from the bus. She wore her drab brown uniform now.

"I wish them well," she said.

Markov nodded and put his arm around his wife's shoulders. Incredibly, she let him get away with it.

"They have the future of the world in their hands, Marushka," he said to her. "Our future, the future of Russia, of America—the whole world."

Maria looked up at him. "They'll be all right," she assured him. "The launch will go well. Come, we can watch it from inside the control center."

As the sun crept over the distant hills and the morning mists of Rome began to burn away, the Pope got up from his knees and walked slowly to the door of his private chapel.

Cardinal Benedetto would be out there, he knew. And Von

Friederich and so many others. The television people. The paparazzi. He had to simplify it all, bring it down to a few strong words that all could understand. He spoke not merely to the cameras and the newspapers, but to hundreds of millions of believers and—strangely enough—to billions of non-believers, as well. The Papacy was a heavy burden, global in scope. Now it was about to become interstellar.

That is what I will tell them, the Pope thought, nodding slowly to himself. God in His mercy and wisdom has seen fit to reveal more of His creation to us. We are indeed fortunate to live in these times. This alien object reaffirms Christ's truth, that all men are brothers.

Fleetingly, he wondered again what the consequences would be if the alien turned out to be evil, devilish.

It cannot be, he told himself firmly. That is something I cannot believe. God would not allow such an evil to fall upon us.

He reached out boldly and threw open the doors. Television lights glared around him and the crowd of news reporters strained against the velvet ropes that had been set up.

The dazzling lights even reached back into the chapel chamber, where, above the altar at which he had prayed, a Medieval mural of the Flood showed a sinful mankind being chastized by a wrathful God.

Halfway around the world, on Kwajalein, it was early evening. Reynaud sat by Schmidt's bedside and watched the countdown's progress on the hospital television set.

Cronkite was showing a view of Cape Canaveral. A NASA Space Shuttle stood gleaming white in the glare of floodlights, its nose pointing into the Florida sky.

"And at Kennedy Space Center, American technicians are preparing to launch the tanker that will refuel the Russian Soyuz, deep in space, as it nears the alien craft.

"The tanker itself is a Russian vehicle, flown to the United States six days ago as part of this intricate joint American-Soviet effort to make contact with the alien spacecraft."

Schmidt, sitting up in his bed, asked through his wired jaw, "Do you think they'll make it?" His voice was thick and slow.

"I believe they will," Reynaud answered. "Stoner won't let anything stop him."

The General Secretary also sat propped up in bed, watching the final moments of the countdown on his private television set. Borodinski sat next to the big, heavily blanketed bed.

"It is going well, Comrade Secretary," the younger man said without taking his eyes off the screen. "You must be very proud this morning. The whole world is watching Russia lead the way to a meeting with the alien."

But the General Secretary had closed his eyes. His chin slumped to his chest. His final breath was a long, soft sigh of release.

Stoner lay on his back in the cramped spherical capsule of the Soyuz spacecraft. Helmet on, visor locked and sealed, gloved hands resting on his knees. And sweating. His legs dangled up above him. Like a turtle on its back, he thought. Useless and in danger.

He turned his head to see Federenko, in the left seat, but the helmet blocked his view. He could hear the cosmonaut, though, in his earphones, chatting happily with the launch control engineers in Russian. Stoner guessed at what they were saying.

"Internal power on." A row of lights on the panel a few inches over his head winked on, green.

"Life support systems, on."

"Guidance computer, on."

"Air pressure, normal."

The cosmonaut's gloved fingers flicked across the switches of his control panel like a pianist testing a new instrument. One by one, the banks of lights lit up.

"Shtoner," Federenko's bass rumbled.

"Yes?"

"You can pick up the countdown at Teh minus one meenute, at my mark . . . *Mark*."

T minus one minute. Stoner heard the Russian words in his earphones. He appreciated Federenko's taking the moment out to give him a translation. Now his own mental clock could click off the last sixty seconds in cadence with the Russian launch controller's voice.

Stoner's eyes flicked over the control panel. Every light and switch had been hastily labeled in English. He had crammed a year's worth of orientation into a few weeks. But I can fly this bird if I have to, he told himself. They can maneuver it remotely from the ground, of course, but I can override them if I have to. I can fly her.

His hands were slippery with sweat inside the silvered gloves. He hoped he wouldn't have to take over control of the spacecraft.

T minus thirty seconds.

Jo stood on the roof of their barracks building, peering into the brightening sky and the rocket booster, several kilometers away.

Don't let anything go wrong, she prayed silently. Don't let anything go wrong.

The loudspeaker boomed in Russian for several moments, then in English:

"A MESSAGE FROM THE PRESIDENT OF THE SOVIET UNION. GOOD FORTUNE TO THE TWO BRAVE MEN WHO GO TO MEET THE ALIEN SPACESHIP. THE HEARTIEST ADMIRATION AND GOOD WISHES OF THE SOVIET PEOPLE FLY WITH YOU ON YOUR GALLANT MISSION."

Before the echoes could die away, the voice added:
"T MINUS FIFTEEN SECONDS."

T minus ten seconds, Stoner counted mentally.

He could feel his heart pounding wildly as he went on, Five, four, three . . .

The booster trembled beneath them. Pumps starting up.

" . . . one, zero . . ."

He heard the Russian word for *Ignition!* and felt the whole capsule shudder. A dull growl from somewhere deep within, exploding into an ear-shattering bellow as millions of demons howled their loudest and a heavy, implacable hand squeezed down on his chest, pressed him into his seat, shook him with bone-jarring violence.

Stoner felt the breath forced out of him. His eyeballs were pressing back in their sockets. The noise was overpowering, a solid wall that pressed his eardrums flat. He couldn't lift his hands from the armrests. His spine was being crushed. And the noise, the noise and vibration rattling him . . .

Across the whole world hundreds of millions watched the gleaming rocket climb upward on its tongue of flame, straight and stately as if guided along an invisible taut wire, rising slowly, majestically, then accelerating, higher, faster, into the cloud-flecked blue, faster now, arcing over, flame bellowing from its rocket nozzles, racing across the sky, dwindling from view.

In Moscow a huge roomful of hardened correspondents broke into cheers as the booster hurtled across the sky.

In New York, Walter Cronkite stood up at his desk, startling the cameramen, who abruptly jerked their cameras upward to keep him in frame. Millions of viewers thought they heard Cronkite mutter, "Go, baby, go."

Jo watched the rocket lift off, its exhaust flame brighter than anything she'd ever seen before. The booster rose in eerie silence, up and up, higher and higher, without a sound to be heard. Then the overwhelming roar reached her, washed over her rooftop perch, wave after wave of solid white noise, making the whole building shake. Jo imagined she could feel the heat from the rocket engines, knew it was all in her mind, but felt it anyway.

Good-by, Keith, she said to herself. Somehow she felt, deep within her, that she would never see him again.

> **Man will not always stay on Earth. . . . Earth is the cradle of the mind, but one cannot live in the cradle forever.**
>
> **KONSTANTIN EDUARDOVICH TSIOLKOVSKY (1857–1935)**

CHAPTER 41

The mind-numbing roar eased away and finally died altogether. The pressure dwindled until Stoner saw that his arms were floating free of the seat rests. He felt light-headed, and for a moment his innards told him that he was falling. Squeezing his eyes shut hard enough to make them tear, he opened them and he was no longer lying on his back but sitting upright in the Soyuz capsule. Nothing had changed but his perspective.

"Shtoner," Federenko's deep voice rumbled in his earphones. "You okay?"

He nodded. "Okay, Nikolai. I'm fine. You?"

"All good."

Stoner's vision was blurred. "Okay to open my helmet?"

But Federenko was on the radio, checking back with mission control. Stoner waited until he was finished, then asked again.

"Yes, yes. Cabin pressure is normal. All systems are good, ground control confirms."

Stoner slid the visor up, pulled his gloves off and wiped at his eyes. The gloves drifted out toward the control panel and he grabbed at them, grinning to himself.

"Zero gravity," Federenko said. "You remember? Do not make crumbs when you eat."

Stoner laughed and took a deep, easy breath. For the first time in nearly two years he was weightless. The pleasure of it was euphoric.

"Was a good launch, no?"

"Perfect," Stoner said.

"Now we make contact with Salyut by radio, then go EVA to dock with equipment and supply vessels."

Stoner pulled out the clipboard that was mounted on the panel to his right. In both Russian and English it listed every task they must do, the day and hour it must be started, and how long they had to complete each.

"You make the first EVA," Stoner said.

"Da."

"I'll watch the store."

Federenko peered from around the edge of his helmet. "Watch store?"

"It's an American expression." Stoner tried to explain it to him.

Federenko listened, frowning deeply. "But there is no one here to steal from store."

Shrugging inside his bulky pressure suit, Stoner said, "Well, Nikolai, you know how it is in a capitalist society. So many thieves that we expect them everywhere."

It made no impact on the cosmonaut. "But no thieves in orbit. No thieves aboard Salyut. They are both good Soviet citizens; officers in Red Army."

Stoner grinned weakly and gave it up.

Borodinski was on the special picturephone that the General Secretary had set up in his quarters. The beefy-faced man in the viewing screen wore the collar of a soldier with the tab insignia of a major general.

"This line is scrambled and secure?" Borodinski asked in a near whisper.

"Yes, comrade. Of course."

"I have heavy news that must not go beyond your ears until I call you again."

"I have kept state secrets before, comrade," the general said, a slight smirk twitching at the corners of his mouth.

"Our great friend is dead."

"No!"

"Just a few minutes ago. The doctors have confirmed it. There is no hope of resuscitation."

The general's face fell. He seemed genuinely grieved. "He was a good man. A fine man. A strong comrade."

"You understand why this news must be kept secret for the next several hours?"

"Of course, comrade. You have many calls to make, many . . . details to check on."

"I have called you first," Borodinski said, "because I want to impress on you the fact that the General Secretary's policies are still in effect, still to be carried out exactly as he desired them to be."

"Yes, comrade. Will the Presidium . . . ?"

"That's none of your concern at the moment. Of utmost importance is the question of the missiles. Are they ready to be fired if we should need them?"

"The strategic strike force is always prepared, comrade."

"I mean," Borodinski explained patiently, "the missiles that are being held ready for the alien spaceship." Is the man being deliberately doltish? he wondered.

"Oh! Them! Yes, comrade, they are prepared for launching at an instant's notice. The tracking radars have precise data on the alien's position. The warheads are armed and ready."

Borodinski nodded. "Very well. Keep the missiles in readiness. And yourself as well. I will call you, personally, if we should need them."

"I understand, comrade. They will be ready, and so will I."

As Borodinski clicked off the connection and the general's face faded from the screen, he looked across the bedroom at the body of the General Secretary, arranged carefully on the bed, eyes closed, hands clasped on his chest.

"So much to do," he muttered to himself. Now the real work begins, he knew. And the real danger. It was one thing to be handed the reins of power; it was quite another thing to hold onto them.

Borodinski shook his head. For a fleeting moment he almost envied the peaceful slumber of the General Secretary.

Stoner turned in his seat as Federenko opened the hatch that led from the orbital module and crawled back into the command section. The cosmonaut wormed his way into his own seat and gave a weary sigh of relief.

"It took longer than the schedule calls for, did it not?" He was breathing heavily, and his zippered coveralls were dark with perspiration.

Stoner glanced at the clipboard floating by his knee. "Eighteen minutes longer. Not bad. We still have plenty of slack in the schedule."

Federenko passed a hand over his eyes. "It is so different out there . . . hard work."

"I know."

Outside the viewing port above his seat, Stoner could just make out the stubby outline of the Salyut space station. The two cosmonauts who had been living and working in the Salyut for the previous month had taken over the task of connecting the supply modules to their Soyuz.

My turn next, Stoner knew. Working in zero gravity sounded effortless, but he knew how easy it was to exhaust yourself. Every motion made in weightlessness had to be consciously, deliberately counteracted by a counter-motion. No friction to bring motions to a "natural" halt. No subliminal visual clues of distance or orientation. No up or down.

Years earlier, General Leonov, the first man to "walk" in space, had advised his cosmonauts, "Think ten times before moving a finger, and twenty times before moving a hand," when working in space.

Still, Stoner felt eager as a puppy. Impatiently he waited and watched the two Salyut cosmonauts at work, while Federenko went back into the orbital module of their spacecraft for a squeeze bulb of hot tea and enough room to stretch his aching limbs. Stoner sat alone in the cramped command module, surrounded by the Soyuz's instruments, his eyes on the crewmen working outside.

Finally the digital clock on the control panel showed it was time for him to suit up. A radio command from ground control confirmed the time.

Federenko came back into the command module and took the pilot's seat as Stoner unstrapped and wormed his way weightlessly into the orbital module.

The orbital module was a globular, womb-shaped section that

served as a workroom, bunkhouse and air lock. Stoner slowly pulled on his pressure suit, carefully testing each zipper and seal, forcing himself to be deliberate and patient. The module was a clutter of bunks, lockers, cabinets and two airtight hatches: one that connected with the command module, the other that opened onto vacuum.

Federenko came in to help him into the backpack of oxygen tanks and maneuvering jets. Finally Stoner lowered the fishbowl helmet over his head, sealed it to the metal collar of his suit. Federenko connected the hoses from the oxygen tanks to his helmet. Together they tested the suit's radio, oxygen pressure, heater. Stoner flexed all the joints, then nodded to Federenko and slid the visor down over his face. The cosmonaut ducked back through the hatch into the command module, and closed the massive airtight hatch behind him.

Stoner was alone now in the metal womb. Reaching out with his gloved hand, he opened the safety latch and then pressed the button that started the air pumps. Through his helmet he heard the machinery stir to life, sucking the air out of the orbital module, into storage tanks.

The telltale panel light went from green to amber, and finally to red. Stoner slowly opened the outer hatch, then drifted out of the metal womb head first.

And gasped.

He had remembered all those months on the ground how beautiful it was in space, but the memory was a mental image, not the visceral passion. Now he saw it again, felt it in his guts again, and all the breath gushed out of him.

Before his eyes the ponderous bulk of Earth curved, glittering blue oceans streaked with dazzling white clouds, huge and overwhelmingly lovely. Turning slowly, Stoner saw the depths of infinity, utterly black but flecked with so many stars that it looked like diamond dust sprinkled across black velvet.

O Lord, I love the beauty of Thy house, and the place where Thy glory dwells.

The words welled up in him as he turned slowly, effortlessly, surveying the heavens. And then he saw the squat, bulky space-craft sections that hung a few dozen meters from his Soyuz. Beyond them the Salyut space station rode calmly through the sky, its panels of solar cells looking vaguely like a gull's bent wings,

while the Earth passed majestically behind it like a slowly
unreeling backdrop.

Work to do.

Using the maneuvering unit in his backpack, Stoner jetted
over to the equipment and supply vessels. They had been joined
to each other by Federenko and linked by rigid steel cables to
the Soyuz by the Solyut cosmonauts. Stoner's task was to check
all the connections, make the final inspection. They had saved
the least demanding job for him.

He moved like a man in a dream, slowly floating, each motion
a long, deliberate, weightless glide. He didn't fight the weightlessness, he enjoyed it. Better than skiing. Like floating out in
the ocean, riding the heaving swells out beyond the breakers. Go
with the flow, Stoner reminded himself. Enjoy it while you can.

He chatted with Federenko over the suit radio as he inspected
one by one the connections that linked the Soyuz with its new
equipment and supply modules. They checked out perfectly; the
cosmonauts had done their work well. The Soyuz was ready to
move outward toward its rendezvous with the alien.

And Stoner realized that he felt reluctant, rebellious, un-
willing to leave the freedom of space and return to the metal
confines of the spacecraft.

"Shtoner," he heard Federenko's voice in his earphones.

"Yes."

"Checkout is complete. Return to air lock."

He gazed at the Earth, huge and glowing and heart-achingly
beautiful. Turning, he looked out into the depths of starry space.
He knew what Odysseus heard when the sirens sang their
beckoning call to him.

"Shtoner! Can you hear?"

With an effort he wrenched his gaze back to their tiny, lumpy
spacecraft. "Yes, yes, I hear you. I'm coming back in."

But even as he ducked into the air lock and swung its hatch
shut, his eyes stayed fixed on the stars until the heavy metal
hatch cut off all view of them.

Jo sat at the computer console and watched the numbers and
symbols flashing across the glowing green background of its
readout screen.

The Russian computer technicians tolerated her at the mission control center. They had given her a console to sit at where she could watch the progress of the mission, one of the hundreds of computer consoles that stretched in long rows across the vast, buzzing room. Up at the front of the control center were huge picture screens and an electronic map that showed where the various spacecraft—the Soyuz, the Salyut orbital station and the alien ship—were in relation to the Earth and the Moon.

The technical staff tolerated an American woman in the center, but the security authorities were clearly on guard. Jo was escorted by armed, uniformed policemen to and from the command center. Markov sat just behind her, nervously smoking cigarettes and tugging at his beard. Often his wife would come in and sit beside him. She also wore some kind of uniform, although Jo didn't know which branch of the service she was in and didn't really care.

The controls at her console were for readout only. Jo was here as an observer, and the Russian authorities had made it clear that she was not a participant in the mission. Even the way they said "observer" made it obvious that the word was semantically equivalent to "spy" in their lexicon.

She could watch, she could observe, but she could not help.

She looked around the huge control complex. The tension of the first few hours had worn away. There was a quiet, almost drowsy air to the center. Even Markov seemed more relaxed, in the seat behind hers. The Soyuz had passed the Moon's orbit nearly forty-eight hours ago. Stoner and Federenko were farther from Earth than anyone had ever flown before.

Trailing behind them, she saw on the huge electronic map, was the unmanned tanker that had been launched from the United States. It was moving on a different track, one that would converge with the Soyuz a few hours before Stoner and Federenko came within sight of the alien.

They'll be busy then, Jo knew. And so will we.

In another twenty hours the control center would be crackling with activity: first overseeing the link-up with the unmanned tanker, and then the actual rendezvous with the alien itself.

But now all was quiet. Half the consoles were unoccupied, and the technicians who were at their posts seemed at ease, al-

most nonchalant. Even the few who were speaking into their lip
microphones or fingering the switches and dials of their consoles
had no appearance of urgency about them.

It's going well, Jo thought. He's safe. And it's too late to sabotage the mission. All the boosters have worked perfectly, all the
vehicles are on their courses. Keith is safe, nearly a million miles
from Earth.

Stoner scratched drowsily at his stubbly beard. It was starting to
itch, and he longed for a hot bath. Federenko, just as grubby
and tired-looking, sat calmly in his seat at Stoner's left, checking
the mission schedule. The command module smelled of sweat
and body heat.

"Separating supply module is no problem," Federenko was
explaining. "Explosive bolts snap cable and push it away."

"That's the fourth time in the past hour you've told me,"
Stoner replied. "It's worrying you, isn't it?"

"No, no. Is no problem."

"Something's bothering you, Nikolai."

The Russian's unshaven face sank into a dark frown. "Not
worry, Shtoner. But I see problem."

"The tanker?"

"Da. We must link with it before attempting to rendezvous
with alien, according to flight plan."

"I know."

"But latest radar shows tanker is not in best position for us.
Trajectory is deviating from plan."

"We can still reach it, can't we?"

Federenko nodded somberly. "But will take more maneuvering fuel than planned. Leaves less fuel for making rendezvous maneuvers with alien."

Stoner thought a moment. "We could let the tanker go and
save our maneuvering fuel for the rendezvous."

"And have no propellant left for return to Earth," Federenko
said.

"They could send up another tanker."

With a grim laugh, Federenko said, "In how long? Two days?
Two weeks?"

"They've got a backup at Cape Canaveral; they were holding it in case the first tanker didn't get off okay."

"By the time backup tanker is launched we would be on same trajectory as alien—heading out of solar system. Second tanker not reach us at all."

"Shit."

"We must link with tanker," Federenko said firmly, "even if it means no rendezvous with alien."

"Christ, Nikolai! We've come all this way to make contact with that bird!"

"Is true," the Russian replied calmly. "But I have no desire to meet alien and never return to Earth. Do you?"

Stoner did not answer.

"Don't worry," Markov said. "They can easily reach the tanker. They have plenty of fuel for that, according to the mission controllers."

He was sitting next to Jo at the dining table in the common room of their barracks. Maria sat on his other side, spooning cold borscht to her lips. Across the table one of the Chinese physicists picked at his dinner.

"But they won't have enough fuel left to make contact with the alien," Jo said. Her bowl of borscht sat in front of her, untouched.

Markov shrugged and said lightly, "So they will get as close as they can, take a few thousand photographs and then return home. If that's the best they can do, then that is what they will do."

But Jo could feel cold tendrils of fear tracing along her veins. "Keith won't settle for that. He wants to get aboard the alien spacecraft."

"Federenko is an experienced cosmonaut," Markov insisted. "He won't allow anything that would jeopardize their safety."

"But Keith . . ."

"What can he do?" Markov asked, gesturing. "Overpower Federenko and steer the Soyuz to the alien? That's nonsense."

"I wouldn't put it past him," Jo said.

"Besides," Markov tried a different tack, "Federenko is a fine pilot. The pride of the Soviet cosmonaut corps. I'll bet you that he links their ship with the tanker and still has plenty of fuel afterward for their rendezvous with the alien."

"I hope you're right," Jo said, not believing a word of it.

COCOA BEACH, FLA.

"But why do *you* have to go?" she asked.

He gave another exasperated sigh. "For the twentieth time, Marge: I've been *ordered* to go."

"But you're not an astronaut. They can't order you to fly off into space!"

"The hell they can't."

"You're a medical doctor, not an astronaut."

"I'm a colonel in Uncle Sam's Army, and when the orders come down from the White House, I salute smartly and say, 'Yes, sir.'"

"You *want* to go!"

"I'm scared green to go! But I'm under orders. What can I do?"

"You're too old to go into space."

"Not on the Shuttle. I'll just be a passenger, like on a plane. . . . Look, Margie, it's only for a couple of weeks. We've got to set up a quarantine for those guys after they contact the alien . . ."

"You'll catch alien germs! I know you will!"

"Don't be silly. It's all a lot of fuss over nothing. Alien organisms are *alien*. They can't infect us. Just because the goddamned White House is jittery, we've got to go through the motions of a two-week quarantine. In orbit, yet!"

"I'm afraid, Sam."

"It's nothing to worry about, honest."

"Alien germs . . ."

"I won't even be in contact with the guys who make contact with the alien. We've got a whole sealed laboratory for them to stay in. All the tests will be done by remote control and anybody who goes into the lab will be wearing a space suit."

"But why you, Sam? Why'd they have to pick you?"

"Don't you worry, honey. When I come back I'll be an important guy. They'll want me on TV and everything. We'll retire in style, Marge. Real style."

CHAPTER 42

Markov sat by the bedroom window, smoking ceaselessly as he watched the long summer twilight give way to darkness.

It was cloudy out there, and would probably begin to rain soon. It made no difference. Even on a clear night the floodlights surrounding their barracks made it impossible to see the stars. And the spaceships were all so far away that they couldn't be seen from Earth anyway.

The first drops hit the windowpane and trickled down across the reflection of Markov's long, brooding face. He took a fresh cigarette and lit it with the end of the butt in his lips. The fire glowed bright red for a moment, reminding him instantly of the devilish machine that Maria had back on Kwajalein.

Where is she? he wondered. She had gone out right after dinner and hadn't come back yet.

Restlessly, Markov glanced at his wristwatch. Six hours to go before they rendezvous with the tanker.

Jo was right, he knew. Stoner would never settle for anything less than physical contact with the alien spaceship. Not without a struggle.

He sighed, then pulled deeply on the cigarette. The rain was spattering down now in big, fat drops. In the reflection of the window Markov saw that he was tugging at his beard again. Annoyed with himself, he got up from the chair and paced across the little room, jamming his right hand into his trousers pocket.

He heard Maria's clumping footsteps out in the hall and went to the door. Opening it, he saw that the rain had caught her. She looked soaked and bedraggled, hair dripping down across her face, uniform hanging soggily on her stocky body.

And then he saw her eyes.

"Marushka, what is it? What's wrong? You look as if you've seen a ghost."

She came into the room and shut the door tightly, then leaned against it.

"I have," she whispered, her voice strangely harsh and breathless. "Two of them."

"What do you mean?" Markov asked, lowering his own voice unconsciously.

"Federenko and Stoner," she whispered. "They are both dead."

"What?"

"Not yet," she said, raising both hands to quiet him. "But they will be. In six hours."

Markov felt as if a tiger had clawed out his guts. "What do you mean? What are you saying?"

"The tanker," she said, glancing all around the room, as if she could see a microphone if one had been planted. "The one launched from America. It's been rigged to explode . . ."

"The *Americans* did this?"

"No." She shook her head impatiently. "Our own people, a faction, very high up . . ."

"They're going to kill our own cosmonaut? And Stoner too?"

Maria looked frightened, terrified. "You don't understand, Kir. It's a power struggle. Inside the Kremlin, they are fighting for control. We're only pawns to them, Kir. Less than pawns."

"When will the tanker explode?" he demanded.

"When they make contact with it. The timer was set by one of our technicians just before the tanker was loaded aboard the American shuttle."

Markov sank onto the bed. "Maria . . . to kill them, kill them both, because of their power games . . . it's monstrous."

"I didn't think they would kill Federenko too," she said. "I never thought they would do that."

He buried his face in his hands. The cigarette fell from his fingers to the bare wooden floor, glowing in the shadows.

Maria went to him, knelt by his feet. "I'm sorry, Kir. I risked my neck to find out for you, and now I'm sorry that I did."

"It's not your fault, Marushka." His voice came out muffled, tearful.

"There's nothing we can do," she said. "Nothing."

But Markov put his hands down and straightened his back. He looked down into his wife's eyes.

"Yes, there is," he said firmly.

"Kir . . ."

"There *is* something we can do, Maria. We can warn them."

"But then they'll know that I . . . Kir, they'll kill us both." She was beyond terror; the absolute certainty of it made her voice flat with hopelessness.

"Then we'll die together," he said. "Better that than letting those two be killed in space."

"You are sulking," said Federenko.

Stoner pulled his attention away from the computer screen and looked at the cosmonaut sitting beside him.

"You don't look so happy yourself, Nikolai."

"How can I be? To come all this way and miss the alien . . . it is not happy."

"I've been checking the computer figures against the latest data on the tanker's trajectory. We can still make it—if you can dock us with the tanker on the first pass."

Federenko closed his eyes for a moment, as if rehearsing the problem in his head. "Not easy, Shtoner."

"You want me to try it?"

The Russian laughed. "You? You are not pilot; you are passenger."

"Then it's up to you," Stoner said flatly.

The laugh died. "I see," Federenko said. "You make trap for me, eh?"

"I want you to understand how important this is. You've got to dock us with the tanker on the first try. Otherwise we miss the alien."

Federenko nodded unhappily. "Hokay, Shtoner. You make point. I dock with tanker on first pass. You watch!"

Breaking into a grin, Stoner said, "See? I wasn't sulking at all."

Blindly Markov raced through the rain, his long legs propelling him by instinct toward the command center. Zworkin. The old man had not been in his bedroom when Markov had pounded on his door. He must be in the command center, Markov told himself. He must be.

Maria was somewhere behind him as he raced along the

gravel path that led to the command center's massive windowless building. The rain lashed at him and he slitted his eyes against its cold sting.

Zworkin is the only one who can save them now, Markov thought as he ran. If I try talking with the security police I'm lost. Zworkin! And through him to Bulacheff.

Stoner couldn't understand the babble of Russian coming through the radio speaker, but from the expression of Federenko's deeply lined face he knew it was bad.

The cosmonaut spoke almost angrily back to ground command, and more urgent words burst from the radio.

Stoner turned to the radar screen, a small orange-glowing disk on the panel between their two seats. It showed a strong blip almost dead ahead of them. He stretched slightly to search through the observation port and—yes, there it was. A silvery crescent of metal against the starry blackness.

The tanker. Close enough to see it.

But Federenko's gloomy frown sent a chill of apprehension through Stoner. He looks as if he's just been ordered to attack the whole Chinese Army with his bare hands.

"What is it, Nikolai?"

Federenko turned toward him, defeat smoldering in his eyes. "The tanker. We must not go near it. Malfunction."

"What?"

"Very strange, they tell me. Malfunction in tanker self-destruct circuit. It can explode, they think."

The cosmonaut's hands reached for the stubby levers that controlled the Soyuz's maneuvering jets.

"Wait!" Stoner yelped. "If we don't link up with the tanker we can't complete the mission!"

"If we do link with tanker—boom!"

Stoner sagged inside his restraining harness. "I don't believe it. How could . . . ?"

A flash caught his eye and they both craned toward the observation ports. In total silence the tanker blew apart, a trio of small flashes followed quicker than an eyeblink by an enormous fireball that nearly blinded them.

Stoner squeezed his eyes shut. Federenko growled something too low for Stoner to catch.

The fireball faded into darkness, leaving a burning afterimage against Stoner's eyes. There was no shock wave, no noise, no debris pattering around them. It was as if they had been watching a silent picture. Stoner couldn't believe it was real.

"Gone," Federenko said heavily.

Stoner rubbed at his eyes, then looked out through the port again. Nothing but the unutterably distant stars.

"Gone," he admitted. "And where does that leave us?"

"We are dead men, Shtoner. Without propellants from tanker, we cannot get back to Earth."

It took a few moments for the realization to sink in. Finally Stoner heard himself say, "But we have enough fuel to make the rendezvous with the alien, don't we?"

Federenko gave him a long, solemn look. "Da," he said at last. "Plenty maneuvering fuel now."

"Then let's do it!" Stoner said. "That's what we came out here for, isn't it? Let's do it!"

Federenko's bearded face almost smiled. "I knew you would say that, Shtoner."

"What else is there?" Stoner asked, feeling strangely excited. "Let's go!"

"Hey, it's quittin' time, man!"

Hank Garvey planted his ponderous bulk on the computer analyst's desk and leaned toward the skinny youngster.

"We got an emergency on our hands, boy," Garvey said, his voice murderously calm and deep, like the throaty warning cough of a lion.

"The next shift . . ."

"Uncle Sam wants *yew*," said Garvey. "Yer the best goddam' computer jockey in the Center. I know, 'cause I've had to lissen to yew tellin' me 'bout it a thousand times or two. Now yer gonna prove it."

"But my ol' lady . . ."

Garvey laid a hand the size of a football on the analyst's bony shoulder. "Our man Stoner and his Rooskie pilot are in trouble. Their tanker blew up on 'em."

"Jeezus!"

"They ain't hurt. Their spacecraft's intact, no damage. But they cain't get back home—not unless some damn smart boy comes up with a new flight plan for 'em—damn fast."

"Holy shit!" the computer analyst said. "Why didn't you say that in the first place? Okay, okay, get your fat ass off my desk an' lemme get to work."

Garvey grinned like a Poppa Bear. "That's mah boy."

CHAPTER 43

The communications center on Kwajalein was in an uproar. Even the technicians at their consoles were yelling at one another in confusion.

Jeff Thompson, standing beside Ramsey McDermott's chair,

was hollering into the old man's ear, "We can't let them go on! The farther out they go toward the alien, the more impossible it'll be to get them back!"

McDermott's jowls sagged. He had lost ten pounds and aged a decade in the months since he'd first seen the aurora mocking him. His shirt collar gaped around his wizened neck. His hands shook uncertainly. His eyes had lost their fire.

Edouard Reynaud, his arm no longer in its sling, gripped Thompson's arm. "You must call them back. You must make them come back!"

"Can't . . ." McDermott croaked.

"But they can retrofire into a lunar orbit," Reynaud insisted. "I have the numbers in my head. They should have enough fuel for that."

Thompson brightened. "Right! If they can get themselves back into an orbit around the Moon we might be able to send something up there to ferry them back to Earth."

But McDermott shook his head weakly. "Stoner won't listen . . ."

"QUIET!" an amplified voice roared.

Everything stopped. People froze where they were. The room went silent, except for the electrical hum of the communications consoles and the buzz of the air conditioners.

Lieutenant Commander Tuttle was standing on a desktop, microphone in hand. He gazed around the room and, satisfied that all attention was on him, let the hand holding the mike drop to his side.

"This is a Navy project," he said, voice sharp and loud enough to be heard across the stilled room. "And I am the Navy officer in charge."

Thompson stared at the little lieutenant commander. For the first time since he'd met the man, Tuttle was making his uniform look good.

"The goal of this project is to make contact with that alien spacecraft. Stoner and the Russian are on their way to do just that. So you will all get back to your jobs and stop the yakking."

"But they won't be able to return to Earth!" Reynaud shouted, his chubby face going red with either anger or embarrassment, or perhaps both.

"That's a problem that we'll have to tackle," Tuttle snapped. "Stoner is aware of it. He's the only one of you who's kept his head. If he's willing to risk his life to make contact with the alien, the least we can do is see to it that whatever he discovers is received here and properly recorded so that the whole human race can study it. Now *get to work!*"

They moved. Numbly, sullenly, with grumbles and whispers they turned back to their jobs.

Reynaud, trembling in his perspiration-soaked white shirt, glared across the big room at Tuttle as the Navy officer climbed down from the desk. For the first time in many years, Reynaud knew real anger. He also knew that Tuttle was right.

"There it is!" Stoner shouted. "I can see it!"

Federenko took his eyes from the radar screen and leaned across to look through Stoner's observation port.

"It glows," he whispered.

They had come up on the alien craft with the Sun at their backs. The radar image had been fuzzy, almost nebulous, at the longer wavelengths. But when Stoner turned on the microwave radar the image cleared up and showed a smaller but much sharper blip.

Now he saw the spacecraft itself.

It glowed with a strange, eerie, golden light, like a shimmering aura that surrounded the solid craft. The spacecraft was imbedded in the glowing light. From this distance it was still too far away to make out details, but it appeared to be roughly oblong in shape, with a smooth surface and rounded corners.

"No wonder it looked like a comet to the ground radars," Stoner realized.

"What is the light?" Federenko asked.

"A screen of some kind?" Stoner guessed. "A screen of energy like a magnetic field, maybe. To protect it against cosmic radiation. Maybe a shield against micrometeors, too."

They were closing fast on it. Stoner floated out of his seat and wormed his way back to the orbital module of the Soyuz. Taking the stubby, compact telescope from its clips on the equipment rack, he focused on the alien ship through the nearest observation port.

"If it's come all this way from another solar system it must have been in space for hundreds of thousands of years, at least," he called, loudly enough for Federenko to hear him on the other side of the open hatch. "But its surface looks smooth and clean. No meteoric erosion. No pitting."

"What is color?"

Squinting through the telescope, Stoner said, "Hard to say. The light around it makes everything look kind of golden."

"Are cameras recording?"

Stoner glanced at the equipment monitor panel. The camera lights were on. So were the video transmitter lights. "Yes," he called.

Stoner watched for what seemed like an hour as they glided closer to the spacecraft and Federenko spoke to ground control. The spacecraft's surface was absolutely featureless, and as smooth as the skin of a supersonic aircraft. Not a rivet, not a seam, not even a line of decoration.

Then he realized that they were not getting any closer. Leaving the telescope hanging weightlessly, he ducked halfway through the connecting hatch.

"You can get us a lot closer, Nikolai. It won't bite us."

"No closer," Federenko said firmly.

"Come on, we . . ."

"Orders from ground control. They are working on new course for us, get us back to Earth."

"Terrific. But in the meantime we're *here!*"

"Not to use maneuvering fuel," Federenko said. "Take photographs, describe spacecraft for radio and tapes."

"But we can rendezvous with the thing!" Stoner insisted. "For Chrissake, it's only a stone's throw away!"

"Too long a throw. You are Olympic champion, maybe?"

"Come on, Nikolai!"

"Must not use maneuvering fuel," the cosmonaut replied stubbornly. "Orders. Our lives depend on this."

Stoner pulled back into the ovoid orbital module and peered out the observation port at the alien craft. It was close enough now to make out clearly with the naked eye. It hovered against the stars, tantalizingly near, its golden energy screen glowing, pulsating slowly, like the deep eternal breath of God.

They seemed to be at rest now compared to the alien vehicle. They rode alongside, about a hundred meters off its flank, riding silently against the stars, close enough to touch, too far away to touch. Stoner knew that their placid, seemingly motionless encounter was an illusion. Both craft were hurtling away from Earth, flying farther from safety each second. The alien was heading out of the solar system, back into the unthinkable gulf between the stars, and unless they broke away and took up a new trajectory, Stoner knew that he and Federenko would also leave Earth's grip forever.

He stared hard at the alien spacecraft, knowing that a million miles away, men and women were working frantically to find a way to bring them back home safely.

"Fuck it," Stoner muttered. He reached for his pressure suit, hanging limp and lifeless on the opposite wall of the orbital module.

"What you do, Shtoner?" Federenko called from the command module.

"I'm going out," Stoner said, yanking on the pressure suit leggings. It was no simple matter in zero gravity. "I'll use the backpack maneuvering jets to get to it."

"Not enough fuel in backpack. Alien is too far away."

"Nudge us a little closer, then. Close enough for me to reach it."

"No."

"You've got to, Nikolai!"

Federenko appeared at the hatch, his dark face set in a solemn frown. "I want to save our lives, not kill us foolishly."

The exertion of wriggling halfway into the pressure suit made Stoner bob weightlessly across the orbital module. He put a hand against the ceiling to steady himself; his feet dangled inches from the floor.

"Sit down, Shtoner," Federenko said. "Calm yourself."

"Listen. I could take both backpacks—yours and mine. One to ride me out there, the other to get me back."

"Foolishness."

"But it'd work!" he said. "There's enough fuel in the two of them to make it okay, isn't there?"

Federenko turned away from him.

"*Isn't there?*" Stoner grabbed him by the shoulders.

"Yes," said the cosmonaut. "But I forbid it."

Stoner went back to struggling into the pressure suit.

"Shtoner, I am in command."

"And I'm a third-degree black belt," he said, reaching down for his boots. "Are you going to help me or do we fight?"

"You will kill yourself."

"Nikolai, if we get back to Earth I'll have to live with myself. Do you think I could, knowing that we got this close and didn't go the rest of the way? That sonofabitch has traveled *light-years* to reach us! The least I can do is cover the last hundred meters to meet him."

Federenko said nothing. He solemnly watched as Stoner pulled on his boots and began zipping up the suit.

"Well, are you going to help me or are you going to just stand there and sulk?" Stoner taunted.

Scowling, Federenko pulled his own backpack from its rack and started adjusting its shoulder straps.

"You are killing me also," he said. But he helped Stoner into the backpack.

The television screens at the front of the control center showed the alien spacecraft glowing against the star-flecked heavens. For long minutes now the Soyuz radio had been silent.

Jo sat at her computer console, every nerve tingling, stretched taut with tension, a headphone clamped over her glistening black hair.

"Go ahead, Houston," she said into the lip microphone. "I can hear you clearly."

Markov stood tensely behind her, and beside him Zworkin hovered like a protective mother hen. Uniformed security police armed with machine pistols stood a few yards off. Other men, bulky, hunch-shouldered, scowling men in dark suits prowled all through the huge command center, eying everyone suspiciously.

Jo watched her computer screen fill with data: numbers and

symbols flashing across the tiny screen faster than any human eye could follow. She glanced up at the smaller wall screens flanking the main picture of the alien spacecraft. A new booster was being fueled hurriedly out on one of Tyuratam's eighty working launch pads. A new tanker to be launched into a high-acceleration rescue trajectory. The Americans, with their faster and smarter computers, were working out the flight plan that would get the tanker to the Soyuz in time to save Federenko and Stoner. Jo had become the liaison link between Texas and Tyuratam.

The command center was astir with quiet, organized frenzy. Computers and humans were working their hardest. Markov gazed around the vast room and saw the security police, their steely eyes constantly moving, their hands never far from the guns they carried.

As if shooting up the place would help, he said to himself.

Zworkin had spent an hour on the phone with Bulacheff in Moscow. Great upheavals were taking place. Maria had been called off for questioning by her superiors. She'll either be made a Hero of the Soviet Union for foiling the saboteurs or we'll both end our days in prison, Markov knew. It all depends on who wins what in the Kremlin.

"Very good, Houston," Jo said into her microphone. "The data's coming through. Thank you."

She yanked the headset off and let it clunk on the console's desktop, then leaned back in her chair.

"They've got the big NASA computers working out the high-energy trajectory," Jo said.

"Will that be enough?" Markov wondered. "Can they get the new tanker into position for them?"

Jo looked up at him, her dark eyes shadowed with fatigue and fear. "If they can't, no one can."

"What if ground command send up new orders, a new flight path that will get us back?" Federenko grumbled as he checked out Stoner's suit. "You will be out there . . ."

"I'll be in touch over the suit radio," Stoner said.

"Da. And when I say to come back, you will say, 'Not yet. One more photograph.'"

Stoner chuckled. Satisfied that the suit was sealed, Federenko handed him the helmet. Stoner pulled it on, locked it in place, slid down the visor and sealed it.

"I'll come back when you tell me they've got us a new trajectory that'll get us home," Stoner said, his voice muffled inside the helmet.

Federenko looked unconvinced. He held up one finger, then squeezed back through the hatch into the command module and swung the hatch shut.

Stoner was alone now.

"Radio check," the cosmonaut's voice rumbled in his earphones. "Can you hear me?"

"Loud and clear."

"Very good."

Stoner glided over to the controls that pumped the air out of the orbital module. Nikolai's giving me his backpack for this, he thought. If his rescue depends on going EVA, he's just thrown his life away.

"Shtoner."

"Yes?"

"Good luck, Shtoner."

"Thanks, Nikolai. I appreciate . . . everything you've done."

"Say hello to alien for me."

Stoner laughed. "I will."

He cycled the air out of the ovoid chamber and opened the outer hatch. Pushing the extra backpack out ahead of him, Stoner stepped out into nothingness. He drifted free of the Soyuz, then turned and surveyed the situation.

The Earth was far away. No longer a huge smear of awesome girth, it was now a crescent of blue and white hanging in the star-scattered dark. Stoner put out a gloved hand and covered the planet of his birth with an upraised thumb.

He could see the Moon, too, a smaller crescent. The Sun's fierce blaze was over his left shoulder; he had no intention of looking in that direction, but he could see at the corner of his vision the glowing disk of the Sun's zodiacal light: cosmic dust, rubble and debris left over from the formation of the planets, eons ago.

A slight soundless puff from the thrusters at his waist and he squarely faced the alien spacecraft. It floated serene and aloof inside its golden, pulsing aura of energy.

Slowly, tugging the spare backpack on its tether, Stoner approached the alien spacecraft.

"Nikolai, do you suppose that energy screen could do damage to a slow-moving object, like an astronaut?"

"Could be," Federenko's voice responded. "Keep talking . . . everything is relayed to Tyuratam automatically."

"Okay."

Describing what he was doing as he did it, Stoner pulled up the tether that held the extra backpack, reeled it up until the pack was in his grasp, then pushed it out ahead of him. The effort slowed his approach to the alien spacecraft as the backpack sailed out ahead of him, the long tether gradually, slowly unwinding.

"The tether's insulated," he said. "If the screen causes an electrical discharge it won't run back up the line and zap me. I hope."

He held his breath as the backpack glided into the glow of energy, then passed through it with no discernible effect.

"Did you see that, Nikolai?"

"Nothing happened."

"Right. Good." Stoner licked his lips. "Now it's my turn."

"Cameras are recording. Television transmission is working."

Stoner touched the controls at his belt and felt the thrusters push against the small of his back, gently, for just a flash of a second, like the encouragement a schoolteacher gives a reluctant child. He glided toward the golden, pulsing light.

"Almost there . . ."

The glow seemed to be all around him for a moment, there was a brief sharp *crack!* in his earphones, and then he was clearly inside the screen. He twisted around for a view of the Soyuz.

"I'm through it! Can you hear me?"

"Da."

"It's like being inside a gold-tinted observation dome. I can see through it. Doesn't obscure my vision much."

"I see you also." Federenko's radio voice was as strong as ever, although a slight background hum now accompanied it.

Stoner could feel his heart pumping. "Okay," he said. "I'm going to . . . going aboard it."

"Be careful, Shtoner."

The extra backpack, still drifting at the end of its tether, bumped into the curved side of the spacecraft and bounced harmlessly off it.

"It's cylindrical," Stoner reported into his radio microphone, "with tapered ends. Sort of like a fat cigar. Light tan in color. Looks like metal. No protuberances, no antennas that I can see. Very smooth finish. About twenty, twenty-five meters long; five or six deep."

He was coming close to it. The craft loomed before him, dominating his vision. Stoner's lips felt dry. His innards burned.

"Kind of light brown in color . . . I said that already, didn't I? Looks like metal. Definitely metal. Well machined. No sign of rivets. No seams. Like it was made whole, cast out of a mold or something. No markings. Hasn't been pitted *at all*—like it's brand new. That screen must eat up micrometeoroids and any other junk it's encountered . . ."

As he reached the curving side of the massive spaceship, Stoner instinctively put his hand out. He touched it, rebounded slightly, and with his other hand pulsed the thrusters that gently pushed him against the craft's hull again.

"Yeah, it's got to be metal. Feels like metal."

He planted his boots against the ship's hull. They clung.

"Hey! I think it's magnetized! My boots are sticking to it." Stoner pulled one boot free; it took only a slight effort.

"Boots are non-magnetic," Federenko said flatly.

"Well, something's holding them," Stoner answered.

He stood erect on the curving hull, a lone visitor on a world twenty-five meters long. He took one step, then another. It felt tacky, as if he were walking across a freshly painted surface that hadn't quite dried.

"Going forward," he said. "At least, I think it's forward. Could be aft—this thing looks the same at both ends."

Carefully, Stoner planted one booted foot in front of the other.

And felt the breath rush out of him.

A line of light suddenly glowed the length of the ship and his earphones gave out a low-frequency whining hum. Not loud enough to hurt, just loud enough to make certain that it could not be ignored.

The line of light flickered through every color of the spectrum. It was like watching a rainbow rippling under a stream of water.

"It's color!" Stoner shouted, describing it. "Then it goes dark . . . I think it goes into the infrared and ultraviolet, beyond human vision."

The whining in his earphones also wavered up and down in pitch and Stoner realized that he could only hear it during the few seconds when the line of light was off.

"It's going through the whole electromagnetic spectrum! Visible light, radio frequencies . . . must be putting out pulses of x-rays and gamma rays, too. Can you hear me, Nikolai?"

The cosmonaut's voice came through despite the background noise. "I hear you. The high-energy detectors on instrument panel are silent."

Stoner watched the flickering light, fascinated, almost hypnotized. "It's saying, 'Welcome aboard,' in all the colors of the rainbow."

Federenko's unruffled voice replied, "Switch to radio frequency two. Perhaps hum is not there."

They went through all four channels on the suit radio. The whine persisted on all of them, running up and down the scale in contrapuntal rhythm with the line of light.

"Hold everything!" Stoner yelled. "It's . . . something . . ."

Up at the nose of the craft the line of flickering light suddenly split into two parallel lines, then looped around to form a circle. The metal of the hull inside the circle seemed to brighten.

"Something up at the nose." Stoner described the circle. "Maybe it's a hatch."

"Be careful, Shtoner."

"I'm going up there."

Trembling, throat dry, too excited to be afraid, Stoner stepped slowly toward the glowing circle.

He stood at its edge as the whine in his earphones worked its way up to a shrill screech and then cut off completely. The line of light cut off too. But the circle of metal continued to glow dully, almost as if heated from within.

"It's glowing," Stoner reported. "Could it be radioactive? A nuclear heat source? Maybe I've cooked myself."

"No radiation counts from detectors here," Federenko replied.

"Maybe the screen blocks it."

Federenko said nothing.

But the glow was subsiding now and Stoner saw that the metal inside the circle was becoming milky, translucent. He strained his eyes at it.

"I think I can see something . . ."

Slowly he got down on his hands and knees and put the visor of his helmet against the hazy surface.

"You look like religious pilgrim," Federenko called, "at prayer."

Ignoring him, Stoner reported, "It's clearing up. It's becoming transparent. I can see inside . . . not much light down there, but . . ."

He peered through the glassy surface, forcing himself with sheer willpower to see what was inside. Then it hit him with the power of a physical blow.

"Oh, my god in heaven," he whispered. "It's a sarcophagus."

Deep inside the windowless bowels of the ABC News building, the FCC official shook his head in wonder.

"A sarcophagus? What the hell's he mean?"

The network vice-president, a bright, dazzlingly intense young black man wearing a maroon cashmere jacket, answered, "Whatever it is, we've got to get it on the air. *Now.*"

Hugh Downs was on the monitor screen, anchoring the ongoing coverage of the space mission. An image of the alien spacecraft as seen from the Soyuz's cameras was displayed behind him.

"On the air? Live?" The FCC man blanched.

"Got to."

"No! Too risky. Suppose he finds something . . . awful? The panic . . ."

The network VP jabbed a finger toward the monitor screen. "Half the country is already scared stiff of this thing and the other half don't really believe it exists at all! We got to put it on live, man, let them see for themselves. Otherwise nobody's going to believe it!"

"I'm not sure . . ."

"Well, I am." He picked up the phone and gave the necessary orders.

The FCC man said gloomily, "If you do it, the other networks will go to live coverage too."

"Good. Long as the Russians are feeding it to us live, we oughtta put it out on the air live. This delay crap is for the birds."

"But I don't have the authority to allow live broadcast! I shouldn't be involved . . ."

"Listen," the VP snapped. "Why do you think the network brass put me on this hot seat? Part of their affirmative action program? I get paid to make decisions, man! If this works, I'm a genius, I'm on my way to the top of the heap."

"And if it doesn't work? If there's a panic or some kind of reaction from Washington?"

"Then I'm on my way back to Philadelphia, with my death certificate in my hand."

CHAPTER 44

"I can see right through the metal," Stoner said into his helmet microphone. "The metal's become transparent."

"He is dead?" Federenko asked.

"Must be. Or frozen. Maybe he's just preserved . . . you know, cryonically."

Stoner's pulse was racing and he felt sweat trickling along his skin, inside the pressure suit. It was difficult to make out details of the alien's form—he saw a long, very solid-looking body stretched out on a bed or bier of some sort. There was a head, shoulders, two arms. He couldn't see the lower end of the body.

"Speak!" Federenko commanded. "What do you see? Your words go straight to Tyuratam."

"Okay, okay . . ."

Stoner pressed his visor close to the transparent hatch again, to get a clearer view. And there was no hatch. His helmeted head sunk an inch or two below the rim of metal that framed the circular hatch.

"Oh no . . ." He pulled back, then ran his gloved fingers around the rim of the circle. It was open, as if the metal that had been there moments earlier had dissolved.

"Nikolai," he called, fighting to keep his voice from climbing too high. "The hatch—first it went transparent, now it's disappeared altogether."

"Disappeared?"

"Gone. Vanished. Just an open hole where solid metal was a minute and a half ago."

Federenko asked unbelievingly, "It is open?"

"Yes. I'm going inside."

"Wait. I check with ground control first."

Stoner shook his head inside the fishbowl helmet. At their distance from Earth it was taking nearly six seconds for Federenko's messages to reach Tyuratam, and another six for their responses to get back to the Soyuz. Plus the time in between while they screw around trying to make up their minds, Stoner thought.

"I'm going in," he said.

"Wait, Shtoner."

But he already had his hands on the hatch's rim and started gingerly lowering his legs through the opening.

"I'm halfway through. No problem."

"Shtoner, it could be dangerous."

"I don't think so."

He floated down inside the craft and touched his boots to the soft flooring. They stuck gently, just as they had on the outside of the hull.

He turned slowly in a full circle, taking in the interior of the alien spacecraft.

"I'm inside," he said, his voice unconsciously hushed. "Can you hear me?"

"I hear you." Federenko's voice in his earphones was weaker, streaked with sizzling static, but clear enough to understand easily.

"It's a lot smaller in here than the ship's exterior dimensions. This must be just one compartment. All the machinery's hidden behind bulkheads." He shivered. "And it's *cold* in here. Colder than outside. How can that be?"

"What do you see?"

Stoner turned to the elevated bier and the creature resting on it. He took a step toward it, then stopped.

The curved walls of the compartment were starting to glow. Not like molten metal, but like the soft radiance of a moonlit sky. As Stoner watched, slack-jawed, the hull turned milky white, then translucent, and finally as clear as glass.

"Shtoner! Answer!" Federenko was bellowing. "Can you hear me?"

"I can *see* you, Nikolai," he answered, awed. "The whole

damned hull has turned transparent. Just like the hatch did. I can see right through it!"

A pause. Then Federenko grumbled, "It is the same as always from here. Dark metal. Not transparent."

"A one-way window," Stoner mused. "Christ, what'd that be worth to Corning?"

"Who?"

Stoner giggled as he stood beside the bier and looked across the hundred or so meters of vacuum to the Soyuz. It looked squat and ugly to him now, a primitive artifact from a primitive world.

"They have one helluva grasp on materials sciences, I'll say that for them."

"Describe, Shtoner. All is being transmitted."

He swallowed hard and looked down at his gloved hands. They were trembling.

"Shtoner, talk."

"This whole section of the interior is about four meters long—say, twenty-five feet. Almost the full five meters wide, but only two and a half, three meters high. The floor is solid and opaque. So's the back wall of the compartment. But the nose and side walls are perfectly transparent. As if there weren't any hull there at all. I can see right through it."

He stepped to the edge of the floor and put his hand out, timidly. The gloved fingers touched the invisible hull; it felt spongy, giving.

"Hull's still there, though. Hasn't vanished completely, the way the hatch did. And it's very cold in here, as if energy can go out through the hull, but none can get in. This thing must've been designed by Maxwell's demon."

Turning back to the alien, Stoner took a long look in the dim starlight. Then he remembered the lamp hooked to his belt and turned it on.

He leaned over the alien's body. It was very long, but thin, emaciated, desiccated.

"He's more than two meters tall, I'd say. No clothing. Very slim, plenty of ribs showing. Body's covered with some kind of orange-brown fuzz. Not hair, really. Looks more like a nap on velvet. Almost."

"The figure is human?" Federenko asked.

"Sort of. Two arms, one head. Body's much longer than ours . . . legs start where our knees would be. And there are four of 'em, four legs. Little knobby ones with round hoof-like pads at the ends."

"Wait . . ." Federenko said. "Tyuratam reports, your words being broadcast all across Soviet Union, Europe, America, Asia, many other places."

"I'm on live, Nikolai? In Russia?"

Federenko hesitated, then replied, "In U.S.S.R., broadcast is delayed fifteen minutes so censors can make certain nothing harmful is let out."

"And in the States?"

"Live, I think."

"I'd better watch my language."

Federenko said nothing.

Stoner turned back to the alien. "Arms are longer than ours. The hands have only two fingers each and the ends of the fingers look like suction cups—suckers, like on an octopus."

"The head? The face?"

"Seems to have two eyes, but they're closed. I don't see a nose of any sort, but there's a mouth—lips, at least. Wide and thin." Stoner couldn't bring himself to touch the creature, although he badly wanted to see what was behind those lips, those closed eyelids. "Same kind of nappy fur covers the whole face, even the eyelids. The head is rounded, large-domed, very smooth. I don't see what he breathed with."

"Is it breathing?"

"No," Stoner said. "He's dead. I can *feel* it. There's no atmosphere in here. This chamber's been in vacuum for millennia. Cold, too. Frost is forming on my visor."

"Turn up suit heater."

"Right. I'm doing that." The miniaturized fan in the helmet's collar hummed a bit louder.

As the tendrils of frost cleared from the edges of his visor, Stoner saw that there was writing on the bier alongside the alien's body. And artifacts: a metal cup, a translucent sphere the size of a child's ball, a rod of something that looked like wood. He tried to pick up the rod but it stuck fast to the surface of the bier. As he described it all into his microphone he tried to dislodge the other objects. None of them would move.

"This is a sarcophagus, Nikolai. A tomb. I know it is. This guy died a million years ago and had his body sent into space—like an Egyptian pharaoh. He had himself sent out in a sarcophagus."

"But why?"

"As an *ambassador!*" The answer hit Stoner's conscious mind as he pronounced the words. "Of course! As an ambassador! What better way to make contact with unknown intelligent races scattered across thousands of light-years?"

"Ambassador?"

"Yes!" Stoner knew he was right. "He's saying to us, 'Here, I want you to see me, to know that I exist, my civilization exists. You aren't alone in the universe. Take my body. Study it; study the artifacts I've brought along with me. Study my ship. Learn from me.' What better way to share knowledge? To show that his intent is totally peaceful, benign?"

Federenko was silent, thinking.

Stoner went back to his description. "He's got a jaw that looks like it hinges the same way our own jaws do. No ears, but there's a couple of circular patches on the sides of his head . . . they look almost like outcroppings of bone. Not horns, they're flat. Sense organs of some kind."

"What sexual organs?" Federenko asked, then added, "Biologists want to know."

Stoner grinned. "They would. Nothing visible in the usual place, but there's some kind of protuberance halfway down his torso. And his fuzz is a slightly different color around there, more yellowish." *Christ, it looks like he died with a hard-on,* Stoner thought.

"Wait," Federenko said. "We are getting a transmission from ground control."

Stoner walked around the raised platform, bobbing in the zero gravity as his boots clung slightly to the spongy flooring. There were more artifacts on the alien's other side. A straight edge, a square covered with dots that were connected by thin lines. An astronomical map? he wondered. This ark is a damned treasure house; he's brought his whole civilization with him.

Federenko's voice interrupted his musings. "Switch to frequency two, Shtoner."

Stoner clicked the suit radio switch on his wrist and the Russian's voice said, "Shtoner, this frequency is for private talk. Not for broadcast."

"Okay."

"Ground command is working out new course for us, to get us back. New tanker is being launched."

"I knew they'd figure something out," Stoner said.

"We will fire retro-rockets to break present course. Very soon."

A tingle of alarm went through Stoner. "How soon?"

"Computers working on it. But you must be ready to return to Soyuz when I give command."

"Sure," Stoner replied.

"Photograph everything now," Federenko said. "Time is short."

"Yeah, okay. I'm switching back to frequency one now. I want everybody to hear what I've got to say."

Federenko grunted. "Tyuratam estimates more than one billion people hear your voice."

Good, Stoner thought. Now they'll know.

Unhooking the bulky 35 mm stereo camera from its case at his belt, Stoner said for broadcast:

"I think it's clear now that this alien has come in peace. He's offering us his body and his treasured possessions, giving them to us, for us to study. He's telling us that we have nothing to fear—that there are other intelligent races scattered among the stars. We're not alone. The universe is filled with life, and it's civilized, intelligent life."

He was starting to babble and he knew it, but his hands clicked away with the camera while he chattered on:

"We have nothing to fear! This isn't the end of our world, it's just the beginning! Do you realize what that means? Intelligent civilizations *don't* wipe themselves out with wars or pollution or overpopulation—not always, not inevitably. We have a future ahead of us as wide and bright as the stars themselves, if we strive for it, if we work together, all of us—the whole human race as a species, as a family, as one family unit in the great interstellar community of intelligent civilizations . . ."

In Rome, St. Peter's Square was thronged with tens of thousands who stood in awed silence, watching the giant TV screens that had been set up there by the government. Finally the Pope appeared, not at the usual balcony, but at the head of the cathedral's steps, flanked by red-robed cardinals and the colorful Swiss guards.

The mammoth crowd surged toward the Pontiff, its roar deafening. He smiled and nodded and gave his blessing to them all.

In Washington the President watched the rendezvous with the alien spacecraft in the privacy of his family room, with his wife and children clustered close around him. Downstairs in the West Wing the staff watched, too, and for at least a few hours all thoughts of the upcoming national conventions were suspended.

In Moscow, Georgi Borodinski phoned the commander of the Red Army missile forces and personally told him to deactivate the pair of hydrogen-bomb-tipped missiles that had been ready to intercept the alien spacecraft.

A few blocks away from the Kremlin, the Minister of Internal Security picked a small pistol from his desk drawer and, with a sardonic smile twitching at his lips, he placed its muzzle against his temple and pulled the trigger.

At the control center in Tyuratam, Jo's face lit up as she watched the readout glowing on her computer screen.

Turning to Markov, who still stood by her side, she said, "It'll work! We can get them back! They've got to break their current orbit within the next half hour. If they do that they can coast until the new tanker reaches them."

Markov whooped and lifted Jo out of the chair and kissed her. One of the uniformed guards behind them twitched at the sudden noise and leveled his gun at them.

"I love you like a sister!" Markov proclaimed loudly, as the guard's partner silently pushed the muzzle of the machine pistol down toward the floor, with a reproving frown.

Oblivious to what was going on behind him, Markov added in a whisper for Jo's ear, "I never did believe in that silly taboo against incest, you know."

Stoner was hoarse, his throat raw, but still he talked, minutely describing each artifact arranged along the alien's sides as he snapped stereo photos. Questions were flooding up from Tyuratam and Kwajalein.

"No, no sign of other life forms," Stoner answered, his throat rasping. "No plants or seeds or other animals. Maybe they're in other compartments of the spacecraft.

"I've tried to get into the rest of the ship, but it's no go. Just a smooth blank wall that won't open up. It's going to take a lot of study to figure out how they work their entrances and exits.

"The biggest discovery among the artifacts, I think, is this star chart. At least, I think it's a star chart. I don't recognize any of the constellations, but there's writing on it . . . looks like writing, a lot of circles and curlicues."

Federenko's heavy voice broke in. "Shtoner, we have new trajectory data. Tanker is being sent to meet us. We must retrofire in eleven minutes."

"Eleven minutes?" Stoner's heart stopped in his chest. His voice nearly cracked.

"Ten minutes, forty-eight seconds, to be exact."

Stoner's gaze flashed to the alien resting on his bier. *He's spent thousands of years to get here and I have to leave in ten fucking minutes?*

"No," he protested. "We need more time. We can't . . ."

"No more time," Federenko said flatly. "Come back to Soyuz now. There is no other way."

"Nikolai, I can't! Not yet!"

"Now, Shtoner."

He looked through the transparent hull of the sarcophagus, toward the distant stars. Then at the shrunken Earth, so far away, and finally at the stubby Soyuz.

"Nikolai, please . . ."

"We must go, Shtoner. Or die here."

Stoner's lips were dry and cracked. He felt the chill of death breathe on him, and he turned to stare once again at the alien. *All the distance you've come, to offer us your body, your knowledge, everything that you are and you represent. So much to learn from you . . .*

"Shtoner."

"No," he said quietly. "I'm not coming back with you, Nikolai."

"Shtoner . . ."

"I'm going to stay here, with him. Maybe in another few million years some other civilization will find the two of us."

And he turned off his suit radio.

The noontime sun beat down on the silent, deserted street. Inside the air-conditioned offices, bungalows, house trailers, every man and woman on the island sat transfixed before their television sets. The same scene showed on every screen: the alien spacecraft floating in the void. The same voice came from the alien craft: Stoner's.

"No, I'm not coming back with you, Nikolai."

In the bustling communications center, everything stopped. Men and women froze at their jobs and stared at their screens.

Only Reynaud reacted.

"No! No, he can't do that! He mustn't, it's not necessary!" The cosmologist rushed across the room, red-faced and puffing, toward Tuttle.

"Let me talk to him!" Reynaud screamed. "Give me a link to him! In the name of Christ, let me talk to him!"

Everyone tore their attention from the communications screens to the florid, screeching madman. Tuttle put his hands out in front of him, as if to protect himself from the wild-eyed Reynaud.

"You want to talk to Stoner?"

"Yes! Quickly! Before it's too late! I can save him! I know I can!"

CHAPTER 45

Stoner felt strangely calm. All the big decisions were behind him now. There was no more need to struggle. No need to worry. All his life had pointed to this ending, he realized. He would finish life alone, untouched by anyone, away from them all, lost in the starry wilderness with his member of an alien race.

Another loner, he thought, gazing down at the alien's strange, immobile face. Were you like that in life? Is that why you chose this way to spend eternity?

In New York the FCC monitor was screaming, "Get him off the air!" while the ABC News vice-president grabbed at his flailing arms to keep him away from the master control panel. In Moscow the Soviet censor, livid with anger and fear, slammed his heavy fist into the button that cut the Soyuz transmission off the worldwide broadcast. TV screens all around the globe still showed the picture of the alien spacecraft as seen by the Soyuz cameras, but suddenly there was no voice transmission coming from space.

Stoner had relaxed into an almost fetal-like curl, hanging weightlessly a foot or so above the floor of the chamber. Through the transparent walls of the ship he could see the distant crescent of Earth and the Soyuz, still parked about a hundred meters away. It seemed to be staring at him accusingly.

Stoner flicked on his suit radio.

". . . you *must* return," Federenko was saying, with frantic determination. "That is an order. Only seven minutes remain . . ."

"Nikolai, I've just realized something," Stoner said. The cosmonaut fell silent. "This spacecraft—this tomb—must have been built to seek out G-type stars, I'll bet. Our friend here came from a star that's similar to the Sun."

"No time for philosophy, Shtoner."

"And once it reached a G-class star, it searched for planets with strong magnetic fields. That's got to be right! That's why it headed for Jupiter first: the strongest magnetosphere in the solar system. And then toward Earth, the strongest magnetic field among the inner planets."

"Six minutes and thirty seconds," Federenko growled.

"The strong magnetic fields are targets for two reasons," Stoner went on, ignoring him. "First, the spacecraft taps electromagnetic energy to recharge its batteries . . . or whatever it uses for energy storage. But far more important, it's likely that only planets with strong magnetospheres can support life. Life *needs* a strong magnetic field to act as an umbrella that shields the planet's surface from cosmic radiations!"

"Shtoner, stop this foolishness. Come back."

"Did you get all that, Nikolai? Was it sent to Earth? It's important."

"Yes, yes. Now come back."

At CBS News, Cronkite was putting on a bravura performance, talking over the static image of the alien spacecraft, filling in with facts, conjectures, history, opinion, while his top aides phoned frantically to Washington to see if there was any way to pick up the live radio transmission from the Soyuz again.

In the White House, the President had rushed down to the communications room, where the radio transmission was coming in over the private link from Moscow. A wide-eyed aide told the President that Walter Cronkite was on the phone. The President took it immediately, and frowned with disappointment that it was actually only Cronkite's producer screaming incoherently into the phone.

A few calming words and Cronkite himself came on. They chatted hurriedly and the President agreed to have his technicians relay the words being spoken in space to CBS. Cronkite hesitated a moment, then asked that the same favor be done for the other networks, as well. The President smiled and nodded.

"Barbara's going to love you, Walter," he said.

It sounded to the President as if Cronkite sputtered. "Thank you, Mr. President," said that famous voice. "If you'll excuse me now, sir, I should get back to the cameras."

"Certainly, Walter," said the President. "God bless you."

Jo sat stunned at her computer console. All through the vast control center everything seemed to groan to a halt, as if each of the hundreds of men and women working there had simultaneously stopped breathing.

She looked up at Markov's stricken face.

"He's going to kill himself."

"You must stop him," Markov said. "You must!"

"How can I . . . ?"

"No one else can," Markov said, bending over her, gripping her shoulder, speaking urgently. "He loves you. You are his only link with life. Speak to him! Quickly!"

Numbly, Jo answered, "But this console isn't wired for transmission . . ."

Markov turned to Zworkin, fidgeting nervously beside him. "Do something! Please! She must get through to him!"

Zworkin licked his lips and glanced uncertainly at the guards around them. "I'll try . . ."

"You're all going to have to work together from now on," Stoner was saying. "All the nations of the world. It can never be the same for any of you. There are others out there, other races, other intelligences—and they're just as curious and brave as we are."

"Five minutes, Shtoner!"

"Five minutes, five hours . . . it doesn't make any difference, Nikolai. It doesn't."

"Wait . . . communication from ground. On frequency two."

"No," said Stoner. "I don't want to talk with them."

"A personal message, from a woman. Miss Camerata. She sounds very upset, Shtoner."

He debated within himself for half a moment, then pressed the button for frequency two.

"Keith! Can you hear me?" Her voice was shaking with anxiety.

"Yes, Jo, I hear you."

Silence. Stoner realized it would take nearly twelve seconds for her answer to reach him. I'm already so far away that it's impossible to hold a normal conversation with her.

"Please don't do this! Don't be a fool, Keith! Come back, please!"

"I can't do that, Jo. Not now. If I stay here, I can send you more details about this ark, about our visitor. It's a treasure-house of knowledge. I can't just leave it after a few lousy minutes and allow it to sail away from us forever."

He stared hard at the distant blue-white crescent of Earth as his word sped to her and her answer came back.

"But you'll kill yourself!"

"I'll have more than an hour's time before Federenko gets too far away to pick up my suit radio and relay it to you. I can describe everything in this chamber in detail."

He waited, counting the seconds, preparing what he would say next.

"And then you'll die!" Jo said. "You'll die up there!"

"That's not such a terrible thing. My life hasn't meant very much to anyone."

It was better this way. He had time to think, time to get ready for her voice, to freeze his emotions and guard against hers.

"Your life is important, you damned idiot! You can't just throw it away!"

"I'm content to die out here, Jo," he said. "It's not such a bad way to go."

He noticed that frost was forming on the edges of his visor again, despite the suit heater's highest setting. The cold was seeping into him; he could taste its metallic bitterness.

"No, Keith, no!" There were tears in her voice. "Come back! Come back to me! You have so much to live for . . ."

"No, I don't, Jo. This is the climax of my life. This is what it's all been leading up to. What would I do for an encore?"

"You can't throw away your life like this! We have our whole lives ahead of us!"

"You have your life, Jo. You're young, the whole world lies ahead of you."

The time stretched, and then, "But you said that the world can never be the same now that we've contacted the alien." Her voice was fever-pitched. "We're not the same! I'm not and you're not. It's a new world, Keith. We need you here. I need you here, to be with me."

"Three minutes, Shtoner."

Before he could answer either one of them, a new voice spoke in his earphones:

"Switch to frequency three. Priority message from Kwajalein."

Almost glad to get away from Jo's voice, Stoner clicked on frequency three as if cutting an umbilical cord.

"Go ahead Kwaj," he said flatly.

"Dr. Stoner?" The voice was breathless, familiar. "This is Dr. Reynaud, from Kwajalein."

For a moment Stoner felt almost giddy. He wanted to laugh. *Reynaud, our chubby monk. Is he going to try to save my soul?*

"Listen to me, please!" Reynaud shouted in his earphones. "I've examined the plot the computer has made of the alien spacecraft's course. It will not be irretrievably lost once you leave it. Do you understand me? It will not be irretrievably lost!"

"You mean we'll be able to track it on radar?" Stoner asked. "What good is that?"

"That is very important! Vital!" Reynaud's voice was shrill with excitement. "We can go out and reach it again. We can recapture it and bring it back into an orbit near the Earth!"

Stoner shook his head inside his helmet. "It would take years to build the hardware to retrieve this craft. We just barely got this far and it took six months of planning. And we screwed it up anyway."

"But we have years!" Reynaud insisted. "The alien will slow down as it moves outward, away from the Sun. We have perhaps five years before it reaches the orbit of Pluto . . ."

"Five years," Stoner echoed.

"We can recapture the alien," Reynaud repeated. "There's no need for you to stay there."

Federenko's heavy voice interrupted. "Two minutes, Shtoner. I must start automatic sequencer now."

"Yeah . . ."

"Bring back camera," Federenko commanded. "Must return photographs to Earth. They are too valuable to throw away."

"We can recapture the alien ship," Reynaud said again.

Jo's voice broke in on the same frequency. "Come back to me, Keith. Please come back."

And Markov's. "Keith, dear friend. Don't be so stubborn. Dead heroes are of no value to anyone. From what Reynaud is saying, you can fly back to our visitor within a few years."

Shuddering from the growing cold, Stoner realized he still held the stereo camera in his hands.

"The photographs, Shtoner. Now."

He reached out and touched the spacecraft's bulkhead, pushing himself toward the hatch. Where the hell is it? he asked himself. The entire hull was so transparent . . .

He felt it, a circular rim, open to space. Clipping the camera to his belt, he started to pull himself up and out of the alien ship.

Markov was still talking, "We can build new rockets and train new crews. And you will be the natural leader of such a program. You must come back and lead us. We all need you."

"Please, Keith," Jo's voice pleaded.

He was halfway through the hatch when he looked back at the alien, resting silently for countless ages. And his mind filled with the bickering voices and flint-eyed faces of all the bureaucrats he had ever known. And McDermott. And Tuttle. He saw Dooley in his mind's eye, the agents and policemen and politicians who didn't understand, who feared, who resisted, who would not accept reality even when it was thrust at them.

And he saw Cavendish, twisted and destroyed by them. And Schmidt, smashed into a pulp with his own hands.

"Shtoner, retrofire is in one minute. All is automatic. I cannot stay."

"It's all right, Nikolai," he said quietly, sliding back inside the spacecraft's transparent hull. His boots touched the springy floor at the alien's feet.

"You get back to Earth, Nikolai. I'm staying here."

"Keith!" Jo's strangled scream.

"Don't commit suicide," Markov pleaded.

"It isn't suicide," Stoner said to them all. "You think I'm killing myself, but I'm not. I'm giving you an incentive, a double reason to come out as quickly as you can and recapture this treasure-house. Because I'll be here—frozen. Maybe I'll be dead. But just maybe . . . maybe, I'll be preserved, suspended, waiting to be brought back to life."

"What are you saying?"

"It's a vacuum in here. No air. Temperature's pretty close to absolute zero. It's preserved the alien for god knows how many millennia. It ought to preserve me for a couple of years."

He took a breath, realized their reply couldn't reach him for many seconds, and went on, "It's cold enough to flash-freeze me once I turn my suit heater off. I'll ride with the alien for a few years. If you really care about me you'll come out and get me before the two of us leave the solar system altogether."

"Keith, you can't . . ." Jo's voice broke into sobs.

"I won't be dead," he told her gently. "I'll be waiting for you, frozen, suspended between life and death, waiting for you to reach me and bring me back to life. Like the tale of Sleeping Beauty, only with our roles reversed."

Markov's voice was filled with grief. "She can't speak, Keith. She wants to, but she can't."

"Kirill . . . Jo, listen to me. Make them work together. Create a global space effort, make the politicians do what needs to be done. Get the whole human race involved in this. We have the chance to reach the stars, all of us, to come out of the cocoon that we've been living in. Make them understand, make them look to the stars."

The delay seemed to get longer with each exchange.

"How can we?" Markov's voice pleaded. "We're only ordinary people. We need you, Keith. You must return to lead us!"

"No, Kirill," he said firmly. "You'll have to lead them. It's all up to you now. You and Jo."

He waited for a reply.

"Ten seconds to retrofire," Federenko's glum voice tolled.

"I can't do it," Markov answered at last. "You must come back. You must!"

"Too late, Kirill. It's in your hands now. You've got to change them—all of them. Change the world for me, Kirill."

Federenko broke in, "Farewell, Shtoner. You are a very brave and very foolish man. Good luck."

"So long, Nikolai. Stay in training."

"Keith!" Markov's voice begged.

Stoner turned off the radio and watched the Soyuz. Its retrorockets puffed soundlessly, a brief flare against the dark, and the craft slid away, silently speeding off, dwindling until it was lost against the stars.

He turned back to the alien, swallowed hard against the rawness in his throat. He tried to rub his aching eyes, but his hand bumped against the sealed visor of his helmet. Shrugging, he went back to describing everything he could see.

And as he did so, he wondered, Could *he* be frozen too? Not dead? Can we revive him someday?

He knew that human medical science knew of no way to revive a frozen body, not without rupturing the cells and killing the person. That was for the future. With a grim smile, Stoner thought, Maybe I'll shame them into making progress on that front, as well.

Jo sat stiffly in her chair before the communications console, the tears dried from her eyes, leaving no trace of emotion on her face except the smudges down her cheeks. The other technicians, row after row of them at their consoles, tried not to glance in her direction as they directed Federenko's return flight toward the landing area at Karaganda, some six hundred kilometers to the east.

Markov sat beside her, blank-faced, his eyes a million miles away. Stoner's voice was weaker as it rasped, static-streaked, from the console speaker. He was describing the spacecraft's interior as emotionlessly as a lecturer detailing an archaeological specimen.

Markov seemed to shake himself into awareness. He reached into his pockets for a cigarette, muttering, "He's made his decision. There's nothing we can do about it."

She looked at the Russian and saw that his eyes were filled with tears.

"He isn't dead," Jo said softly. "He won't die . . . not unless we fail him. We can reach him, bring him back to us, bring him back to life."

Glancing at the armed guards still surrounding them, Markov said, "We have much work to do, then."

"Yes," Jo agreed. "But we can do it. We can change the world."

Markov nodded grimly. "I never thought I would become a crusader . . . an evangelist."

"But you will be, won't you?"

"For you," he said softly. "For him."

"No," Jo corrected. "For yourself. For all of us. For Russia and the whole world."

A slow smile spread across his lips. "You are just as bad as he is."

"Worse," Jo said. "I'm here on Earth. I can watch your progress."

Markov got to his feet, drew himself up to his full height. "It will be an interesting battle. I've never been inside the Kremlin, you know."

Jo smiled up at him. "We'll win the battle, Kirill. I know we will."

He nodded and put the cigarette to his lips.

Jo turned back to the console. Stoner was still patiently describing the contents of the spacecraft-tomb:

". . . there doesn't appear to be anything like a periodic table of the elements, or anything else that I can recognize. If there's a Rosetta stone aboard this ark, it'll be some piece of scientific information that the alien civilization has worked out similarly to the way we've worked it out . . ."

Suddenly Jo heard herself telling Markov, "I've got to talk with him. One more time. Before . . . before it's too late."

Markov nodded.

"Alone . . . just the two of us, with no one else on the frequency."

He grinned down at her. "You expect Russians to allow you to speak in private?" With a tug at his beard, Markov said, "Well, if we're going to change the system, we might as well begin here and now."

The messages were coming in from all across the Earth now. Stoner hovered inside the alien crypt, utterly spent, feeling the eternal cold of infinity congealing around him, turning him to lead. He listened to the voices that called to him.

The President of the United States sent his thanks and prayers and an assurance that America would bend every effort to reach the spacecraft and bring him back to Earth.

The head of the Soviet Academy of Sciences, speaking on behalf of the peoples of the U.S.S.R., praised Stoner for his dedication to science and his bravery and promised that the Soviet Union would participate in any program to reach the spacecraft.

His Holiness, the Pope, spoke personally to Stoner, promised that he would work unceasingly to save his body and would offer daily prayers for the preservation of his soul.

The Secretary General of the United Nations, the Vice-Chairman of the People's Republic of China, Jeff Thompson from Kwajalein, politicians from Britain and Japan, scientists from other lands, people Stoner had never heard of—all the voices of Earth spoke to him, one by one, growing fainter, farther removed, whispering against the crackling background radio noise of the cosmos.

And then a voice he recognized.

"Keith, Keith, this is Kirill. Can you hear me?"

"Yes, Kirill. Faintly."

"Jo wants to speak to you . . . privately, on frequency four. No one else will eavesdrop, I promise you."

A burst of static from some unseen star rasped in his earphones. Stoner waited it out, then answered, "I'm switching to frequency four."

For long moments he heard nothing but background hiss and crackle. Then:

"Keith . . . oh, god, Keith, what can I say?"

Say you love me, he thought. But he replied merely, "I'm here, Jo. I can hear you."

The time waiting for her response was an eternity. "Why, Keith? Why have you done this? Why didn't you come back to me?"

He smiled sadly. "I'm a blackmailer, Jo. I'm holding a hostage to force them to come up here to the rescue. I'm shaming them into it."

Silence, except for the sibilant whisperings of the stars. Finally:

"And what about me, Keith? Don't you care about me?"

"Farewell, Roxane," he quoted lamely, "for today I die. . . . And my heart, so heavy with love I have not told, cries out . . ." But he couldn't remember the rest.

He flexed his gloved fingers as he waited for her reply. It was getting difficult to move. His blood was turning to ice.

"Did you mean that?" she asked shakily. "Do you love me, Keith?"

It was safe to tell her now. "Of course I do, Jo. I've loved you for a long time."

He waited for response. The seconds ticked by, longer and longer.

"And I love you, Keith." Her voice was faint, barely discernible above the background static in his earphones. "I love you."

He had nothing else to say. His lips were growing numb.

"We'll come for you, Keith! We will!"

"I know you will, Jo. Don't let them stop you, kid. Don't let them forget. I'll be here, waiting for you."

With a final shuddering breath, he clicked off the heater in his suit.

CHAPTER 46

Jo stood alone in the twilight shadows on the roof of the barracks building. She had gone up there to cry.

The floodlamps weren't on yet, and an evening star hung low over the horizon, shining brilliantly. For a moment she fantasized that it was the alien spacecraft bearing Keith inside it.

The breeze sighed down from the hills, dry and warm. She could hear the faint, tinny noise of a radio somewhere off in the gathering darkness. With a startled shock of understanding, she realized that the voice on the radio was speaking English. An American broadcast, she said to herself. They're letting an American broadcast through!

It was a news broadcast, of course. "Reaction" stories to the long day's events, now that Stoner was permanently out of reach.

Jo listened, despite herself. The announcer was reading an item about a flying saucer organization in Missouri that indignantly maintained that the alien aboard the spacecraft was *not* of the same race as the aliens who had been sending UFOs to Earth.

"According to the Missouri saucer experts," the announcer said archly, "we have found the wrong aliens."

Instead of crying, Jo smiled. There are so many fools in the world, she thought. So many. She lifted her face to the heavens, to the stars that were starting to appear in the darkening sky.

"Thanks, Keith," she whispered into the night. "They'll have to send a team of astronauts to pick you up and bring you and your friend back to Earth. It'll take a few years to put it all together, but when they go out after you, I'll be with them."

Then she turned and headed downstairs, dry-eyed, head high, determined to get to Houston as quickly as possible to begin her training.

Few will deny the profound importance, practical and philosophical, which the detection of interstellar communications would have. We therefore feel that a discriminating search for signals deserves a considerable effort. The probability of success is difficult to estimate, but if we never search the chance of success is zero.

GIUSEPPE COCCONI and PHILIP MORRISON
1959